THE BOOK OF APÓCALYPSIS

THE BOOK OF APÓCALYPSIS

APÓCRYFA

ANDREW J PIXTON

unmapped
THE KINGDOM REPUBLIC OF NEVERMORE
KARAQUIOK VALLEY
BARBATHOR MOUNSTAINS
here be monsters
SHRUUMOTH FOREST
MAOLGON
TROISACK MOUNSTAINS
CANTLGRYM CASTLE
VOIUM
MANTLGRYM
OVIEDOM
KOURII MARSHES
unmapped
BOGGORN
THORNWOOD FOREST
CASTLE COVADONGAR
TOLGRYM
ONIS
CANTABRYN

CHAPTER ONE

HOT IN THE FORGE

Based on *Leyta's Journals*, cc bastica 334;
The Hunter's Parchments, cc bastica 356;
Annals of Syago, cc bastica 299;

15th of Akril, 247

Grim days birth out savage nights
Ancient evenings age new wights
As the stars fall at
   Iron-made world's end

Knowledge surpasses capacity
Ability breeds rapacity
All yield to filth in
   Slow psyclopean end

Necromancy for unsane wiles
And strange tides bearing oddsane smiles
Dies even death at
   Apocalypse end

Cold eclipse celebrates the start
Fateful fires shall forge last art
Creation's fade dream's
   Long psyclopean end

—*Iron Psyclopean Apocalypse* by Goyabeksinski de Chambercraft

1

Tentative knocking tapped the door of Leyta's room. "Leyta, may I come in?" Priestess Katti asked.

"Uh no, I'm indecent," Leyta lied. She'd not been sleeping, just wishing she had been. It was a poor lie too, for it only bought her a few seconds time. She looked at her forearms; the cut marks were still dark red. Just trying to feel something and distract from painful thoughts, it had helped a little. She drew her sleeves over them and sat up on the bed, then threw her hair to one side with a few quick comb-throughs. "Enter."

Katti entered and before she closed the door, Leyta glimpsed Syago and Qosku in the hallway. Katti sat on the bed next to her, then felt her head. "You don't feel hot, but you're still unwell?"

Leyta hadn't the time—or the motivation—to prepare a fake fever. Lately she didn't have the motivation for anything, not since she'd used up all her sentiments to power her dyne at the Battle of Tiakanawu. The allies had fought two enemies at once, the Royal Chaos and the Razhod, and she'd drained herself to keep either side from taking the allies' piece of the dydatris, an ancient relic that supposedly held tremendous power. Each effort she made to recover only sapped more energy that she didn't have. But everyone else didn't need to know that, they couldn't or she'd lose her position. At least she hadn't gone mad, that common ending to dynasts had passed her over for now. Katti straightened in puzzlement. "Well, I think the fever has faded, but my stomach and energy is still down. What faces us today?"

"They're calling a war council of leaders in Upper Voium in an hour. You should hold a council of your own first, to prepare."

She sighed. She knew a portion of the Chaos army sat outside their gates, waiting for an opportunity to attack or for instructions from the troupe leaders, King and Queen.

Probably won't get out of this one. I suppose the breaking point was to come eventually. I either resign or continue.

Perhaps one more effort. One more day. If I can do one more day, maybe that'll break the spell of my disabling void.[1]

She forced her eyes to meet Katti's. "Tell them I'm coming. The leaders, I mean, but I'll be late."

---

[1] See *Moonspell Hell Light de Lostregos* for further guidance and encouragement. Because this does not end well.

The priestess nodded. "Shall I help you prepare?"

She almost replied no but knew that as soon as Katti left the room, she'd lie back down. She nodded instead.

The only sentiments she bore were occasional bouts of sorrow or anxiety, but even they faded. She would give anything to feel even those sentiments again.

The other elementists had also spent themselves in battle, but they had soon recovered themselves, if with some trauma and fragility. She'd not, she'd gotten worse. On top of that, she was haunted by the guilt of her past, of the people she'd hurt through caustic treatment and cruel neglect, both as Castellan and across her personal life. But worst of all was abandoning their Kimoc allies at Tiakanawu. She could make excuses, all of them hard decisions in a complicated world. It reminded her of Jester, who'd told her when she was his captive of his struggles as an injured, blind boy. Was she the same kind of person as those who'd treated him cruelly? She hoped not. Yet the words of her old friend turned rival Camila, a victim of Leyta's neglect, tumbled in her brain. *You put pain into society, Leyta, and it doesn't just disappear when you're done.*

No, it didn't. Instead it continued on and went into circulation, coming back to her, or spreading out through everyone else. As if those things weren't enough for her to deal with now, there was also the weight of her new, hope-crushing heresy sitting on her. Robbing her of the refuge of faith. They'd always been taught the world had been made cruel as a punishment on humanity, and that their only recourse to prove themselves worthy enough to their savior, Deova Bondua, was to fight the world's cruelties with dyne. But Leyta's research showed that the faith they'd built their entire society around was wrong. The monsters hadn't always been as terrible as the scriptures claimed, but rather had been made terrible by dyne itself. Dyne pushed sentiments out into the elements, usually negative sentiments like fear and anger. This process twisted the plants' and animals' growth over time. They were now in a trap: dyne was necessary to fight monsters, but doing so only made more monsters. Dyne, her passion and profession, had doomed everyone. And she alone knew this, unable to tell anyone else for fear of excommunication and sanction as well, maybe even pillory. She'd tried to tell Balgor, who'd brushed it aside without serious thought.

Under all these weights, she couldn't recuperate her power or will—though she wondered how much, if any of it, was the hopeless fear of making the outside worse.

Katti helped her dress and wash her face. It was all motions with no intention behind them. An act, but one that served its purpose. Why not just resign? It would've been the smart thing to do, a dutiful act. Yet her duty was also the only thing that moved her. She couldn't act on her own, but when duty pulled at her, it eventually got a response. If she stepped down, she'd be able to teach children more often. This might also restore her energy; seeing the children during public festivals had inspired some light in her. She'd been so occupied by her Castellan duties that she couldn't spend as much time with the little ones.

They were just finishing up dressing her, Katti combing her hair and lamenting that they'd not had more time to wash it first, when a hurried knock rattled the door. "Enter," Leyta called.

"Enemy at the gates," Syago said, bursting through the door. "You're needed."

"The Royal Chaos followed us here," Leyta said, brow furrowing. "What's so urgent about another assault on our wall?"

"No, that army moved back. We're being hit by a monster, a feldinal." His knuckles tightened on the pommel of his sword. "A really big one." Just then she noticed the window tremble slightly, and a sense of urgency shot through her for a moment. Taking heart in the feeling, she nodded. Her staff in hand, they hurried out.

The screams, booms, and frantic struggle of battle sounded through the streets of Voium, the silhouette of the monster visible at southgate between columns of smoke. Already she could see Syago, who'd run ahead, jumping high as if flying. His soulsword, Alexandre, had almost magical powers to heal and make spectacular leaps or cut through stone. But Syago seemed to realize he wasn't hurting the titanic creature and ducked for cover. They quickened in pace, rising up to the battlements some few paces from the assault. Qosku, her monk bodyguard and friend, stopped some debris from falling on her with his arrow quick arms. Dyne powering the dynfist friar's body, he cleared the air before her and then they continued into the monster's range.

Most mabin'guarik were three feet taller than a man, this giant was over forty more, making it one of the biggest feldinals on record. The Asturion word for monstrous aberrations, feldinals like this one were beasts of abnormal size and form, and it towered over the thirty foot wall in furry bulk.

The moment she saw the creature, all urgency inside her died. The evidence of her heresy was staring her in the face. Mabin'guarik were large and strange creatures to begin with, a mouth on its stomach and one eye on its small head. But instead of the belly-mouth, this had a human face, devoid of expression, on its torso. Its humanoid deformities bespoke human sentiments affecting its enormous growth. And seeing the elementists throw dyne at it, unknowingly furthering the activity that had changed it over time into the aberration that stood before them—it was too much for her. She dimly thought somebody should tell them to stop, for the dyne wasn't even deterring it. Demons and devils often had human parts attached when they invaded from the other-worlds, but feldinals were natural animals from this world, with human parts occasionally grown out. In fact, otherworlders had previously been the only explanation for feldinals. Her heresy provided an better explanation, it was dyne that made them. *Here we meet the consequences of our actions. How odd and terrible our sentiments must be, to twist this creature so.*

Katti shaking her snapped her attention back. The creature was claw-ing the battlements to pieces. Fires burned around the wall, patches of its fur smoked, but it paid no heed. Dynasts were in retreat and had all but stopped their attacks as it only targeted them. If nothing changed, it'd break the whole wall down. All she had to do was distract it so that the scattered defenders could regroup.

Standing on the wall, she raised her staff and pointed it at the air around its massive human eye to use darkfire and freeze over its eye. But with only a little bit of anxiety to project, she made only a little poof of the freezing darkfire in the air. She had despair, sorrow, but that wouldn't cause anything useful. She saw in the Vision swirls of yellow fear in the air and smoke. She put her own fear into the wind, harnessing what fear was already there, to blow smoke into its eye and produced even less of a reaction. And then nothing else. Not even defending others rekindled her powers. Deova had abandoned her.

The great monster turned to her, spotting her through pillars of smoke. It snorted through the pudgy human nose. The human mouth on its stomach growled as its feet thundered toward her. With each step, the wall shook violently. Everyone around her ran for cover until she stood there alone.

Now right in front of her, the lifeless human eyes gazed at her through the haze. She prayed again, rote with no feeling, and waved her staff uselessly. But it only grunted with foul breath that blew her hair back. She was nothing but a failed dynast, an impotent leader who held her pain in secret.

She whispered to it, "Please, just kill me. I can't do this anymore. I want to die." She closed her eyes in wait of the release.

It grunted again, blowing hot breath over her, then turned away, rejecting her plea. The army had regrouped, launching a feeble new assault, but it abandoned its attack altogether, walking away from the city with a dull thud at every step. She watched it go, dumbfounded. Through the swirling pillars of smoke and dust, she felt the sun shining through. Felt Deova Bondua seeing her, blessing her. Maybe she wasn't so lost yet. Maybe she could do one more day. Then another day. Then another. With the Deova pushing her, she could do it. She realized tears were streaming her eyes, and she wiped them away as Katti ran up with Syago and Qosku in tow.

"How did you do that?!"

"You turned it away!"

"I've never seen anything that incredible before!" They all seemed to speak at once. She shook her head in wonder. She'd been denied her deathwish, and she felt surprisingly glad for it. That very sense, however faint, seemed like hope on the horizon, and she clung to it.

The war court of Voium was filled with the tension of a losing war and tremendous fear of what lay ahead. Candles dimly lit the room along the wall and from the chandelier above. Leyta's forces had been cut in half and put to flight and now remained holed up in Voium, along with refugees from the siege on Mantlgrym. Having fled to the closest city after the battle at Tiakanawu, she only waited for the opportunity to break out for Cantlgrym, where she needed to be as its Castellan. The enemies at the gates, and need to recover, had prevented their move.

Cantlgrym had ceased responding to light signals and gurow messages, not always reliable anyway but usually useful in emergencies. Their communication was being shut off, and they were boxed in their own protective walls.

Leyta looked around the packed hall. Syago appeared lost in thought, as he often did. Once, he appeared to be whispering to himself, probably to the soulsword. Something had been bothering him, although he assured her it wasn't her.

Neither Tek'ouk'iek nor Lil'iek had come; none of the remaining Kimoc had. She hadn't spoken with them; she'd been too afraid, too weak. She'd heard they were being watched but not imprisoned. Although they had done nothing wrong—had fought ferociously alongside the Asturions—they had reason to seek revenge. The Asturions had abandoned them at Tiakanawu to be surrounded by the enemy as the rest of the forces retreated. She and Syago had tried to warn them of the sudden retreat, but at least forty of their Roah'Riik had still died because of it. She knew the court had been ready to defend against their accusations, but instead vacant seats stared back.

Though he waited outside, Leyta knew several things clearly bothered Qosku, but he hardly spoke about anything anymore, much less what bothered him.

Across the aisle, Captain Alfonsor, a thin man from Mantlgrym, considered their summary with skepticism. "And you're sure the Razhod are back at full power?" he asked.

"Yes," Balgor said, leaning his bearded bulk forward. "Or at least they're summoning greater spirits and using the soulweapons. It's possible they don't have all the old weapons or spirits at their command, but they have enough to destroy a sizable army." Balgor's cycloptic eye looked intensely at the leaders who'd not gone, not judging them for it but urging their understanding.

"And the assassin networks?" Alfonsor pressed, lips thinning. "Or what about the heightened battle proficiency?"

"The heightened proficiency I can attest to," Virgow said, voice hollow. The Unakan's eye patch and scars belied his many years of battle experience. He'd been the head general at Tiakanawu and the one who'd given the final order to betray the Kimoc, reproaching her for hesitating. But Leyta doubted any of the remaining Kimoc knew that. "I saw it all from my vantage point up the hill. They fought as they used to, experts in every way. I've seen no assassinations yet; it might be too early for them to infiltrate us. So far, they're everything we remember except the numbers, but it's only a matter of time."

"But all of the devils are gone?" Alfonsor asked, and everyone looked at Syago. "The ones they'd released, I mean."

"Yes." Syago cleared his throat and leaned in from his corner seat down the hall. He'd personally hunted those devils and come away with many deep scars, something that still amazed her in spite of her numbness. "They released six, and we destroyed six. That is, until they let more in."

"They'll try for more eventually," the new leader of the chamands, Andala, said firmly. A veteran of the summoner coven that wore armor, the Order of Quokketh, she had replaced the slain Bartolina. "But it appeared that most of their disciples fell in addition to two of the six Razhod, so they'll have few to sacrifice now except themselves and the captive children."

She'd forgotten about those. *Rood's blood, I can't keep all this straight.* She needed to free the children, and she prayed to Deova Bondua to aid her and protect the children. But she also knew the dydatris piece still in her possession would outweigh the captive children in importance.

"—and we know they aren't beyond any of that," Alfonsor said, closing the ledger before him. "Though if what you say is true, the devils were only the beginning. I too will never forget what it was like fighting them. I'm sorry you had to do so without our aid for so long. Tell me of this mix of rebels and barbarian giants led by the Royal Chaos. How can we pit them against the Razhod? We have no other option."

"The Chaos? Impossible," Count Cantarchar of Voium said. He was one of the few leaders who'd actually gone in person to rescue them from the fight. Though he'd delayed much. "The giants are too savage to think beyond fighting us, are driven by King and Queen... Excuse me, Queen was torched at the battle, wasn't she? Jester, too, keeps them under control with his dynal songs. The demon, Knave, and giant, Knight, I assume are still there as well. They'll fight the Razhod, but they're pounding at our gates for a reason. They want our relic piece more than they want our allyship, and it's not a worthy exchange to make either."

Virgow agreed. "We're an object of conquest with a particularly valuable treasure. This power play is zero sum for the blood. None rest until winner takes all. We need the rest of the kingdom here." She hated hearing him, especially speaking like that. It only reminded her of their argument over the betrayal.

"I'm not sure the barbarians are so far beyond us," Balgor said, himself a Fomorion who'd converted to Deova Bondua and taught at Castle Cantlgrym. "The rest of the Royal Chaos might be unreachable, but the

Fomorions only joined their side, not their cause. The way the Razhod tore into them, they already see the damned Hellfaces as the greater threat, and after the battle they might want more revenge against them for what happened out there. If we can convince the giants to focus on the Razhod at the same time we do, we might have a chance."

"But what will that serve?" Syago said quietly. "The witchlords came back, again, after everyone thought they were gone for good. If we destroy them, they'll just come back again. How can we stop it completely?"

"A mystery for another time, lad," Virgow said. "Such a puzzle has gone unsolved for the century and more that we've been fighting them. Right now immediate survival is the struggle. We can certainly petition the Fomorions, but with them under wraps of their insane leaders, I'm sure it will fall on deaf ears. Of course, if the remaining Kimoc would stop whimpering in their rooms, and instead confront me, man to men, we could get their input too. But until they've the balls to face us, we'll have to decide without them."

"And my congratulations on reducing the Kimoc," Alfonsor said. "Though we're left with a radicalized few to beware of, it's still impressive work from you and Leyta."

It took all of Leyta's remaining will to not physically attack them both. She should've denounced what they'd done, but the acceptance she'd needed, even longed for, had finally come. Efforts to wear down her power had ceased, and denouncement would accomplish little. She felt a cold calculus settle in. She was equally angry at herself but knew that this would be the only way to protect, even advocate, for them. They were a hair's breadth from spurious execution. But the kindled rage, such a rarity now that she would need later, promptly faded into despair. Couldn't they see it was all hopeless? Even without the heresy, the doom of dyne, they were all dead. There was no way they were going to get the relic pieces from either enemy, much less hold them off for long.

"So we wait?" Syago asked. "You want to sit here in Voium for the other armies to show up, if they do? What happened to the forwardness? We can't leave the initiative to them, we have to move."

But I can't move, Leyta thought. *But we must. Deova aid me.*

"We need to take control of the situation," Leyta said.

"If you've any ideas on how best to do that," Alfonsor began, hands splaying out, "by all means propose them and we'll put it into motion. As I see it, we've no good option, but fortifying here is the safest until things change outside."

"Well it seems Kask still leads the Razhod," she began, improvising the thought. "He was the one who assaulted the castle with Davagis. I believe they'll have more spite for the crude thuggery of the Royal Chaos; Kask was even tortured by their mob before he attacked us that first time. I'm sure we can pressure them against each other." She nearly choked on the idea, but to win security for her people, she'd have to swallow many more painful things.

"Unlikely," Virgow said. "They'd know our game from the start."

"The outside is changed," Syago said. "Darkemorg season is ending. The nightly rising of bodies is giving way to the blooming of the forests as the land moves to the season of darkelan. Not only does that mean the Razhod lose their army of lifeless, or the part they don't raise through ritual, but both foes will be vulnerable to the blooming as we remain protected in our cities."

All around the court, heads nodded their agreement.

Leyta liked the idea of waiting. It was easy, something she could do. But it was also morally wrong. Castle Cantlgrym remained vulnerable to both enemies without her and her soldiers. Of course, everything about the situation was bad, but the proposed strategy let the enemies take the initiative and all but surrendered Cantlgrym. Once again, duty pulled her into action. "Gentlemen of the court, I hear your strategy and agree. But I must return to Cantlgrym or we lose it to the enemy. We can't cede ground."

A quiet fell on the room. "What of the dydatris piece? If you are here, we can protect it, but if you leave..." Alfonsor said in concern.

Balgor hummed, "Perhaps we can hide it, so they don't know who or which place has it. Only those of this room will know."

Virgow said, "We'll work out a plan with good timing and move out. If nothing else, it's harder to flank several armies rather than one. Dispersal will be a danger only if we let it."

The consent was unanimous and rare.

"So that's the present decision then," Cantarchar said with finality. "Fortify, watch, test waters, guard the relic, and prepare a split. And may Deova

Bondua save us all in these precarious times. At least She'll have our thanks for the unity."

Leyta was just glad for an excuse to leave. After the meeting, she went to the Kimoc quarters, no longer able to put it off. An armored guard stood outside the door. On seeing her, he reached for the knob.

She raised a hand to halt him. "No, I'll knock."

"My lady, it's not necessary," he said.

"Well then it should be. They're guests and allies, not prisoners."

She knocked, then realized they might not understand the sound as it was purely an Asturion custom. As her hand turned the knob, the guard whispered in her ear, "They *weren't* enemies, my lady. But now I get a different feeling." She entered the room.

The six Roah'riik, Kimoc hellhunters, sat on couches or leaned against furniture, forming a half-circle around the room and facing her with cold gazes. When she saw the paint on their faces, she drew breath in and took a step back, but they didn't move. Only watched as she looked from one to the other. Their weapons hanging at their sides, wounds mostly bandaged up beneath black leather, furs and feathers still stained red.

"I, uh, came to see to your well-being in the city," she said and would have been quavering but even fear was faint in her. Yet she was nervous and unsure. What was this; why the face paint? "I want you to be comfortable and safe here... and, well, I assure you I had nothing to do with the guards. I've asked for them to be sent away, but I've no authority over them."

She paused, hoping for comment or response. Prepared for anger. But they said nothing. She felt as though she were standing in a court of judgment. They didn't need to interrogate for they saw right through her.

"I- I am so very sorry for what happened at the battle. I hope my letter of condolences was well received..." She felt her diplomatic will and training withering away under those glares. "Virgow thought it was necessary. I swear by my Lady Deova that I argued against it. I tried to help you, but I had no more power and the enemies were coming and we had to retreat. I-I know I should've done more still, I just- Rood's blood, I'm so, so sorry."

She thought she saw Lil'iek breathing heavier, perhaps even a rage burning beneath that stoic surface. But then it faded. Tek'ouk'iek had tilted his head somewhat, as if growing bored of her talking. They did not respect her, or trust her, so what would more apologizing serve? She supposed she couldn't blame them either. All the excuses in the world didn't change that she had, ultimately, supported the betrayal.

"Well, I have to go check the ramparts and- I'll- I'll be in my room after if you decide you want to talk, or send a message. I will listen. I do mean to make it up to you in what way I can." With them still staring at her, she turned awkwardly and left.

CHAPTER TWO

The Murderer Within

Based on *The Hunter's Parchments*, cc bastica 356;
Annals of Syago, cc bastica 299;

15th of Akril, 247

"Do you believe her?" Tek'ouk'iek asked, running his fingers over his worn crutch-scepter, its intricate symbols chipped from only months of battle.[2] His other hand touched the feq'uok necklace around his neck. It held hairlocks and teeth from his family, connecting him to them.

"No," Lil'iek said. She folded her arms and furrowed her brow. He saw the fire still blazing in her eyes. Even in mourning, she remained fierce. "She might be sorry, but only in front of us and because she has to be. Once we're out of sight, they neither think of nor care about us."

"I was actually asking about Virgow," Tek'ouk'iek said. "Though in regards to the apology, I do believe she feels remorse, I just also feel that being sorry is not enough."

"She clearly made that Virgow shit up to shield herself," Klom'oth said. The only one to wield a sword, he now kept the Asturion weapon hid behind his quiver on his back. "It's a convenient truth, weak and cowardly."

"Convenient but not unlikely," Tek'ouk'iek said, but their hardened faces didn't agree. He felt like Fal'iek must have, always making the most rational point no matter how unpopular it made him. Though for Tek'ouk'iek it had more to do with his academic background than Fal'iek's faithless skepticism. *Try every possibility until you whittle it down to the necessary,* they'd taught him at Castle Cantlgrym when he'd guest-studied as a dynast. "He

---

2 The truth is always worse. See *Gybiaaw Blackbraid: Born of Winter,* 12

13

was the top command, after all. Besides, he seems more the type. Syago did come down and warn us."

"He should've been prepared to die with us then," Dar'miir said, the tallest and normally quietest one.

Tek'ouk'iek looked at Machi'guenk and Guaran'upik, who didn't seem to disagree with the assessment. Lil'iek as well, though he knew she held back on Syago, knowing him better from his old friendship with her dead previous husband, Fal'iek. The trouble with righteous anger and grief was that they justified all manner of irrational thinking, and any action became permissible, no matter how mutually destructive. *We are few; our options extremely limited. We need to focus our revenge, for some justice is better than none.*

"We'll confront Virgow first," he said. "We'll need to do it right with a public charge. If we just walk up and attack him they'll hang us all. A pretext they'd welcome. I doubt we'll ever win enough people over to finish him with a trial but the public needs to at least understand why we're killing him. I want them to know who he really is."

They nodded and left down the stairs. The guards followed not far behind, but Tek'ouk'iek was not worried. He did fear the mob, however. He'd been the victim of one before, it took his leg from him, and he hoped his impulsive wife kept that in mind as well. The last thing they needed was to incite a mob.

The streets were busy as ever, and people watched the hellhunters more warily than ever. Tek'ouk'iek suspected they didn't know about the betrayal or even that these six Kimoc were under guard. It'd be buried in the annals as had previous betrayals. The suspicious glances likely had more to do with the face paintings of mourning than anything. Other than the spectre of mob, Tek'ouk'iek didn't care. *Let them fear my grief, for to them it is rage.*

Rage with caution, a difficult balance that he was reminded of when he saw the Asturion door wreaths being changed. *Shit, it's the season of poison now! We didn't celebrate at all. How the golkaw did we miss it?* Caged up in the city, outside of the motherwood, even their grief paint was late. But the ancestors and eternals would forgive them this, in light of things.

They found that the leadership they sought was not at the Voium court. For a time they didn't believe the guards, thinking it was a ploy to dismiss them. But one eventually informed him Virgow was on the wall.

The wall's damages from the furacán mabin'guarik were immense, and people already busied themselves with repairs. They saw Virgow, Syago, and Leyta all together. And many other soldiers besides, to witness. *Perfect. We can demand answers from all three.* But as the Roah'riik approached the stairs, violent noise began on top of the wall.

As more Fomorion giants joined the mostly rebel group camped outside Voium's wall, Syago had noted the absence of Chaos leaders even now, sixteen days after their return. Though, the gaunt white form of Knave had been seen flying around, and Knight was sighted as well, which meant he'd somehow escaped from the Razhod's necromantic spell. It wasn't a big enough group to surround the city walls, but their speed would make up for it. It was obvious even to Syago, watching on the wall with relative disinterest, that the Asturion rebel portion of the encampment was wary of their savage partners.

The conflict weighed heavily on everyone's minds, but in the stillness of wartime intermission, the truth and trauma of his family legacy was what pressed at him. He had based his entire path on being worthy of his father's legacy, of embodying it. Odiru, the hero warrior of the Holy Judgment Sword Alexandre which could heal and cut through stone or wood like sand. Yet it was a lie. His father and Fal'iek had sacrificed people to be slaves to a devil in the old war. Lil'iek had insisted it was a necessary evil that they had regretted ever since, but that didn't make it right. Syago agreed hard decisions occasionally had to be made, had done them himself numerous times over. But there was a difference between the sacrifices he'd done and the horrific ones he'd learned of. He felt lied to and let down. He'd so often ignored stories of his mother in preference for anything related to his noble father, favoring his heroic Asturion line over her pagan Kimoc one. It was despairing enough on top of his trauma and nightmares, and the impending conflicts. He regretted things, being so careless with other's lives, leading them to horrific deaths in his quest for the devils, and he feared that if the war continued, he would become just as stained as his father before him. He already was in a way, having gotten too familiar with the devil arm attached to his left shoulder. Its appetites and impulses competed with the hard discipline and purity pushed by the Holy Judgment Sword. The two crowded his already crowded mind, pushing and pulling in a way that exacerbated his other troubles.

He snapped out of his thoughts as Leyta appeared at the parapet beside him. Evening sun, weak through the clouds, shone beautifully on her face. He knew she'd also been weary from trauma and illness but wondered if something else ailed her. She smiled faintly, fakely even, and looked out over the plain. Qosku stood further down the walkway, also looking out.

Moments passed before Syago spoke. "Do you enjoy being here in Voium?"

"No," she said, still looking across the plain at the setting sun. "I have fond memories here, but this place held me back. Being the only daughter of adopted rich parents can do that. I miss them, but this isn't the Voium I remember either. It used to be the academic center of Nevermore even more than Cantlgrym and Bokhor, which have a military or spiritual focus. Voium is intellectual for its own sake, I came to miss that at Cantlgrym. Now with Voium being the new military center, what I loved is gone."

Syago suspected that wasn't the real source of her disquiet but said nothing, thinking about his home in Tolgrym. Parts of the town remained after Kask and the devil's burning of the forest town, though the citizens found asylum in Mantlgrym until repairs could be fully completed. With the pressures of the war and arrival of the darkelan blooming, that could be a long time. Darkemorg, the season of bone, was better for construction in its predictability: at night the monsters hid and corpses rose to shamble about. Darkelan, the season of poison, was unplannable: monsters and plants and fungi took free reign of the land night and day. Even after being rebuilt, he didn't think he could ever return to Tolgrym. But neither Voium nor Cantlgrym felt like his home now.

"You'll always have a place at Cantlgrym, Syago," Leyta said, reading his mind somehow. "If you don't want to go back to Tolgrym, I can always find a position for you."

He smiled, but instead replied, "Leyta, I'm sorry but I need to leave again. With your permission."

"For what?" Her face didn't show the expected disappointment or anger, but more trust and curiosity.

"The blinding on the summoners from Bokhor," he began, choosing his words carefully. "I heard the chamands talking about it. They're certain the Razhod, or their disciples, did it somehow. They're trying to figure out how to lift it, but the irony is that they won't know how without talking to the spirits, which they can't do because of the blinding. It might be that we need to kill the disciple or witchlord who did it, whomever that is, to undo it. We need their summoning for this fight. Until then, I have an idea to figure it out."

She nodded, saying nothing. It stunned him a little that she didn't fight him on it or pick apart the theory he'd suggested. But something else had been on his mind. "Also, that and another question. The Razhod, something about the full induction changes the disciple on ascendancy from the cult to the coven. I fought Kask in Tolgrym and again at Tiakanawu. I could've beaten Kask the cultist the first time fairly easily if not for his pet devil, but the second time, only two months later, not only was he a full Razhod, but his swordsmanship was far ahead of me. Nobody makes that big an advancement in so short a time, especially when switching from a regular sword to a soulsword. I remember Fal'iek talking about this once. He didn't understand how they accomplished it either. I'm just wondering if there's not some secret to unraveling their power, if not them, and if any cha-mands or spirits know. The- the mystery of their powers. But"—he became uncomfortable under her blank, steady gaze—"well, there is a summoner in Boggorn. It's not that far and could answer both questions. I shouldn't be gone more than ten days."

"The witch?" she asked, skeptical but not incredulous. They'd all heard tales of the witch as children, more tales than could be true. "You want to go into the marshes alone after the witch?"

"Yes," he said, meeting and holding her gaze. "The enemies are distracted now, and it might be impossible later. With how long our dispersion is taking, you might even still be here. For the troops, you can tell them whatever you want, that I'm on a secret quest. I'll back you up. I am sorry about leaving before, but this time it's different. At least it beats sitting and waiting for them to take initiative." He almost mentioned the oppor-tunity this would provide to sort himself out and to reconcile himself to his dead ancestors. The sense in him grew that he couldn't succeed here until he became whole.

She nodded. "All right. Would you like someone to go with you, any supplies?"

He shook his head. "You're really fine with this?"

"You eliminated three large devils nearly all by yourself, I'm sure you can handle it. And I don't like the waiting either, so I trust you. Perhaps on your return just go back to Cantlgrym."

He was about to respond with something sweet and witty when he noticed a wall guard walking up. Syago didn't know him but thought the man's halting gait to be strange. The man doubled over, clutching the parapet. Leyta looked at him too. She moved to the man, who stumbled toward her. "What's wrong?"

Syago saw the glint of steel and his heart leaped. He pulled Leyta away just as she slapped the dagger-arm aside. Not deterred, the guard stabbed toward her repeatedly and hard. Syago's mind nearly froze with fear for her safety. She caught the arm as the knife bit into her shoulder. His gaze narrowed at the blood streaming from her wound, and his own blood pumped furiously through him. Syago moved around her and tackled the man, rolling on the floor. Then Qosku was there, pulling the knife away and throwing it off the wall. Leyta fell to her knees, clutching the wound and using a handkerchief to stem and bandage it.

Syago rolled with the guard, whose distant eyes rolled back in his head as his jaw clenched and head twitched. The fury with which the man struggled somehow put him on top of Syago. The man drew another knife, Syago's hidden blade out of his boot. *What?! How?* Alexandre jittered commands and suggestions through Syago's head, complaining that he'd not drawn it instead. Syago's left arm, the devil arm, now free, shot up, and he felt a thrill as he gripped the fool's neck. A moment later, Qosku broke the man's attacking arm with a push to the elbow, and tossed the second blade away. Syago rose up, using the strength of his devil arm to lift the struggling man by the neck. He dimly realized he'd fogged up in anger.

"Put him down," Qosku said as he grabbed the other arm. "I bind him."

Syago tried, clearing his head, but found that the devil arm wouldn't let go. He willed it lower, trying to temper the rage and worry he still felt coursing through him. Instead, the large hand, bulging beneath his glove, tightened around the man's neck. He pushed his will into it, commanding obedience, easing the anger that fueled it. Instead of just clouding his mind, it now worked in spite of him.

"Syago, let him down," Qosku urged.

"I'm trying," he growled. Slowly it lowered the man, who wriggled wildly until the hand gave one last hard squeeze. The traitorous soldier died, limp.

The body dropped to the ground, and Syago and Qosku stared at it in bewildered repulsion.

Syago turned away from the body, still foggy and now trembling, and prayed. It was the only recourse he could think of as both Alexandre and the devil's arm were abuzz in him with conflicting thoughts and feelings, overwhelming him. The devil arm was getting worse, acting without Syago's approval. Alexandre normally held it off, but so far its power had not regressed. For a moment, he couldn't hear himself think, couldn't even create thoughts of his own in that noise.

"Is one of you going to help me?" Leyta asked, snapping Syago out of it. She leaned against the wall, bleeding all over her dress.

Virgow, who hobbled up from nearby, offered her a clean rag and said, "It was only a matter of time before the witchlords tried this, but well done stopping it. Having the soldiers and townsfolk see this will boost morale and trust at least." They bound her wound and walked her down, only then seeing the small gathering of people who cheered them. But in the middle stood another group: the six Roah'riik, their faces still painted. Lil'iek's mouth opened to speak but closed as the cheering grew. They looked at the oblivious Asturions around them, annoyed, then walked off.

By the time Syago and the others got her to the infirmary, word had spread. Constantin and Balgor entered as Katti and Lügos laid her down, preparing to work on her. "Who was it?" Constantin asked. The veteran warrior monk had just recovered from his own wounds from the battle enough to get out of bed, but barely more than that.

"We don't know," Syago said, watching Lügos prepare his items, then looking away as Lügos gently moved her clothing. Qosku continued to watch uncomfortably. "I asked the captains to look into it and report to me as soon as they learn."

"Describe the attack to me," Constantin said.

Syago did so as Balgor pounded a large fist against the wall, shaking the building. "It's happening again," Balgor muttered. "The Razhod assassins. We could never figure out how they infiltrated our ranks, or turned our own against us, but as you said, someone would suddenly turn on you in a rage. Somehow they get their fanatical disciples in, spying, then trying to kill everyone around in an insane rampage."

"You're sure? He didn't say—"

"Absolutely, every detail you said lines up with what it was like before. The disciples aren't full Razhod, but they're still well trained and radically devoted. It's no surprise these are no different. Someone you know well and trust, not just for their loyalty but also competence should remain on guard with her. And each of you, watch your backs. This isn't the last."

After they left the room, Syago excused Qosku so he could spend the night as a werebeast in his "territory," wherever it was. Syago sat down to hold night watch, thinking of how his mind had buzzed from the devil's arm. He felt disquieted over the way its love of violence had consumed him.

The scaly red flesh now took up half his chest, a little more than the month previous. And he wasn't sure how to stop it, though he had to admit, dangerous or not, it had its advantages. He was much tougher, stronger, and quicker. Its appetites and impulses competed with the hard discipline and purity pushed by the Holy Judgment Sword.

On top of that he was hungry more often and in greater degree. Always hungry.

Leyta slept, so he pulled out the old journal he'd been reading. Written over a hundred years ago by his five times great grandfather and namesake, Iagon in the year 113, it read: "It was midnight. I ran lait through the raini streets of Mantelgrom to our secret council. I was missing my son's birth to stop Barthandeon from becoming king. I new he was becom the leader of that cult of the razor. He was becom a witch of sorts, though I cannot imagin why found this coven when you have a duchy to rule. But he murderd to do this and would lose it all. I had to stop him, Alesandre would stop him. But I was too lait on arryval, they alredi ordered it done when he arryved speeking cunning blasfemia with eyes transformed into hell, but I feer it is not done. The cult is still there, my spyes tell me, still venerating him."

Leyta stirred, startling him.

"You're still leaving," she stated softly, not asking.

"I shouldn't now," he said, closing the book. "With the assassinations and you wounded."

She scoffed, "I don't need your protection. I could've handled that myself. I only let you men protect me for your own egos."

"If you think so." He smiled.

"We need to understand the Razhod more than ever now. I think your quest is important. Better than the nothing we already have."

He looked over her face, more serene now than tired. And in her eyes, he thought he saw a hint of the interest he'd thought they shared before all this—Alexandre, the devil arm, Tiakanawu—happened. It would've been the perfect moment to kiss her. She was pretty and they'd practically courted each other since meeting in Castle Covadongor. He'd had doubts after their disagreements, but they seemed resolved now. "You know, I've been thinking," he began, "I'm tired of all the politics, so I'll just say it: I do like you and wish to court you."

She actually smiled. "I've thought the same. I'd wondered if you could be the only man I'd ever be able to live with. But I think maybe the timing is poor."

He hid a sigh of relief and nodded, feeling the blush and accepting its inevitability. "I agree… But don't you think the trying times require strong commitments that make us happy? If we don't know how long we have the nice moments, why not make the most of them when they're here?"

After a moment, she nodded. "Perhaps. Kiss me then."

He leaned forward and pressed his lips to hers. The soft warmth of her washed everything else away, just for a moment. Then he pulled away, and the feeling faded. Her closed eyes made her look more at peace, but when she opened them, he saw her weariness had returned and wondered if she was disappointed by it.

Before he could question it, she changed the subject. "You're scared to go out again?"

"Yeah." He leaned back in his chair. "It's different now that I'm not driven by anger. Hellhunting is lonely, and terrifying. I never should've left the Roah'riik to go after the devils. At least before I was always within a day's reach of any city and I knew what to expect, but now… I'll be heading away from the cities. Away from people. At least I won't make the same mistakes again." He tapped his devil arm.

"It's your choice. But it's only going to get worse here, that's what scares me. At least you'd be away from *them*." Everyone had nightmares of the monsters outside. But since Tiakanawu, most of that had been replaced by nightmares of the Razhod witchlords summoning dark spirits and tearing through the allied forces.

"Well, I could also use a break from some people here," he said, half smiling.

She scoffed again. "In that case, go already and have a good time." She rolled over, pulling bed covers over herself. "Leave before dusk. Remember to wake me before you go so I can protect myself if none come to relieve you. Just promise to come back." And she left him to confront her own nightmares. He quietly promised, then kept guard by the bed, mulling his questions, past, present, and future, of who he was and who he was becoming.

Lil'iek had watched the unfolding assassination attempt first in surprised bafflement until she realized what it was, then with some hope that it might work and rid her the trouble, then with guilt and ignited memories.[3]

Long ago, she'd witnessed a similar event. Had been standing beside Fal'iek on a battlefield outside the forest when a woman from a rival tribe sprung at her with knives. But Fal'iek had seen it before and cut her down. It'd have been better to tie the woman up as proof against her tribe, but there'd been no vines or ropes. And the ferocity was uncontrollable. Lil'iek remembered that now, seeing the struggle. Then seeing Syago perform that execution of the soldier sent chills through her spine. He was a cursed man already.

As bystanders became aware and watched, stunned but happy the attempt was foiled, it became increasingly clear that this would not be a good time to levy a public charge against them. When Syago, Leyta, and Qosku descended the stairs, the people cheered. Lil'iek looked up, seeing Virgow on the wall clapping. On his hard, dark face of scars and eye patch, his shrewd eye seemed pointed at her, noting his political victory and estimating their reaction. It served as a reminder of how dangerous an enemy the aged veteran could be, but at least this confirmed to her his direct involvement.

When she turned to leave, the others followed.

<hr>

3 See *Sol Sistere de Selbst* by Himetuks Himi'n and *Gyibaaw Blackbraid: Mutilated Tyrant*

CHAPTER THREE

The Blight That Was Bottomless

Based on *Writings of Qosku,* cc bastica 340;
The Dark Fortress of Mephorash, cc bastica xxx;

19th of Akril, 247

Qosku's hands trembled. He sat on his bed, stood up, walked a circle, sat down again. When they'd arrived in Voium after the battle of Tiakanawu, Leyta had insisted he and Syago stay with her at her parents' mansion, and she'd given Qosku her old room. Syago stayed in the guest room and Leyta in the "red room" even though it'd given her nightmares as a child. In fact he wasn't sure why she'd not let him take the red and she stay in her old one. Being her guard, he waited for her to rise, but as she delayed it daily, this allowed him more time than he needed or wanted.

He would've preferred to be in any other room, as the femininity of Leyta's old one racked him. He'd come to accept that he'd never change his own femininity. Things would never get better, would probably get worse. It was time to learn to live well with that instead of waiting for a happy ending. He'd assumed it was an imbalance of his yanantin, of losing his twin sister, Chaska. But he'd felt this way when with her, too. He wasn't sure yanantin was even real, or the dualism would've been practiced universally instead of just in the mountains. In any case, denying it had only hurt him and not helped.[4] It even threatened his ability to protect Leyta and the realm. Robbing his focus and power for sorrow. One could be angry at it for only so long, and neither Deova Bondua nor the old Unakan eternals aided him. He could no longer bury it, but had to face its inevitability.

---

4   *See Losnin Liberado Kani, 33*

23

It was no longer about making the depression go away, but dealing with it. He'd gone from forcing himself to be a boy to pretending to be one, adapting to the sad reality.

I'm not man, but woman. In soul if not body, somehow. So what do I do?

He couldn't become a woman; he knew of no curse for that. He was imprisoned by his own body, surviving only by not thinking about it. He considered leaving, starting over again in a new town disguised as a young woman. He thought he could pass, but it seemed like such an impossible if not silly charade. Besides, he needed his friends and they him.

He trained in the small room to keep his combat forms perfect. As a dyn-fist friar, though more of the Takanaku tradition of the Unakan mountains than the Deovan of the Asturion lowlands, he found both power and solace in fighting with fist and foot. Speeding up his movements, he channeled his sentiments through his body. Driving anger for speed and hate for strength, but these were weak as sorrow inevitably took over. Bubbling up from recent memories of the battle, he didn't need to heal his body now, but he couldn't avoid it, especially with the room's mirror reminding him of his maleness. He took a deep breath and went into Leyta's old closet, there finding old dresses that no longer fit her. They were all pretty, with frilled laces and silky coverings. The longer he'd been in here, the more jealous he'd become of her wardrobe and her ability to just be herself. One gown in particular reminded him of the traditional dresses of the moun-tains, with its red and white colors and its gold linings. His shaking hand pulled it off the shelf.

"Am I really doing this?" he whispered as he returned to the middle of the small room. The mirror made it look as though the dress belonged in his hands more than his worn tunic belonged on his own body. He quickly switched into it, just to see what would happen. Briefly avoiding the mirror so he wouldn't have to look at his own naked body. The dress was on. He looked great, authentic, real, true, though there was no miraculous change inside or out that he might've hoped for. Even so, tears fell from his face. He was beautiful, except for the wet cheeks and red eyes. He liked it still. Would Lügos like him in this dress? He wanted his friend to like him, but couldn't risk opening up. Couldn't ruin the friendship and tenuous stand-ing in the army, not again. Nor could he do that to Lügos, one of the few understanding people good to him here, and definitely not in the middle of a terrifying war. It was a forbidden, corrupt love anyway. He was supposed to like women, not men, but he'd never been able to correct this. It'd helped that he hadn't seen the young apothecary much; Lügos had been about the barracks treating wounded soldiers while Qosku stayed close to Leyta. He'd never get out of his head the image of Lügos in a frenzy of treating soldiers at the battle. A brave warrior of a different sort. He so wanted Lüg to desire him as he really was inside. Validation from anyone would bring so much relief, but from him especially. *So what do I do with myself now?*

She? No, not yet.

A knock at the door startled him, and Katti's voice called out. He answered too quickly, "Uh yes, wait a minute."

He hurriedly removed the gown, donned his tunic, and returned the gown to its place in the closet, taking care to make sure it looked just as it had before opening the door to leave with Katti. Instead it was Lügos, Katti standing behind him.

"Hi Qos," Lüg said. "Might we come in?"

"Oh, uh yes you might." He drew the door open wider and closed it after them. For a moment they stood awkwardly in the room.

"It is an odd room," Katti commented.

"I couldn't sleep here," Lüg said. "But I bet Qosku can sleep in anything with his training."

This wasn't wrong. Qosku shrugged.

"Katti and I were talking," Lüg began. "She thought you get your powers from praying to the Unakan eternals, but I recall it being more like dyne. You just facilitate it with prayer sometimes." But Lüg's dashing vest, not yet stained by his day's work as apothecary for the armies, called Qosku's attention.

"Not that it matters," the priestess cut in. "Though I do worry about calling on them, especially in a city blessed by Our Lady Deova Bondua. But I was only curious and am glad you have faith in any case."

Lüg continued, "And I thought why don't we just go ask him and he'll speak for himself?"

"Both are sometimes correct," he began, taking heart she was less aggressive than their first meeting. At least she'd not embarrass him in front of Lüg. "Is truth I use dyne without prayers. I do pray to eternals, but not often because they no help me anymore. I also pray to my ancestors who probably don't listen. And to myself, the only one I have left." This was the most he'd admitted to anyone about his struggles, he'd not meant to but he wanted Lüg to sympathize.

"But you have us Qosku," Lüg quickly added, to Qosku's heart's fluttering content. "Always us."

Katti's eyes also shared Lüg's earnest sincerity. "Yes yes, always. Pagan or not, I'm glad you're here." He nodded his belief of them and they left to attend their duties.

Later that day, church bells again tolled assault as he followed Leyta through the town's cobblestone streets to the wall, remembering with pain when a third of the city died or disappeared. The deepwraiths who'd used a black fog to lure him and Fal'iek in still had not been caught. Such a trick couldn't happen now, not with the city full of soldiers and dynasts ready to counter it. Leyta, now mostly healed in the days since she was stabbed, though still weary from her sickness, kept him close in light of the assassination attempts. Arriving at the top of the wall, Qosku had a sinking feeling. He didn't understand large scale tactics very well, but it was obvious that they couldn't last much longer. Food stores would soon run low, and the enemies were many. Normally they'd be able to rely on the neighboring towns for aid, but the towns were buried in their own problems and too afraid to draw the attention of the barbarian giants.

Several guards met them atop the wall, and Qosku viewed them all with suspicion. The Razhod hadn't been seen, but it was clear they had infiltrated Voium and their deepwraith servants had attempted to steal the relic at night.

From atop the wall, he saw the Chaos faction taking up arms, but it was the single Razhod walking toward Northgate, with dark cloak and scarf covering all but the top of his face, that Master Constantin pointed their gazes to. He was a burly Unakan man, bald except for a knot of black hair that trailed down his brown skin. Leyta muttered that the soulgauntlet weapons, Fobos and Diemos, were on his arms.[5] A disciple followed behind like a friar in prayer. Although unnerved by both, Qosku had to admit to jealousy. These hated men did not hide who they were but bore it openly. Making it a statement.

---

5   *Fobos and Diemos, or Panic and Pain in old Asturion.*

The men walked calmly as archers and elementists poised to set loose. Not far away, the Chaos faction prepared a charge on him. The Razhod either didn't care or paid them no heed. *He must practice Takanaku as well, or their evil version of it.*

The soulgauntlets disappeared, and the man held up his hand, a long knotted blackwood staff materializing in his grasp. A piece of odd metal gleamed from the top like a gem. Someone gasped while Qosku asked, "What is it?"

"Vilekor," Virgow said. "The staff Barthandeon used to lay the Seeping on an area.[6] But I'm surprised to see others using it."[7]

"What this mean? Seeping?" Qosku asked.

"In the old war, it was some kind of invisible blighting curse," Leyta said, glancing at Virgow and Constantin, who watched below, "that affects large areas with slow decay. It's like a wasting disease, making you feel as if your whole body is bleeding, inside and out, from burns." None of the veterans around her disputed it. Qosku recalled elders in the mountains talking of something similar, though they'd called it the Canker.

"Glory to the Crimson Covenant and all those of its name," the disciple shouted, drawing their attention again. The witchlord himself said nothing, walking in range of the archers, where he planted the staff in the ground. The attendant continued, "May the Great Lord of the Deep rise again and slaughter that you greet agony with open mouths and greet death with dripping wounds."

The witchlord said only, "Suffer."

Before they'd finished Virgow called for all to fire at will, but it was still too late. Qosku watched in horror as the Hellface brought a knife up to slit his own throat, blood gushing out on the shining staff head. The Razhod's body fell as arrows and bolts plucked into it and the dirt all around. A hot light seared from the staff's metallic head. Plants put forth lethal pollen swells, but this felt more unnatural to Qosku. Wrong. A stale wind blew at them as all ducked below the parapet, covering their heads. The older dynasts also covered their mouths as they raised their staves to push the

---

6 Brings to mind the old plague, but lacking the black bubons.

7 He's wrong here. Vilekor the Rule of the Grave, or Blightmaker, was a foci for all Razhod dynasts, not just the Dark Sage.

wind away. Qosku tasted the tang of rusting metal on the air, feeling nauseous from it. *This evil wind must be the cause of the Canker.*

The winds diminished, and they looked over the parapet. The solitary staff continued its menacing light; the disciple stood mute behind. Qosku moved to the wall. "I go and stop staff."

"No, Qosku!" Leyta yelled and put a hand on his shoulder as he mounted the parapet.

"Someone needs to, Leyta," Virgow said. "The longer that's there, the more it will poison us. Get on it, lad."

Qosku dropped down from a rope and ran ahead, aware of the army nearby and those on the wall covering him. His mind ran through painful memories to stir up anger for a burst of speed, moving his legs faster than any man could normally move. He expected to feel more of the blight, but only the odd rusting taste in the air met him. He grabbed the glinting staff, the metal tang strong on his tongue, but the staff shocked him, jolting him backwards. It then vanished in a puff of smoke, and the dizziness caused him to hurl into the grassy dirt. The disciple snarled, "You are not worthy to touch the—" Crossbow bolts plucked into him. Qosku used sorrow to heal the burns on his hands, as well as the nausea and dizziness, then returned with a burst of rage in his limbs to get him back up the wall where he vomited again.[8]

The winds stilled further, but he could still taste the metal in his mouth. After some moments to catch his breath and let the rest pass by to descend the stairs, he vomited once more, this time with black bile, and he tried to recall what omen this meant. Everyone else made the sign of the wheel cross while he continued the balm of sadness sentiments in his body. It felt like it worked, but somehow not enough against this new intangible force.

When he felt stable enough, he stood. Master Constantin was instructing Leyta. "The Seeping was always like that, at first there's nothing, then come the ulcerations. Exposure worsens it, and not just us but the air itself is poison now. We should get inside." He pointed at Qosku, his student. "You especially should get treated by your apothecary and use your training, or you'll be dead in a day. Although even our dyne won't save us completely. It never did."

---

8   Nausea, dizziness, and vomiting appear to be the most common first symptoms. But they wouldn't have started for him just yet even being so close, according to all the records I find. Eventually, ulcers form as the body 'seeps' blood.

Leyta led them down the stairs toward her infirmary. "What happened? What this mean?" Qosku asked her, his voice raspy. She also bore signs; everyone from the wall was showing bronzed faces and hands as if from a day in the sun.

She turned to Constantin, who said, "Because that wind touched our water and our buildings, we cannot stay here or the place will add to what the wind did to us. All things are now inedible, they'll make you sicker than starvation would. We are already showing signs of the sickness. By late tomorrow, or perhaps tonight, it will be worse."

"And there's no way to divert it?" she asked. "What can we do?"

"None that we've found. Although there was an instance the priestesses were able to pray it away, completely. But short of waiting on that miracle, or the time necessary for it to fade, we'll have to be out of the city by tomorrow, sooner if possible, or the sickness will consume us. The entire city must evacuate."

From Leyta's concerned face, Qosku gleaned that meant not just the armies but also the citizens had to leave early next morning. Luckily, being a new war outpost, the citizenry was smaller, but that still created a huge burden. The lack of time for such a big move was dangerous during wartime and the season of poison.

Constantin continued, "We who were on the wall will have to do a full wash from canal water before vacating to cease further contamination. Those of us who were at the wall will already be sick, we can treat them with herbs and dyne but ultimately much of the sickness will stay with us for the rest of our shortened lives, barring some miracle. We can migrate to Mantlgrym, Bokhor, and Cantlgrym, as we'd already intended with the dispersion plan. The good thing is that this will also affect that Chaos army waiting outside, however the Razhod will no doubt be waiting for us. We might be able to mount a defense against the Razhod but not if the Fomorions are also waiting us out."

Someone called for Constantin and he left to it on his crutches. Leyta gave commands for people to start preparing for the evacuation. Entering an inn turned barracks, after finding the infirmary already full, she sat on a bench with a sigh. Grateful for a moment to sit, Qosku joined her. He followed her gaze to a victory cross hanging on the wall, though she looked not at it, but beyond it. The cross made Qosku think of his parents' religion, much of which had been lost since the Asturion conquest of the Unakans. He fell back into the healing prayer, meditating to stop this Canker curse. "What do you think about, Qosku?" Leyta asked after a moment.

"What?" he asked, surprised at being addressed. His skin felt hot with blushing.

She looked at him. "You're so quiet all of the time, you must think about something. I'm just curious as to what, enlighten me with your thoughts."

His thoughts were filled with heroic daydreams, Lügos, and painful memories mostly. But he couldn't tell her that. In any case, her interest seemed bland. Not insincere, but flat. He sensed he knew her struggle then, having flitted through something similar before. His initial pity turned to empathy and resolve to lift her out of it—without revealing himself.

"I don't know," he said, searching for a suitable way to avoid the question. He responded, "Fighting."

"That's all? Surely you think of other things too." Her eyes bore into him with rare interest, making him uncomfortable. He looked away. *At least the perpetual weariness in her face is gone.*

"Yes, well... sometimes poetry," he said. This was true, he'd actually written some in Unakan. But warrior men weren't supposed to make poetry, so he destroyed them after, except for the ones he loved too much to eliminate.

It was women's work to create powerful words that empowered men in fighting enemies, but he made up for it by rhyming in the style of Pelagiod the Conqueror and avoided softness. Words of strength and toughness that gave Qosku both when he imitated them. Love poems he shunned completely except in weaker moments. Lately his style shifted to darker moods, ruminating on his cruel dilemmas and inner pains. It was all he could do to adapt to the bleak world ahead, face it instead of flee it.

"What kind of poetry?" she pressed gently, frustratingly not letting up.

"Strength," he responded, maybe too quickly. "I don't really—"

A strained yell from behind made him jump to shield her. A soldier from the wall was rubbing his reddened face and vomiting. Qosku realized that his own skin was burning, his red face itching as if sunbaked. He'd let his guard down, stopped healing before finished. He noticed others were coughing and vomiting now as well, some with bloody noses besides, but only those who'd been present during the Hellface incident. Leyta included, but Qosku was the worst. He doubled over and coughed up more black bile. He'd begun to feel sick but ignored it. He focused the sorrow in his body to move to the worst parts, summoning memories to make it as strong and constant as possible. Recalling sorrowful and grim songs and poems added further strength. It all helped, but the queasy feeling was remained. He could self-heal only minor wounds and very gradually. After a moment, he opened his eyes to find Leyta leading Katti and Emilia carrying him down the street to a new infirmary setting up in St. Casilda's Chapel. There was a shout for them to first hold an emergency mass in order to stem the curse with prayer and song.

However, before they could get there, a scuffle began in the streets. Five Asturion men were shoving an Unakan man, yelling at him. Qosku's initial reaction was to keep his head down and stay in the safety of Syago's arms. But Katti and Emilia set him down, then went up and pushed the Asturions away from the man, making Qosku feel embarrassed for his own cowardice. Yet the problems didn't stop there.

"In the old war, the Razhod were mostly Unakans," one of the soldiers said, "and they are again. That one out there was."

"That doesn't matter," Leyta began, walking up to join Emilia and Katti.

Another picked up, "These pagans are in on it somehow. They're the assassins and spies."

"You don't know that," Katti echoed more forcefully. "You can't just attack him. Either bring charges or get out of the city."

But they weren't listening, instead looking past them at Qosku, who felt as though he was going to puke again. "That's why you defend them," the first soldier began. "One's with you. Did he cast a spell on you or is it blackmail?"

"Or bribery?" the other said.

Leyta looked weary of this but still put a hand to Katti's shoulder. "No, don't." Katti, surprisingly ready to slap him, held it. Leyta never failed him as a friend, Syago too though he'd already left for the bog, but Katti was different. The normally sweet archpriestess had not only loosened up but angrily defended him. Leyta turned to them. "If you want to—"

"Yeah, we'll be watching you," one said as the five started walking away. Then he pointed to Qosku, smiling. "And we'll be watching him. Don't let him trick you."

In the chapel infirmary, Qosku tried to avoid being helped, and certainly didn't want to lie down with all the goings on, but the nausea and now headaches on top of internal bleeding made him realize the need. He told them all he needed to do was pray it off, which did help, but not enough. Of those sick with the Canker, he was the worst.

He faded in and out of sleep, waking more fully as darkness set in. He sat up, feeling the weight of the dark room and other wounded sleeping. The moon waned this night, so he could avert changing into his werebeast form if he'd wanted to. But he wanted his beast form. Not only would the dangerous transformation heal him from the blight faster, but it was his escape from his body confusion. It kept his mind off of Lügos. Since the Battle of Tiakanawu, he'd come to terms with his desires, his identity—that he could not eliminate it. While he couldn't switch his body out for an-other—the wrongness of his body being male had no cure—he could embrace his nightly turn under the moon. This had always been a dangerous and incomplete solution, but short of a magic spell, he was stuck as is. Still, he could not yet openly embrace being she. Embracing it had gotten him in trouble in Chuqi'kirau. Would it be any different here in the lowlands? He wasn't sure of anything, lost in a time of total conflict.

If he did transform into a beastspawn, he'd need to find a reason to leave the infirmary without raising suspicion to the others—there was no private quarter he could use.

An armed guard stood at the door, a priestess prayed in a corner, and a wounded nobleman read a book from his bed. He heard people outside, moving about in preparation to exit the city. No, it wouldn't be a good night to roam.

The change pressed at him, but he turned within himself, focusing on keeping it at bay and healing through his meditative prayer, in between fits of bloody coughing and itching. He lay back down when Katti and Lügos entered.

Katti was the only priestess he really knew and still felt surprised by her change of heart. She'd gone from just another dogmatic priestess enforcing the Church's will to a genuine friend and defender. She spoke first, "Qosku, I just want to tell you that your pure and humble example has made me rethink my faith. You always help others, even those not good to you, and today you were willing to sacrifice yourself for the city without even being asked to. And then when persecuted, you didn't react in anger. I'm going to be more giving and true. And I'm sorry for the way I was rude to you when we first met." Without waiting, she began the prayers over him, then moved on to the others. Qosku barely remembered that first meeting but admired the gesture. As Lügos sat in the chair next to his bed, Qosku froze. He looked beautiful and concerned, melting Qosku's heart, and he knew this distraction would only diminish both his healing and his resistance to the transformation. Qosku shook his head. "No, is bad time. I need sleep."

"Qos, I just need to check your bleeding. And probably apply a salve to your burned skin," he said, placing a hand on his bare chest and another on his face. His hands were gentle and slightly cool, and the feeling of them made Qosku's stomach flutter. Qosku slapped them away, harder than he meant to.

"Qos, I need to clean it," he said, his tone somewhere between irritation and surprise. "I'll be gentle."

"No, I—" He looked around for an excuse.

"What's wrong?" Lüg said. That look of concern only made it worse, so beautiful. The life Qosku wanted was right here in front of him, yet if he reached for it he'd lose it all. He prayed in his head for his ancestor's aid and understanding. Yet all he felt as Lüg prepped a new bandage was more yearning, and the monster pried at the corners of his mind for the change. "Your transformation?" His eyes widened slightly, and he looked behind him quickly, then dropped his voice as he said, "If you can hold it off at least until I clean it, then you can leave. Might be good for you actually." He grabbed the bandage and peeled it off.

"Yes- no, I can't hold it." Qosku grasped at it as his excuse but it fell short. Lüg ignored him and again the questions persisted: Did he know? Did he feel the same way? Lügos came close, his bare arms against Qosku's chest, a sensation that Qosku'd longed for. For a second he lost himself in the feeling. Then old revulsion at the moment swelled in him, and the monster's change came on. He'd accepted himself, consciously, but disgust buried was disgust that remained. To his relief, and horror, he couldn't stop it. Fast in its lateness, his whole body grew, hairs sprung, and his mind, full of longing and affection, faded into the fury of lost concentration. Having focused his prayers on healing instead of conscious change, he felt his memories fade. Lügos stumbled back in surprise, becoming just a boy to the wereozor monster. The bed broke beneath as a guard ran at him, drawing his sword. The hackles on the ozor beast's neck rose; he didn't know the creature with the sword but he knew he could handle its threat. The boy moved between the two, placing a hand on his large hairy arm, annoyingly distracting the beast from the challenge.

He slapped the boy against the wall in a soft thud, then threw him at the guard, then the chair at the other soldier who came in. The guard's armor and reflexes allowed him to deflect it. Three more came in after, charging him. Something awful cried inside himself as he thrashed them, clawing and breaking them. A terrified woman prayed nearby and he roared at her for silence. He turned back to the carnage in front of him, numerous guards lay about, conquered by his ferocity. Then he saw the boy lying at an awkward angle, neck broken, dead. The sight wrought something terrible in him that he couldn't understand. He shrunk, fading out of his beast form to crumble to the floor over his friend in human sorrow as realization dawned. Sobs consumed him, and he cradled the lifeless, beautiful body of a true friend.

Yells and shouts brought him out of his mourning. The wounded guards stirred around him, their armor protecting them where Lüg had not been. People surrounded the place, torches and weapons in hand, talking loudly and pointing at him. The soldiers picked themselves up, then scrambled out of the room in fear. There was no denying what he was, too many people saw him come out of it. He stood naked before them, and their anger and fear lay on the brink of eruption. The mob yelled for his execution.

They charged into the room, filling it with shouts. "Hang him before he corrupts us with his plague," said a man.

An old lady pointed her finger at him. "We shouldn't have to suffer for your bad choices, filthy dugger!"

He shouted back that he hadn't been in control, though normally he was in control or safely isolated, but it was drowned out by their shouts, and his own inner voice that agreed with them. For a moment they only surrounded him, afraid to come closer. Then the rage boiled over and two men with gloves grabbed for him. He tried to escape but the room was so full and he was still trembling with grief. Large rough hands clenched his arms tight, someone whipped and kicked him as they carried him. Others spat on him. They dragged his naked form out of the house toward the town square where gurows pecked at the criminals already hanging there on wooden gallows in front of the chapel, all illuminated by his cursed moonlight. The blackbirds flew off as they carried his small form up to one of the corpses, cut the body down, then strung up a new rope.

"Don't let him eat you," said an old woman, which struck him as particularly ridiculous since he was now in his human form. They continued the slander against him, saying the Unaka were always bringing filth and that the Razhod had probably sent him in for this. Then one complaint stood out to Qosku.

"I'm talking to Leyta and Alfonsor about this. We shouldn't have to deal with this wretchedness, as if we haven't enough already. His mistakes need not be ours."

"But he's Leyta's personal guard!" yelled one.

"That's right. Did she know of this all along? A werebeast among us this whole time!" Whispers followed the question with more suggestions of a Razhod plot.

Another sinking realization fell upon him. This could end her, but she wasn't here yet. He had to take the blame, all of it, before she arrived to try and defend him.

"My secret," he said. "Not Leyta's. She never knew."

But they barely heard him. He was at the noose when he raised his voice. "She didn't know or she would have exiled me already! Do you think she wants the curse on her as well?" This caught their attention. "Being around me gets you the curse. Those who've carried me might have it already."

They backed away from the platform and he hid surprise at how easily this worked. "I've fought for you, fought beside you, with only the good intentions. Now, I go exile myself so you not get the curse."

He didn't wait for them to part for him, but climbed the gallows, then jumped up a nearby wall, easily scaling it. Some of them shouted but most seemed keen to just let him escape to the outerwild. A couple chased him with weapons as he scampered over the rooftop, coming down only to grab his belongings from the chapel infirmary. He grabbed his sack of spare tunics and armor, and with one last sorrowful look at Lügos, bloody and broken, he walked out the door, breaking into a run as it started to rain. The droplets snapped at his shoulders and head. Shame haunted him too strong.

Tears streamed his face, mixing with the rain, as he raced through the streets, changing back into his werebeast as he reached the nearest wall. Scaling easily up the fortification, he flew over it, over the malwolves and

Fomorion giants below, to race across the land. He found a forest of brambles and, in a pure rage, lay waste to any logs and rocks in his path, unsure why but the image of a dead boy centered his mind.

CHAPTER FOUR

TREACHERY, TREACHERY

Based on *Milgalic's Journals*, cc bastica 70;
Leyta's Journals, cc bastica 247;

19th–20th of Akril, 247

The cider ran down Milgalic de Culon's throat, warm and tart but refreshing. He laughed better at Fernandeon's jokes this way. They drank as if it were their last night alive and almost felt as it were. Supposedly the food and drink could make them sick. Well, strong drink did that anyway.

Fernandeon slammed his mug down. "Let's just go."

Algernon scoffed. "At night? They'll gut us."

"Prolly gut us anyway," Machen said between swigs.

"Naw, they want us," Fernandeon said. "Need us. Listen, I can get us out past the guards. The Fomorions won't do anything to us, jus' walkin' up to 'em. At least we know the other Asturions with 'em won't let it. They'll take us in; I got friends."

Milgalic didn't like the idea of desertion, especially to the enemy. But the feeling of impending doom frightened him in ways he admitted to no one. A blight and two enemies that had beat them in battle and now sat at their doors. They could not survive. At least defecting would keep him with these friends. He faked a laugh with the others, having missed the joke.

Fernandeon stood and raised his mug in a toast. "To new armies and new beginnings. And may we each drink better cider next time too!"

They all rose, said "aye" with a laugh, and clanked their mugs before gulping down the rest. Fernandeon surprised everyone by throwing his at the bar. None tended there, in these last days of civilization, so it only clattered off of other empty mugs. The others cheered and threw theirs. Milgalic threw his, wishing he'd meant it.

They stormed out of the tavern, laughing, but resumed silence and speed in their rooms gathering the last of their things into packs. Their escape came surprisingly easy. Two went ahead to pretend being on gate duty. The guards eagerly took the opportunity to leave, and with that, the gate was cracked open and they slipped out, pulling it as shut as they could from the outside but not worrying about a full seal and lock. That alone could earn them the gallows.

Darkness fell and campfires already burned ominously in the near distance, obscured by tents and bestial giant humanoids. The Fomorion giants watched them with evident hunger, but given the small size of the non-aggressive group, they did not charge. Some rebel Asturions ran up and vouched for them to a lead barbarian, a cycloptic ohancanu with a thick red beard. The barbarian giant grunted and resumed sharpening his massive battleaxe as they walked past. A wookalar moved in front of them as if to bar passage. Its eyes shimmered in the firelight over the swine face of tusks and horns. They made to go around, and it blocked them again. The Asturion leader didn't face up to the hairy giant, but looked down to the ground. Finally the ohancanu grumbled at him in a gutteral language. The wookalar stared them down a moment longer before moving aside.

They were led to a small corner of the Asturion rebellion area. Milgalic knew none of the rebels there but had hoped for reassurances on meeting them. However, he found none. They looked, or didn't look, at the giants warily, out of both fear and disgust. And he agreed. He also saw signs of the blight among them all, bloody coughing, vomiting, and diarrhea, and the red skin. The Fomorions for their part disregarded the rebels completely, or so it seemed. It was difficult to tell since the two groups never interacted. The monster barbarians frightened Milgalic, and it wasn't even late into the night. They never stopped being violent or loud, frequently breaking things or yelling, and they smelled terrible. Only the drums and horns drowned out their hitting each other or themselves. Their sex was loud and unconcealed, bestial and brutally inescapable to those who wanted nothing to to with it. Their food was revolting; they ate all of the monster, not just its holier parts, and it was fouled by the Seeping anyway. Only their drink was redeemable, though also sickening. Too strong for anything more than a sip.

As the night wore on, Fernandeon discovered the camp entertainment and invited Milgalic, who moved through the crowded area in search of a better viewing spot. The rebel Asturions had started a fight ring for the older, idiot recruits. The dumbheads, who'd been the servants and caretakers of the Royal Chaos leaders from the start, were gullible enough that, with enough pushing, they got into the middle of the circle and started fighting each other. The rebels running the show took bets.

The ringleaders got the dumbheads riled up, gave them some drink, and pushed them in against each other while everyone watched, cheering and laughing. The swings began clumsy and tactless, but hard and mean. Dull-mouthed taunts and grunts got swallowed up by the raucous gamblers. Milgalic saw two men, Arturon and Bartolu, if he remembered right, pound into each other. These two, normally gentle, now turned brutish and violent under all the coaxing and drunkenness. Tears streamed down Arturon's face as he struggled weakly against Bartolu's headlock. Bartolu's taunts were unintelligible. He didn't speak very well even without drink. Milgalic felt a stab of pity for both of them, soft men made animal. Fernandeon tapped Milgalic's shoulder and handed him a mug of cider with a big smile. He took it, though he still felt something awful about what had been done to the two otherwise kind men. But he had to admit, it was fun once he stopped thinking too deeply, and more cider helped the guilt go down easier.

A shout and a crash from behind Milgalic got everyone's attention. He was surprised to see Jester walking toward them; it was believed that he'd not been in camp. In fact Milgalic might not have come if he'd known the powerful lunatic clown was going to be present. He jumped slightly as Jester upturned another makeshift betting table, throwing up the ledgers. The noise quieted though the fighting in the ring continued.

"HOW DARE YOU!" Jester boomed, and a chill shot through Milgalic. "They make your food, clean your clothes, run the camp, and this is how you repay them?! Damn your games and your drinks. I did not suffer for this, they did not work for this, and I will kill anyone before I let them—"

"Aw c'mon, Jesterman!" said a ringleader, as he moved up to Jester and towered over the clown's scrawny form. "We was just havin' some fun. We thought it'd be good for 'em, train 'em and give 'em fun times. Nobody *made* 'em do it. And they're all fine."

"Yeah, sit down and watch with us. You'll like it," said another ringleader, clapping a hand on Jester's shoulder. A couple others joined the call but remained in the crowd as the two towered over Jester, trying to intimidate the wiry, masked bard into conceding.

Before any of them finished cajoling, a low humming filled the camp. Milgalic noticed some of the dumbheads walking toward Jester. The tone rose in pitch, and the idiots charged in, pummeling the ringleaders, who shouted and struggled to get away. But they were outnumbered by the even bigger men entranced by Jester's music. The two ringleaders fell down, clutching themselves, trying and failing to block or swing back, yelping for it to stop. The song was powerful enough that Milgalic also felt its pull, urging him to join, and many others besides, judging from their expressions. The beating continued, and yells turned into screams and whimpers, and then finally silence—broken only by the sickening sounds of bones crunching and fists pounding flesh slick with blood. Milgalic watched in horror while the ringleaders were beaten to a pulp long after the men were dead. Jester's unreadable mask sustained the tune, his sorrowful mask unreadable. When the men were unrecognizable lumps of blood and viscera, he changed the ethereal tone to one more soothing. The beating stopped as the dumbheads became gentle again, chests heaving, faces flush and tear-stained.

"Anyone else?" Jester asked, daring. "Any more that like to watch them fight or don't like the way we do things here?"

Fernandeon shifted next to Milgalic and said, "You- you didn't have to do that. It was just fun and games."

Jester backhanded him hard across the face. Fernandeon spun and would've fallen off the rock he'd been sitting on if Milgalic hadn't caught him. Jester continued, "I am ashamed of you, all of you. You forget the purpose of the Royal Chaos, our tenets prohibit games of torture and humiliation, except for traitors, which is my task, not yours. You do not rule each other. If you don't like them, then get out. You can die with the rest of the world. Now apologize to my people and clean this mess up." He walked away and the dumbheads, their spell ended, followed him out.

Milgalic turned to Fernandeon, who rubbed at his head. He drank the last few drops of his cider, which had mostly spilled when he got hit, then threw the mug. Milgalic had never seen him so furious.

"Are you all right?" Milgalic asked.

"No!" Fernandeon spat. "Stupid tightass clown. He doesn't have a foding clue for shit. Who cares about this stupid fight? He's just like the foding priests and noblemen he hates, telling everyone what to do, giving all these rules and shit. Stupid hypocrite motherfoder!"

Fernandeon got up and started pacing, still rubbing his bruising face. Milgalic wanted to say something but couldn't think of anything that wouldn't upset him more. Milgalic had mixed feelings about the incident. He felt Jester had a point, but the savage execution of those men churned his stomach. Fernandeon growled in frustration and kicked a discarded mug. It hit the leg of one of the other guys who was reluctantly cleaning up the place and rearranging things.

"Hey, watch it!" the man said. "An' are you gonna help clean up or what?"

"Foda you!" Fernandeon retorted. "I'm done with this stupid place. Milgalic, let's go."

Unsure of what he meant, Milgalic stood up hesitantly. "All right, where?"

"Away. C'mon." Fernandeon turned and left. The bloody bodies caught Milgalic's attention; he couldn't tell if there were two or three. He felt a pit in his stomach and walked after his friend, now wishing he'd never left.

Early that morning before the evacuation, Leyta couldn't get herself out of bed again. This time not just from lack of will or energy, she felt sick. The nausea everyone else on the wall experienced had come to her, along with some vomiting. Katti's prayers did help ease it, as did herbs from the apothecaries. Additionally, the dread of leaving the security of the walls and fighting again turned to a dead numbness inside her. And the ordeal of losing Qosku to self-exile and having to cover up her involvement in the incident only made it worse. Consequently, she lacked the energy to try in full the two deserters, Milgalic and Fernandeon, now returned. Count Cantarchar annoyingly had left them to her. She considered a more forbidding option proposed by Constantin: calling upon the cosmic gate Osmos for aid from Heaven to help them cleanse the Seeping. She could offer the criminals to the gate and rid two problems at once. But she shuddered at the thought, not only of dealing with Osmos but also the angels who tended to harm more than help. Absurd thoughts and an emotional void, maybe she was going dynast insane after all.

After another morning of Katti pushing her to get up and dressed, she made her way to the city dungeon where the deserters were held, having to stoop slightly to walk in. The dark, wet, odorous cellway suited rather than worsened her void. She paused in front of one cell that held a number of people who'd preached too far out of line with the Church, alternate paths to salvation and endings of the world. Heretics. She didn't know what would become of them, but saw a potential future for herself in there. How many of her own friends would throw her in here if she tried to convince them of the sentimental poisoning of the world?

She passed to the next gated cell. Kneeling in front of her on the brick floor, the two soldiers sat with hands in chains. She stared at them, letting the uncomfortable silence weigh them down a little. Their faces were shadows beneath long grimy hair. Fernandeon had complicated her position ever since he'd arrived at Cantlgrym. Though an excellent soldier, she had to admit, she now felt glad he could be out of her way. A month ago she'd have relished the opportunity to punish him, now she just felt light relief at one less thing requiring her effort. Memories of the two executions she'd done haunted her: her first a murderer she killed by fire as a young girl—too young; the other a rapist whose body she drained of water in an execution gone too far for an experienced leader. She wouldn't do it again here if she could avoid it. Normally, she'd not be able to do anything but expel these two children of wealthy families, but their crimes were many and severe and this was war.

"I can give you information on them," Fernandeon supplied, his voice small in the dungeon. "If you give me leniency."

Doubting he could provide anything of value, she rubbed her face. She was too tired to deal with this. "What do you have?" she said.

"They're moving soon," he said.

"We already know that," she said. "We just don't know when."

"And the demon Knave," he continued. "He's a distraction whenever the leadership move, sometimes transporting Jester directly in a supply sack."

She perked up. "What do you mean? Explain."

"The demon transports messages and supplies because he can fly, right? I saw- I wasn't supposed to- but I saw the demon bring in his sack, so I decided to take a look. I saw it through a crack in the tent, Jester stepped out of the sack, he was crouched in it and got out." His eyes flickered up to hers, and she saw hope in them. And an eagerness to please.

She turned to Milgalic, who only stared at the floor. "Milgalic, can you verify this?"

He looked at his companion, then back at the floor and shook his head. Nausea began returning to her, and she decided to take the claim just so she could get out of there.

"Keep them here for now, shared cell is fine," she said to the soldiers.

"But I gave you good information!" Fernandeon protested as she turned.

"That's still to be determined," she said, walking back along the dungeon hall. "And in any case, I never promised it would save you from anything."

He protested further, but she ignored him. Milgalic, to his credit, stayed silent. She returned to the court and slumped down in a chair, but she only stared at the exit plans, feeling no push or pull to review or build them. In what the old her would've considered a terrible dereliction of duty, she skimmed them, made only three corrections, then left to retire. But duty nagged at her so she first turned to check on her men at the wall. Climbing to the battlements, she could see the enemy camp. A small force of Fomorion giants and rebel Asturions sat not far from the wall; archers could shoot for them with minimal accuracy and the force could charge any exiting group with ease. The evacuation depended on who buckled and left first. She'd all but forgotten Fernandeon's information, which she'd thought silly as they'd seen Knave carry Jester openly before. But as she stood on the wall, she saw that wretched thin white creature, wearing the head of a human boy on its neck, rise up out of the camp carrying a bag. She turned to Virgow, who stood nearby, and pointed at it. "We need to shoot the demon and catch that sack. I received information that it could be valuable."

Virgow looked at her, slightly puzzled at first, then quickly responded, putting his men into focus with arrows and crossbows. Leyta attempted to join by raising her scepter. But again, her efforts produced nothing, so she pretended to be commanding the wind with hate. The other dynasts' winds seemed enough, though, blowing Knave back toward them. A group of soldiers prepared the roped ballistae, and they moved quickly, as did Knave, who dove then rose, trying to slip past the drafts. As the agony rose up, the soldiers moved along the ramparts and fired corded spears at the sack. One caught, causing Knave to lose his flight pattern just before veering away. The soldiers pulled on the rope, slowing Knave's escape, and as the spears began to tear free, three more plucked into it. The carrying handles shredded under Knave's talons and the bag swung down, already being pulled in by the men.

Knave screeched a childish "NOOOO!" and dove after it. Leyta reacted quickly, grabbing the rope to help pull the sack up while others joined in and the elementists focused wind bursts on disrupting the demon's flight. He fought it, but more dynasts joined in, sending him into a spiral. He fluttered and dodged as the soldiers pulled the sack up the wall.

Once over the wall, they hurried the sack down the stairs to take it into the city. The white agony came at the parapet, diving at the remaining soldiers and dynasts. Its wings propelled it along the walkway, tearing with its front claws, ramming with its human head, and lashing with its sickle-tail. Dynasts threw fire and darkfire at it, but nothing stopped it. Their defenses were insufficient against an otherworlder. It dove into the city, scampering after the sack. Watching Knave escape into her city, Leyta knew she should be leading the attack. She followed soldiers down, not feeling urgency but acting as if she did, and when she saw Knave whip its tail at a Cantlgrym soldier's neck, her gut wrenched. Still, she had no sentiments to use.

The soldier clutched his neck as red squirted out. A pair of soldiers put up a shield wall, holding against the demon's charge. It scratched and whipped at their wood and metal, ignoring their return spear thrusts. Then Leyta heard Lil'iek's war cry undulating above the shouts. She was fast behind it with the hellknife Ravenger, coming out of nowhere and jumping on Knave's back to plunge Ravenger in.

It screeched and scrambled, shaking her off, then leaped up the side of a building and flew off. Leyta felt a brief pang of envy, and also concern, for that meant the woman had been there, could've attacked her, and she hadn't noticed. But Lil'iek hadn't attacked her, and that was something. Lil'iek impassively watched the demon fly off, then she vanished into the crowd.

With Knave gone, Leyta went to the sack and tore it open. There lay Jester, seemingly unconscious, among a sheath of papers. Had he abandoned the army here? She couldn't tell if he was even breathing. She looked at the soldiers. "Take him to the dungeons and set a guard on him, three guards, make sure he's no weapons. We'll determine his physical state later, but for now let the Chaos think he's alive and well so we can bargain."

Even as she spoke, she wondered why it mattered what they did or what Chaos thought. *It's all unraveling; we humans can barely live together much less deal with all these outside threats.*

They dispersed and she saw a small boy watching curiously from a doorway, chewing his finger. And finally she felt something, a lasting plume of love for the adorable child. She put on a smile and went to him, crouching to be level with his glassy eyes. "Hello, I'm Leyta. What's your name?"

He mumbled out, "Tomas."

"Tomas, that's a nice name. Is this your home?" He nodded faintly, and her heart melted. Children did that to her. "Did that monster scare you? Or the clown?"

He didn't respond, just stared blankly, chewing his finger. She continued, "You know what I think—"

"Tomas, come inside!" a voice shouted from within. The boy turned from her, closing the door in her face. The love faded.

The guards dragged Jester through the dungeons and threw him into the cell across from Milgalic and Fernandeon, then locked his legs in shackles. Through the iron-bar doors of the tiny cells, Milgalic could barely see him lying there, back slumped against the wall. His masked head hung awkwardly to the side as the belltails jingled dully in the shadows of his cell. As they left, the guards muttered something about being unable to remove the clown's hood. Darkness returned as they took the lantern with them, leaving the prisoners with only the steady sound of a dripping leak, the scratching of a rat, and the stench of rotting food and old shit.

Milgalic concluded that Fernandeon's information must've been true and strangely well timed. What did he care? Fernandeon chuckled to himself, looking at Jester's limp body. "I got him back in the end. I accomplished more in this war by deserting and trying to have fun than anybody else."

Milgalic hugged his knees to his chest, not looking at Fernandeon. Milgalic kicked himself inwardly for following this pathetic excuse of a friend. He buried his face in his knees, wishing he could just go to sleep and forget the whole thing. He hated that he was so weak in those moments of moral significance. It pained him that he couldn't take those moments back, and now his conscience seared him.

"You don't have to be bored in here you know," said Jester from his cell opposite them. His body remained prostrate, still and quiet. "I know some games we can play."

"Shut up," Fernandeon said. "Nobody cares about you."

"There's this one game where you two fight each other," continued Jester. "And I watch. You fight, and I'll place bets on who wins. Then when the guards stop us, I go tattle on them and lock them up so you can keep beating each other. Doesn't that sound like a fun game? I love that game. I'll take the loser."

"Shut up, damn you!" Fernandeon yelled.

"Fun and games," said Jester. "That's all it is. Just fun and games."

"Guards," Fernandeon shouted. "Come make him be quiet. He's bothering me."

"Howsabouts you both shut it," a guard said as he walked past their cells. "Or I give you a new whacking you never forget."

When the guard passed, Jester resumed his conversation. "You see nobody understands me. What I've gone through, why I'm so motivated thus. 'Tis a tragically sad but inspiring tale."

He went abruptly quiet for a moment, which Milgalic thought odd. Then he spoke again in a slightly harsher tone. "You must understand that these struggles, this insanity of life and the world, it's enough to make your head explode. And these bars, well, I've never liked cages, so this cell is just making it worse.

"I'm losing my mind. In fact, I think I'm ready to pull my head off," he said as he reached up to his head. To Milgalic's horror, Jester's masked head popped off his neck. "See, all better."

He tossed the head toward the bars but no blood flowed or splattered. The head bounced and turned to face Fernandeon, whose face froze agape. "I wish I could see the world through your eyes. I just want to laugh again.

"So here's another anti-joke for you," Jester's head continued. Behind, the headless body reached one arm over to grab the other arm and pull it off. The arm fell to the ground, then reached up and grabbed the remaining one. That too plopped off. "How many arms does it take to screw the head off of a traitor?"

The clown head, moving in small hops, squeezed through the prison bars and bounced into the hallway. Apparently finding the coast clear, it crossed to the cell of Milgalic and Fernandeon. "None; traitors screw themselves, over and over again." The arms followed the head. Body trembling, Milgalic stood and pressed himself into the corner. Fernandeon started to stand once he saw that the arms were coming for him, but he was too late.

The voice filled the air, "Don't you get the joke? Why aren't you laughing?! IT'S FUNNY!"

The arms sprung and grabbed Fernandeon at the neck, fists wrapping around him, choking him. He struggled against them to no avail. The arms bashed his head into the stone bricks. Blood flew. Milgalic cowered, then recalled his need for courage. He tried to pull them off but got whacked in the face by an elbow. He saw a guard staring into the cell, mortified.

"Help us!" Milgalic shouted. The guard pulled out his keys and fumbled with them at the lock but his trembling hands couldn't get the key in. Milgalic returned to Fernandeon but failed to get a hold of the arms as his once friend rolled and bounced about the cell, eyes bulging.

During all of this, the head continued its rant in harshly surreal tones. "Don't you like the game?! Are you having fun now?! I thought you liked fun and games. IT'S WHAT YOU WANTED!"

The door swung open as Fernandeon went limp. The guards rushed in, but it was too late. Their eyes followed the detached arms as they crawled back into Jester's cell with the head. "I just want to feel laughter again," the head said as the arms put it back in place, the Mourning Jester now an unmoving whole.[9]

---

[9] Milgalic was later hanged with a few others in a rushed ceremony before the exit and probably without Leyta's knowing. She seems to have forgotten about him and the gaolers didn't want to manage a prisoner of no value to the enemy, or themselves, so they rushed him and a couple others to the gallows.

CHAPTER FIVE

Alone in the Dark

Based on *Writings of Qosku*, cc bastica 370;
The Nordvargor Testaments, cc bastica 913;

dates unknown, 247

Qosku crouched in a small hole of dirt, rock, and root in the Kourii Marshes, looking out across the wetlands at Boggorn. The marsh area stretched out, a series of ponds and grass patches. Deeper in, it turned to bogs, where Syago had gone in search of the notorious witch shortly after Qosku had gone to the infirmary. It was said that none returned from the bog wholly sane.

What if he found Syago? Would his stupidity kill that friend too? No matter the power of the Holy Knight, Qosku's ill fortune reigned supreme.

Currently he struggled with the simple task of lighting a fire. Qosku had killed some type of white rabbit with antlers that had nearly skewered him, which would make a survivable evening meal if the logs he'd gathered would catch. His bowels had calmed enough to try food, but he'd felt new fatigue, either from the Canker or the sorrow. At least he was able to use the fur to make a coat against the cold. Since turning into a monster had destroyed his tunic, he'd covered mud all over himself, crotch to chest, to avoid seeing his body. Even out here his naked wrong body still bothered him, but the fur helped. When he'd lost his friend in Chuqi'kirau because of his sex perv- confusion... thing, he'd questioned the eternals and apus on why they'd done this to him. He'd never gotten an answer, leading him to doubt them. He'd written a poem on it and prayed on it now.

THE GRAND GIVER GIVETH THEN TAKETH AWAY

Drop me and I break into a thousand thoughts

Scatter them to the winds and clean out my soul

Bring my pieces back together

Bit by bit, I'm roughly renewed

Assembled as a conscious console

Universe, thou art full as the tipping hourglass

Oh Maker, why hast thou made me?

You've given me all the answers

But all they do is ask me questions

I've studied the wisdom of the ages

But when I open those great books

I find the writings reading me

Oh Mover, where hast thou moved me to?

When I search out what's true

I'm blinded by thy example

Oh Master, servitude hasn't served me

When I attempt to solve riddles

I'm speechless as they resolve me

What do you do when puzzles are puzzled by you?

Content only in ignorance

What has Truth done for us?

I only see it questioning me

And judging thee

Because thou madest promises no longer kept

Because I maketh promises that never slept

Because I never strayed from waiting in thy pew

Because thou art ever fading from inward view

Because the more thou takest, the less thou givest

Because the said blessings are just a life well lived

I've journeyed deep, far, and wide with you at my side

Now all I can do is lay bare in this thy snare

Or be free from truth in thee

In me[10][11]

10 The language in this poem doesn't fit Qosku, it's very late century Asturion and so I've heard debates rage about it being copy errors, a misattribution, or a mistranslation.

11 I disagree. Qosku was well read and even invented many words; it's possible some of those later words actually came from this now famous poem.

He retched up the rabbit, with what he suspected was congealed blood. Why was the sickness making his intestines bleed? *What is this Canker thing anyway? Just one more curse for me.* He'd kept with the prayers of healing, but his wereozor had healed it most, though not completely. His skin was completely better but the internal bleeding persisted.

Speeding up his arms didn't counter the wetness in the wood he spun. Again and again, he contemplated just walking into a den of malwolves. What had happened with Lügos, it haunted him as never before. More than the betrayal-to-save Chaska and more than sacrificing her, since she at least might still be alive. He'd thought her dead but then he'd glimpsed her at Tiakanawu, at the cult camp with the other captive children, which seemed almost as bad. He wasn't sure if his seeing her had been a dream or not. And it was his fault, whatever her situation, it too was his fault. What right did he have to live now?

He wondered if Syago also was cold and starving out there. Then he understood that while he could not live for himself, he had to for those friends. He'd committed to aiding Leyta and would commit now to also aiding Syago. And Lil'iek. He'd not been part of her betrayal, had been on the other side of the field, but maybe she'd need him too. In this he hoped for renewed purpose.

Part of him still wished for something to kill him as he went, rid his feminine soul of this male body. But what if they didn't kill him outright? Some monsters fed their living prey to their young. It was not only the unknown creatures of the bogs that scared him, but also the unknown hereafter. After dying, would he be slave to an eternal because of his curses or loss of tradition? He hated this, everything. Himself for the path of destruction he'd walked. Ending Lügos's and Chaska's lives. He decided now that he'd loved Lügos, though the remorse didn't help. Training, meditating, writing his journal, poetry, none of it had worked. There was only the beast, which he now hated for what it'd done, even as it offered him his only solace.

He'd found an old spearhead wedged deep in the mud, metal he could use. Roasting the last of his rabbit's meat from earlier, he choked down several bites. Hard and stringy, the wiry animal tasted bitter but at least it tasted. At least he could feel.

Did he want to feel? So much pain pressed at him. Anytime he recalled why he was out here, it incapacitated him. At least here he no longer had to pretend, not until he rejoined Syago. He even tried wearing the meager rabbit fur more like a dress, but switched to his back for the warmth.

He left the hole to search more through the fetid land of mud and grass and puddle. A cluster of mushrooms gave him pause. They sprouted out of a large rotting blackbird corpse, yet they weren't ejecting spores at him so he was able to douse and pluck them safely.[12] It was the season of poison and so plants and fungi came out in assault. There was no way to know if the mushrooms were toxic except by trial and error.

A green haze hovered over the watery plain from evening fog, the sun just disappearing behind the mountains. To his left sat Thornwood and its swamp. Behind, the Apugaka Mountains rose. And to the right more marsh and mountains. What a terrible grave to lie down in, but he deserved no better. At least he was near his mountains, being so close to them again made him wish he'd never left. But he really needed drinkable water. It was everywhere, mossy and muddy and full of algae. Up the mountain sides might be fresher streams.

He walked around and up the hill, yellow moon waxing overhead, which he resisted to focus on finding water, and Syago. Some ways up the hill, the slopes turned more rocky and full of vines and ferns. In the growing dark, he noticed two shimmering orbs ahead. Orbs that glinted like predatory eyes in the dark. He froze, then crouched.

The large beast approached, the body of a large hairless black wolf becoming more clear, but it was not wholly alive. The yellow blossoms of wormwood protruded out of its gaunt body, a corpse host controlled by its alerha plant parasite. The verdant lifeless shambled toward him and whimpered. So this one wasn't completely dead. But a recent and incomplete germination had left it barely alive and under the plant's control. Qosku debated: run, fight, or die? It gave another whine then pounced, almost too quick, but Qosku's reflexes adeptly made the decision for him.

He jumped, swinging a hook at its head, funneling rage into it. The hit cracked the skull sideways and life seemed to go out of those eyes, finally. It twisted the head back, now crooked, to bite at him. He jumped to avoid its jaws, finding himself suddenly sliding and rolling down the muddy hill, the alerha wolf rolling with him. He bounced and splashed through a stream,

12 See *Blut Aus Nord* but mainly the later mlsss

dashing back, out of reach of its snapping jaws. He just had to be sure the pollen didn't infect his blood, for he did not want to die that way.

In an icy splash, dirty water enveloped both him and the wolf flower corpse. The stream had given way to a pond, bottomless in its blackness. Darkness swallowed and surrounded, and ghostly eels reached for both of them. He tried to bend down to attack the creatures but they only yanked them deeper into Boggorn's abyss. Down and down they pulled to unseen depths, forever.

Accepting his fate, one which he deserved, he opened his arms. Let judgment be done for what he did to Lügos and Chaska.

But they wouldn't have judged him, would've tried to save him. Would even accuse him of surrendering, weakening down, instead of helping in the war.

Full of purpose, he turned to grab the flower corpse's mottled fur as it clawed feebly at the muddy surface. The grip on his leg loosened as he kicked free and achieved the surface in a gasp of fresh air. Scaling the flower corpse, he jumped free onto land and rolled away through the mud.

Sopping wet and muddy in the cold night air, he felt free. Though still grieving, he at least felt some forgiveness from Lügos. Sitting up, he saw a human skeleton clinging to a log. He stripped its tunic, gauntlets, and greaves. *See? Tough as stones, you can handle anything.* But it would only last until next transformation. He thought of ways to fix that dilemma, maybe a belt or bag that would carry clothes and gauntlets with him.

A large part of his dilemma, he thought, wasn't just having the wrong body but not being able to get the right one. He considered what he'd heard of other, older monasteries did with circumcision, even castration. Would being a—what was it called?—a eunuch, get him close enough? The more he dwelled on this thought, the more appealing it became. It wouldn't get him a woman's body, but it would at least rid him of most of his man's. It would bring him halfway, he felt he could live with halfway.

But for such a bloody and dangerous task, even with clean tools, his powers could only heal so much. He thought on this as he wandered, not wanting a hasty decision on something so permanent. But the endless blackness of the bog forbade anything good. *And why isn't morning coming?* Then he saw the lights.

Small and faint, far away. First one then two, then many blinked into existence. They glowed and pulsed dimly, almost fading out before returning back to strength. *Is it an enemy camp?* he wondered. Approaching carefully, he soon noticed the lights didn't seem to come closer. But as he approached, the warm feeling told him not an enemy camp but perhaps a solution somehow. But how? That didn't make sense. Still, the warm feelings persisted.

The vague promise of the lights was too good, too simple. His skin and hairs prickled with danger. He recalled the old Unakan wisdom: Fording a new path with a human guide gets you to a human destination, fording a path with the mountain eternals as guides gets you to an eternal destination. *But what if I have neither as a guide? I've been left alone on this path to walk it blindly. Do I just create the way?*

He finally neared the lights. They hovered several paces away on either side, with only darkness below. They pulsed tantalizingly, hard not to look at. Hypnotic even. He shook his head, realizing he'd been walking without meaning to. In front of him was a pit of black mud, or peat, or tar. He wasn't sure, but his mind concluded what his feelings did not: they offered none of the relief he'd been desiring and only death. Even knowing, he still felt such a pull to them. *I've got to get out of here, or at least find somewhere safe to pray.*

He walked on until he found a cave with a small pond to bathe in. He built a fire, stars looking in. He placed the old spearhead at the edge of his fire then took the one uncooked mushroom, examining it. A vision from the eternals could guide his decision, even walk him through it. That is, if they spoke through it. Perhaps they wouldn't and he would simply see for himself. If he couldn't be woman, at least he could cease as man. But could he survive it? Maybe it was clear already, he'd killed people. Nearly killed himself. Wished he'd just die. It might kill him, but so too might not doing it. He was already dying and wishing for it. *So why not try it and if I fail I die as I'm meant to be?*

Fire crackling before him, he ate the mushroom, and prayed.

Hail to the Flame!
That burneth before me
Bring me light, bring me warmth
Feed my soul thy power

A blaze so full
Raging, purging, surging
Accept my offering
Take my blood, take my flesh!

Hail to the Flame!
That burneth within me
May'st thou mirror that fire
As without, so within

Burn in me, burn!
Cleanse my meat, wash my soul
For through thee, I shall have
Salvation or sweet death

Hail to the Flame!
Open my eyes, light of Land
My blood for thee, oh Stars!
That the Sun find me new

Burn in me, burn!
Light within, light without
Grant me birth, grant me will!
Free me oh fire, free me

Blessed be

The bleak cave of dark green and bitter brown began to swirl with other colors, many of which he'd never seen before. The Eternals' shadows danced along the walls, he danced with them. The moon shone into the cave. All was bright, the colors brilliant. He roared with the Fire.

He looked down to see a snake, but he feared it not. This serpent had been an old companion, wrapped around him for as long as he could remember even though they didn't belong together. However, the snake would not let go. But it was time to part ways. The Eternals chanted him on. The Moon smiled. The Stars shimmered. The Fire raged.

He wept as the Fire handed him the spearhead, hot in his hands, and with another roar, he ran it through the serpent's coil. He howled in pain. Sweet, blinding, consuming pain. A fountain of blood surged out of them both; he drank of its thick darkness and threw his old companion into the flames. The Fire roared, purifying and accepting his offering of flesh. Trembling, he put the blade back in the blaze, deep in there. The fire within him also raged, consuming him fully until he was unsure if he could move for the pain. Shadows danced on the walls. He took that hot blade and pressed it back on the snake's stump until the fountain and pain slowed.

Steam from his flesh cleared the vision away. Alone again in his cave, with the smoldering Fire, blood still leaking out of his crotch, vomit hurled from his throat, tears fell from his eyes. Taking ash of the Fire and clay of the Ground, he mixed them together and rubbed them on the stump as he sat down for a prayer of healing.

Again, he howled at the Moon, for agony had never felt so good. Whether he would survive or not. And when the Sun rose at last, its light peeking at him in his blood-painted cave and finding him alive, his pain finally began to subside.

Morning Sun on his face, he wept with joy.

CHAPTER SIX

THE RUN

Based on *The Hunter's Parchments*, cc bastica 357;
Leyta's Journals, cc bastica 370;
The Dark Fortress of Mephorash, cc bastica xx;

20th of Akril, 247

Church bells tolled evacuation. Lil'iek and the Roah'riik archers exited the portcullis of Southgate at the front of the caravan in a warwagon surrounded by soldiers. With the Chaos army still at Westgate, the Cantlgrym group couldn't leave that way. The Roah'riik, having been inside during the blighting winds, were among those hit less hard by the Seeping. They had some nausea and felt starved, all of which made them even more homesick for the healing shelter of Motherwood. Leyta had to get back to Cantlgrym and Lil'iek wasn't done with her yet. They'd sought to accuse Virgow both publicly and privately but the astute general had evaded them at every turn. Now in the evacuation, they could hunt through the crowded caravan until they found and either accused or killed him. She wanted to just finish him, but they remained wary of the public perception and its ramifications. With so few warriors left, their people hung by a thread.[13]

They'd been positioned in the front, where the rest of the caravan could see them, and where the old general would see them coming from his place the rear. It was a shrewd move.

Lil'iek knew the wisest move was to simply retreat home, but she simply couldn't. None of them could without more justice from the enemies let alone the rage against Virgow and his palemen pawns. Lil'iek watched Leyta crawl into the back of an armored wagon not far down the line. Beside

---

13 See *Sol Sistere de Selbst* by Himetuks Himi'n

Lil'iek, Tek'ouk'iek, Machi'guenk, Klom'oth, Dar'miir, and Guaran'upik watched it all impassively. *Good, this way he can keep an eye on her.*

Of central concern to the Asturions was the preservation of the dydatris relic piece, which the Kimoc no longer cared about. As far as they were concerned, either of the two enemy camps could take it and then break the Asturions. Assuming it had any power at all. She knew nothing of it, few did, but Tek'ouk'iek believed it to be a kind of scepter that magnifies the power of any individual, possibly making them unstoppable or incredibly destructive. She knew their tribe would likely have to go into hiding with the other tribes either way; they had too few warriors to sustain the village for any extended time and were already risking them by staying out this long.

The Asturions' plan, the Roah'riik had gathered, was to hide and protect the relic piece, and this secrecy centered around Leyta. Additionally, they had Jester in chains, several chains due to the bizarre murder incident earlier that morning. The clown could be their key to evacuating without a fight. Or it would invite greater fury than before. A gamble they couldn't avoid, and in the latter case Leyta would execute him. But Lil'iek's focus was on keeping her people safe until they could personally take down Virgow and possibly Leyta as well, then slip quietly away in the ensuing madness. Of course, she still wanted the deaths of the shadowmen who'd slain her husband, and she would have them at any opportunity. But her heart demanded justice more immediately from treacherous friends than cowardly enemies.

The Asturions could make Cantlgrym in a day, maybe less if no fighting happened during the journey, but it would. Even if neither army attacked, some group of beast or plant would set on them, hoping to pick off weaker members or stragglers. The season of poison swung in full now, the mushroom forest had plumed, so the bodies wouldn't rise at night but instead the beasts and plants hunted in force.

She turned to examine the spore cloud, a large fuzzy mass of dark brown hovering over the mushroom forest to the north. Mushrooms usually had one of two kinds of spores: one a glittery green that caused hallucinations or trauma to lure a creature into the feeding trap of its hypha filaments. The other a dull yellow spore that infected creatures into fungal hosts, usually only on those hypnotized by a cap's psychosomatic aura after wandering too close. This brume was the first kind. Its brown color indicated it was still new.[14] The poison cloud would expand and turn more green and sparkly, then move wherever the wind took it.[15] All of their elementists together wouldn't be able to hold off a cloud that big if it descended on them. Hence, they left the city through the southward exit, putting the Chaos between them and the cloud. And hence the Roah'riik's need to finish their task before the cloud and enemy converged on the escaping allies.

"Sound the trumpets!" Leyta shouted behind, which would confirm to the eastern battalion of the exit so that the two sides could leave at the same time. The heavy blaring ended, then blaring from the other side could be heard. The Chaos army only watched as the allies' wagons and carts rolled out before the iron portcullis slammed shut. Lil'iek felt a deluge of relief at leaving behind the crude and crowded place. The Chaos army didn't charge them, but followed, likely as ill and tired from the Seeping as they.

Leaving Voium behind, the two enemy armies maintained their parallel paths. Lil'iek saw no sign of anything else from her perch atop the wagon, nor of any Chaos leaders among the enemy group. At least their proximity served as a deterrent against any assaults from the wild. The Asturion rebels looked weary and sick, the barbarian giants, all half-human half-beast, or cycloptic ohancanu, and didn't look ill at all. But they had to be, nothing was immune to the Seeping. That deep dissolution of flesh.

She watched the caravan behind, guessing at where Virgow might be hiding and how to reach him. She saw no way in daylight to get to him and wondered if waiting until they arrived at the castle would be best. The march continued and so did the growth of the spore cloud. She watched it warily, now moving in the same direction, like a third army. Indeed, as the late day waned, having left later than planned, it now became evident to her wind-wise eyes that the poison cloud would catch them. On realizing this, she saw an opportunity and hopped down from the wagon, mentioning her intention to Tek'ouk'iek, who nodded for Dar'miir and Klom'oth to go with her. She walked down the line of surprised soldiers to Leyta's wagon. "She is occupied right now," the soldier walking before the door said.

"Then where might I find Virgow?" she asked. "I need a commander."

He pointed at the wagon right behind it, waving at the soldier by its

---

14   See again, *Blut Aus Nord*

15   See *Gybiaaw Blackbraid: Mutilated Tyrant,* 8

cabin door. That soldier stepped inside for a moment before opening to let her in. On entering she realized the few present, Virgow, Constantin, Balgor, and a couple soldiers, all knew of the betrayal already, might've even had a hand in it as well. Each bore hard, haggard faces.

She began, "That cloud is going to meet us before we get to Cantlgrym, and we can't get caught in it, certainly not at night."

"What else can we do?" Constantin asked, though his face was more weary than worried. He'd become one of the sickest from the Seeping, often coughing up blood. "We can't outrun it, not at the pace it's moving."

Then Lil'iek had another idea. "No, but the Chaos army doesn't seem to be aware or concerned about its trajectory. We might trick them if we act as though we're camping for the night. They'll continue on to Cantlgrym but will get hit by the cloud before they get there."

"That assumes the cloud won't switch again," Balgor said, large fingers mulling his thick braided beard. "Or that we won't encounter anything else while sitting here." Lil'iek watched his one large eye. The Fomorion ohancanu had always been perceptive but now he acted as if oblivious to the tension between her and them. Constantin seemed keen on it, but he was nearly doubled over in age and with the cough. Virgow held his own, resisting illness, keeping his good eye on Lil'iek, his mouth silent. *Your suffering is not enough.*

Lil'iek shrugged. "It is risky, but we don't have to stay camped. We could use the opportunity to follow the cloud from the southeast as the army converges with it from the northeast. We could avoid the cloud and the winds that carry it, then once the army is hit, we pin and flank them behind its cover. We could finish them!" *And I could slip away after killing you while your people fight each other.*

"They won't fall for it," Virgow said from his seat next to Leyta. "The Fomorions are sea raiders, they know the wind."

"They know the winds of the sea." Balgor stroked his beard, now smiling. "But not wind on this land. The rebel Asturions might, but they're not in charge. If the cloud does return back from that west wind, we need to be south. The Fomorions, or the rebels, will likely catch on eventually, but by then it might be too late. We can move in and catch the aftermath. That will be the hardest part, following the poison cloud without getting hit by it or anything following us."

Lil'iek looked at everyone as they digested it. She cleared her throat. "So... we camp now?"

"Yes," Virgow said, motioning to the men. Pleasantly surprised that she'd managed to persuade them, Lil'iek wondered if this was one more trick. But Virgow's gaze told her that he was considering if he'd overestimated her rage. It wasn't an obvious trap, few better solutions could've been put forward. They slowed to a stop silently. The barbarians would notice but not worry over it as it only gave them a lead on obtaining the castle. They moved equipment about, though not in a way that would be difficult to gather up again in haste. Lil'iek returned to Tek'ouk'iek, who watched the enemy army, noting a few had stopped to watch them. There was a moment of tension in the camp for fear that the army wouldn't keep going as hoped but instead turn and attack.

But they didn't; the giants continued on instead for a perceived advantage at arriving at the castle first. Night fell, the spore cloud now invisible save for the blocking of the moon and stars. After a couple hours of rest, they picked up camp and resumed the march, slower. But what else followed them? Lil'iek wasn't naïve enough to believe the Razhod weren't watching, waiting, or moving. They could only prepare for it, and otherwise focus on what they could see and do.

She and Tek'ouk'iek prepared themselves for another long night of moving, commanding, and fighting instead of sleeping. Being together made it more bearable and, at Lil'iek's urging, they made brief, hard love to each other. They talked through the night of the children. They slept some in the rolling wagon, taking shifts, while the other Roah'riik tracked the cloud by watching the winds and the stars, leading the navigation of the allies.

Lil'iek was one of the first to hear the dull rustling. The audible movement of a swarm of... something.

As the first rays of dawn edged in on the horizon, the Asturion soldiers looked around nervously, jumping at shadows. The Razhod had finally come for them, but with what? She and the Roah'riik looked north where the silhouette of a great spirit loomed in the dawn, an unknown emaion of the witchlords. The silhouette of sharp antlers blocked out the low hanging moon. Only glowing eyes were visible at first, until the rest of her dark brown-furred form came into view under the rising sun. The nameless horned hag had never been seen or heard of before by any of the allied forces.[16] Her gentle laugh echoed through the area just as the reason for the rustling became apparent. A swarm of poisonous flower corpses. The mindless flower vines that had infected the bodies shambled together under her spell, a great writhing flowerbed. A few trees also walked among them, shambling and clawing with the rest. Such a coherent group was unthinkable without the greater spirit. Some corpses were so overgrown they resembled nothing more than a bushel of flowers, other bodies only had sprouts out of noses and eye sockets.

The miracle of the overgrown beasts not stampeding, but coming in a steady pace toward the human armies sent chills up Lil'iek's spine.

The dark emaion's presence meant the witchlords themselves weren't far away. Their summoning brought her and kept her there, acting on their behalf, and they must've sacrificed something to her to gain such a favor. When the sun finally broke the mountains, she and her ride disappeared with another low laugh as the swarm continued against the armies' rear, north of a large boulder field. The allies, now in ideal position to attack the small Chaos force east of Cantlgrym, were themselves flanked. Luckily the spore cloud now occupied the Chaos force. Their screams and roars from within the haze rent the early morning air. They were caught then between a spore cloud that could cause lethal hallucinations or pollen from the alerha flowers that would consume the physical body. Either one would've been perfectly survivable in a normal season, holed up in their homes. But this was now the time of apocalypse and all were refugees.

The allies turned to face the gathering foes in the north. Although the emaion had vanished, the swarm appeared to remain under her spell. They halted completely. Facing each other, two Razhod rose up on a tall rock, their hands raised and shaking their summoning bells—two figures of red and black above a colorful flowerbed. Their coal eyes simmered in the fading dark. Another emaion shadow took shape, accompanied by a deep reverberating hum. The shadow coalesced into a gigantic clay figurine she'd heard of but not seen before, almost more of an old temple than a statue and with a burning furnace inside its eyes and mouth holes. Barduum the Golem materialized, the humming chant booming across the field. It

---

16 She, it, appears to be a new emaion and has come to be called the horned hag or witch of the wild.

grindingly raised stone arms slowly to bless the two Razhod. The ground vibrated, grating on Lil'iek's nerves.

Fighting the fearful trembling in her hands and knees with the rage in her heart, Lil'iek stood in line with the archers, infantry in front and elementists behind with Tek'ouk'iek. The entire war caravan was in motion preparing for attack. The betrayal now a secondary thought, this was survival time. Tek'ouk'iek joined the dynasts under Leyta's direction. A trench tore up the ground in front of them, then another one in front of that, then a third as the elementists created as many obstacles to their front as possible. They had a retreat line open behind, a way to edge around the ever moving venom cloud toward Thornwood which stood in sight, but such would be risky. The two goat-riding Razhod began to charge and the rest of the horde trailed behind, slowly giving distance. One Hellface waved his arm and whooped in delight as his ride carried him fast and hard to their front. She watched for what the Golem, still looming, had done for them.

Tek'ouk'iek's heart thundered in his chest, more frightened than he'd cared to admit. As the two Razhod charged in, boulders and rocks in the field rose up out of the ground behind them then followed the two leads like an avalanche, preceding the verdant stampede behind. Rocks and dirt rolled and bounced behind the two racing Hellfaces, eventually rolling past them. Tek'ouk'iek searched frantically for a way to brace against it. The trenches alone wouldn't stop the barrage or the Razhod, and the elementists brought up a wall of dirt and stone that would avail little. The ground thundered, a storm of stone. He leaned on his crutch-scepter then told the elementists to try and push the assault away from themselves, to deflect it, and ordered for the archers to instead back from the wall and scatter while Leyta had her dynasts hit the Hellfaces. This all happened only in time for the first impacts.

Boulders smashed through the trenches and barriers and the Razhod leaped from the goat's backs in the ensuing mayhem. The men scattered and dodged as ordered, getting clipped and smashed by the bigger ones while the smaller rocks and dirt clods hit the rest. Tek'ouk'iek ducked while pushing anger into the rocks he couldn't, blasting them away. Dirt smacked him in the face then a larger one clipped his shoulder but he rolled back to his knees. He saw the Razhod evading the avalanche with ease while cutting into fleeing soldiers. He tried to get at them with dyne, tried to turn the rocks against them but was hampered by the utter chaos of the scene, too many allies in front and around him, bustling, bumping, and fighting only two Razhod. Gritting his teeth, he maintained a tight focus until he was knocked down, then helped up, then knocked down again. *Damn leg!* And in all this could not see his wife. *But focus!*

The allied force scattered and moved back and back. Some fell to the rocks, some fell to the Razhod, and the rest fled. However, this left them open to the poison stampede. The barrage of stone faded as the alerha swarm came in, hampered but not stopped by the obstacles that the boulders had beat down. This descent only pushed and scattered the allies further. Tek'ouk'iek called for regrouping but knew it would only happen in patches. He looked around him and saw only allies jostling each other in the stony, muddy grass until one soldier was cut in two, his shorn body falling apart in a fountain of blood. Another beside him was pierced through by a rust-red sword, then that same blade sliced through him and into another. The field cleared around this wavy soulblade and its bearer. The allies backed off save three soldiers who took to the Hellface simultaneously. The long haired Asturion Hellface held them off with Grievore the Violator, the two-handed flambard, and only barely holding ground as the great blade whirled around the central figure. Tek'ouk'iek tried to hit him with lightning, but the sparks deflected off of the blur of the soulblade. He muddied the ground around the man's legs, but his feet moved too quickly. Of the three soldiers, one lost his legs; a second lost his head; a third was cleaved in half down the middle; then back to the first as a thrust of the blade drained his remaining health. He withered in his armor, blood flew everywhere, while the Razhod's wounds sealed up.

This happened before Tek'ouk'iek could finish loading the crossbow he'd picked up. He simultaneously was pushing rage into stones on the ground to shoot them at the Hellface to small effect. His eyes met those red on black of the Razhod, who Tek'ouk'iek recognized as the one that had whooped, and the Hellface smiled. A grotesque sight with those coal-eyes, why was there always one who was more insanely cheery than the others? The Hellface pulled Grievore from the corpse and came for him. Fighting panic, Tek'ouk'iek hurried his crossbow lever into place while leaning on his scepter-crutch. But the Razhod came too fast, ripping the crossbow from his hands before he could pull the trigger.

"I know you," he muttered, smiled again. "Tell me the best way to a man's heart." He raised a ritual dagger to Tek'ouk'iek's chest as the Roah'riik gripped his crutch and threw all his anger into the ground at their feet. The ground beneath them exploded.

Lil'iek was surrounded by flower corpses. Most of them baingoats and daemog, but a malwolf with roses coming out of its black body pursued her through the deadly garden. She chopped its leg with her axe, then side-stepped a black baingoat, which was sneezing, somehow still alive. After cutting more legs off of a daemog with black lilies, she had to jump over the tusked flatnose of a muru'unkuy, then halted before a mewil'ishyuuks so covered in white lilies all she could see were the antlers. All was chaotic frenzy, but some of the emaion's spell was wearing off as they began to turn on each other. The ground exploded off to her right. She discarded her now damaged shield and picked up a second axe, then her bow and quiver, placing them across her chest, her small pack hanging on her hip. She glimpsed one Hellface, who looked to be dead or dying on the ground, and to the south she saw another Razhod taking Leyta, staffless and alone, away from the battle and toward Thornwood.

For a moment she hesitated. *What's that bitch to me?* Leyta had allowed her companions to die at Tiakanawu, almost Lil'iek as well, so she'd deserve whatever he gave her. She shook her head. She needed to find her husband, whom she couldn't see. He was her primary concern. But her husband was likely behind her in the slowing fight, or already dead and beyond her care. Leyta was fast fading from view with nobody else available much less paying attention. The thought of facing a Razhod alone, again, terrified her, but that same fear made her sympathize with any woman taken captive by them. *And I'll not betray anyone to my enemies, especially not the Razhod.*

Lil'iek ran after Leyta.

The Razhod held Leyta's arm tightly and walked swiftly. She struggled to keep up, but he didn't care. He would've dragged her without slowing pace. She vaguely recognized him as one of the disciples who'd stormed Cantlgrym, now a full Razhod with the helleyes to mark it. He was Unakan but older and leaner, with scars lining his brown head, bald except for the black hair-tail. He yanked her arm as they went deeper into the forest.

He'd gone straight for her; she and the elementists threw everything they had at him. Fire, lightning, even reflecting the moving rocks back. He'd blown through them with the soulblade double-axe, Zurrogiath the Desolator, and broke her staff. Then in the madness of the fight, dragged her away from her armies. He'd patted down her body aggressively in search of the relic. That much gave her relief, that he thought she still had it.

She tripped over a log and got jerked forward. She asked, "Why are you doing this? What do you want?"

She felt a sharp pain in the side of her head as he smacked her, then the roiling nausea from the Seeping swelled up and she dry-heaved.

"Shut up. I have nothing to explain to you," he snapped.

Light fog blanketed the fern-covered forest floor but sunlight made it less dark. She nearly stepped on a mound of dangerous-looking ants and watched the forest thicken around them as they crossed deeper in. He made no effort to hide their presence, and the odds of a monster attack rose every moment. Being weaponless, it would be of no benefit to her. He had nothing to fear, and she thought back to some of the old accounts, how the Razhod had talked of the painful life they live, of their punishments. But didn't the Church teach this of everyone? She waited till he was ahead of her, so less likely to strike again before asking, "Is it the pain? You want revenge or a way to end it?"

He stopped and turned to face her, those inhuman eyes bore into her, and the killer whispered, "You have no idea."

Words written on them echoed in her mind:

Fear that darkest star

In our vast night sky

"I'm sorry you have to go through that," she said, hoping to calm him. She had no illusions about surviving this, she just wanted the shaking in her limbs to stop, she wanted it to be less terrifying. Wanted to go back to feeling nothing.

A far light so dark

It blots out all else

"No, you're not. Not sorry enough," this whisper almost a snarl. "Now kneel, the Lord of Pain commands it."

"But what does your pain have to do with us? Did we cause it?" He ignored her, looking over his shoulder, eyes flickering about the forest. She pressed him, "Why take this out on us, on me, if I had nothing to do with your misery? Maybe we can help—"

He shoved her to the ground with surprising strength, and she dry-heaved once more. She tried to roll to her feet, but he kicked her in the shoulder, knocking her down again. Nausea overtook her again, but she felt the sharp pain as he sliced into her upper arms. Once, twice, countless times. As he went, he traced the blood to a design. He'd begun some sort of ritual on her.

Slashers that wage war

On hope, on refuge

Her head swimming, she tried to grab a rock or a dead branch, but got kicked down again. "You'll hold still while I paint," he snarled. "Or tell me where you hid the dydatris piece." He drew another thin line across her other arm.

They open you wide

And play in your blood

He tore open the top part of her bodice, the one loose part of her dynast gambeson. She struggled, having a mind to make her rape as unpleasant as possible. But rape wasn't in his eyes—no lust for her breasts, that much she now saw in their smoldering coldness. He punched her in the side of the head, and stars flashed.

There's no fight nor flight

That saves from this doom

He drew another knife and raised as if to throw, this one serrated and more rusty in contrast to the elegant ritual blade in his other hand. Was she to be sacrificed?! To Belfegor the Behemoth or Nimrød the Reptilium or maybe one of their soulweapons?

The twang of a bow sounded just before an arrow glanced off of his shoulder pauldron, and he swerved slightly. "Too late," Lil'iek's voice rang from the brush. Leyta couldn't see her, but the Razhod clearly did. She followed his gaze to see Lil'iek perfectly situated in shadow between two towering thorntrunks, another arrow already drawn at her bow. "I've got you, now release her."

Amazingly, Lil'iek's aim on the Hellface was steady despite those eyes that'd haunted her nightmares for over two decades. *Motherwood and the eternals be with me.* "Another move and you'll have an arrow through your throat."

"I've survived worse. Fight me or I finish painting," he replied with a glare, not removing his knife from its new place at Leyta's neck. Lil'iek held the pause, drew it out, before slowly entering the small clearing. Wordlessly, she removed the arrow from the bow as he removed his knife and stepped aside. Lil'iek's head motioned for Leyta to get further away.

"I'm surprised you came out here alone," said the Hellface.

"That's the point," Lil'iek replied, coming closer and dropping her bow, quiver, and bag. "It's time—"

"I've been looking forward to this," he interrupted, clanging two knives together. Leyta moved away, looking for a rock, a stick, anything to aid her, Lil'iek hoped. "For some time."

"As have I," the Huntress said, drawing her two hand-axes.

"Liar." He smiled and leaped. She barely got her axes up in time to fend off the rapid offensive of the knives. His arms were a blur she could barely follow. Finding herself pressed against a low thornbranch, she nimbly hooked her feet on the thorns to walk up its slope, out of reach of the knives. *Praised be the motherwood!*

The Hellface attempted to follow, but she now had the high ground and barred his advance. He called back Zurrogiath and, with a grunt, sliced clean through the thick branch, the soulblade leaving a burst of rotting

---

17 *An old folk saying. Origin unknown.*

splinters. The branch Lil'iek stood on tipped and wobbled, but the Hellface didn't even wait for it to collapse. He began hacking at it, splinters and leaves falling everywhere, rotting them as it cut. She leaped to another thornbranch, but the Hellface attacked that one, bringing it down as she jumped to another. He sheared through the new branch right as she landed, causing her to fall. She rolled to her feet as the Hellface came swinging fast. Trunks and branches crashed all around them with each swing. The cacophony deepened as she darted around and under the collapsing forest, only to be faced with another attack or falling thorntrunk. She searched in vain for a path and found none. This was her zone and yet he'd trapped her in it. The berserking wasn't without control; he deftly parried her attacks while nimbly skipping between two boulders, avoiding stepping on an acid slug before rebounding at her. Lil'iek could barely get away. She couldn't maintain the semblance of confidence and rage she'd entered with. Not with the panic bubbling up inside her. All she felt now was fear.

Seeing the woman's confidence and control shatter alarmed Leyta. She tore her gaze from the fight to the rocks in her hands and began throwing. The first throw hit his back and he didn't seem to even notice. The second one, she aimed instead for his leg. The Razhod stumbled and the Huntress darted to his open side with a low swing. But he whirled around and severed Lil'iek's hand-axe before it reached him. He chopped through another thorntrunk, bringing a mess of thornbranches down on them all. Through showering leaves, Leyta saw him walking between the fallen wood, and hurled her last rock at the Razhod's head. He caught it easily and, with a snarl, came for her, vaulting over logs with the swing of his soulblade. Suddenly he was very close, his dark face feral, his blade slicing through the thorny logs that separated them. Leyta stumbled back as the soulaxe grazed her dress. Zurrogiath swung back in and Leyta dove backwards, barely avoiding being cut in half. In the dirt and ferns, she rolled, the blade chopping down beside her, sundering the ground into an exploding fissure. As dirt and twigs showered on her, she rolled down a slight incline, thinking this was the end.

Then Lil'iek stood over her, bow and arrow ready for release. The two warriors faced each other across the clearing.

A loud crash came through the brush as a gigantic cat with horns charged in, slashing its great claws at them, roaring.

The warriors jumped away from each other, and it plowed past them toward Leyta. Its claws knocked her down as she backed away. She rolled in the brush, beneath the newly fallen thorntrunks. Licking its fangs, the dark beast came at her, gouging grassy dirt all around. She rolled out from under a fallen log and beneath another, then back out on seeing the carrion crawling beneath it. Sharp claws reached for her, but the mess of logs blocked it. Her hand fell on an old spear, half buried and worn out, but she lifted it to prick the paws. They retreated and she crawled beneath some ferns, looking for another weapon, but the beast had shifted focus to Lil'iek and the Razhod.

The monster didn't look like the hunting cats she'd heard of. Its size and ferocity had concealed its lack of real fur. Rather than bristly hairs, it had little spikes all along its scaly body. The strange monster charged the Razhod, and Lil'iek ran to Leyta, who retained the old spear. They ran away from the bloody thrashing in the brush. Leyta didn't see what happened, but they were not followed as they ran on.

"Lil'iek," she shouted, almost breathless as they sprinted through the wood. "What was that thing?"

"I don't know, I've never seen it before." Forest cleared before them, then ended quite suddenly. They crested a ledge that sloped down into a vast plain of green and brown ponds and streams gleaming in meager daylight. The Kourii Marshes, vast and stretching into haunted Boggorn. She knew they'd been close in that corner of the forest, but the abrupt arrival surprised her. Even with the proximity of the marsh to Cantlgrym, she'd never ventured near it. Impossible to hunt or gather in, with every forbidding tale one could imagine, it remained an unmapped and unknown area.

She looked to Lil'iek and pointed north along the forest edge toward the castle. "We should be able to make it up there—" A roar came from behind. Too close, and followed by a second.

"The Razhod is still coming too," Lil'iek said. This confused Leyta at first; how could she know? Then she noticed the woman's hands rested on the thornstalk. She saw through the eyes of the forest. "We have to go into the marshes. They're coming."

"But if we hide or run up—"

"No, run! Now." Lil'iek pushed her into motion. The brush behind moved, cracked, and hissed. They slid down into the marshes, muddy and mossy, and Leyta let the dirty wetness come, knowing that it would only be the beginning. She didn't look back to witness the commotion above as they made their way into the wetlands.

CHAPTER SEVEN

THE CAVE

Based on *Annals of Syago,* cc bastica 350;
The Nordvargor Testaments, cc bastica 906;

dates unknown, 247

Tall stalks of reeds rose out of the wetlands and opened into leafy spans, reaching for the yellow moon above. Deep in Boggorn, the water congealed into what looked like several ponds grouped together, but was really more of a lake. One full of grassy islands and mucky peat that smelled terrible, and sometimes burned with acid, but which provided fire for a torch. All the water eventually emptied into the sea after passing through leagues of this rotted vegetation so slowly the current was nigh undetectable. Sparse brambles populated the area as well.

Traveling alone provided too much time to think. Or rather, too much time for Syago's mind to wander between the poles tugging at his sanity.[18] The only things to attack him were the caimons snapping at him from the water. But he'd had to mind the flowers, shrooms, and strange lurelights floating over mudpits.

He walked through the light fog, illuminated by sickly moon, toward an odd structure that had appeared seemingly out of nowhere. For a long time it seemed as though it wouldn't come nearer. Alexandre had guided him to it, possibly having been here before, but the sword still was vague on its past.

Like an old tower in disrepair, the structure bent and twisted up through reeds with candlelight in a window. All wood, with some planks or sticks

---

18 Lustmord comments, in the *Atriom Carcerio y Cryo,* extensively on this place. I wonder if it was just delirium caused from dehydration and sleep deprivation in a gaseous swampland.

protruding. He soon realized it was more of a wooden hut than a tower. Though he had to admit the structure was an impressive stack of wood. Staying quiet became difficult as both Alexandre and the devil arm exuded confidence that crowded out his caution. Alexandre in hand, he went low, brush crunching beneath his boots, until he crouched behind a density of reeds. Through them he observed the tall hut. A single lantern hung outside, providing dim light in the area during what seemed to be an un-ending night.

The hut sat upon a floating platform, as best he could tell, on the marsh-lake. And crawling all over the flat were little dark brown duendes, no taller than his knee. Bushy and naked except for painted wooden masks, he couldn't think of them as human. They even had horns, like tiny goat-heads, but with the general form of human. Using tools, they cleaned a dead animal to eat, dancing and clicking as they did so.

A drape over the hut's door shuddered and there emerged the witch. A beautiful woman stood tall with sleek golden hair and a silk dress. She said something to the duendes then looked right at Syago. He ducked slightly, but there was no mistaking that she'd seen him. He stood, and she twirled a strand of hair then changed. Her face transformed, aging into an old hag with more wrinkles than he'd thought possible to fit on a human.

Something poked him in the side, and he spun, guarding with Alexandre. Duendes surrounded him with small spears, clicking through their masks. Though impressed by their stealth, he did not fear them. He stood tall, Alexandre's blade hanging low. Suddenly the hag stood on the other side of them. She opened her arms wide. "Welcome, child. Please, to our home. We do insist."

"If you wish," he said, hiding his surprise. They walked around the grassy island to a wooden walkway that stretched to the hut through reed stalks.

She stopped him at the porch, bidding him to sit down in a wooden chair before entering her hut, and a duende jabbed him in the leg before he could respond. He sat with his bag on his lap and Alexandre across his knees. The chair barely held him in his armor, creaking as if it might break any second. The duendes stared at him, a new sight out here. He returned a calm glare that affected nothing in their dark eyes.

"How do you get these py- brownie duendes to obey you?" he asked loud enough for her to hear inside.

"They're not brownies," she called back. "Or pygmies. Brownies maybe if you stretch the word, but pygmies I've seen, they're human and these are not. I call them the Kourii duendes, as most do, or urisgs. But what's in a name? Only sound and symbol, a collective dream shared by humans and some beasts. They don't call themselves anything, for to them, only they exist and need no name. Only us, the illusions they toy with, do."

"Then why respond to you?"

"I'm an interesting enough illusion for them to pay attention," she said. "And they've learned I'm an illusion better pleased than crossed. Or did you not find the same from those lurelights on the way here?"

He said nothing, musing over the oddity and the way they moved about him. She continued from inside, "My congratulations on arriving here safely, mind you. You're the first this decade. The lights usually get what the caimons don't. These duendes haven't seen many humans other than me.

"And I am something to behold," she said, emerging from the hut with a clay plate of two steaming cups. Her face was different, more a motherly crone now with less wrinkles and more teeth. She handed one to him, which he accepted but didn't drink, and she sat down opposite him on a stump. She drank hers, but he looked his over warily. Alexandre didn't think it a good idea either. The devil's arm wanted to brave it, or throw it in her face. Both were too many voices in his head.

"Scared?" Her toothy grin certainly inspired such. "I've other ways to kill you."

"And I've ways to fend them off. Still, Boggorn isn't a place for risks. I'm here to see you for something specific. Are you the Kourii witch?"

"They call me that. They've also called me a great many worse things even when only seeing my form of beauty. Pfuh, what do they know about beauty."

"And what do you call yourself?"

She smiled, toothy, then sipped her drink.

"Can you summon and speak with the dead or not?" he pressed, getting impatient.

"I can and have been this entire time," she said.

"Then we need your help. The Razhod have returned and they've blinded all the chamands."

"So I've heard." She sipped again, amusement in her voice.

"Well, can you help me lift the blinding?"

A low, soft laugh crept from her mouth. "You wish for my help. The *Holy Knight of Nevermore* asks for my blessings. What will you do next? Beg? I help no one, especially Nevermore."

"Do you realize what is happening? What the Razhod can do?" he urged.

"Of course I do!" she snapped. "I know better than anyone what they're like. They're half the reason I'm out here."

Syago noticed something in her visage shimmer as she spoke and narrowed his eyes at her. "This isn't your real appearance, is it?"

Another toothy smile. "Very good. You got me to let it slip and noticed too. The first face wasn't either, but I don't suppose it's too late to convince you the beauty is the real me?"

"Yes. Then who or what are you really?"

She gave him a challenging look. "I emerged from the hut as what you weren't expecting, then changed to what you were, the hag. Of course, if you really want to know, you'll drink that tea in your hand."

He looked at it, then at her. Still not worth it. He set it down.

She grunted. "This is the problem with your civilizations. All of you, leaders and followers of all stripes, are caught up in avoiding truth that doesn't befit them. They're as afraid of uncomfortable realities as they are of any monster. Afraid of the risk, of being misled, of being hurt by it, of what the truth, when actually had, will do to their peace. The decision that you're safer, happier, with what you have now than with what you might have by taking the leap makes a virtue out of ignorance. If you're not going to be brave enough, you don't deserve to know."

Thoughts of his struggle with the truth about his heroes, his father and Fal'iek, pressed his mind. Bitterness still clutched at him, as well as an ache for answers or some kind of resolution. "Maybe being happy and healthy under a mystery or even a lie is more important than risking an abusive truth. The happiness is true, and the goal, so why shake it up? Why change what is good?"

She watched him over her cup. "You don't really believe that, nobody does. Or at best, you're not sure. Well, I suppose it's better than the reverse. Someone who thinks they're unafraid and seeing through the illusions when really they don't. That delusion takes others down with you. I'd argue any joy not based in reality can only be temporary, constrained by the limits of the illusion."

He leaned forward. "Help me against the Razhod, please. At least tell me what to do, point me in a direction."

Rather than respond, she casually took a sip. "Your fear of a drink doesn't surprise me really. An entire life inside walls will do that to you. I am surprised you haven't asked for what you really want."

He stared at her for a moment. There would be no hiding things from this one. "Will you call someone for me? Call up a family spirit to talk to me."

"No," she said, directly and firmly. "I will not, and you don't need me to. Fortunate because I doubt the ones you seek would answer my call in any case. No, the cave has what you need. Deep inside, the surface to the Otherworld weakens and even non-summoners can call the dead and speak with them."

Syago thought on what she said briefly, then asked, "What else is in the cave?"

"Evil. All of it," the witch said. "And nightmares. A darkness more pure and real than anything you've seen before. You'll likely either join the dead you seek or if not, lose your sanity trying not to."

"I'm prepared for whatever may be waiting," he said as he rose from his seat, sheathing Alexandre and returning the pack to his back.

"No. You're not." She finished her tea, then rose as well.

He realized his growing irritation with her stemmed more from the devil arm than anything else. He forced it into quietude. "Then show me. Give me what I need."

"Alexandre may help you, but nothing else will aid you in there. It is a place unlike any other. I'll show you the entrance, but that's it." She walked around the hut to a small raft and stepped on.

"You'll tell me about it," he said as he followed her, "and take me there, but not call up spirits? Your ethics are confused." He boarded the raft, along with a few duendes.

This brought out a low cackle from her. "Ah, ethics. The greatest illusion of all."

She grabbed a long stick that held a lantern and stuck it into the water, guiding the raft, which started moving before she'd even done so. Looking down, Syago realized the raft, or what sat beneath it, was alive. A giant scaly back that swerved in the water. A dark green head with elongated maw peeked above the water before submerging again. As it gently slithered through the water, he envisioned it snapping him up whole.

"If I'm going into this cave alone, how do I know when I've found it? The summoning place, I mean."

"You won't. But you might figure it out."

"How big is the cave?" Syago asked, a plan forming in his mind, a preparation.

"Too big," the witch's voice became more hoarse and emphatic. "And too dark."

"How do I get out when I'm done?"

"You can't."

Syago scoffed. "Can you offer any advice or hope at all?"

"There is none!" The great caimon they rode increased speed. "Reasons abound why none go in there."

After some time, the islands around them increased and a large hill emerged in the night. Syago saw a large rock formation jutting out of the earth.

The witch breathed deeply. "The cave is there. Take all that you have and are. Rely chiefly on your sword and your wit and you'll get far. But be warned, older enemies common to both of us have used this place. It's more to their liking and never forgotten to them."

"Thank you," Syago said as he leaped from the platform to the muddy bank, nearly slipping into the water. When she didn't respond, he turned to see her already drifting away. Turning toward the rock formation, he opened his pack to eat the last of his rations when he saw that it was gone. As were some of his tools, including alcohol and flint for a torch. The duendes had stolen his things and left in their place a rotted fruit, a prank of theft. About to drop the fruit to the water, he thought better of it and kept it in his pack.

When he crested the sharp rock ridge, he saw the cave entrance: a black hole wedged into the middle of a twisted peak, as if nailed in. The hole seemed like something from a nightmare. It gaped at him, sucking him in. *I've grown up with nothing but nightmares my whole life. I can do this,* he told himself. He noticed that Alexandre began to glow bright, strong in its hatred of the hole. Here he had his light then. A holy torch that would burn through danger. His devil arm itched, pulsing slightly. He decided to use it as little as possible; the risk would be greater here. Holding Alexandre in his hand, he strapped the empty pack tightly to his back where his shield normally would be. A better tool for fighting other people rather than monsters of the wild, he'd left it in Voium. He checked himself, his armor was tightly strapped, though he'd lost his helmet, again.

The hole seemed so bottomless. On a thought, he pulled out the rotted fruit and dropped it down. He thought he heard a wet *thump* after a couple seconds. He had no rope to belay down with and grabbed the ledge to lower himself in.

He paused, hanging, then jumped into the dark and landed no more than six feet down. He raised Alexandre to illuminate the shadows, finding no clear path onward. Instead, all along the rocky walls sat ruined camps, aged clay pots, and old armored skeletons, some of them chained to the walls. Behind the skeletons were small clay statues of people and monsters in various positions of agony or battle. Alexandre's light projected their shadows against the cavern walls behind them. But Syago's attention was quickly drawn to sounds of feasting. A white rabbit sat hunched over a... dead girl? Her blue and pink dress was marred by blood, as were the claws and face of the rabbit that ate it. Syago's stomach churned. *But rabbits don't eat meat.* He picked up the rotted fruit and threw it at the rabbit. It looked at him and hissed, but he lunged for it, beheading it before it could resume its feast. Alexandre's enhanced speed jerked the blade into the stone floor and the blade stuck. He yanked it out then pulled aside the white hair of the girl before stepping away in shock. The girl, or boy, had no face. Just a pasty white blank space where a face ought to be. Then she sat up, and the faceless head turned to him. Almost purely on reflex, he swung Alexandre through her neck and she fell back down, dead. He backed away, shaking as he looked at the rest of the cavern, wondering what he'd gotten himself into. Alexandre and the devil arm buzzed both buzzed with nonsensical alarm.

The growing sound of rushing waters made him pause. He turned, raising Alexandre to see the source. Above him, a small stone door slid open and a dark liquid came gushing out too fast for him to evade. Blood. The crimson flood swallowed him, quickly engulfing the area, immersing and baptizing him, then pulling him away as he clutched Alexandre and a piece of wood. He panicked about being pulled under but eventually kicked to the surface, managing to climb on top the wood's shaky stability. Alexandre's light only let him see immediately around him of about a pace. He thrust the soulblade it into the stone wall to stop but it didn't catch enough, cut through. It glowed fiercely but the darkness fought back, resisting the light much like the black fog had.

The crimson tide carried him down a narrow corridor he'd not seen as he struggled to maintain balance atop the wood. Cold from the uncomfortably wet clothes whose smell would surely lure predators, he shivered and sought land. It was not long before he saw a ledge nearby and jumped for it, using Alexandre to glide himself safely on. Edging away from the river, he saw no walls and wondered just how vast this place was.

Walking a bit deeper in, he found himself in a cavern with no way out but the way he came in. He raised Alexandre, thinking there had to be some way through, when he saw a large crack in the wall, just big enough for a person. He glanced around for what options he had but the light of his sword had small range. A shuffling sound behind made him jump. He held his sword out, but the sound stopped. Heart racing, he turned and squeezed through the pass as shuffling renewed behind him till he came out on what appeared to be a thin stone bridge that stretched across a dark abyss. Screeching rent the air above him, like a massive swarm of bats except not so high-pitched. He took a step forward, and as he did, furry monsters with wings and fangs flew at him, hundreds of them fluttering too fast for him to get a good look. Covering his head with his own claw while swinging Alexandre in overhead arcs, he ran forward on the bridge. They stopped coming directly at him, now flying over him. But he heard them coming around. This wave hit from behind, forcing him to lie down, still using his claw for cover and sword for random striking. One creature whose wing he'd clipped dropped in front of him. To his horror it had the form of a furry human baby with leathery wings. The six-month-old infant of fangs, claws, and dark eyes crawled toward him, growling and salivating. Something about it reminded him of the devils he'd fought, but these creatures looked even more human than beast. Syago kicked it off the bridge; it squealed.

He wondered again at the nature of the place, and Alexandre shared his wonder and disgust. Syago listened for the swarm's flight path and leaped up with a great slash of his sword. The stream of menaces parted to circle around. Syago took the opportunity to hurry to the other side of the long bridge, where he found another wall with a tight crack just as they came on him.

He held his sword up behind him to repel them from coming in after him as he edged inward, hoping this would bring him to the summoning area, if it even existed. Given his ill fortune, it'd be back there. But checking here first would give him time to breathe, self-orient. So far he felt like he was just fleeing for survival rather than hunting for a specific thing.

The crack finally opened up to a small cavern with a sloping floor. Alexandre's holy light revealed an emaciated human clutching his head. Syago reflexively raised his blade to strike, then paused as the man looked up. But before Syago could see his face, his body exploded, blood and intestines flying everywhere. Syago's mind flashed to when this had happened before, hunting the devil with a concussive flail. Now, as then, he retched. Another was approaching on two feet, and on entering Syago's light, his gaunt frame rippled, then burst. Syago fell to his knees, clutching his eyes and wiping gore from himself, the trauma flashes overcoming his trembling body.

Come on, Syago, stand up and fortify. You did this before, you can do any-thing. Just remember to close your eyes in time. Gripping Alexandre, he rose and moved toward noise on his left. The swordlight revealed one crouched down and sucking hungrily on an arm. Syago was so surprised that he wasn't ready for its burst.

"Whoa!" He jumped back and his feet hit something slick and lost their grip. He found himself sliding down a slope of gore, unable to stop his now rapid descent. Bracing his arms against the sides, he tumbled out over a cliff, hurtling toward a dark abyss. He swung Alexandre above to slow the fall. He submerged into a cold lake. Terror gripped him, for he couldn't swim well and feared deep water. Alexandre calmed him and coaxed his kicking until he surfaced. He had to kick hard to keep his head above water, tiring in his armor.

He realized how vulnerable he was, barely keeping his head above the surface, kicking in a large body of water that could be hiding anything in its bottomless darkness. He dipped his head back under water to see around for any threats and saw something flicker by his bubble of light. He returned his head above for air, heart thundering.

Something yanked him under, then let go. Before he could swim up, a tentacle wrapped around his chest. At the end of it was what looked like a human hand. Horrified, he swiped Alexandre up through it. Another came in, and Alexandre severed that one too but only barely.

His lungs burned, and he surfaced for a gulp of air. Then he was pulled down again, a hard yank on his leg from another hand tentacle. Two more

grabbed his sword arm. He cut at them all but more came in; he was surrounded. Though despairing, he resisted still. His destination forgotten,
only getting out of the water mattered.

As he fought to regain the surface, large luminescent eyes appeared far
ahead. They shone soullessly until arm tentacles again obscured his view.
Panicking, he went into a frenzy of twirling and cutting with Alexandre.
Even using his devil's claw.

The tentacles still holding him, he used Alexandre to propel himself
upwards. He swung and cut more, twisting in the abyss. Suddenly his head
was above water, and he gasped for air, then was pulled back down. A hand
pried Alexandre free of his. He reached for it but it drifted away. His lungs
burned, his body was cold, but the tentacles had released him. Free, he
swam for Alexandre. The tentacles parted to reveal those luminescent eyes
coming close, a span away. The tentacles withdrew onto the head, as if its
hair. It drew near, five paces away, and opened its mouth wide, so wide it
could easily swallow him whole. He couldn't swim away in time, drifting
into the mouth of rotted teeth. He reflexively opened his mouth in a scream,
"No, no, NO!" He was inside the maw now, total darkness enveloping him as
it closed shut. What must've been a tongue hit him, pushing him deeper
into the throat, swallowing him. On the point of numb resignation, he gave
up on his unuse of the devil arm. In one last desperate act, he grabbed the
tongue, holding on as it struggled against him. The arm, somehow able
to work without air and no friend to this place, was keen to help him. He
would've been screaming and crying if above water, but as it was, he could
feel himself falling unconscious.

He shook himself, regaining a last bit of mental clarity, and called for
Alexandre to fly to him. For a moment he lost himself again in burning
suffocation and cold blindness. Alexandre pierced through into the giant
head, spearing to his hand, rejuvenating with warm light. With a final
snarl, he swung Alexandre, using the motion to carry him. Alexandre flew,
cutting through the thing's mouth. With another swing up, the sword took
him straight to the surface, then another swing lifted him out of the water and gliding away as he gasped for air. He landed not far from a stone
outcropping that glowed, unable to go further by sword. Splashing behind
him alerted him to more danger. He swam frantically before arriving to
the piece of land, where he collapsed on cold stone, panting and weeping.

His body burned sharply from where Alexandre healed him. Even the devil arm now kept him warm. Out of the corner of his eye, he saw a faint glow, and he felt his blood freeze at the thought of more danger. But as he turned his head toward the threat, he breathed out in relief.

The glow was concentrated atop a hill, emanating from dozens of faintly visible spirits.

He'd arrived.

CHAPTER EIGHT

Horns in the Haze

Based on *The Hunter's Parchments*, cc bastica 234;
The Nordvargor Testaments, cc bastica 916;

20th of Akril, 247

A brownish green haze of poisonous mushroom spores drifted over the field of immobile bodies. The cloud thinned and dissipated after stalling and churning over where the Chaos encampment had been, the spores now seeding into the ground would be later gathered by Cantlgrym as newly budding mushrooms if they survived. Tek'ouk'iek hobbled on his crutch among the bodies and boulders, looking through the wounded. His other hand held a cloth up to his face. He knew his cloth wouldn't fully block the venom, he already felt some effects as his vision swam with swirling colors, but with the brume thinning out, he would survive. He couldn't outrun it in any case.

He grunted in frustration as his crutch slipped on another rock. Corpses, poisoned and normal, littered the plain in every direction. He moved his fear into the wind, to make it flee from him and gently carry the haze with it. The elementists, gathered together again, raised their staves and, on Balgor's call, began moving the winds to blow away the spores now that the wind had ceased.[19]

The air cleared and brightened, and when the winds died down, he thought he saw Lil'iek's body. It turned out to be one of Andala's chamands, from Bokhor. His head was swimming and he really needed rest, but there was too much work to do, peace of mind on Lil'iek being first among them.

---

19 See *Sol Sistere de Selbst* by Himetuks Himi'n

The silhouette of Castle Cantlgrym was now visible and blackbirds hovered in wait of the haze further fading.

Although they'd assured that the relic remained secure, a sickening worry filled him regarding Lil'iek's disappearance. He trusted her, not only that she made good decisions, but that she was more than capable of fulfilling them. But with both Razhod missing from the end of the fight, nothing could worry him more. With the spores he'd breathed in during the battle, it was hard not to see Lil'iek in every corpse he came across. In fact, his vision had become tinged with unreal images and an urge to walk north-east.

Recalling his own fight with the Razhod, it brought back memories of the old war, and Tiakanawu. They rarely ever knew the witchlord's names, them being mostly loners and outcasts from the fringes of Asturion and Unakan societies. This time they knew two, Davagis, who'd been seneschal at Cantlgrym, and the vagrant Kask, who'd befriended Syago and led the raid on Cantlgrym. The rest were a mystery, but they always seemed to fit types of people. A cackling, poetic witchlord, or an intense, pain-focused warrior, and sometimes an overly religious one acting as a priest might. It'd been the former type that he'd just fought. Most of them were quiet, brooding, and loathing, and switched out weapons often. Are they just selective of whom they pick? Or is it only these kinds of people that join them?

He pulled out his blackbird skull, and now with the spore haze fading, he found a quervosk not far off. The connection was faint but there. Its poisonous mind of hunger and sex itched at him, but he maintained himself, pushing it to look around. He saw nothing notable yet when pain began racking its body and thus his mind as well. He realized it was infected by the spores and was being driven by its hallucinations back to the forest, where it would fall into the feeding traps. He jerked himself out of the trance, gasping for air and shuddering. He tripped on a rock that brought him down onto a dead soldier, and cursed gierra in a stream of profanity that would've disappointed every one of his ancestors. He rose to his knee, then heaved himself back onto foot and crutch, taking a moment to breathe deep. *Forest Mother, River Mothers, and all other Eternals I haven't been as attentive as I ought. I swear I'll offer more when I return. I'm sorry, but please help us now.*

A commotion ahead distracted him: soldiers fleeing a monster. Through the retreating haze he spotted a particularly large tree, a willows so big and twisted it was clearly a furacán aberration, come to eat what's left on the field. It slurped up the corpses beneath its roots, almost oblivious to him as it gorged. He pulled out his twig, bonding his soul to the tree's through it as with the skull. He'd never tried this with a furacán before. Once his mind touched it, instead of the usual dull hunger, a thousand shrieks wailed in his head. He pulled out in shock and nearly fell back.

But it appeared content to feed on the corpses already strewn on the ground. With a shiver, he hobbled back to his three Roah'riik.

The dynal wind continued so he spoke over it. "I counted only one dead Roah'riik. Dar'miir, our Brother of the Bone, and a few dead Asturions that I don't care about, none that we want dead. And still no sign of Lil'iek, which makes us down to four until we regain her."

Klom'oth and Machi'guenk muttered similar accounts, each also clearly resisting their hallucinations. Guaran'upik kept his silence. All had heard the mixed rumors of Lil'iek and a Razhod following Leyta, or something to that effect.

"Perhaps she's exacting revenge of Leyta," Machi'guenk speculated. "Or of the Razhod."

"That gives me so much comfort," Tek'ouk'iek said drily. *Though I wouldn't put it past her. Come to think, it would've been a good opportunity to take out Virgow. Golkaw the chaos that prevented it.* "Did anyone hear what direction they were heading?"

They hadn't.

"Our best chance is to see this through here," Machi'guenk said. "They know where we are and can come to us, if they're still alive."

"Or they'll die in need of our help." Tek'ouk'iek rubbed his temples. "Who's in charge of the palemen now?"

Klom'oth rubbed his chin while glancing back at the Asturions. "Probably Virgow again, though I couldn't find him. Balgor and Constantin are here too. They were sort of all giving orders at once. There's also Andala of the chamands, what's left of them. I'm not sure, they've too many subgroups in their structure for it to make sense to me."[20]

The dynast winds subsided and midday light allowed for better view as the poison cloud moved behind them. And what the cloud revealed was

20 *See Gybiaaw Blackbraid: I Don't Conform*, 10

a camp of barbarian giants still living, moving, and standing. Eerie yellow eyes peered at him through the haze. They'd been hit hardest by the cloud, sat inside it the longest, and still walked sane. How? Childhood stories of the monsters rose to the front of Tek'ouk'iek's mind.

And in a sickening revelation to that observation, the body posts became more evident. Around the enemy camp stood the mushroom stools of Asturions crucified to their eternals and remind Tek'ouk of his feq'uok necklace, which he touched, thinking of his own people's wisdom. It was difficult to tell if the cloud really had taken all the humans, but the only ones seen were dead. "None of the Asturion rebels survived," he breathed. "Only the giants."

"Let's move!" Balgor shouted to the other allied groups as the Fomorion party also left their camp toward the castle. Virgow was now at his side, hunched over and vomiting, either from the spores or the Seeping. "Let's move now!"

Tek'ouk'iek's gaze darted around for signs of Lil'iek. *What do we do? A mere four of us alone are too vulnerable either way, may not be able to get revenge or return home. I certainly wouldn't be able to flee after. And if we attack, then finding her will be impossible.*

The other Roah'riik watched him consider it, clearly hoping he'd order the attack, but it seemed too foolish. His hesitation allowed the army to make a decision for him as they moved past. They accepted his shrug to wait a little more with a tinge of disappointment but no insubordination. He felt shame at being weak but also relief at having the decision taken from him. Abandoning their broken wagons, they rolled out of the area with the elementists setting fire to the field of corpses and sprouting fungi as they exited. The Roah'riik stayed at the back of the broken caravan, evaluating it. Jester remained captive to the Asturions, unharmed as far as they could tell, on his chain-wagon.

The dydatris relic still hid safely in its place, he assumed, or there would've been more of a stir. And despite heavy losses, most of their forces remained strong.

They arrived at Lake Laomain with the island castle in full view as the barbarian war party gathered around the docking fort on their side of the lake. Tek'ouk'iek wondered if they were planning to siege the castle wall, but was surprised to find the wall had giants on it too.

The Asturions were surprised as well. The allied camps gasped in astonishment at the realization that the castle already lay under Chaos control. Rather than cross to the castle, which would've made them vulnerable, the barbarians around the docking fort faced the approaching allied war group. Tek'ouk'iek supposed it wasn't a huge surprise after all.

Tek'ouk'iek walked up to Andala, the only leader he trusted or respected anymore, her group having suffered a similar fate in the alliance at Tiakanawu. "They'll want to bargain and we might have to," he said. "There's no laying siege to Cantlgrym, especially not as we are. The question is will they ask for the relic or Jester."

"The leverage is ours," Andala said. "We can't give up the relic, but we've kept Jester for reasons such as this."

"I don't see the castle being worth Jester to them," Tek'ouk'iek said. "The relic yes, but Jester... they know we won't kill him yet. And they're probably more interested in rescuing him."

"Yes," Andala said, stroking her chin with one hand while the other casually rested on her spear. "They'll start by asking for both and then we bargain it down. Unless of course we begin with a proposition. That would bring us up stronger despite having our own place controlled by them."

"And I've got just the trick," Balgor said, moving up. He had a serious limp from an injury in the last fight, and some from Tiakanawu. Bandages covered his left arm and leg, which he now tore from their places to drop on the ground. The friendly Fomorion's deep voice continued its rumble. "I'll talk them down, they'll listen better to me." None argued his point, though several of the allies moved to go with him, but he said, "No, this I must do alone."

Striding forward and shirking the last of the bandages, making himself raw to his former people, he walked up to the group surrounding the fort.

"Stand ashore with arrows and scepters ready," Virgow shouted, hobbling up behind. He didn't look at Tek'ouk'iek, but undoubtedly noticed the hard gaze on him. If Lil'iek had been there, she'd have confronted him. Tek'ouk'iek felt too prudent with the new situation to do it. Perhaps if she showed up, but on his own he'd keep pushing it back. He despaired at this thought, thinking himself a terrible advocate for his people. *I'm too cautious. If she doesn't come back by tomorrow, I'm going after her.*

"He will get their help," Katti commented, not a question. And her sudden appearance at his side struck Tek'ouk'iek as oddly creepy.

"If they don't kill him first," Andala said.

Balgor spoke Fomorion to those in front of the fort and after a tense moment, they stepped aside for him to pass through and take a boat to the island. The quiet paddling of the small boat amplified the tension. Once it reached the wall, his bulky form shook the craft as he stood. His head tilted back to look up at the wall. His wounds, no longer bleeding, sat open on his body. Tek'ouk'iek didn't know him well, but the scholar had never looked more the hardy warrior to him than that time. *But he still supported our betrayal, I'll never forget that.*

Barbarian giants lined the wall above, beastly faces unreadable. Two in the middle parted, and King stood between them as did several Cantlgrym prisoners. Tek'ouk'iek noticed no sign of Knight or Knave, or of Queen, supporting the hope that the fire from Andreis's spear trick had finished her at Tiakanawu.

"You've finally come to join us, I presume," King said, his strange voice echoing across the lake. "Excellent. Upon surrendering us your weapons in good faith, we'll enter you into our blessed society. Of course we'll take the relic and Jester back as well. You have no other options in any case. Everyone's better for this wise decision."

Balgor ignored him and called out again in Fomorion, loud and gutteral. It sounded rough and dark. Tek'ouk'iek understood none of it other than his posture and presentation. By Balgor's own later account, he spoke of the battle of the relic, of the affliction of the Razhod, and the need to unite against them. He spoke of the Fomorion losses in the conflict, one that had initially only been a grand raiding party now out of hand. He told them the allies didn't want a conflict with the Fomorions, but would share whatever spoils recovered in the defeat of the Razhod, and that the need of vengeance was urgent and the Royal Chaos would not hesitate to abandon them on this foreign land.

King watched in silence, then when Balgor's speech ended, he proclaimed, "You will not have special aid from us. The Razhod are your creation. Your authoritarian society creates scum such as they. We fight them as we fight you. Unless, of course, you join us with that relic. Then we'd have reason to protect you from—"

As King spoke, the giants whispered among themselves. Then one near the middle turned and spoke to King. After an exchange of words none below could hear, the giant turned back to Balgor, raised a fist in front of him, said one word, and then followed the others down, behind the wall.

As they moved past him, King turned to Balgor. "We've decided to consider your offer with the guarantee that you will not attack us until we reach a decision. That includes not harming Jester. We'll bring you into the castle to discuss it further." Then he too descended behind the wall. Balgor rowed himself back to shore and an applause ensued as two Roah'riik welcomed him back into the allies.[21]

"Applaud the circumstances more than me," he said, walking farther into the lakeside camp. "The Fomorions took heavy losses in fighting the witchlords, many more than they expected to an enemy new to them. They don't seem to even care about raiding anymore, only the vengeance and termination of the Razhod. Luckily, it is enough to make them push back against King and break with him over it, forcing his hand since they are his army.

"The rest of this struggle will not be easy. If they agree, and I think they will, you'll have to work alongside the barbarians. They've killed and wounded us, and we them. Watch them and keep your distance, especially the Chaos leadership. And do not offend them. We may need to call on what respect we've earned from them when the Razhod threat is finished. This new alliance will effectively end after the Razhod. I know you fear them, but endure this, please, as it is our only chance." He finished with a roar, "Now will you with me?!" The allied armies cheered.

Andala turned to Tek'ouk'iek. "We'll have to meet with them to form a strategy, but we don't even know where the Razhod are."

"North," Katti said pensively. "In the mountains or Shruumoth Forest whence the last army came."

"North seems most likely but we can't just go north," Tek'ouk'iek said. "That's walking into a trap. They want us to come to them."

Andala looked north. "If we can appear unallied, they might just move on us. But until then... their spies would tell them about our alliance ahead of time."

And not just their spies, Tek'ouk'iek thought. *Like any other summoner that can speak to spirits, they see and hear much more than we do.*

---

21 Tek'ouk'iek's claim about Roah'riik being the first to welcome him is suspect. They'd had a good relationship before the betrayal, but not after, so it's likely embellishment from the author.

"Our best hope is that the giants know something of where to go and how to approach," Tek'ouk'iek said, wishing there was a way for all this to include a search party for Lil'iek.

Trust her. She'll be fine. Trust her.

As he ruminated in his pain and worry, Katti surprised him by putting a hand on his forearm. He glared at her, but she either blissfully didn't notice or care. The priestess continued, "She's alive and fighting. Leyta too. They're the two most dangerous people I know, they'll be fine. The Lady Deova will protect them."

Tek'ouk'iek brushed her hand off and muttered, "Thank you." *And keep that name out of my ears, she's your eternal. Not ours. Quoak will not be the next Tolgrym.* And just to counter-balance it, he prayed to his 'pagan' eternals for Lil'iek and their children.

They'd ended up exchanging Jester for the Cantlgrym hostages; tactically not the best move, but Tek'ouk'iek sensed the Asturions feared for their safety, and also feared Jester even in captivity. Later that evening, after a loud and frenzied supper from the adjacent barbarian camp and a quiet one from the allies, a group was selected to go to Cantlgrym and speak terms with the Chaos leaders. The boat carried them out over the quiet lake, fog-filled and black. Tek'ouk'iek hated the rocking of it, if something beneath attacked, he'd have a harder time swimming to safety. Nearby, Virgow held his unease better as they watched each other. He wondered if Virgow was feeling the same nausea he had from the rocking, probably more as the traitor had been on the wall during the winds. Tek'ouk'iek hadn't asked if he could go, he just went and none stopped him. He didn't want his people to miss out on the high stakes meeting. He had a suspicion Virgow would sell the tribes out in exchange for something if he could. He took gratitude in at least having a task he could handle. Cripples did just fine in meetings. Boring, but safe. He sighed.

Jester sat in front of him while Constantin and Andala rowed, the wind blowing her bushy black hair and fading sun shining off of her armor.

Once they docked, a tall goatman led them in through great, grim halls, the tapestries pulled down and art marred, then up stairs and into the private meeting quarters in the rear tower. Tek'ouk'iek struggled to keep pace with them but managed it, sitting between Jester and Balgor, with Andala on the other side of Jester. Opposite them sat King and next to him a grizzled and burly Asturion whom Tek'ouk'iek correctly guessed was Tomas de Pelaion, the current rebel leader. Beside them the goatman took a seat, saying nothing. His skull necklace indicated he was likely a hell-hunter or tamer, one thing he and the Kimoc had in common.

"We'll begin with a joke from Jester to set the mood," said King. His bulky costumed form turned slightly to face his companion.

"What has two arms and a burnt body?" Jester paused, waiting for an answer even though clearly no one planned to do so. "Our dead queen."

An uncomfortable silence filled the room. "It's best that we leave the past battles behind us for now," Balgor said. "We can and will discuss that another time. We're here to discuss beating the Razhod, a conflict of the living and not the dead."

"Oh but that is not dead which can eternal fight," spoke the high-pitched voice of Queen. "And with strange powers, even death can die."

A collective gasp filled the room and hopes fell that she'd been deposed. Tek'ouk'iek was disheartened but somewhat less dumbfounded; they'd already seen King somehow recover from an axe wound to the head. How they did it was beyond him, be it new armor or dark magic, but he suspected the Chaos must have limits, just not ones they'd found yet. King, Jester, and Tomas rose from their seats as Queen walked out from behind a long curtain, still wearing parts of her red, gold, white, and violet costume but much of it blackened and burnt, or just cut off and patched up. She wore an ornate shawl of royal purple design to cover up the holes in her dress. Tek'ouk'iek suspected it was an old piece stolen from the conservatory. Worse, her white mask had partially browned and melted. The hair was mostly gone, in stark contrast to the crown she still wore. Her graceful stride was lost, and one of her arms was held up by stitched threads. Now visibly weaker, she made an even creepier sight than before, but the most eerie aspect to him was the apparent lack of pain that she must've been enduring. She daintily took a seat beside Jester, bringing the table to a full circle. Inhuman. *How does one kill you, then?*

"Of course, I'll still behead those responsible for this when I get the chance," she said, folding gloved hands over each other on the table. King, Jester, and Tomas resumed their seats, although Tek'ouk'iek noted the goatman hadn't even risen. *The rift is real then.* Tek'ouk'iek hadn't seen the attack that had hit her, but everyone reported the burning was complete. Another benefit to their allyship: they would now have the opportunity to get close to this mysterious enemy, observe and then learn their secrets.

"I'll cut to it then," Virgow said. "We move parallel but separately, staying in sight of each other. We keep to our own supplies, to be shared at discretion as needed. Information on the enemy and the conflict alone will flow freely between us, and all of it will flow."

"Oh, but that's no fun," said Queen. "Who taught you how to war? Poor parents indeed. We prefer game rules. Majestic husband, tell them."

"Rules can only be enforced when you're caught breaking them," said King. "In the end, rules are less useful than leverage. If you want to make rules of true alliance and pretend they're real, you can, but you're only fooling yourselves. Better to work at the same time on the same thing than pretend to be working together."

"Or have you forgotten whom you're meeting with?" asked Queen. "Have you learned nothing in all our games?"

The room fell silent as the implications of this meeting settled. Effectively, they met not to agree to terms but to clear up the misconception that there would be any. Tomas leaned back in his seat, thick hairy arms folded over his chest and a smug look on his face as his eyes scanned theirs. He clearly enjoyed having bosses such as these. The allies scrutinized the enemy leaders with intense gazes during this deafening pause.

"Would you rather I have a meeting with your army again," Balgor said, turning his eye to the goatman. "I suspect the Fomorions will be more cooperative."

"Do you?" said King. "You swayed them this one time, my congratulations. But how far do you think they'll go with you? These barbarian tribes are as numerous violent storms swirling beside each other, shaping into a single tempest. We've been riding this storm for some time now, and you've just jumped on during a lucky break. Go ahead, try and see how hard you can keep pushing them against us."

The goatman said nothing, gave nothing away, only stared with those eerie eyes. Tek'ouk'iek was about to push this division, but then he remembered he didn't golkaw care about their conflict. He just wanted to make sure his people weren't sacrificed in it.

"Where are the Razhod?" Tek'ouk'iek asked, wanting to get this moving and over so he could sooner find Lil'iek.

"That we will give you," said King. "Because we want you there with us. Some have scattered to separate ventures, but the main force if further north, hiding in the mountains. However, our last sighting put them coming toward us to finish us off, although they won't try for us in here. We have only to surprise and meet them."

"Then we march out at dawn," Andala said.

"That is if we decide to move on them with you," said Queen. "It may be more beneficial to us to let them wipe you out while we stay in here, then move on the finish."

"But you can't while we retain our relic piece," Virgow mused, half-smiling. And Tek'ouk'iek watched him too; the man's eye had left Tek'ouk'iek for the Royal Chaos. "Your piece is useless as long as we hold ours hostage. And it would gain you nothing against the witchlords. How long then must we wait on your gracious word?"

"We'll announce our decision two hours before dark," said King. "Then move soon after."

"But they see in the dark," Tek'ouk'iek said. "They could wipe both of us out, they'll probably attack before then under cover of night."

"That's unlikely and no concern to us," said King. But the sense of imminent betrayal brought flashbacks to Tek'ouk'iek, and an idea. King continued, "You'll have to figure it out for yourselves."

"What you must be careful with, however," Tek'ouk'iek began while his hand fingered the skulls on his necklace, mirroring the quiet barbarian giant, helltamer to helltamer, "is pushing your allies too hard. I've learned the hard way to not make myself a minority to a larger group with different interests. Better to take charge and determine the path than have it determined for me."

"Puh, try and betray us," King said. "We've more tricks than you. And you're too scared of the enemy anyway."

Tek'ouk'iek kept his face from smiling. King had thought he was talking about the allied forces betraying the Royal Chaos when he really meant it a subtle hint for the goatman. His eyes fixed on the giant's, opaque and brooding, and the giant gazed back, watching him finger his skull necklace as if seeing the hint. Hopefully he noticed and understood it as "help us, be *my* ally, you clever goat, and I'll help you. Betray and bully everyone else but me." Virgow too seemed to miss the hint, or pretended to.

"What we can't count on is the size of their force or what kind of attack they'll bring in," Virgow said, more to the allies than the enemy. "Be prepared for anything."

"Preparation is key for a hearty meal or respected funeral," quipped Jester.

"Then let's retire until it's time," Balgor said, ignoring the clown. Tek'ouk'iek voiced agreement with the others, grateful Virgow was distracted and the conflict was in full motion again. He gave one final look and a faint nod at the giant before leaving, unsure if any of it had worked but praying that it had. For Lil'iek, he prayed that she'd return but prepared himself to find her dead body, or not find her at all.

CHAPTER NINE

A Dark Way Down

Based on *Writings of Qosku*, cc bastica 380;
Annals of Syago, cc bastica 350;
The Nordvargor Testaments, cc bastica 906;

dates unknown, 247

Qosku dropped down to the platform of the witch house, ghost quiet. He'd seen her return on the caimon raft, then enter her hut, but there was no sound from inside. The little maskers had gone off. *Muki, weren't they?* Finding the towering hut had been a confusing and frightening endeavor. Wandering lost through unending night, waking up one moonlit hour to see it there, looming in the fog. This after a day of barely any progress, so sore and tired from his amputation that he could barely walk. His relief swallowed up his confusion.

The boards creaked gently under his weight on the steady waters. He had no armor nor weapons, but a quick glance in the witch's bizarre shadowy mansion showed no alternatives. He grabbed the long wood pole she'd used to steer the caimon. Its lantern still carried a flame, but he grabbed some flint and dry peat as a precaution. He climbed onto his makeshift canoe—a kind of reptilian shell he'd found—then startled to see the old hag standing on a ledge facing the hut. Had he not seen her go inside?

He hurried and pushed off in the direction she'd come from, but instead of stopping him, she cackled a strange laugh. Qosku used the pole to draw himself through the still water. He wasn't sure of the direction but as it turned out, there was only one clear path north between the reeds. It brought him to a rock island, and he paused at the lip of a forbidding hole. He was sure he could've found the place without seeing it; powerful sentiments emanated around it, yet the hole itself was a void. He couldn't normally sense sentiments outside himself save the strong ones, but this entire place was of absolute hate and misery greater than even he'd felt inside himself. Yet it felt as though the cave pushed him away, or was it his subconscious that repulsed him away from it. Had he still the mountain of self-hate inside him, he might feel at home here, but he'd cast the last of that into the fire. If he could do that, he could do this. He could do anything. He was free, if still really sore.

He didn't need to call out for Syago, or look further. He knew this was where Syago had come; there was no sign or sound of him, however. Qosku yelled into the cave but heard no response, not even an echo. *Well, it can't be worse than anything else I've been through*, he thought. Lantern-pole in hand but lacking any other weapons, he hesitated at the lip. He tested the drop with a rock, and after a quick clatter, he jumped in.

The swinging lantern revealed desiccated corpses and distorted statuettes all along the wall, casting monstrous dancing shadows behind them. His eyes fell on one such soldier with gauntlets and greaves. They were old, rusted and covered in cobwebs, and lacked the claws, but cursed or not they were in better condition than the ones he wore. After all, Qosku was already cursed or damned. He peeled them off the skeleton and, keeping eyes on his surrounding, placed them on himself. He wasn't brave enough for the chestplate, however.

A whimper caught his ear. In the center of the small cavern lie a baby with gleaming white skin. But this infant had large bloody eyes. It whimpered again, and Qosku stared at it blankly until it started to scream. He crouched and realized its face was Chaska's. He tried speaking to it, but it was clearly nothing to do with her, so he punched it, killing it. Certain that he'd not killed a real baby, he stood. The sound of grinding stone snapped his attention upward to the walls, the grinding turned to sounds of rushing water. He kept the lantern straight up, searching for higher ground. A red waterfall gushed out of the stone opening, quickly filling the small area and picking him up. He struggled to keep his only light aloft as the mighty current pulled him completely under in a baptism of blood. While maintaining a hold on the pole, he kicked to push himself upward till he breathed air. As the blood river took him down a small tunnel, he saw an opening, a cliff. He couldn't stop due to the strong current, so instead leaped from the edge without sight of a landing. The still-burning lantern swung as he flew then fell. He stumbled onto a stone ledge that caught him as blood rushed past, a cascade of gore. He shivered as the smell and taste of it revived awful memories.

Soaked in the viscous liquid, he moved forward, not daring to call out for Syago but unsure how else to find him. He went quickly through the cavern expanse until he nearly tripped on something, an array of odd rocks. No... heads. They littered the ground everywhere and a closer look revealed they were Lügos's heads. Gaping in expressions varying from anger, fear, and plain dispassion. Bloody at the neck stump, all had their eyes open blankly. And so real, clammy to his touch. Seeing his face, so many of them, sickened him, and he choked down bile. He noticed other faces too, his own and more of Chaska's. Reminders and reflections of everything that hurt him, that he wanted to change but couldn't: Chaska, Lügos, Qosku. He was trembling and gasping in uneven breaths. He increased his pace, refocusing his dynal flows throughout his limbs, and more and more heads appeared, even behind him somehow. He crawled over them, which was easier than trying to stand on their slippery surfaces even with the pole in one arm, slick from blood and sweat that he was. The swinging lantern light showed the heads multiplying. As their numbers grew into a mound, they fell off of each other, rising like a wave and arcing over onto him. Pushing the only thing he felt, fear, into his legs, he sprinted and stumbled over the field of heads with the wave growing, rumbling behind. It finally dropped, barely missing him and splashing a thumping, thunderous surge of heads that bounced around him and knocked into his back and legs. He eventually cleared the field and took a moment to catch his breath and get his bearings. He had no idea where he was going, or how off course he was. *Mother's shit, this is too much.*

The lantern still burned dimly, and he felt drier from the blood bath. He walked quickly, hoping he would eventually find a wall he could navigate or some sign of Syago's path. He walked for some time through endless darkness but found no wall, and began to wonder if he was even in the same cavern. This expanse unnerved him deeply and stories of being in the underworld, ukhu pachan, resurfaced, though less gruesome than this. He paused to look around, considering shouting in search of an echo, when he felt something brush his arm, making him jump. Then another, its softness bothered him more than pain ever could. Gentle, a furry hand rubbed his bicep, reaching out of the shadows for him. He moved away and another arm grabbed at his other shoulder.

All around him long furry arms reached into the light, grabbing at him. Not wanting to see the rest, Qosku hurried forward, but the lantern revealed only more arms in his path. They closed in, grabbing violently. Qosku spun with his pole, knocking the arms away. The light spun around wildly, and lacking an opening, he dashed into them, ready to elbow or kick anything solid. Arms covered him, and he beat them away as much as he could while powering through. They followed but no bodies appeared. He finally broke through and ran until they were far behind him.

To the side he could see a different light down a branching tunnel. He turned to it, thinking it might be Syago but then recalled that Syago probably would use the white light of Alexandre. This was yellow torchlight. He heard faint noise, maybe talking, and cautiously moved closer. As he neared the tunnel, the sounds became more distinct. Sounds of sex. Harsh panting, moaning, and... growling? He stopped and saw that, although he moved not, the tunnel drew slowly closer to him. Qosku turned away, and as he retreated, the tunnel followed, its light seeming to pulse. He saw a hole in the floor, and with the other tunnel roaring at his heels, he jumped down. The lantern swung on the pole, throwing shadows everywhere in this placid but crowded room.

He reached up and stilled the lantern and saw people everywhere, standing stalk still. A chill shot through him. On a closer look, he realized these were not people, these were mummified corpses.

Each of them was wrapped in cloth and leather and stood up unsuspended, a chilling reminder of the terrifying battle at Tiakanawu. The leather on their heads opened at the mouth, each of which hung agape toward the ceiling. The smell of the damp air fell beyond description. A shiver ran up his spine as backed away. He felt his pole touch something and cursed himself as he heard the first groan. It reached up to claw off the coverings, revealing pale white skin with no face, but numerous holes all over. Porous and blind, it was not a corpse, probably had never been a living human. Qosku flinched, but it didn't come for him. It walked away. All around Qosku, the others jolted awake, then pulled off their wrappings and walked off into the darkness of the small cavern.

Confused, Qosku walked after the first one, slowly, quietly. A sharp pain lanced up his leg as an iron trap latched onto his foot. The old greave protected most of it but not the back. He clutched at it, trying to pry it off. He almost had it when the white ones returned, bearing chains in their clawed hands. Qosku pried his foot out and tripped, falling backwards. A manacle latched onto his wrist. He tried to draw the chain in, capture it as a weapon, but this distracted him from the chains clamping down on his legs. Then they had his other arm and neck.

No! Shit, no!

Trapped, he twisted and punched, used dyne for extra speed and strength. But they didn't draw near him and the rusty chains held, stretching him out. One of the hollowed ones planted Qosku's lantern in the ground, but most worked just outside the light, only their porous arms were visible as they used hammers, stakes, and hooks to prepare what came next. His stomach shrank as he saw no way out and wished he'd used his time better, moped less and fought and laughed more. Maybe he didn't deserve to live, but why did that really matter? He would live anyway. He could save those that did, if nothing else.

Qosku prayed to his eternals, prayed to the mountains, prayed to Deova. He struggled against the irons when he heard the clanking sounds of a rotating crank in the darkness. As the hollow ones turned their levers, the chains raised up, lifting him into the air. An old tin pan was slid beneath him and a large mirror was placed in front of him, reflecting himself in the dim light. For a moment he just hung there, powerless and wondering at the point of having him just hang belly down in front of a mirror? Then the white hollows came out of the shadows bearing more chains, these chains now smaller and with stained hooks on each end. Thoughts of those hooks and their placement in his body made his head swim with nausea.

The manacles tightened and Qosku couldn't move. The first hollow stabbed and laced a hook through Qosku's hand, the point jutting out his palm. He held off screaming or even so much as a grunt, focusing on healing, until the second hook went through his shoulder, snagging just under a collarbone. The nausea became too much, and he retched. Another hook went between his forearm bones, another in the other shoulder, another in the other forearm, then his other hand. Each stabbed and lanced through his arms. He could no longer help it, but winced and wept. He was dripping sweat, blood, and tears into the pan below. His body was swimming in pain and waves of nausea, and they weren't even done. They put two more on the backs of his ribcage, with each of these chains raising up on more cranks to tighten. His upper body hooked, they undid the manacles and he sagged. The metal hooks rubbed against his bones and tissue. His skeleton was on fire.

They then resumed their silent, painful work on his lower body, placing hooks into his lower spine, femur bones, calves, and feet. The agony began to dull, but the nausea only grew as his body lost precious mortal fluids. The last manacles removed, he hung completely on these bloody metal hooks, suspended in total darkness. The pale hollows faded back into shadow.

Eternals, please! I'm sorry for being an abomination, or being harmful to myself. I'd just found peace with my body. Please save me, get me out.

Something emerged from the darkness, slow, resembling a gigantic slug. But as its glistening bulk lurched near, Qosku saw that it wasn't a slug, but a man so bloated and swollen his eyes bulged and arms protruded like feelers. The gaunt ones ratcheted the hooks to pull at Qosku, stretching his body and sanity tight. He saw no way out, would've accepted a quick death to just end the misery, but instead kept his mind in meditation. The slugman was served a tray of strange needles with straws. A grubby hand picked up one of these crude attachments and plucked the needle into Qosku's back and began sucking the blood out of him. The tray was passed around as several others drew up needles, stabbing him, and, hungrily, mindlessly, began sucking him dry. Others drank of the pan below. They bunched up around him and the blood loss began to make Qosku delirious. Instead of welcoming unconsciousness, he instinctively focused on healing. Using sorrow to seal up the wounds and stop the leak of blood, and joy to produce more blood, he pushed back the delirium. This also pushed back the hollowed ones who, apparently on tasting blood filled with sorrow or joy, spat it out. The slugman waved his oozing arms and slurped with a thick tongue. Qosku continued this and, in the distraction of his parasites, focused on easing his hand out of its hook. The task was difficult, nigh unbearable, but he unhooked both hands, then undid his forearms. The hollowed ones were so preoccupied with their rare feeding opportunity being interrupted that they didn't notice until his arms and shoulders were free. As some of the hollowed ones retreated and brought in a table with spikes on it, Qosku rose up, wrapping his chains around those still close, hooking them to each other.

Once the table reached him and more thin hollows grabbed for him, he snapped a hand at the lantern and brought it down on the old wood of the table. It caught fire and spread along the leaking oil. The hollowed ones retreated from the heat, and he released himself from the last of the hooks. Completely unchained, unhooked, and bloody all over, he grabbed the lantern's pole and moved to the other side of the fire, then ran at the slugman and planted his pole at the base of it, vaulting himself toward the entrance he'd fallen in from. He grabbed the ledge and raised himself up, rolling free of the smoking hole. Slick with blood and sweat, he sat up, feeling glad to be alive. It was such a new and refreshing feeling, and the achievement of his escape helped. He tended to his aching wounds, the holes all over him, bandaging them up and praying them shut. He saw no moving tunnel or furry arms. But he did see the faded images of spirits walking down a more normal looking tunnel, the only thing he could see in the darkness. He noted the strangeness of having entered and exited the same place yet now sitting in a different area. This could only be the summoning area Syago had been looking for. He'd found the path to Syago.

Spirits walked about the mound like glimmers on the surface of a pond. Vague reflections that shimmered then disappeared. Syago couldn't tell how many there were and couldn't imagine who would want to be in this place even as a spirit. Still wary, he walked up to a dais in the middle of the glow, a large stone platform with intricate markings like the interlacing knotwork Leyta had been interested in. He missed her now, needed her comforting presence and imagined she'd be fascinated by this place and know all kinds of things about it. Syago knew nothing and could only guess this was the calling spot. The dais was worn, old, and crumbling.

"Father," he said as he stepped onto the circle. "Odiru Parlain, I call you. Your son, Syago, calls you here to the cave, now. Please come and come quick that we may speak."

The air in front of him shimmered and he thought the spirits in the area looked at him, he heard them like muffled whispers. "...not here... look at you... will never... give up."

Syago waited, then called again for the father he'd never known. He'd often dreamed of doing this, back when confined to his village, young and ignorant. But he'd not dreamed it to happen this way and not with such trepidation instead of anticipation. The air rippled again and a single spirit appeared vaguely at first, then surfaced into a more distinct image. The spirit of Odiru stood before Syago. He looked like an older version of Syago finely sketched on a pale canvas, wearing a plain tunic and no weapons or armor.

"I heard... son?" he asked. "My son, Syago? Is that really you?"

"It is I, Father." Syago wanted to say more, he felt like he should, like there were certain appropriate responses expected, but he didn't know any of them. He felt strange even addressing someone as "father." Odiru's image flickered briefly in the quiet. "Father, I- I called you here, to talk to you."

"I'm glad you did, I really am," Odiru said with a sort of emotional calm, the kind that holds back a flood of complicated emotions. He looked as Syago had always imagined him. He'd only seen a few drawings, of course and had been told they looked alike, though Syago had darker skin, hair, and eyes. His mixed feelings on the occasion along with the lack of confident strength he'd expected to see in Odiru didn't help Syago's despair and sudden uncertainty. This man was simple and quiet. On seeing Syago hesitate, Odiru continued, "How fare you? I see you have Alexandre. That makes me proud. I watch you sometimes, though I can't see you very well, I can still find you. Sometimes."

"I wanted to ask," Syago blurted out. "Why did you sacrifice those people to the devils? And what else have you done that..." He trailed off, unsure of what to say and the best way to say it. It wasn't what he'd planned on asking first; it felt rude given that they'd never actually met before.

Odiru seemed slightly surprised, then smiled gently, the confidence Syago had expected appearing then. "Ah, so you've heard of some of my mistakes. I was never perfect, and conflicts like that bring out the worst in people, even you have made some, I hear. Perhaps not as great, but none can escape evil when these kinds of threats chase you. That's what makes them so bad, not what they do to us, but what they get us to do. The sacrifices we made in desperation. We felt out of options and time. We also took many Unakans and tortured them, I regret to say. We'd noticed that most Razhod were Unakan and so were mistaken in thinking that they would know, or had some connection to it. We thought they as a people were responsible. All of it was wrong."

"Why did you do it?" Syago asked quietly.

"I did what I thought I had to, something I now regret. I could make excuses, but that doesn't change what happened. Instead I have repented and moved on and so have the people it affected. Son, you must stop focusing on me as your grand hero and be your own champion. I'm not as important as what's happening to you now. Learn from my mistakes and improve on them." He said this gently but firmly. An apology with some reproach.

Syago nodded. It wasn't something he hadn't thought about, but for some reason hearing it made a difference. It felt better. He wanted to ask about his mother, how she fared. Perhaps ask after the darker questions that'd been floating further back in his mind: if Odiru had tricked her into marriage, or enslaved or abused her in anyway. He shifted weight from one foot to another, unable to think of the best way to phrase it, so he said, "There is something else I came to ask you. The Razhod are back. One named Kask leads them. I've read all the accounts I could find. No matter how many times they're wiped out, they come back some years later. How did they come back this time? How do we beat them once and for all?"

At the mention of the old enemy, Odiru grew serious. He replied quietly, "I don't know. I'm not sure we can."

"But where do they come from? Haven't you learned anything as a spirit? Do they have some hide-out somewhere with the ceremonies written down? Or a hidden reserve of followers to replenish their numbers and resources?"

"That would make the most sense. We destroyed all the haunts we could find, numerous times." His tone changed to something more urgent. "They do have a secret, Syago. I don't know it, but it's something their loyal spirits wonder about, but they don't know it either. I don't think anyone but the Razhod themselves know it. They're powerful, Syago. So powerful I... I haven't seen my wife in several years. I don't know where she is, maybe they have her. They hunted her like they hunt me. Them and their dead followers. They want me because of what I did to them. I escaped them once, and I can't keep it up for very much longer. You must beat them, Syago! You have to find a way, please."

Taken aback by Odiru's sudden despairing plea, Syago said, "I'm trying to. Just- can you tell me anything about them? Anything you know will help me do that."

"I don't know anything. I always thought I could figure out their secrets if I investigated, but they're too powerful and too cruel. And I'm so tired of running and hiding. Please help me."

"I will beat them, Father," Syago said, hoping to push some hope back into them both. "Somehow, we will beat them."

Just then a sharp pain shot through his chest. He looked down to see the handle of a blade protruding from his upper ribcage, a shiny redness barely visible between his chestplate and gambeson. A voice whispered in his ear, "No. You won't."

A hand pulled the thin blade back out. Odiru yelled, and spirits rushed around them and then disappeared. Syago fell to his knees, staring in disbelief at the gushing hole in his chest. At least it'd not touched his heart. The Razhod now stood in front of him, long silvery hair draped an amused pale face. Stealth of death and shadows, he knelt to level his face with Syago's, who thought he saw a dark spark of joy in those insidious helleyes. The Razhod smiled, a familiar smile on an unfamiliar face. "See, dead before you even started. You're even more pathetic than your father was. Well, now the butcher has come and you're both expired. Are you crying? You think your life matters?

"*Behold, the Creature*

Bipedal maggots that leech

Bulging in excess,' saith the poet."[22] The smile deepened.

Syago tried to disbelieve that this was happening. Tried to wake up from the nightmare, and yet already his consciousness began to slip, body sinking closer to the floor. Alexandre had already begun to heal him but for the seriousness of the wound and watchfulness of the Razhod, Syago knew it would never finish. How could he sneak up and stab him so simply? He was breaking his promise to Leyta by dying. Qosku would be let down and alone, he'd not made up to Lil'iek, stopped the Razhod. The Razhod drew a curved sword, then raised his hand and slapped Syago hard across the face, throwing him down. "Prepare yourself for a great honor, a tributary sacrifice. One of the few occasions where I'm forced to acknowledge that you humans are useful. I'll be sure to let Odiru watch the show." He pointed the sword at Syago and a second one, the red wavy flambard Grievore, materialized in his other hand. He stepped forward, then looked up as something landed solidly right in between them.

---

22 This is clearly a poem, but nobody knows from who or where. Even the style is foreign to me.

"I am Qosku," said the small figure in the dim light. "Step away." Relief swelled in Syago's chest, or was that just air coming into his lungs? Syago exhaled then inhaled more sweet air, with great pain.

"A friend," the Razhod said, sheathing the curved sword. "Good, you'll die together. More blood for me to use."

Qosku jumped forward with two quickened kicks. Either of the kicks would've dropped a seasoned soldier. But the first kick missed, the second got caught and upturned by the Hellface's free gloved hand. Qosku flipped in the air and landed on his side, then rolled back to his feet. Syago noticed to his surprise that instead of passing out, he felt much better. His chest hurt as the hells and he could barely lift his arms, but the bleeding had slowed. Alexandre flared brighter than ever before, as if recognizing the enemy gave it more desire for Syago to fight back and healing him faster than ever before. If Qosku could give him a few more seconds, he would be able to stand and swing his sword.

Qosku's recovery, quick and graceful, only barely prepared him for the onslaught of the Razhod's counter-assault. The long wavy red blade whirred, the black form behind it darting and twisting, only visible in the dark by his silvery hair and pale skin. Grievore came around lightning fast, and Qosku narrowly ducked under it, then over it, vaulting upward as the Razhod swung the blade faster than anything Syago had seen before. Somehow Qosku stayed just ahead of that terrible edge. Syago saw him attempt to use his gauntlets to deflect the cuts, but the attacks were too jarring, quick, and risky. He wouldn't be able to last much longer. *Just a few moments more, my friend,* Syago thought.

Qosku's dodging, equally a work of battle art, kept him alive until he slipped on the damp stone. The blade descended, and, seeing his friend's death upon him, Syago gripped Alexandre and leaped forward with a roar, using Alexandre to knock the blade aside.

Ignoring his pain, Syago pressed in close, where it would be harder for the Razhod to maneuver the long blade. But somehow, the Hellface did manage it. With perfect skill and swiftness, the great flambard seemed to fly around him while nimble feet carried the Razhod away and around. Even when Qosku joined, darting in with reaching kicks or punches and dodging when necessary, the Hellface kept both of them from a full flank, forcing them to backpedal till they both backed out of his range.

The Hellface ceased cutting. Panting, he drew a small blade and his summoning bell, then sliced his cheek. His helleyes widened with madness. "Agony. A gift I know well and must share with you. I will teach you—"

"We both already know agony well enough," Syago growled as he threw his hunting knife, drawn in the enemy's fury of broad slashes, "because of you." The Razhod raised his sword to deflect the knife as he rang the bell. But the knife was only to distract as Syago ran forward with Alexandre, and Qosku with his fists. The bell jingled in the Razhod's hand as Syago knocked aside the rising soulsword and Qosku crashed into him. Grekiask the Slayer appeared behind them, a cloaked bird skeleton, but it disappeared as Qosku rammed his fists into the Razhod repeatedly and Alexandre stabbed in the Razhod's belly with searing light. The Razhod landed on his back, coughing blood.

"No! Not like this," he snarled and drew another knife, trying to stab Syago's leg with it. "Not this time, not again. You don't deserve—"

Syago hit the knife away and thrust Alexandre, shining fiercely, into the Razhod's back. He choked, eyes wide, and went still. Syago withdrew Alexandre, letting the body drop to the floor, and wiped the blade on its clothes. He recognized the silver hair as one of the newer disciples, so he'd recently joined the cult and ascended to the Crimson Covenant only in the past few days.

He looked at Qosku, sitting breathless among partially visible spirits, who, returned from his banishing, numbered more than before, now watching them in their victory. He offered a hand and pulled Qosku up, then turned to see one spirit, slightly more distinct than the others, standing over the Razhod's body. This one a young woman he didn't recognize but she had the Razhod eyes, perhaps an older one long dead? Or a follower? With a cold look of rage, she growled, "I hate you!"

"You don't need to follow them," Syago said. "We have a better way, a happier way if you'll listen."

She smiled cruelly. "I'll see you dead for this, maggot."

Then she was gone. Syago called again for Odiru, but he'd gone and none of the few remaining spirits knew where. Nor any others they asked for, including Goidiberic, his mother, Camila, or Qosku's ancestors.

After asking the spirits how to get out, they climbed the slick wall up into a muddy hole And emerged out far from the Kourii lake. Syago was sure they would never have exited so easily without their help.

Once they'd climbed out of the disgusting hole, sitting somewhere in the marshes, the mud gurgled and dripped until the hole sealed itself up. Qosku asked, "Syago, what was that place? Was it real?"

"I don't know, Qos," he muttered, also looking at the mudpile in wonder. "I hope not."

CHAPTER TEN

IN THE LAND OF LOST MINDS

Based on *Leyta's Journals,* cc bastica 370;
The Hunter's Parchments, cc bastica 360;

dates unknown, 247

The two women fled into the marshlands, keeping a northwest course so as not to stray too deep. They ran much farther than Leyta would've liked but given the openness of the area, she understood. Eventually they stopped behind a patch of tall grass to catch their breath and bearings, warily avoiding the ponds. But as they crouched, they felt their feet give way on the mud. Unable to find purchase, they fell into a ravine that was deeper and more slippery than the appearance warned. Once down, they waited, hoping that being out of sight would keep them from being hunted further and bracing for what new predators might stalk them.[23] The steep, slick walls prohibited climbing back up.

After a moment of stillness, Lil'iek and Leyta walked through the mossy ravine quickly. Being in a deepened area gave them a distinct disadvantage if attacked. They came to an area that opened up like a bowl, its walls slanted enough that they might be able to climb out with Lil'iek's grappling rope. A web-like fungus covered the far end of the bowl and in the center sat something that resembled a stumped tree or growing mushroom of about six feet high. Its sickly green color with dark spots, short feeler branches, and small blue bulb sitting on top made it seem less threatening than other fungi Leyta had seen.

---

23 Lustmord comments on Nordvargr and the strangeness of the wild, citing rumors of creatures believed to be mythical but more likely twisted versions of what's common.

107

Lil'iek set her bow and small bag down at the base of one side. "I'll try and get us up out of this spot. Watch that fungi."

Leyta nodded but said nothing. Lil'iek had been quiet and brusque. Leyta knew the woman hadn't liked or trusted her since the siege at Mantlgrym, and following Tiakanawu probably wished her dead. But then why save her? That she had both surprised and moved Leyta, a welcome feeling. Then with a start, Leyta realized she cared. *So all I needed was some more danger to push me back? Wonderful.* Though it was an inconvenient time to start feeling again—more than the fleeting moments meeting that child or kissing Syago—scepterless and in need of being tough. She wasn't sure she was completely back, and wouldn't know until she got her scepter to try dyne.

She shivered and rubbed her arms, the old spear leaning against her. If the humid air and acrid smells weren't enough to make her uncomfortable, the eerie sight of an unknown mushroom was. It reminded her of the heresy, made her wonder how different, if at all, the fungi would be in a world without dyne? It didn't have the anthropoid mutations, but certainly was a bizarre and menacing thing. Maybe nature was strange and cruel to begin with.

She looked around the rim of the bowl and noticed how unusually quiet the area was. No bugs or birds, a good thing normally, but it made the place feel wrong without the ambiance. Her skin prickled. She noticed an odd log next to her on the slope. On closer inspection, she realized it was a human corpse covered in moss and overgrowth. She jerked back from it, then noticed several others, mostly animal, lining the bowl. Frowning, her gaze went from the fungi in the middle, to the desiccated corpses that surrounded it, and back.

Lil'iek growled in frustration. "This damn hook won't catch. Place is too slick."

"Lil'iek," Leyta said. "I think it's growing."

"What?" She turned and looked where Leyta pointed. The mushroom in the middle remained still, but the bulb on top was clearly larger than before. Its bluish, porous membrane gleamed. Leyta searched Lil'iek's face as she watched it for a second, then Lil'iek said, "We have to go."

Too late.

As Lil'iek turned to grab the bag and hookline, Leyta heard a faint hiss, and the bulb on the fungus began shrinking. Lil'iek grabbed Leyta's arm and shouted, "Run! It's a culicida, which are poisonous. Hold your breath and close your eyes."

She did so after marking the path out of the bowl first, not far to go. Then an earsplitting screech shot through their heads. Lil'iek stumbled and went down. Leyta put both hands over her ears, but the shrieking, like a thousand screaming children, was in their heads, blocking out everything.

She stumbled on toward their exit. When she realized Lil'iek wasn't following, she cracked an eye to see her struggling to get up, weeping and muttering apologies while clutching her head. Leyta ran back to pull Lil'iek and the bag up and felt the gas from the bulb on her skin. It burned like fire, adding to the pain in her head. Her lungs ached from holding her breath, and she knew they would pay for worse if she opened them to the miasma.

She longed for her staff more than ever before. A simple gust of wind would push the gas out, but instead it scratched at her skin. She helped Lil'iek up, glimpsing that the woman had a cut on her leg and her face had blotches. She hurried and closed her eyes, pulling her along, not much time left. Then another screech came, this time over the whispering of children.

A crack of her eyes showed that the culicida had somehow moved closer, and pulsed with dull violet light. She closed her eyes again and tried to move around it. The screech cut off, and she heard the sucking sound of its feelers as they brushed against her, sucking hungrily with a long thin needle.

Remembering the spear she still held in her other hand, she snapped it forward. It screeched anew, this time with a pained gurgle then hiss. And they ran. When they finally cleared the miasma, they fell to the floor, coughing and rubbing their skin.

With the miasma cloud still pressing forward, and the creature still alive, they crawled down the ravine, using moss and mud to rub their skin clean of the poison. Leyta knew the burns would remain as scars, on top of the Seeping burns, but felt more relief at getting out, and contentment that she could once again feel such relief, however brief it might last.

They'd circled around back to the castle, or what direction Lil'iek had thought was the castle, but the ravine must've turned them around somehow.

"I don't understand it," Leyta said, rubbing her arms in the chill fog. "We should've been able to return that way. We didn't go far."

Lil'iek gave no response. Didn't give away that Leyta was stating a conclusion she'd already reached long ago. They were lost, and Lil'iek was at a loss for what to do.

"Can't you find it through the animal skulls?" Leyta pressed. "Try that."

Lil'iek was about to whip a response back about how she already had tried that and the princess needed to quit whining and giving orders, but a light ahead stopped her. Not the pulsating lights they'd seen before, but more of a flicker, like an actual lantern. She started for it and Leyta followed. The silhouette of a misshapen tower emerged in the mist, dim lanterns glowing from its crooked windows. Tall reeds added cover to the fog, but Lil'iek still crouched low. *Could this be the witch? But she's in the center of Boggorn and we were just in the outer marshes.*

The sun, frustratingly, hadn't moved all day. Lil'iek knew the rumors of illusions and phantoms, but this struck her as ridiculous. *What if this caimon hag is doing it?* She preferred that explanation to the tales she'd heard. The sun's fixation forced her to rely on intuitive direction, which she had but didn't wholly trust. She did pray, repeatedly blowing prayers on the winds to the Great Ones, but wondered if those would even reach them out here. Aside from the pond reeds, the marsh was an open field. But open in the wrong way, hiding creatures lurking beneath the mud and water. And it could only get worse during the nighttime, if that ever came. Especially with that spiny cat on the prowl.

The area, quiet and motionless, unnerved her. She crossed several more wetland patches and old boardwalks until she stood on the front deck of the towering hut. The floating shack, made of wood, reeds, and mud, stacked high, appeared to be empty.

She looked back at Leyta, who held her old spear, hiding her shivers, then back at the worn curtain hanging on the door. Axes in hand, Lil'iek brushed the curtain aside and entered slowly, silently. Flasks and bottles lined the walls. A small cast-iron cauldron hung against a far wall over a small fire pit. The single room seemed the very kind a witch might have, though Lil'iek had expected shrunken heads adorning the walls. As she looked around, going up a couple floors, it struck her as more odd to see no bedding. Did she not sleep as the Razhod were rumored not to? They, as punishment for joining the coven, were said to be unable to sleep and so entered a meditative trance at half the effect. Being a dark summoner as well, maybe the witch faced a similar curse.

Lil'iek shook her head; she was starting to believe horror myths. The room had nothing for her, not even better weapons or armor, and no trace of Syago as Leyta said she'd hoped, or of a compass with which they might navigate home. Although she did notice with interest that the cauldron was full of stew, now cold.

She exited, looked at Leyta, and shook her head. She looked skyward again then left. "Well, I believe that way is north, so a northeast path that way would take us to Cantlgrym."

"That's fine," Leyta replied after a pause. She rubbed her arms as they moved back along the planks. Lil'iek sighed inwardly. Leyta had been better after Tiakanawu, but that didn't change what the woman had done or allowed to be done to them. Lil'iek was frequently tempted to either leave her or let a caimon snap out of the water and drag her down in its jaws. But the girl seemed so innocent and defenseless now, had even helped her flee the culicida, but she knew the feeling was likely more her weariness and frustration speaking than any rational thoughts of resolution. She was also getting tired of the long awkward silences between them. Leyta could be more helpful if Lil'iek talked to her more. Perhaps the dynast would come to regret what she'd done, make the change to instill better treatment of the Kimoc people.

Start the change you want to see, Fal'iek had often told her, and the echo of it stung. *Instead of waiting for change, create the society you want to live in by how you treat others. Only us saves us.*

She sighed. Once off the reed-filled lake, she broached the subject. "You've been quiet. What's on your mind?"

"Nothing and everything," Leyta muttered after a pause. The mud and slime covering her gambeson dress didn't seem to bother her, nor did the cuts on her arms and legs from crossing the marsh and bog. A tough young Asturion woman, Lil'iek noted with some begrudging admiration, not that she hadn't met hardy women like this before in Tolgrym. But a pampered noblewoman and scholar such as Leyta surprised her out in the wild.

"Are you despairing after Syago," Lil'iek pressed as they tried once again to leave the cursed bog. "Affections that aren't mutual?"

"No. We agreed to court more fully when all this ends."

"Qosku," Lil'iek asked. "What happened with him still bothers you?"

"Yes," Leyta said. "He hid so much from me, even knowing of his curse, I could tell it wasn't all. He'd become more and more reserved and melancholic. I'd wondered if it was the battle trauma. Or the Razhod using Unaka and then our own people targeting him. I'd meant to ask but then his werebeast blew up. Before I even knew about it, he'd gone. I keep wondering what more I could've done."

Lil'iek opened her mouth to tell her of the secret, that he was a twist, and remembered Qosku's request for secrecy. She still felt sympathy for the boy, and maybe a little for Leyta now. She said, "I asked myself the same thing after losing Fal'iek. I think there's always more we could've done, always mistakes that fed it, but dwelling on it is no good. Doesn't help us now. You did more than most would've done in your position. I'm certain he understood that."

"I think I realize that. I do worry about him now. Sometimes he looked so forlorn, I got the impression he was just teetering on the edge. I can't imagine what exile has done to him, if he's even surviving it. When I first met him, he said how glad he was to be in a new place and start over. How much he liked it here and appreciated us, his friends. He always went back to that, and then it was ripped away from him. The one out of all of us who had the least to begin with. He did so much with so little—"

She cut off and stopped as did Lil'iek. Not far ahead, they could see a body impaled and propped up by several thin javelins. Recognizing it as a Fomorion tactic, Lil'iek looked around, gripping her axes tighter. She wondered if she should string her bow but, not seeing any enemies, knew that would be irrational. Hardly even a blackbird had flown over them the entire walk, though a few now pecked at the body before them.

As they approached the corpse, Lil'iek prepared her blowdart pipe to shoot down one of the quervosks on the corpse until Leyta yelled them away, not noticing Lil'iek's effort to feed them for the night. She sighed and switched it out for her axes. Red, purple, and white, the body had been flayed maybe an hour or two earlier, just barely drying now. Several pin sticks protruded from it, like tiny javelins. The skinless face was a grotesque smile, teeth yellowed and crooked with some missing and some sharp. Fanglike. One eye hung out of the socket while the other gushed fluid from the quervosk beaks. Lil'iek blew a prayer on the winds to the Great Ones.

"Fomorions?" Leyta whispered, crossing herself.

"No, they don't flay their victims," she replied, also breathless. Then less certain, she said, "I think." She looked back the way they'd come from, the lake of reeds still visible. The body was clearly that of a woman, due to the skinned genitalia. "This must be the witch. Golkaw me."

"What could do this?" Leyta asked.

Lil'iek thought of the menacing creatures that lived out here, duendes. She'd always considered them a myth made up. This sounded like the outlandish tales she'd heard of them, though it also struck her as something a Razhod might do, but this lacked the ritualistic markings. She could only shake her head in disgusted bewilderment. Then she noticed something white protruding from the corpse's crotch. A large piece of bone had been jammed into it. *It looks like it came from a skull, perhaps I can use it.* Fighting revulsion, she pulled the bone piece free. The blood on it already dry, she sensed nothing through it and so stuffed it into her small pack and mentioned it was for potential later use. They moved on.[24]

Lil'iek pondered what kind of justice she ought to demand of Leyta. The woman had turned out more friend than enemy, even if out of need, but she still participated in a betrayal that resulted in the deaths of so many kin. The revenge she had to enact on Leyta was less than what Virgow deserved, and the shadowmen also. Her list grew long. *Will any of it make my life better? Or those of my people? The shadowmen will, for they continue to threaten us. But Virgow and his palemen supporters will only extend the cycle of bitterness unless I can demonstrate their wrong.*

Leyta seemed to have warmed up to her. If Lil'iek truly wanted a safe world for her family, she needed to work with Leyta, not against her. Such diplomacy was another thing Fal'iek had been right about.

If Leyta had Kimoc blood on her hands, then maybe it was in part resolved by saving Lil'iek, and aiding her along this failed wandering. She had restored justice between them.

Restoration, how could I have forgotten about that? It was one of the Kimoc's oldest traditions, yet they'd suspended it when it became obvious the shadowmen and Royal Chaos wouldn't allow for justice to be restored. The Asturions might, though.

Then, like the snuffing of a candle, the sun went out and the moon was there. The shift was sudden and unsettling to the point where Lil'iek hoped

---

24 This description fits what little I've been able to learn about the ursig duendes, better known now as the Kourii duendes. Though why they would do this is beyond us; perhaps the witch's hold over them wasn't as great as she thought.

it was just a trick of the Kourii Marsh and not a physical reality, though the stories of marsh-induced insanity didn't offer more comfort. Should they start a fire to cook some food and stay warm? Nothing would draw the cat, or something else, quicker, but they couldn't walk in the dark and it was getting cold. There was one other thing on her mind before daring that.

"Leyta, there's something I need to tell you." To her credit, the dynast didn't stiffen or slow. Lil'iek continued, "I'm going to seek retribution from you, and from Virgow. I just haven't decided what or how."

"Oh," Leyta said after a pause. "I understand. I am sorry, if that helps. I don't know what else you would want of me than true remorse, but I have it."

"Apologies are worthless without changed behavior," Lil'iek said, though she did believe Leyta felt remorse. "Words are cheap and empty in a land where violence is the ultimate law. But I'm trying to be less violent. I want you to give me Virgow. Then I'll accept your apology and we'll be restored to friends and allies."

"Give him to you? What will you do with him?"

"I haven't decided yet, and no doubt it will depend on the situation in which I find him." Lil'iek turned her gaze from the soggy path they wove to Leyta walking beside her. "But honestly I don't think it's any of your affair. Do you deny that it's his fault we're having this conversation at all? By your laws, he, as a criminal, doesn't belong to you, but to us. He's mine, to borrow and return, or keep forever as I see fit."

Leyta shivered beside her, and they decided on walking farther then trying a fire. In the distance, dim lights hung, blinking. They regarded those lights warily, but didn't even consider approaching. Still, the lights seemed to pull at them.

At some point, Leyta halted, pointing. "Lil'iek, I think that one's a campfire."

She looked to where Leyta indicated; all she saw was the eerie blinking lights. Lethal lanterns of the dark bog, she knew. "I only see the fake ones."

"The yellow one, right there. The others are more white but this one's more yellow and flickers different."

"Is it by any of the fake ones or isolated?"

"Isolated. It's in a dark gap between those two groups."

She tried to see what Leyta was pointing at, but her gaze always drifted to the eerie lights. She shook her head. "I still don't trust it, not here."

"Then trust me. Syago is here, if it isn't him then we'll know before we arrive." She grabbed Lil'iek's hand to lead ahead.

Lil'iek hesitated against someone not attuned to the wild leading her, but rather than be pulled by Leyta, she broke free of her grasp and followed her. Trusting her.

As they neared the camp, the forms of Syago and Qosku became more evident. Leyta quickened her pace almost to a run as she saw, but Lil'iek stopped her, clamping a hand over her mouth. Looking into her eyes, she smiled. Partly to hide her misgivings about this good fortune, but the mischief also felt badly needed in so grim a land. Creeping up on Syago proved so easy it was disappointing. Though to their credit, Syago and Qosku noticed as she was a pace away and the firelight revealed her. Jumping at Syago, after nearly getting stabbed, the two embraced, laughing. Not far off Leyta embraced Qosku. Then they switched. After a moment of this, the four sat around the fire, eating some tender roasted meat Lil'iek didn't care to know the identity of. They ate together and laughed as they related the stories of what brought them to this point. The last vestiges of Lil'iek's anger at Leyta and Syago faded away completely, and she let it go.

"Never heard of it before," Lil'iek said of the cave. "But it sounds a lot like that time you showed me the Tolgrym privy." She ducked under the bone Syago threw at her.

Even Qosku laughed and joked, or attempted to. "No, it's more as his room." They laughed anyway.

"Maybe that's how you survived," Leyta said. "Or the cave was a manifestation..." She trailed off, staring at the fire. No, not at the fire. Lil'iek followed her gaze past it to some furry creature between Syago and Qosku. They startled when they noticed it too.

A wooden mask, large and painted with small eye and mouth holes, covered most of the tiny body of dark fur, horns protruding out the top. This small humanoid creature carried a stick akin to the tiny javelins they'd seen on the flayed body earlier. The masked head tilted and clicked several times. Then more of them came into view, surrounding the group. They swarmed in, moving so silently and quickly, that Lil'iek didn't notice her axes were gone from her belt until she reached for them. Alarm ran through her head as they danced and clicked and cartwheeled about. Qosku and Syago looked about them with wary amusement, not seeing the threat for what it was, but Leyta shared the expression of fear that Lil'iek was feeling. Lil'iek couldn't count how many they numbered—they were too many and too everywhere, cartwheeling and twirling in some type of tribal dance. Almost playfully. She thought she saw one of her axes being passed around in a play fight. As she moved for it, one raised a hollowed reed to the mouthhole in his mask. Before Lil'iek could so much as duck, her shoulder pricked painfully, burning. They jittered and cartwheeled and spun. She plucked out the dart and several more stuck into her. Her skin and muscles hurt, she would've screamed if not for the contortions freezing her jaw up.

They continued to shoot at them, clicking and dancing in between and around, as if this were only a game. Two fought over her blowdart pipe, even though it was far too large for them to use. She couldn't see or hear Leyta. Syago fell to his knees, covered in their needles as he futilely punched at the ones dangling Alexandre in front of him. Qosku concentrated in anguish against both the poison and his beast form. Herself too weak, Lil'iek put her hand on the skull piece she'd taken from the witch's body earlier and held it up. Focusing on that, she reached out with her mind and found the great spiny cat. It took all her will to muster the strength and ignore the jabs from their javelins. If the cat came, it'd likely eat her too, but it was all she had.

The duendes were dancing atop her now while others rolled her toward the fire. Preparing her to be eaten, they tied her up. She could sense the creature nearing, through the skull piece. Its great cat eyes appeared in the dark, glowing malevolently from the firelight. She struggled to move this mysterious mind to eat the duendes. On seeing the face, the small creatures stopped, stared at it in a long continuous chant of rattling. They bowed down in evident worship. It licked its fangs, then pounced. It devoured them as they clicked and jittered, dancing, bowing. Lil'iek's connection to the cat's mind waxed and waned as did her strength. Knowing that they were also easy prey for this new predator, everything rested on that tenuous bond. A wild and puzzling mind beyond anything she'd encountered before, but strangely, it didn't resist her as the wild usually did. It almost welcomed her, toying with her in return, perhaps because she satiated its hunger with other prey.

It slowed, licking its paw. The remaining duendes resumed their adoration but there were still too many. She searched a way to get them out, and they didn't noice as she struggled to sit up. The poison was wearing off, but not quickly enough still. Clenching her jaw, she grabbed the skull piece again, and encouraged the hunting cat to lead the duendes away.

It growled then lowered its monstrous head to hers, sniffing her. The mouth opened, great fangs gleaming and breath hot. A large pink tongue licked Lil'iek full on in the face, rough. Its mind was imperious, strange, ravenous, and opaque. It vanished into the night, and the duendes followed.[25]

Lil'iek slumped in relief and noticed the others weakly picking the needles out of their skin. With the threat gone, they rested, Qosku keeping watch over them in his beast form. The moon waxed thin. They didn't sleep long, picking up early in a quick pace out. They found the edge of the boglands with Cantlgrym in sight at early dawn.

25 Though lacking in accounts of this rare beast, it has earned the names Pumar and Mishipesh.

CHAPTER ELEVEN

WHEN THE VOID COMES FOR THEE

Based on *Leyta's Journals*, cc bastica 377;
The Hunter's Parchments, cc bastica 390; *Annals of Syago,* cc bastica 380;
The Dark Fortress of Mephorash, cc bastica xxxx;

22nd–29th of Akril, 247

Leyta approached her castle physically weary but mentally and emotionally rejuvenated. Nearly being slaughtered by a Razhod, then making the rough trek through the marshes with a woman who'd gone from enemy to ally, and reuniting with Syago and Qosku, had all pulled her out of the emotional drought she'd been in. That things were getting better gave her a glimmer of hope about getting her powers back, if nothing else.

She neared the camp bustle in the burning dawn, and to Leyta's horror, barbarian Fomorions lined the wall of her castle. She prayed and prayed that all those inside remained unharmed. The lack of any siege or defense activity unnerved her. Katti checked in on her as she searched out her scepter, buried in her things she'd left behind, the staff still broken from the fight. Gripping the scepter, she prayed and pushed out a spark of anger at a candle in her tent. The candle flickered to life. But no more. She pushed it to blaze and it flared but barely that. Some sentiments was better than no sentiments, a good sign, but not nearly enough given the circumstances. Seeing in the Vision some brown hate and yellow fear sentiments vibrating through the area allowed her to use those, stoking them with her own. This burned the candle brighter, but still too weak for fighting their present enemies. She hated being broken like this. Even on the mend, it was so feeble and fickle. She had no idea how to speed up her recovery process. She took heart in progress, but it seemed a rotten way to live and lead, just waiting for the power to come to her rather than it being something she could attain with conscious effort.

Hours later after being fully informed of the situation, she felt glad that the Royal Chaos hadn't followed through on their threat to march at night. And also that their dydatris piece was reported safe in hiding.

Leyta and the newcomers took some much needed rest but it was short lived as the demands of determining the next step fell hard. In Leyta's tent, Balgor concluded the discussion. "So the Chaos are either stalling or divided, we're not sure. Either way is to our benefit unless the delay is only until night again."

"I don't like us waiting on them," Virgow grumbled. "If nothing else, we need our castle back and they can wait out here."

"But for that we'd probably have to give up the dydatris piece," Andala said. "We can't do that."

"My question is why haven't the Razhod attacked," Constantin asked. "They speak with the spirits around them, they have spies and power. That delay worries me more."

"I'm certain that the Chaos realized marching means leaving the castle," Balgor ruminated. "They don't want to do that."

"Let's shift the negotiation there, then." Leyta's first comment drew startled eyes to her. She'd been uncharacteristically quiet during the councils since Tiakanawu. But after the past few days, it felt good to have even the smallest hint of her powers back. The madness kept at bay. And she could be with Syago now. "We got our prisoners back for Jester. That also bought us some goodwill and trust. Let's offer a cohabitation of the castle, else we just move down to Oviedom and leave them alone up here with the Razhod."

They agreed and messages were drafted. The Royal Chaos's delayed response was more baffling nonsense. They debated going over them to discuss with the Fomorions again, but saw no way to pull it off. The barbarian giants were more reserved than before.

This carried on again and again, well into the next day. The camps became restless, fended off monster attacks, staved off assassination attempts and the prying eyes of the grimshades, watched the skies for pollen and spore storms. But the only thing they witnessed was another black cloud descending on Voium in the distance, just as had happened before when the summoners' powers were blinded in Bokhor. The sight held everyone's attention. But the black fog didn't stay long, hanging ominously until sunset then vanishing. It made sense that they wouldn't stay there long, the Seeping was known to affect even the witchlords who made it, even their devils and lifeless, though much less so. They speculated about why or what had been accomplished in this second fog assault, but the Razhod remained as opaque as ever. Leyta lamented at the increasing likelihood that their camp would decide to leave for Oviedom.

Wouldn't matter anyway. Even they will eventually succumb to the death-spiral of dyne and what its doing to the world. She sighed, having her powers return would be a blessing but also a curse as she'd be forced to confront the other, more long-term problem of the effects it was having on everything else. Making gigantic, twisted feldinals everywhere. The paradox was that there was no way around it, they had to fight feldinals which only made them worse. They could defeat the Razhod and destroy themselves.

It was the following morning that signs of the enemy attack appeared. In the distant north, stirred smoke and dust from a daemog herd could be seen. A single black and red mantle was sighted, riding the bulls and controlling the herd with a soulwhip. It was here, another Razhod attack. The Fomorion leaders yelled first at King and other barbarians, then at Balgor. Balgor tried to calm the cycloptic chieftain but the chieftain only drew his axe, the rest of the barbarian giants following, pointing at the allies. In response the allies drew theirs. The Chaos leaders on the wall yelled to them as well. Leyta blinked. *What?! Are the Fomorions attacking us?*

To the allies' confusion, battle exploded between them and the giants. Not knowing what was happening, but needing no explanation for the moment, Leyta ran through the ally camp in search of her dynast group. Before she could turn to the combat, shouts alerted her of the threat from the north.

The herd of daemogs broke out of their roiling and fuming cyclone to stampede on the fighting armies. At the center, a witchlord she recognized as Kask lashed Penaga the war whip back and forth to drive them. Three others rode behind and a fifth walked among the herd with Vilekor raised, guiding the rest. Davagis, her old dynast mentor. Five witchlords meant that, of the three known to be slain, two had been replaced.

She called for their army to reform at the northern front but it was too late, the herd came in too fast. The outer field barrier broke as Davagis blew it open with a rock upsurge. The daemogs plowed in, spitting fire and smoke. Syago was there in front of her, and Qosku too, as the herd separated her from the armies. Hellfaces entered the field on flaming bulls' backs, and the Fomorion giants quickly surrounded them, completely abandoning their fight with the allies to fight the Razhod on a southern flank, like trappers circling their prey. *Had the fight been a trick then? They'd not fought us very hard.*

Though surrounded, the Razhod still did not flee. Instead of retreating out the barrier opening they'd created, Kask and the other three jumped off their daemogs to fight the forces directly. The daemog herd swarmed in a confused stampede, until Kask lashed them with Penaga. The herd roiled into the allies, moving dangerously close to Leyta. Grasping at what little rage she felt, she threw darkfire, the field already full of fear and rage for her to build on.

Elsewhere amidst the chaos, Leyta saw the horrid visage of Queen torching the Razhod as King iced the herd with darkfire. She joined her darkfire to his, hoping this would not only obscure her weakness but use it better. Jester sang them all on, a dark surcharge that even Leyta felt. She hated it, but couldn't deny the boost to her sentiments. Having Fomorion ferocity on their side also both encouraged and scared her. The giants warred more viciously than they had at Tiakanawu, roaring and bleating their wrath. Several Roah'riik and Fomorion helltamers used their skulls to steal control of daemogs. They took but few, the rest was mass slaughter.

She saw in Vision terror, anger, and hate in abundance. Then she saw Davagis with hate directing flames into a growing hellish swell with Vilekor. *Here goes,* she thought, taking a deep breath. She pushed her anger at him into the flames to catch his cloak, but he dismissed them with more hate, waving the firestorm outward. His helleyes turned to her. Those red and black eyes alone made him almost unrecognizable, hardly the same person. Her heart hammered her chest. His hate pushed her anger out of the fires, keeping control.

She choked on the surrounding smoke but kept eyes on him as he walked toward her, moving the firestorm around him. As he stopped a pace in front of her, the cold arrogance, the memory of his betrayal, awakened more power within her. It came back! He snapped Vilekor down, and the ground at her feet exploded as she dove to the side. Pain shot up her legs, but she didn't slow in her counter with fury, bringing darkfire from King's steady blast around him. He countered it easily with fire, heat beating cold, and Qosku used the distraction to attack Davagis from behind. He easily blocked that as well, knocking Qosku away.

More anger shot through her, and Leyta blasted rocks at her former mentor, a spray at first then single shots like crossbow bolts from the ground, pelting one after another. Her speed pushed the traitor backward as Qosku rolled to his feet.

Feeling a thrill at a steady increase in sentiments, Leyta angered the air to lightning, but a wave of Davagis's staff redirected her attack back to her, somehow harder than she'd ever seen before. Sparks surged through her body, jolting her as she fell to her knees.

How does he have so much power?

Before the discharge even finished, she threw more darkfire at him from King but Davagis only took control of that too. She ducked down as the darkfire hurtled toward here. Near panic, she drew burning earth up to shield her, then pushed it at him. He leaped over it with the soulstaff.

Even with power I can't win this. Shit.

She backed away between soldiers holding a schiltron wall of pikes. Calls of alarm drew her attention to three Razhod who stood together in the center of the herd, led by Kask. Their hands were raised for the summoning rite, and they were surrounded by praying disciples who'd come in at some point with the lifeless. Their bells tingled. Attacks flew in at the ritual—arrow, bolt, javelin, and dynal—but the attacks were sparse and distant. The complete pandemonium of the herd gave them cover while Davagis shielded them with wind. Syago fought the fifth Razhod, the Unakan with the soulaxe Zurrogiath, whom she saw take three arrows before he chanted something, raised a ritual knife, and cut his own throat, adding his blood to the power brought to bear. Despite her struggle, the allies'd had the upperhand till now.

With his sacrifice, a greater spirit came, an old emaion from lost time who she recognized from the old war texts. Ylm the Void materialized, an ethereal violet cloak held up by endless darkness on the inside, a bottomless abyss that all, even the witchlords, averted their eyes from. A great hush fell over the battlefield. An icy wind followed that sucked the air out of one's lungs. Leyta, however, had dealt with a void inside herself for the past month and fought back. The cowl turned to her and cold winds picked up, sweeping the field of cowering foes. The Razhod resumed their slaughter and Leyta screamed at the dark empty cloak, "I DEFY YOU! LEAVE US!"

The chilling wind made her shiver, and she saw inside the cowl, as if behind parting clouds, a night sky so full of stars and worlds, all dead and empty, that it was blinding to look at. The cold starry picture wasn't fixed, but spinning, fast and endlessly. Endlessly. Endlessly.

Something slammed her to the ground, snapping her out of her frozen stupor. She gasped air into her lungs. A soldier had toppled into her. Fighting had resumed with a more chaotic frenzy; the bulls went mad and the soldiers fought with clear panic. And Leyta saw black tendrils withdraw from the witchlords and back into Ylm's void leaving them wreathed in darkfires, the black flames already freezing everything near.

Another gust of icy wind whipped through.

The darkflames didn't harm the witchlords, but instead froze the ground around them. Fire and lightning flew at the Razhod, to no avail. Their darkflames persisted. Freezing everything around them, they went from defensive to offensive. Ylm loomed over the battle, its void-gusts feeding their darkfires.

Davagis, now wreathed in darkflame and wielding the soulscythe Mordios, sliced down the unruly daemog that trampled between him and Leyta. Its wound froze where the cut was. Qosku ran at Davagis as he came for her, but the darkflames caught and froze on his gauntlets and greaves. A swing from Mordios drove Qosku away. She blasted the ground at his feet, just as an ohancanu charged him. Darkfires burned all around them, the plain now an icy tundra as the flames froze all they touched. The raging darkinferno obscured her sight, and she could no longer see Davagis in front of her, only the darkness and the glitter of its freezing air.

Leyta backpedaled, her defiance gone. She threw her hate for him into the wind and the darkflames blew back, momentarily revealing his hate-filled face. She tried to burn away the moisture that fed his darkfire, but with Ylm still hovering in the background, his power remained dominant. All around these darkinfernos hacked and slashed and froze with fury.

She saw Qosku then, at the same moment as Davagis. The small Unakan raised a crossbow, and Leyta cried out as Davagis rushed him with a fury of swings from Mordios, cutting down two other soldiers in the process. Worry filled her, and she launched more rocks at the traitor until he turned his fury on her. All she saw was a barrage of slashes, glinting metal, coming fast toward her, and she could do nothing but scramble quickly away, ducking behind a boulder. Her sentiments stopped and she fled, shouting, "Help!"

She didn't have to wait long. Leyta breathed in relief as Syago appeared to the side, but deflecting the scythe only splashed darkflames all over him. She extinguished them with fear while a pair of wookalars attacked him then got beheaded.

Finally the great spirit faded, and the darkfires began to subside. Davagis, now just a man in a tattered cloak, defended against Syago while avoiding Qosku, as Balgor approached with a greatclub. As they clamored against each other with blinding finesse, Leyta turned the ground at his feet to mud, halting his retreat. Balgor's darkfire flask burst on Davagis's back, freezing most of him before Balgor shattered his skull with a greatclub. The body crumbled, and Balgor looked at Leyta grimly, nodding before returning to the rest of the fight. She breathed in relief. Her former mentor, the traitor, was dead. That was one less Razhod they had to worry about.

Tek'ouk'iek and the Roah'riik relented trying to trap and kill the shadowmen, grimshade murderers of Fal'iek, with dyne and arrow. These three shadowmen had only attacked the wagons and carts from underneath to avoid the sun, then slid off empty handed. Apparently trying and failing to steal the hidden relic piece. He wasn't part of that secret plan, but he felt certain the Asturians wouldn't leave it alone in a wagon.[26] With them gone, he worked to capture the herd of daemogs but they were in too much of a frenzy, being butchered by Knight's huge sword. The hellhunters became separated so he focused on pulling some of the daemogs out to fight then make a quick escape. But the Razhod hold on them was too strong. He cursed.

He saw Lil'iek darting between soldiers who were corralling the daemog herd and holding off the Razhod attacks. Every time he faced the Razhod, it felt like it'd be the last, but at least he'd had some final moments with Lil'iek. And they'd both survived tighter fights than this, which seemed almost their advantage.

---

26 See *Sol Sistere de Selbst* by Himetuks Himi'n, or would they?

He nearly jumped on seeing a bull coming close, moving slow and quiet enough he hadn't noticed it. He used his skull to join its mind, knowing its isolated state and proximity would make it an easy catch. But when he grasped the daemog skull, he couldn't sense this one. Confused, he backed away and tried again. He found nothing.

Then it reached him. With a lurch, its horn pierced his gut. His eyes widened in shock. Then he saw the flowers protruding out of its rear. That explained why he couldn't connect to it. Its head pushed him, and he fell off the horn and onto his back. The wound wasn't deep, but the flower corpse's mouth and nose dripped saliva, snot, and blood. He held a hope its pollen hadn't infected him with the wound; there was only a small blossom in the nose and mouth that he'd not noticed, but it was too small a chance. He'd be dead within an hour.

The bull tried to charge him again, but Guaran'upik cut him down. Tek'ouk'iek rose to his feet, hiding his wound. "I'm going to see Lil'iek." He moved past as Guaran'upik cut it up.

But seeing Lil'iek in the middle of the fray, as she always was, made approaching her difficult. If he was dying soon, he needed to use his final moment well. Then he saw Virgow off to the side, barking orders and shooting his crossbow. With a snarl, Tek'ouk'iek turned and hobbled toward him.

By the time he was paces away, he could feel roots rapidly forming in his body, clutching his muscles, filling intestines, clogging veins. His mind swam and heart pounded. It clawed at his insides, and he struggled for breath. But he was almost there. By now the Razhod's spell had ended, the Hellfaces were surrounded with too many giants in the way to fire at. But Tek'ouk'iek had one task now that couldn't account for them, and he came to it.

Virgow turned to him with a wary eye, and the two men stared down each other for a moment. The Roah'riik dynast said loud enough for the onlooking soldiers and elementists to hear, "I know it was you. You gave the orders to leave us surrounded at Tiakanawu. You could've pulled us out, but you said to leave us and that's why we're only five now." Tek'ouk'iek grit his teeth against the waves of pain in his torso and head, hoping none watching could tell his agony. With a gentle nod, Tek'ouk'iek put out his hand. "But I can forgive you."

Virgow's eye flickered to his offered hand, then back to his face.

Tek'ouk'iek looked back with a steady gaze, but inside he was brimming with impatience. *Come on, take my hand. Forgiveness comes with a price. You want a clean conscience, you need to put yourself in my hands. That is justice. And I'll only forgive you if you die with me, my reciprocity.* And he was running out of time too, for he knew any second his muscles would visibly ripple and bulbs would protrude out of his wound, then other orifices, and the game would be up.

Finally, Virgow reached out with the hand not holding his crossbow and clasped Tek'ouk'iek's. The Roah'riik yanked him in just as a bulb burst out of his wound. He pushed rage then hate into the grass around them, lighting them both on fire. Virgow tried to pull away, eventually twisted out, but the blaze had already caught him as he fell. Searing pain crippling him from the inside out, Tek'ouk'iek dropped to his knees. Flames ate the flowers that burst out of his nose and mouth, but he focused on what was before him. Seeing the man frantically trying put out the raging flames that took him made it a worthy death.

I forgive you.

Following Davagis's death, Lil'iek saw that the Hellfaces were leaving, Kask having cut a path out for them and the remaining herd of daemogs. She shouldn't be glad to lose an advantageous position over them, but she was exhausted and numb with continuous fear. Her body trembled. As the rest of the allied armies mobilized to pursue them, she turned to regroup with the Roah'riik and ask Tek'ouk'iek what he wanted to do. She expected him to say time to go home, and now more than ever she felt inclined to agree.

But he wasn't with the other three. Guaran'upik had said he'd walked west. She went west and looked about; soldiers avoided her gaze but this was nothing new. She saw the burnt corpse and thought nothing of that either. Not until, as she walked past, she saw a shorter leg and next to it a crutch. Her mind reeled with denial, but the crutch-scepter was unmistakeable. She crumbled as the truth hit her, kneeling and weeping at what was left of Tek'ouk'iek. His ashen body was so completely burnt through that it broke up and blew away in the wind. The grass around him was scorched. She looked to the first burned spot she'd passed, but no remains lay in it.

She couldn't comprehend any of this, couldn't believe it wasn't a dream, until Guaran'upik, Klom'oth, and Machi'guenk stood speechless beside her, affirming it with their expressions. It became real. This was war after all.

She didn't even have bones left to cling to.

A Razhod had found him, or a stray daemog, or Queen had gone ballistic, or perhaps another Asturion betrayal. The Razhod or Queen made the most sense, though they'd been at the center the entire time. But even if they hadn't, just as with Fal'iek's death at Tolgrym, the two enemy groups had created the situation where this had happened.

She had many to avenge, too many, and she knew she ought to return to her children, but her rage was simply too great. Revenge filled her entire being. She would start with the Razhod then work her way down. She had no doubt that the Asturions were complicit in some way.

With the last of the armies marching east after the Razhod, and the wounded staying behind, going to the castle. Trembling with both sorrow and anger, she rubbed his ashes on her face and whispered promises and love to him. She felt his love return to her, and she breathed, then stood up, wind blowing her hair with his ashes.

It was brief comfort in this dark, shaky, and uncertain world. Yet she was still Lil'iek, Huntress of the Wild, Wife of Dead Husbands, Mother of Three Children, Wildflower of Thornwood, Survivor of Colonizing Armies, and she would pursue her justice on through this one last fight. *Avenge my last, for after this I'll have nothing left.*

The three Roah'riik agreed, and they followed the march east.

CHAPTER TWELVE

IN BETWEEN DEATH

Based on *Annals of Syago*, cc bastica 380; *Leyta's Journals*, cc bastica 377;
The Hunter's Parchments, cc bastica 390;
The Nordvargr Testaments, cc bastica xxxx;

22ⁿᵈ–29ᵗʰ of Akril, 247

The witchlords had gained ground in their retreat. It had taken a moment for the allies to collect themselves, and their courage, enough to go after them. Forcing the Razhod to retreat was a rare achievement, and the hard-earned advantage had to be pressed while it was there. Syago sat in the front of one of the closed wagons as they kept pace behind the enemy, watching the cloud of smoke and dust ahead. *Kask is still alive, I saw, but at least Davagis was finally slain.* They expected the enemy to tire sooner, yet the Razhod were known for their extreme discipline. It seemed evident that they were going somewhere, perhaps to a better position or even to set up a trap, for they'd never just fled like this in the old war. Or so he understood, from the histories.

We must strangle them, thought his devil arm.

We must save the world of them, thought Alexandre.

We must cleanse the world of them, thought Syago. No, that was Alexandre. The thought to save was his... wasn't it? Or was he just beginning to think like them? Bondua shit.

It was rare for their voices to make words so clearly, maybe the bond grew their ability. Or made him like them, he wondered how Odiru had dealt with it from Alexandre. The conversation with his father about fighting them stewed in his heart and mind. He felt resolved about his father, now, but not about his mother, Camila. Where was she? Why hadn't she come to the call of her son? He'd shunned her memory, but his father had said he couldn't find her either, so where was she?

Who was she?

He rubbed his eyes, weary but glad to not be sleeping in nightmares after several hours of this pursuit. He decided to talk to Leyta and turned to go into the main box, leaving Balgor to the driving. She rested against Katti, the two trying and failing to sleep against each other. He sat next to her and whispered, "How are you feeling?"

"Fine. Better than usual in fact. I think that bog adventure woke me out of my sickness a little. But, you know, we're still going to die." She leaned against him.

He smiled. "Well, at least your perspective's still in tact."

"Wouldn't mind losing it though."

"'fraid I'm losing mine. It's getting hard to distinguish my thoughts from the rest. But I should be glad I don't have the Seeping. How are you holding up under that?"

"Terrible. Trying to figure out which foods do better with my ulcers but I don't have many options here. Actually, I've been worried about something else." He nodded for her to continue, and she leaned forward to whisper in his ear. "We need to check on our relic piece. I'm worried the Razhod took it from the hiding spot, and you're the best one to do it because Alexandre will heal or protect you."

He paused, thinking it over. Checking on it could also lead their enemies to it, if they're watching. Hiding it in Voium instead of taking it with them so far had worked. But given everything that had happened, there was a chance it didn't. "Do you want me to bring it back?"

"Only if your mission is discovered. Take something else so it looks like you went for that."

He stood and went to the door. "Syago," she said, and he returned to her. "You don't have to. I know this is a lot to ask, going back into Voium could make you sick like the rest of us, even with Alexandre. Or you could be attacked. And you won't have a lot of time either."

He was already shaking his head, tapping his devil arm. She nodded and leaned forward, pressing her lips to his. "Be careful then. Please."

With one last kiss, he stood and left. Hiding the relic piece in Voium had been a brilliant idea the few in the know had immediately latched onto. Carrying it with them, either on anyone's person, or hidden in a wagon, would make it vulnerable.

If the Razhod had found the relic, that would change the upcoming battle dramatically, giving them an impossible advantage. If not, the allies still had leverage. Of course he still had to be careful about Knave following him in and capturing the allies' piece for the Royal Chaos.

Having marched east for most of the day with the army, Voium was back in sight. The first big challenge would be leaving the marching armies and getting to the city without being seen.

Once near enough, Syago walked from where he was at the front of the march to a boulder they passed, hiding behind it. In the near distance, Voium's dark brown and gray walls sat, empty of any activity. He wove his way through the field of boulders, grass, and bushes, staying low. He saw no signs of pursuit, and soon arrived at Westgate. The lock to the individual door was not difficult for him to reach in and undo. The empty battlements above made him uneasy, but worse was that he couldn't feel or sense the Seeping affecting him. It likely wasn't as strong at present, and he had some protection, but he understood it was still there tolling him for his time.

He paused at the doorway that passed into the murder hole, the shadowy in between area inside the gates where any number of traps could be employed to destroy a man or monster. But with nobody there, it was harmless. He still needed to get through the second portcullis without damaging it or making noise.

Looking through those iron bars at the empty town made his spine tingle. His devil arm itched, and he wondered if that was it fighting off the blight. He realized this was his key. With his devil claw grabbing the lowest bar, he was able to crouch and force it up enough for him to roll under, then ease it back down in a dull thud. Afterward, his devil arm throbbed, a pulse that filled his body. The arm rejoiced in offering key aid to his progress. He still felt the constant hunger and mood swings, though offset by its thrill for battle. He wished again that it would stop. Alexandre thought so too, but had come to accept it, mostly. It'd suggested he cut through the wall instead. He brushed their thoughts aside, needing focus.

The houses sat vacant, doors and windows wide open. A light fog laced the cobblestone streets. The city was a skeleton. No, it was a carcass. Food sat rotting in refuse piles or on tables. He walked the streets at a quick pace, feeling the decay of a once great civilization and intellectual center crumbling. Some way in, he saw the first living thing—a city rat. He'd expected it to be mutated by the Seeping, as feldinals appeared to be. Yet the rats were feeble, blotchy, sickly representations of what everyone else would have become had they stayed. So too the gurows he saw, dead and alive as they pecked at the hung corpses in the first square. The prisoners had all been released or hung before evacuation. But at least there was fewer blackbirds than normal.

He went to Leyta's home. Of course the relic wasn't there, but the key was. He stood before the manor, a tallish squat and brown thing, elegant by general standards but still squeezed into the crowded dead city. Shield on his left arm and Alexandre in his right hand, he tried the doorknob, then shoved it in, gently. The darkness of the rooms lightened by Alexandre's ever-glowing radiance were still a haunting image.

He ascended the stairs to the red room, the one Leyta had hated but ended up staying in. He'd hated it too. When he reached that upper landing, all doors closed, the creaking he heard down the hall halted his progress. The red room was the other way, but what was the movement from? He wondered if he should check on it or leave it. It could be one of the enemies following him, or another dying creature, or one of the Voium citizens said to have stayed behind.

Or maybe it'd been in his mind. He turned to the red room and heard shuffling inside. Shield hand on the doorknob, he entered. Nobody was there, only the forbidding red paint of the walls and the furniture. He went to the bed, reached through the sheets into the hay mattress for the old key. As his armored fist grasped it, a creak at the door made him jump. There stood an old woman. No, not an old woman. He recognized her as one of the serving maids who'd been young and happily married to a cobbler. Now? Her pale, blotchy, gaunt visage indicated the toll of the Seeping on her.

"You can't take it!" she snarled, spittle and blood dribbling from her mouth.

"Emilia, it's me, Syago." He lowered his sword, but she ran at him. He sidestepped, and she fell into a fit of bloody coughing. "Emilia, why in hell did you stay?"

"To ssstop—" She was racked again by more coughing.

"I'm sorry for your pain." He held Alexandre to her, to heal, but it instead burned her skin, one rejecting the other. Her ragged breathing turned to a screech. He fled the room, not wanting to raise more alarms over someone he couldn't save.

Checking around him for anything watching, he ran to the chapel. Not Saint Columbar's Cathedral in the central square, which had struck them as too obvious, but the smaller Saint Casilda's Chapel. The hope being that a chapel would be too adverse to a demon to search extensively. And all chapels held secret cabinets, the only way to protect the Church's many treasures from thieves.

The dark building towered, and he made his sign of the sun-wheel cross as he walked through the arched doorway. Yet he still felt apprehension entering Deova's house. She'd not helped much in resolving his questions or struggles, and his devil arm still prickled irritably at entry. Still, he remained a faithful if lackluster servant in spite of all his doubt.

No candles burned, only faded sunlight streaming through stained glass windows gave light to the gloom. The echoes of his footsteps unnerved him, but he couldn't walk stealthy in his boots and hurry at the same time.

As he approached the altar, Father Tomas de Galig walked in from a side chamber. He looked even worse than Emilia had. The man raised a sun cross and smoking censor and yelled in a raspy voice, "Dare you to enter the kingdom of Deova Bondua?!"

"What is with all of you?" Syago asked, breathless. "It's me, Syago de Odiru of Tolgrym. I mean we've barely met, but do I look like an enemy of the Church?"

The man advanced, as if the power of his faith and gnosis would protect him. "You do not. But the enemy is full of deceit. My mission to defend stands true against any and all intruders. Get thee hence in the name of the Lady Bondua."

Syago's left arm twitched and clenched. Sheathing his sword, he moved around the altar, bringing him closer to the relic's hiding place. With the key, he clicked open the shrine.

But the double compartment was empty.

"You will not have it, for the divine wisdom of Deova has preceded you."

"What? Did you move it?"

The friar moved around the altar and broke into a charge, eyes wide and feral. "Yaaaah!" The chained censor swung at Syago, which he ducked under, bringing his shield up to block the silver cross. He bumped the man back and circled around.

"Please, just tell me. Did anyone else take it? A grimshade maybe? Or another friar?"

His throaty shouts echoed in the chapel hall. "The relic of power is back in the hands of the Almighty, where it belongs. Neither fiend nor mortal shall have charge of it save by the authority of Deova Bondua. Rrrrraaaaah!"

Dyne boosted the friar's movements this time, a dynfist, but it was still too slow and weak. Syago avoided drawing his sword and regretted entering with it drawn in the first place. *Maybe that's what set the man off.*

"Where is the relic? I just need to know it's safe—"

The man dashed, the smoking censor swung, the cross swiped, and Syago maneuvered away, wondering if he could just take the man's word for it. Given his evident insanity, Syago didn't think he could risk that chance.

Then the man's charge turned into a tackle against the altar, knocking over a candlestand. While coughing blood everywhere, he clawed at Syago, whose left arm snapped up with a cracking punch. The devil claw drove into the man's skull, bursting it open. Gore splattered and the body fell. Left arm throbbing again with joy, Syago shoved the corpse off him. Horrified, he wiped his face clean, spitting the blood out of his mouth. The pulsing in his arm surged gratitude into his head while Alexandre raged at him, even though he hadn't meant to do it. With the two pulling at his mind, he realized he couldn't form a sentence and they were crowding him out. He looked despondently at the blighted corpse, beginning to feel ill as well. *There goes my chance of finding it; gained nothing but lost time and health to this place.*

And I don't even feel bad about killing him. What's happening to me?

He turned to leave, thinking maybe it was just as well if none knew its whereabouts, and his eyes fell on the blood-sprinkled cloth covering the altar. If he were a religious fanatic, there was one place he'd hide a relic of power.

He pulled the cloth off and felt around the altar for a way to open it. The devil arm, sharing his irritation, finally ripped the top off. "Stop it!" he snapped at his arm. He gave a sincere apology to Alexandre's indignation, then looked in. The usual clutter of sacred objects sat there, and he riffled through them till he grasped the relic. He supposed it couldn't stay there, but he would need to find a new hiding spot. Any new searches would clue somebody in to this place.

He chanced a prayer for guidance when his heavenward eyes met the familiar glint of a grimshade's. Those eyes, like dying candles, fixed him in place, holding him, filling him with cold loss and isolation. The creature of living shadow descended from the archway above on long limbs, carefully and effortlessly avoiding the streams of light from the windows. The unwavering stare continued as the grimshade drew up to him, gazing down into his numb soul. The candle eyes filled him with painful death, finality, eternal end.

His mind managed a prayer just before the grimshade's face touched his, and he barely registered the jerk of his right arm. Alexandre's blinding light flared as it sliced through a shadow-arm. In less than a second, Syago emerged into self-awareness and leaped at the grimshade with a thrust that pinned it against a stone pillar. It squirmed spasmodically as the shining blade-tip sank into the stone pillar. Syago prepared to slice up, but his devil arm seemed to remember its true nature, and its previous allies, and reached over and grabbed his Alexandre arm.

He stood in mental battle as the grimshade writhed in agony against the holy sword's shining blade. Then another grimshade appeared, the lurker's stealth nearly avoiding Syago's notice in his periphery. He looked urgently at his left hand. *You are MINE now, so deal with it! I'm yours, and you're mine. All three of us, together for a little longer at least. Now with me!*

The second grimshade approached with sharp claws, and Syago felt relief as the devil arm eased up then whipped around to grab it by the neck. The grimshade struggled briefly, then lashed out with its arms, scratching armor, but before they reached his throat or face, he brought Alexandre up, slicing through the first grimshade and into the head of the second. They bled inky smoke, darkness dripping from their dissipating corpses.

Syago panted, heart racing from the very near death. He spat onto them both, feeling Fal'iek avenged. And many others as well. He took up some of the Church cloths to wrap up what he could of the odd inky remains to bring to Lil'iek and Leyta. He brought the relic with him, too, but still didn't see it wise to return it to the army. He brought it into Saint Columbar's Cathedral, blessedly empty, and instead of hiding it in a holy place, went straight to the privy, where he hurled it down into a dark, wet, smelly plop. He exited out Eastgate and made his way back to the armies.

Lil'iek leaned forward on the cart. The enemy ahead had disappeared in dust. Now hour from night, they were in danger of losing them or being ambushed. "I think the caravan is slowing. We'd better take a mount to run ahead."

She noticed in the forested hills to the south, four mewil'ishyuuks watching the war party, one for each remaining Kimoc. They grabbed their skull pieces and called. Lil'iek strained under the effort, she wasn't as trained in it, usually more a Roah'riik skill. But she could do it well enough.

After ensuring a solid control over the dangerously proud beasts, the four mounted them and rode ahead of the caravan. Behind, the impassive barbarians watched them leave. Several dynasts commanded the winds to clear the dust ahead for better visibility. Lil'iek had always felt suspicious of the practice, how could one follow the wind's motions and scents if you altered it? They were supposed to listen to the winds, not yell back at them.

They caught up quicker than expected, the enemy having stopped between Voium and Mantlgrym. Instead of going straight, the Kimoc riders skirted around to an elevated ridge that allowed highground and better view. Long before arrival, the steady rumbling of ground and the low hum set them on edge. Lil'iek's heart raced at the familiar, deep hum that reverberated through her. They dismounted and dismissed the mewil'ishyuuks, ensuring they left far away for danger's sake, then focused on what happened below.

The great deep hum emanated from the timeless emaion, Barduum the Golem. The gigantic spirit's burning face holes flared, but the Golem's clay form didn't move. Among the mounds lay a massacre of daemog, the stony hills painted red with their blood. The massive size of Barduum signified incredible power being brought to bear for what lay in the center of the butchery. Dark dust collected into dark bricks, and dark bricks collected into an ascending dark edifice rising over the swirling dirt. A tall black tower reaching several spans high and yet unfinished as it materialized upward under the Golem's direction.

Lil'iek couldn't see any Razhod or disciples but didn't have to, the summon meant they were here somewhere. She resisted the urge to race down and kill them in their summoning ritual, knowing it would be foolish. The tower was nearly finished when the rest of the allies and barbarians arrived. Flying buttresses with jutting spikes and a panoramic platform crowned it, a fortified gatehouse at the base. Barduum disappeared as Leyta, Balgor, and Andala walked up beside Lil'iek. Once the Golem disappeared, the Razhod, visible on the top of the tower now, raised their bells for another summon. They were too high up for any of the allies to reach now.

A cold chill swept through her and those nearby. Once again Bophormothul the Necromancer appeared. The horned goat head surveyed the landscape with strange eyes and nodded. Opening the large tome in arm, Bophormothul raised his other clawed hand to the sky, now turning dark as the low sun went black in an early eclipse, a tenebrous ring of fire in the sky. Nothing happened for a moment, then Lil'iek noticed a tremor in the ground. Faint but stronger around the tower. The mounds, they trembled, then moved. Stones fell, hills cracked, and dirt rolled as mummified lifeless crawled out of them, out of what had long ago been burial mounds. Lil'iek looked to Balgor, the most history wise of all in attendance, and he looked baffled.

All this time, these mounds had been Kimoc burial grounds lost to the Asturion settlements. Even Lil'iek was amazed by the expanse of it. The oral stories had mentioned graves out here but not of this magnitude.

The ground before them crawled with carcasses, brown and rotten. Lil'iek noticed the daemog bodies also rose, not yet rotted; they threatened to trample the others but the sheer number of the human corpses made it irrelevant. The barbarian giants remained impassive, almost calculating in their observance. It became obvious to Lil'iek that the Necromancer wouldn't be stopping soon, that the swarm would keep developing from the spans of mounds as the purpose of the tower was to allow them to maintain the summoning. Leyta beside her agreed, they couldn't wait for morning to come and give them an advantage. They had to move in while the swarm was smaller, and stop the call before it continued longer.

The barbarian calls rang out, and with consensus from the other generals, she shouted her undulating warcry before joining the charge down the hill toward the swarming mounds.

CHAPTER THIRTEEN

BATTLE OF THE GRAVESPIRE

Based on *Writings of Qosku*, cc bastica 388;
The Hunter's Parchments, cc bastica 400; *Annals of Syago*, cc bastica 380;
Leyta's Journals, cc bastica 382; *The Dark Fortress of Mephorash*, cc bastica xxxx;

29th–30th of Akril, 247

As if a dam suddenly burst, the armies descended down to the mounds crawling with bodies. Qosku had jumped to his feet when he saw it. Having departed the march and followed from a distance as the outcast that he was, he'd thought to receive a message from Syago about a battle plan. Now with the battle unexpectedly beginning, Qosku stood in surprise, unsure of what to do. No plan, no preparations, nothing coordinated. Just chaos as the warstorm broke in the lower hills, brutal forces of living violence crashing into the dense mass of stale flesh around the tower. He, alone, couldn't take down the tower or stop the summoning, but perhaps he could aid their drive. As he picked out a plan of attack, he felt the change starting.

Panic. He looked at the surprise eclipse, looming large and full over the mountains before an ascent that promised a long presence.[27] He supposed the eclipse had caused his change to start early, why it was taking him now instead of when full and shining he had no idea. He'd gotten so used to his control over it other nights that he hadn't prepared himself during the fighting and chasing. It took him fast. "No, no no NO!"

His quivering and frightened sobbing didn't help his confidence any. Refocusing, he fought the transformation, but it consumed him regardless. Instead he managed to slip off his gauntlets and greaves in time to stuff

---

27 I don't think it was an early eclipse, they were too occupied to notice the timing. See *Lustmord'a'stigmata de Uada*

them into a sack tied to his belt, a new design purposed to keep them with him during the transformation. The compulsion of this transformation felt as complete as under a full moon, leaving him contagious. His last self-conscious act as Qosku was a prayer for memory. The ozor beast had a mind of its own, a mind of instinct and hunger, that drove his body down the hill toward the fight. So many challengers, so much territory to be won, so many things to… bite. The large shadow by the tower scared him, raised his hackles, so he veered away from it. His limbs grew, hair burst forth, and a roar exploded out of his chest that echoed across the land.

He slammed into the moving corpses that turned to him. Too slow, they merely accepted the pummeling. He bowled into them, slashing and biting, splaying the bodies around. They crawled over him, and he bit the head off of one, then used its body to beat away the others, whipping rank corpses about like weapons. He snarled as more crawled onto him. He looked over at the bigger fighters, giants and their little companions, true warriors to challenge and better for biting, and far from that big shadow. His mouth foamed, vision bloody.

He plowed his way toward them, mauling and trampling anything in reach. As he neared the giants, fearsome in their imposition, a wall of mummies blocked him. He tore into them, snarling savagely. One beasty corpse with horns rammed him in the side, not hard, but the horns prodded. He roared and ripped the head off before throwing the torso in front of him to clear a path. Clutching the head, he jumped over the squirming torso, went up the wall of human lifeless, and leaped into the forces of beastly giants.

Yet he didn't get to gnaw on them the way he'd hoped as two grabbed his arms. He squirmed mightily against their stronger grips. They tried to swing weapons at him, but he moved hard, avoiding the brunt of their cuts, almost biting one in the arm.

Finally two ozormen bigger than he, but less vicious, joined in to hold him while a cyclops readied a greataxe for his neck. Suddenly, ropes swung around him. More and more at various odd angles. The ropes came from the smaller dark warriors, quick but hardly worth biting into. Still, they were better than nothing, and he lunged at them, but they tightened their ropes, restraining him. A woman gave orders to the others. The giants grunted and walked away.

He snarled and fought, trying to break the ropes or slip them so he could reach for that leader. The brown woman, beautiful in her intensity, smiled at him while edging closer. She looked delicious, graceful and so calm in her fierceness. Her soothing voice irritated his mind. He didn't want to calm; he had bonds to break. So close, he could almost bite her arm.

Another figure, brighter in skin and dress, appeared beside her. Dark hair over pale skin, she smiled, and he knew that smile somehow. She walked closer, slowly, softly. She spoke words to him that he faintly recognized. "Qosku, my friend. Come back to me. We need you now. Please, calm and come back."

She ran a hand through the fur on his head, irritating and relaxing. His mouth dried, the foam caked his large lips. She wiped it free, running fingers over his mouth. One last hand through his fur, then she stood, said some things, and he was dragged by several up a hill to where a priestly woman stood. The second woman began yelling at others, waving a stick around. He felt confused, felt many things. A dead boy, that image hurt for some reason. Now, he couldn't stop thinking about it. Any energy he'd had subsided.

The bizarre eclipse raged, seething over the battlefield. It left faint dusklight and the Necromancer's silhouette looming alongside the tower's. Engaged in the non-stop frenzy of fighting, Lil'iek felt a sense of dread about being part of the vanguard deep in this fray, so deep they'd be close to the greater spirit and the tower, and whatever dangers they held. Worse, she and the allies could be cut off from escape. She could be abandoned again.

It struck her then that these ancient Kimoc graves were being desecrated. Again. Only worse now than what the palemen or even Royal Chaos had done, for here the Razhod turned their ancestors' corpses against their descendants. *I shouldn't be fighting the remains of our Fathers and Mothers, but I can't let the Razhod have them either.*[28]

Not far off, she saw King, standing atop a barbarian cyclops and freezing large swaths of bodies with a powerful stream of darkfire. Far back, the rest of the giants pressed with the Asturions. Queen set another lifeless group on fire. With their other Roah'riik beside her, Lil'iek pointed to the barbarian giants as they tore into the lifeless, Knight at their head. Lil'iek

28 *Gybiaaw Blackbraid: Mutilated Tyrant speculates on the Razhod's knowledge of the graves.*

took hold of the blackbirds in the sky, and the three Roah'riik joined her in bringing them down to weaken the lifeless.

Knight made a destructive scene, pushing forward harder than any, leaving the other giants behind. He swung his massive metal sword, sweeping clear a path before him until he achieved the tower base. He attacked the tower, the executioner sword beating chunks out of it while moving around in search of a door. The cultist disciples fired attacks down at them from small windows along the tower. Leaving the animalian minds, Lil'iek realized the Necromancer had vanished. *And what does that mean? Where are the Razhod?*

Though the Necromancer was gone, his swarm continued to seethe and clamor. The long eclipse, however, was ending. The sun dropping behind the mountains, abandoning them and leaving only a red moon and faint stars to suck up the sun's last vestiges. She looked up to see that the distant black forms of the Razhod had jumped off the top of the obelisk and descended gently down using their soulweapons, like twirling flakes of ash.

The roaring army hushed in anticipation of their landing, gradually the black specks became more visible. One man with the soulaxe neared the barbarian tribe, who waited him eagerly, but he suddenly shifted, shooting right into Knight. The Razhod landed with a dull metallic thud as the giant stumbled forward. The Hellface used the axe Zurrogiath to shear the head off, then slid down the back, slicing open the plate-hauberk, which rusted as he cut. He landed nimbly on the ground and sliced both legs at the knees. The tumbling armored corpse giant collapsed into the mess of lifeless. Not far off, another fell lightly but abruptly landed in an explosion that blew away several giants in wait.

The Razhod Kask turned his slow fall to a drop like a black dart onto a charging wookalar with the flambard Grievore. As he drained the giant's life, he yanked an arrow and bolt from himself so the wounds could heal. More giants closed in and he used the greatsword to fly in an arc away from the barbarians deeper into the safety of the field of crawling lifeless. Lil'iek yearned to go after him but saw no way for it.

She and the Roah'riik got pressed by the lifeless and moved closer to the giant ranks, but the giants tightened up, barring their entry and leaving them fully exposed. She shouted at them. Cool, inhuman eyes looked down on them, pitiless at their plight.

Aggravated but unable to do anything about it, Lil'iek's attention went to the black shapes darting through the starless sky. She had many enemies to hunt for the vengeance of her late husband, but these shadow creatures were chief among them. Following what Syago had told her about the chapel slaying of two, she believed there to be three remaining. She couldn't tell what the shadowmen were doing exactly, either observing or dropping objects on the allies. Perfect predators in the chaos. With them up high, she couldn't get back at them until she remembered the quervosks, so hidden by night. She went to Klom'oth, who worked the blackbirds while Guaran'upik and Machi'guenk shielded him from the skeletons. She clutched his arm, the hellknife Ravenger in her other hand, and whispered in his ear, "I'm going after the shadowmen above. Watch for me."

She drew up her skull to find the largest quervosk above, but found one being preyed on by an owl. *Even better, they're bigger and see in the dark.* She switched to an owl skull. Its savage appetite with so many blackbirds at hand didn't sit well in her mind, but her rage against the shadowmen was strong. The dark brown bird lifted up her light form and like hanging bait, drew the first shadowman to her.

Ravenger ready in her free hand, she saw it coming at the last second. She swung away from its arm and snapped the hellknife forward into its chest. The creature's pitch black body was barely visible in the night sky, but its star-twinkle eyes flared wide in surprise. The hellknife didn't drain its life into her, but it did make her sick in the same way drinking mud or tar might. Her body convulsed, but she retained the presence of mind to drive Ravenger harder, slashing up through its neck. The widened eyes flickered and went out as it leaked black smoke, eliciting a vicious joy within her. Then she realized she was beginning to fall, the owl having left her. But another shadowman latched onto her, for a human floating over a battlefield made an easy target. This time it caught her off guard, wrapping around her arms while two wings kept them aloft. Star eyes stared in, paralyzing her in the unwavering stare. It opened a tiny mouth that reached out for hers. She couldn't break out, and it was as though her rage cooled in a vast black ocean. Such despair and loss was so all consuming. But she snapped out of it when an arrow thunked into it from below, from her Roah'riik. This broke the daze long enough for her to tip the hellknife into its tendril. It writhed with her on and began to peel away, leaking smoke. She wrapped her legs tight around it, not letting it escape or drop her, but the slick slenderness of it didn't hold. She frantically dug the hellknife in, but it only cut through, slicing open its midsection. Then she was falling, the strange creature dying above her.

She fell toward the violent mayhem below, grasping her skull necklace.

Then her great owl swooped in and grabbed her, clutching her vest in its claws. She grabbed onto those legs in thankful desperation, full of surprise. Once she realized Klom'oth had sent it to rescue her, she let out her breath in great relief. It was taking her down but she pointed. "No! Over there. I thought I saw the last one over there!"

This was difficult of course, but the owl's eyes made up for her deficiency. Below them in the writhing frenzy was numerous fires, giving them dim light to spot the quick movements of this last shadowman. It was much too quick for the owl to catch, especially with her added weight. With much yelling and pointing, she convinced Klom'oth through the owl to take her over its path. The timing had to be perfect, but she had bravery to match the risk. Well she told herself she did, but her racing heart and fluttering stomach said otherwise.

The moment came, she counted off to three and dropped. It never saw her come down, but she still barely clipped it with Ravenger. The thing shuddered and reshaped as she slipped off only to be caught by the owl again, its dive swinging her around just above the clamoring lifeless. They lost track of it, if it died or not, but none more bothered them in the fight, and she felt content with what was due her, whispering a thank you to the owl and a prayer to Fal'iek and Tek'ouk'iek on the winds. And the winds seemed to respond with a sudden, even violent shift in speed.

Syago felt relief when the eclipse omen ended. He retreated inside the Asturion lines to recover from his wounds. The Asturion soldiers held up the rear of the Chaos vanguard, happy to let enemy on truce be the frontline. He waved away bandages proffered by Katti, better save it for someone that didn't have Alexandre to heal them. The healing was slow and painful but sufficient. Walking through the ranks to take greater stock of the situation, he glimpsed Qosku's beasty form tied up with Roah'riik guarding as they fired arrows.

Syago went to Qosku and on noticing clear recognition in that hairy face, Syago asked, "Qosku, do you know me? Will you fight with me?"

The beast moaned. Crossbowmen keeping a side-eye on him looked uneasy but were too occupied supporting the frontlines to argue.

Syago cut the ropes and Qosku stood, a massive beast of power. "Just don't go near the giants," Syago said as he drew Alexandre and shield before running to the inner swarm. "It's all we could do to get you from them the first time."

Qosku grunted, running with him, barreling ahead of him into the mess of lifeless. He charged between two mounds, bowling over the bodies while Syago cut them down behind. Alexandre glowed bright, and he kept his cuts light to conserve energy. With how many lifeless flooded the hilly plain, he expected a long and exhausting fight followed by a quick and violent one against the Razhod, possibly followed again by fighting with the giants at the end.

If they won against the Razhod in the first place.

They drew near the tower, circumventing the tempestuous barbarians to avoid conflict with Qosku. So caught up in their own work of destruction, they didn't notice the titanic struggle passing just ahead until darkfire froze up a large swath of bodies right in front of them. Iced over, the brittle lifeless tried to move but fell or got cut and beat down by the two warriors. King, riding an ohancanu's shoulder, threw a stream of darkfire at an Unakan Razhod who jumped and slashed with Zurrogiath. Not far off, Queen faced a similar battle, her twisted mask torching everything around her in a reckless effort to keep that Hellface at bay.

Syago and Qosku moved toward King, but carefully as darkfire flew everywhere, even freezing his own subjects in a mad binge to catch the agile Razhod. And agile hardly described it; he used the soulaxe to fly and dart around the icy shards of lifeless piles before cleaving in half the giant bone-axe used by the Fomorion who quickly took up the mace of a fallen ukuku. Syago pressed forward, beating back others with his shield, while working behind Qosku's massive arms. His devil arm snapped out of its own accord, clawing and punching. He felt tempted to just let the fight ahead play out but reminded himself of the goals of this fight: finish the Razhod and amaze the Fomorions.

They were nearly at King's side when the Razhod lashed the soulwhip around the giant's neck and yanked it to the ground. The ohancanu thrashed in agony as King toppled off, and Syago ran to aid King, but he'd already rolled to his feet. The Hellface switched back to Zurrogiath and cleaved through the cyclops to get to where King had fallen. But King was ready; the fake regent hit the Hellface with a raging black inferno. The Hellface vanished into the darktorch. Where the Razhod had stood now sat a human ice shard so complete Syago halted, mortified. Caught blind, the Razhod hadn't brought the soulblade up fast enough to block it. Zurrogiath vanished in a poof of smoke at the death of its holder.

The other giants walked up, surveyed it, then stuck weapons in it as sign of victory for vengeance. Turning away, they looked at Syago, beastly heads unreadable. They raised weapons in mild salute. Surprise and confusion filled him—he hadn't helped in slaying the cultist. Then he looked behind and saw that he and Qosku had destroyed a large portion of the north flank of lifeless in their rampage. He'd effectively defended the Fomorions, freeing them up to fight the Razhod. King watched the exchange hollowly from his mask, then turned to ascend a wookalar.

Their assault forward ended with a thunderous crash as an ohancanu bowled through more bodies to land a few paces off from Qosku. The cycloptic giant lay on his back trying to rise. Queen also rolled to a standing halt. An Unakan Razhod, the one with clawed gauntlets who'd been fighting Queen, jumped atop the giant and, with two mighty punches, crushed his rib cage. Syago moved toward them and realized the gauntlets were soulweapons, dense and black with silver rims and blood flinging from the bladed knuckles. Queen clapped fire at the Hellface, who leaped away.

She showed no concern, took no care for her allies or even subjects, as she set fire to the field. She torched everything trying to destroy the Hellface. Syago ran between the stream of intense fire, hacking down flaming lifeless, looking for the Hellface, but soon had to focus on evading the fires of the furious Queen. For a moment, the melted, hollow mask seemed to turn on Syago, and he considered toppling her. *Give me a reason.*

But the Razhod came through the fires, and she opened her torch on the solemn witchlord. But he was ready, standing atop a Fomorion's torso, he brought forth the soulgauntlets and the palms sucked up the flames. He moved forward, running at her. Because of the powerful torch, she didn't see him coming until he was a pace away, intensifying her torch too late as Syago ran to him.

The Razhod blew back much of the flames as he leaped, landing a kick on her chest and slamming her down. His arms blurred as he tore her apart. Syago was nearly there, but a sudden smack from Qosku's massive fist interrupted this intervention. Syago tumbled away, seeing stars.

The beast turned to face the new challenger, clearly a most worthy foe. The dark man tore the masked lady's head off, then the arms, then threw the rest of the body with dark blotches flying about before facing him. The beast roared at the eerie human.

"I see your pain, I can help you with it." But the man's tone was not taunting. That cold dark face, scarred and fearless with red on black eyes, stared at him dispassionately. "Lügos speaks to me, says you killed him."

That wounded the beast somehow, clawing at something deep inside himself. "He hates you now," the dark one continued. "Syago will too in time, so let them go. Leave them before they leave you, become my disciple and conquer that pain."

The deafening haze of battle raged around them, but without interference.

Qosku remembered himself, briefly lost and recovered by his own pain. Both his love and twin sister fallen to his errors. An uncountable fury mounted him, he remained indebted to Lügos and may not have any right to his friend's name. But if he, the one who killed Lügos, didn't, then certainly neither did this monster tempting him. He snarled and swiped at the ugly man. But his burly claw was halted by the man's small shining black arm. His other arm slammed forward into Qosku's chest, tossing him back into a group of soldiers and corpses. Pain filled the beast and its body shifted back to being Qosku, somehow melting away in spite of the red full moon.[29] Fighting stirred slowly around him, but Qosku only saw his naked form, marred but clean of what he'd overcome. He drew on a tunic and plates. Through the wrecked chaos of the hilly field, the witchlord raised his arms in solemn prayer, making a ceremony of the bloodshed.

Lügos and Chaska.

29 The lunar phases of this battle have been much debated, could all of it have happened that day? I doubt it.

Qosku charged at him again, springing into a forward kick. The Razhod effortlessly brushed him aside.

"I want you as my disciple," the Unakan Razhod intoned. "Accept the honor or suffer further. The old ones, the deep eternals, they bid you. Offer you relief. Praise them."

Lügos and Chaska.

Before Tiakanawu, Qosku might've been tempted to try it, try anything, to be cured of his curse of woman and beast. But now he'd accepted them as part of himself, found small changes to make it more endurable. The woman and beast and the losses, the trauma, the mistakes, the victories, the friends, the poetry, the thrill of combat. It was all him, and he found he could accept it. There would be no more room for the kind of suffering this sick man promised. No more pain for personal relief.

"Praise them, student!" the witchlord snarled.

"No."

The Razhod walked toward Qosku, gauntlet claw raising. Qosku met it with a firm block, all anger through it, but the punch smashed through his block and slammed into his chest like a stone wall, throwing him down and tumbling away.

Dazed and in pain, Qosku rolled to his feet. With sorrow flowing through his body, healing him, he recovered but not quick enough as the Razhod threw him into a mound. Its crumbling vacated structure gave way as he entered the musty old tomb deep inside. Dust, stone, dirt, and the fallen body parts of old corpses worn beyond resurrecting all fell over him.

Coughing, wincing against his dislocated arm and aching back and head, he sat up. Bloody. Sorrow healing him but slow, insufficient. Qosku wanted to pick up a nearby javelin and attack but couldn't. Suddenly a gauntleted hand was pulling him out; the Razhod had come for him while voicing a prayer. The Razhod held him up, cold, grabbed his head by the tied hair, coal-eyes gazing into his.

Then Syago was running up from behind, panting and bloody. He swung Alexandre hard, but a gauntleted arm snapped up to block it. The Razhod dropped Qosku and turned to deflect another strike, then the arms snapped down and grabbed the blade. It burned furiously but the gauntlets protected enough that he tore the sword out of Syago's hands and tossed it far away. Qosku regained enough strength to crawl from the wreckage. Syago

was already backpedaling from the Razhod. As Qosku emerged from the
hole to stand, feeling marginally better, a lifeless pounced on him, clawing and biting. Qosku threw the body at the Razhod's back and followed
with a dash forward and punch that drove through the corpse and into
the Razhod's back.

The Razhod, now covered in torn black clothes that dripped with blood
from several wounds, dropped to a knee and growled. A bloody and shredded wreck, he continued a now hopeless fight, swinging at Syago and
Qosku as they moved to keep the flank and bar escape. He brought his
claws up to his neck and both stabbed him before he could finish the
sacrifice. They looked at his corpse, suddenly unthreatening and broken,
and breathed in relief.

CHAPTER FOURTEEN

The Cataclysm

Based on *Leyta's Journals*, cc bastica 382;
Annals of Syago, cc bastica 380;
The Dark Fortress of Mephorash, cc bastica xxxx;

29th–30th of Akril, 247

From the vantage point of a tall mound, Leyta saw the battlefield layout clearly with the aid of numerous fires spread across the entire battle plain. The vanguard had fought through to the tower but suffered heavy losses on arrival. The lifeless hardly took anyone, but rather served as a constant and pressing distraction while the four Razhod eliminated barbarian and soldier in droves. Masters of the night and of warfare tactics, the Hellfaces flew about the battlefield with destructive prowess even more unstoppable when aided by their summons. Katti surveyed next to Leyta, praying, watching, and praying more. On an adjacent mound, Andala barked commands at her chamand warriors while jumping in with her big curvy sword at the weak points.[30]

The Royal Chaos provided essential help. Jester's singing, she had to admit, gave everyone including herself energy she wouldn't have had otherwise, if a darker more raging mood. She could see him, dancing and singing his song of fearsome strength amidst his Fomorion tribes. She hated the song, but it made her dyne much stronger. In the Vision, the field was a turmoil of fear and hate. Still, the fight couldn't continue as this, Leyta knew, and yet she failed to find another option. The armies focused on killing the Razhod, having taken two already, but the rest evaded them. The Hellfaces need only retreat into their mass of lifeless to rest and avoid getting flanked, and their tower remained another bastion.

---

30 *La Epica de Black Lava Gojira*

The entire scene made her think it the end of the world, and given what was at stake, it may have been, but she knew the same apocalypses had fallen before with no finality. *History is replete with the Iron Psyclopean Apocalypse supposedly coming and going without truly ending anything,* she thought. *Although this looks worse, how do I know it's not finally the one?*

"Pull everyone back," Katti said suddenly.

"What?" Leyta asked, surprised to see the woman not praying or tending the wounded. The priestess had done nothing but pray the entire battle.

"Call everyone back," she repeated without taking her eyes off of the battlefield. "Or have them get low and take shelter in the mounds. Hurry."

"Why?" Leyta asked, her eyes searching about for a threat, scepter ready to blast at the coming danger.

"Because we'll have our miracle. Our Lady Deova Bondua is coming. In force," she said it with a tone more grim than Leyta had ever heard from her before. "Our Lady has heard us, her blessing will reach us from heaven." The priestess stepped forward atop the mound and raised her arms, and two other priestesses joined her, abandoning their wounded to pray with Katti. The winds shifted. Leyta realized Katti knew something, perhaps her prayers for a miracle had been answered. Katti looked at her. "Do it!"

Leyta decided to trust her and raised her scepter. Focusing on the air, shifting and anxious, she spoke to it. "Pull back or fortify down!" She worried that her power wouldn't be enough, but her voice boomed, amplified through the air not especially loud or clear but sufficiently for most to hear and word to spread to the rest.

The wind intensified after this, but not from her, and she realized clouds thickened above, blocking out the moon and stars. The area darkened except for the many fires now getting blown in all directions. The allies pushed past these flames while others took cover. She looked at Katti and saw that the priestess's feet had risen off of the mound, her hair and gown rippling through the air. She and the other two glowed. Arms outstretched, she floated and yelled at the wind, "Divine Light, our Holy Deova, we thank thee for this blessing of destruction. Lay it down at the feet of our foes and we grant thee eternal gratitude. We sing—

> *Oh faint Light, glimmer in darkness*
> *Spear me fade Light through filthy fog*
> *Revive me out of this bleakness*

Then Leyta saw it, above in the dark clouds, forming and spinning fast, a funnel cloud spun down. The tempest tightened, touching the ground, deafening. Dust stirred under whipping winds as everyone dove for cover. Corpses and debris flew as it moved over the rough landscape, rearing up everything in its path. Even things untouched rose and flew through the air or were smashed by something else. Barbarian giants did not escape its reach either, and she feared many of her own soldiers would be hit by this grand display of divine power. She hurried to lay on her belly and clutch the grass. Hair and dress whipping wildly, she watched the terrifying sight and noticed a faint glimmer of white light in the clouds above. *What is that?*

The tempest moved around the battlefield, circling the tower with a deafening roar. The corpses, being lighter and mindless, flew about and rained down with sickening crunches as the tempest passed, one nearly hitting her. Leyta clutched the grass for dear life and prayed for the allies' safety. Amidst this furious storm, she saw a Razhod approaching. He the only person standing and walking against the obliterating winds, darkly glowing coal-eyes fixed on Katti.

"Defend her," Leyta shouted into the winds, herself crawling to intercept. "Protect Katti."

It was Kask. He arrived with the flambard soulblade before any more aid could come. Leyta stood up between priestess and Hellface. Grievore swung at her, but she backed away already moving dirt. She pushed the stones under the mound out at him, throwing him away from Katti. She continued throwing up rocks and dirt all around him, shoving him back closer to the tempest. He deflected and dodged most of the rocks, breaking through in spite of her hits. She had to crouch down for the wind and debris, already feeling drained. To her relief, Andala leaped in, clashing her two-handed blade against his.

Summoner against summoner. Andala brought in a series of high and low cuts designed to keep him defensive more than land a hit. Faster, he maneuvered them aside while starting a forward press, turning her offense to defense. Their long blades clashed as the two expert warriors kept their distance, yet his better speed, skill, and longer blade quickly turned her moves desperate. Leyta sought for a way to hit him. The fierce winds whipped her fires away and she failed at sparking lightning even in the storm. She threw more rocks at him and realized he was pushing Andala toward Katti, now forcing the angle so that Leyta lacked a clear shot, Andala in between them.

Leyta would have to hit them both, she knew. She sorrowed the dirt into thick mud at their feet, halting their movement. This prevented Andala from a needed retreat as Kask began to beat down on her sword while Constantin came in with a spear. Suddenly the wavy flambard blade was enveloped in flames and snapped to the side. The fires winked out, then back on as they ran through the warrior monk, slicing him open in a blaze of embers then through Andala's sword hand. Leyta watched all of this helplessly, her powers fizzled out. Balgor suddenly appeared behind the Hellface with a roar, wrapping him in a hold.

The tempest began dropping pieces of weapons, armor, and bodies on them. *Why is Katti still praying? The tempest has done enough damage and now appears to be leaving the tower for us. Can she not stop it?!* Grappling each other, the Razhod dropped Grievore, freed his good arm, then called in a soulmace, which he brought to the ground in a reverberating tremor that threw Balgor back. He ran up the hill to Leyta and Katti with what could only be Faagul the Waster in hand.[31]

He came to Leyta, helleyes glowing like coals. She reflexively moved out of the way. He brought Faagul down to hammer the ground and stone and dirt surged toward her. Unprepared, the stones rushed and pummeled her

---

31 *Or Faagul the Reflector, primarily it reverses dynal momentum and breaks sentiments.*

but with a quick wave of her scepter, she swept them aside. He disappeared, then she saw him hitting Katti, destroying her body as she sang praises to Deova Bondua, without a single yelp of pain.

Newly enraged, she threw all fire she could muster at him, but he switched back to Grievore and with his remaining arm used it to carry him away as flames futilely chased him, heavy winds whipping everywhere. The storm dissipated as did the lifeless swarm.[32]

On the vague announcement from Leyta, of which all Syago had heard was "retreat" and "down," he hesitantly stopped chasing Kask through the onslaught of bodies. Until they saw the funnel cloud and their hearts nearly stopped. The tempest touched down and they pulled away like the others to lay in between mounds. But the surprising storm passed near and ripped them off the ground, he and Qosku the Beast got picked up and hurled around. Syago twisted Alexandre, using the soulblade to shift himself between other flying objects. Not fighting the almighty wind currents, but navigating them. Dirt and grass blew in his face and as he neared the ground the wind gave a powerful shift and a skeleton crashed into him. Completely in the tempest's power, he tumbled in the air, glanced off of the side of the tower, and lost Alexandre. Disoriented, he didn't call for the return and the approaching ground panicked him. He managed a roll landing, softened by a pile of corpses, his armor, and his ever mighty devil arm.

Lying in that pile of writhing, broken corpses, he breathed and his head cleared. The tempest passed to the other side of the field before fading away. The winds eased up and the black sky rained dust. Sick of the lifeless pieces grasping at him, he regained his feet, battered all over. The tempest had worked in the allies' favor, he hoped, wasting away most of the lifeless and hopefully enough giants to change the future course of the truce. But some enemies still moved, and being in the midst of the swarm he called for Alexandre but it did not come. Nor could he see it but he could sense

---

32 The number of eyewitness accounts to Katti's unprecedented miracle storm make it hard to deny, but it should be noted that the earliest written ones make it appear much less impressive and more dangerous to all sides. Later ones have it bigger, stronger, and harming only the enemies. It grew with time as any miracle tends to do.

it, lying closer to the tower and believing itself to be pinned under debris and unable to come, he grabbed an old, regular sword. Worn but sufficient, he needed some adjusting to fighting with the smaller and slower soulless weapon and he adjusted quickly against the few remaining lifeless that confronted him. In this solitary, isolated struggle, at the end of the storm's rampage, he saw Kask gliding down and land not far off from him. He ceased his fighting and ran in between broken mounds and piles of lifeless after him. He came on Kask, who stood before a tree and stuck Grievore into its trunk to drain its lifeforce for himself. Syago went in stealthy at first then hard and fast. The old foe reacted immediately, eyes in the back of his head. He brought up Grievore with one arm and danced back, away from Syago's heavy pursuit. The fast and unrelenting offensive prevented Kask from switching to a better weapon, struggling from his wounds and large weapon in one hand.

Even given the disadvantage, Kask kept up with Syago by relying more on mobility than anything else to fend off the attacks. Syago also was at a disadvantage, weary, battered, and fighting without Alexandre. Again he marveled that this was the same man he'd fought only months before in Tolgrym.

Suddenly, Qosku the Beast was there with a claw swipe that knocked Kask down. Syago cut the sword hand, getting rid of the soulblade, and Kask dropped to his knees with that haunting face remaining impassive. Syago nearly spat in his face. "What? No more taunts? No strange moral lessons like before?"

"Humans don't speak to ants," Kask responded as Qosku stood by him, watching behind for any other approaching enemy. "The ants wouldn't even understand."

"I'm not so naive anymore," Syago said. "I know as much pain and terror as you do."

Kask said nothing, but in the arrogant way that any further conversation was beneath him. Had he even heard what Syago just said? He shook him, forced his head up, but those eyes looked past him.

"No, my heart is full of vengeance," Syago said, more for himself now. "I acknowledge that and don't need to forgive you, but I will be free of bitterness. Nor does my rage mean that what I do is not just. Justice will have its due regardless of my motives here."

"Do it then." Yet as he looked at the unconquered witchlord, he saw weariness. Not in those unreadable helleyes, but deep inside the man's voice. Even though he'd gotten him to speak, it still wasn't as mocking as previous times Syago had spoken with him. This was a man in pain who wanted to die, to get it over with.

Qosku's roar alerted Syago to the arrival of another Razhod. The man glided down on the spinning Mordios, and Syago recognized his face as one of the earlier disciples who must've ascended to witchlord in the tower. Qosku growled at the man, staying on all fours in preparation for a charge. Syago held his sword up to Kask's neck. "Have you come to rescue your friend?"

"No, I've come to die with him," the new Razhod said as the scythe vanished in his hand and the staff Vilekor appeared. But his other hand was holding up a bell which rang thrice as he whispered to it. Syago picked up a loose spear and hurled it right through his chest. The witchlord, staff in hand, didn't even try to stop or avoid it. *Shit, what does that mean?*

The bell chimes hung in the air, the summoning call was already made and now sustained by his blood.

A large serpentine body of segmented iron came from the ground igniting nearby wood and grass as it snaked into the air above, gigantic. It burned like a furnace in between plates, eyes flaring, and smoke pouring from fanged mouth. Spikes lined the back and four clawed limbs stroked the air. Its head reared toward the Razhod as Syago and Qosku halted their chase.

"*FEED ME*," a deep, grinding voice grated the air.

"Vorogoyod the Helldragon, Lord of Infernos," said Kask, almost forgotten by Syago. "Use the blood of myself and these foes, with my brother, to make me a grand inferno, a sunrise in hell to-" Syago slashed his throat.

Already filling the sky, Vorogoyod snorted smoke and sparks then circled in on himself, coiling in the air around a sphere of fire which burned brighter than any human forge, bathing the field in hot firelight. Already Alexandre distantly warned Syago of the blast so he pushed Qosku to a run. The witchlord's body hung in the air, spear still through its chest, then burned. They ran, darting between the remaining lifeless as the seething ball of fire turned night into day until the concussion threw them down into a nook behind a mound just before the fire raged.

The Hell's Sunrise, a surge of white flame, raced across the land with a heavy wind that threw anything unshielded before disintegrating it. The deafening blast burned Syago's and Qosku's skin even though the flames never touched them, crouching behind broken mounds. It left their ears ringing, heat singing skin and hair, and when the blaze abated and they finally deemed it safe to stand after a long silent pause, they found the entire battlefield destroyed.

All around remained an unrecognizable wreck. Burnt, tossed, overthrown. Ashes and dust and smoldering flames. Syago saw no living thing, nor moving lifeless, and even the tower lay broken and toppled. The last Razhod was dead, the battle was over.

CHAPTER FIFTEEN
THE PIECES SCATTER

Based on *Leyta's Journals*, cc bastica 400;
Writings of Qosku, cc bastica 390;

30th of Akril, 247

The storm clouds fled and dawn approached, allowing more light to re-place the now dying fires across the battlefield. Leyta moved through the wreckage with several elementists. Not far off, she saw Balgor and Andala doing the same, each leading a group to recover what might be saved. They suspected that the final events of the fight had, rightfully, scared off any nearby creatures hungering for living and rotting remains. The gurows had only just started to come for the dead. A gnarled tree emerged from Thornwood to feed on the corpses at the southern edge of the mound plain. With enough carrion to feed on, they avoided the humans, but it was best not to linger; soon this place would be full of blackbirds and trees, and even wolves eventually.

The bodies lay still in the growing light, the Necromancer's spell being over. Leyta was more concerned about the remaining groups of Fomorions and wherever the Chaos leaders might be hiding, waiting to spring the last fight.

In the surfacing dawn, a gentle wind blew ash and torn clothing over the remnants of bodies. Weapons protruded, awkwardly and broken. Sorrow weighed heavily on her; she found few survivors, friend or foe. She didn't know the numbers yet, but the costs of this one would be the highest yet. She took comfort in that her best information indicated complete victory. All Razhod were dead and probably most if not all of their disciples as well. The Royal Chaos also had lost at least two of its principle members and the likely support of their dwindling forces.

She looked north and saw the distant but distinct figures of Syago and Qosku walking over the mounds. Her heart leaped at the first confirmation of their survival. But where were they going? The direction of the tower it appeared, and too far for her to reach at present.

The tower. That tall black obelisk sat mostly crumbled either from the tempest or the blast, or both.[33] Only the base remained in tact. It had been a powerful defensive maneuver for the four Razhod, impressive in a form worthy of all the legends about them.

She angled her search toward the Fomorions gathering ahead on the southwest side of the tower ruins. She didn't want to approach them, didn't want to spark what may be another fight, but she had to know. Had to at least pretend to be a strong and formidable leader even if she thought she would be resigning soon. The giants noticed her approach but ignored her, no hostility, only cold indifference. She hesitated. *Fortify!* And so she did. The other elementists stayed behind, but she noticed Balgor and Lil'iek coming toward the group, so she need not lead alone for long. Andala stood with them, re-wrapping the stump of her newly severed hand.

Walking in between the giants, Leyta's head level with their furry or bearded stomachs, she appeared less scared than she felt. At least, she hoped she did. None looked at her with their inhuman eyes. They talked in their rough language, but one conversation dominated the group at the center.

It was Jester, arguing with them in their language. She understood none of it, but it seemed clear that his command of the language was incomplete and they already tired of him. Or tired of his manipulation of them.

She felt a deeper chill at the sight of Jester than the surrounding barbarians, that hollow mask and lanky body in flashy costume, energetic in its antics but gloomy in mood and horribly outsized here.

Jester finished with a strange bubbling sound as the barbarians closed in. An insult? They fell on him, beating him with their fists, but instead of him screaming she heard a song, which abruptly ended.

The pounding continued after the singing had stopped for a moment, then it too ceased. The giants turned and began walking away. Together, they moved past her. Some glanced down at her pitying, regarding her either with suspicion or distaste, or perhaps warning her. They trudged

---

33 *See Moonspell Hell Light de Lostregos*

past in silence. Then Leyta saw the other figure they'd also left: King tied to a post, or rather a broken spear pushed into the ground.

But King was not dead. She stood before him, and the others joined her side. The masked head of King rose to face her. There was a brief silence, which Leyta broke with, "King, self-described, you are charged and convicted of grave crimes against the Republic. As the leader of the rogue group which brought violent dissension into a stable and functioning society while subsequently eliciting the aid of our enemies, we find you worthy of death."

More silence, then King began, "I—"

Lil'iek's knife interrupted him, shooting out into the neck, up into the head behind the mask. "He doesn't deserve a response," Lil'iek said before yanking it back out. King went limp and Leyta moved to turn away but Lil'iek stopped her. "Wait. Something is wrong."

Lil'iek grabbed King's head and pulled at the mask, fiddling with it before ripping it off. Leyta was exhausted and didn't care what King's true identity was. Until she saw.

King was a doll.

Everyone around gasped. A small sack, with buttons for eyes and a smiling face stitched on it, leaked sand, dyed red, out of the stab area. Lil'iek held up the knife in her hand; it lacked blood as did the shirt below the bag head.

"No," Leyta said as everyone stared in disbelief. "That's impossible." She grabbed Lil'iek's knife and cut open the front of the costume. The elaborate costume was both armor and disguise for a series of sand bags tied together. The costume added puffy bulk to a rather small form. To inspect it better, they untied it from the post and laid it down.

Balgor knelt and pointed at the markings along the bags. "These are archemical, this center one matches the gloves, which explains the darkfire. He, or it, was a walking weapon. Makes sense, Jester also used archemy. But I don't recognize the markings. They're none I've ever seen before."

"Spirits," Andala said, also kneeling to look closer. "These are markings to connect it to the mind of a spirit entity. I suppose it could connect to a living person, who would then puppeteer the doll. But these better resemble the spirit bonding symbols."

"As in a soulweapon?" Balgor asked.

"No." She traced the symbols with her finger. "Soulweapons bond the greater spirits, which have their own unique symbol system. These are more like what you would use to seal a family member or trap an enemy into an object. It's forbidden by all the chamands, but witches will do it. But this isn't a summoner's work, these better resemble elemental markings than spiritual ones. It's a strange combination I've not seen before, but it might explain why a doll was animated. Animated so well we thought it was a real person."

"The bigger question is what does this mean?" Leyta asked. "The entire time we've taken it for granted that King was the leader. I even met with him in the temple. So who or what was controlling it?"

They dwelt on the thought in silence before Andala said, "Could it be Jester? The markings are similar. Or..."

"No." Balgor shook his head while stroking his beard. "Look there, Jester's body is the same. I suppose there is Queen and Knave, but I wager theirs are the same as well."

They stared at it for moments but came to nothing.

"We've wasted enough time on this for now," Leyta said, turning to her soldiers standing around. "Take his body on a stretcher, the other Royal Chaos members too. We'll need to study them, but now isn't the time or place. Bring the Chaos supply wagon and focus on finding the two relic pieces, search the tower as well. We need to hurry. We have a long trek back to our cities."

She turned to head back to the wagons to find Lil'iek in her way, axes in hand. "It's time, Leyta," she said.

"Time?" But Leyta knew what she meant. "Ah, sorry I believe Virgow was wounded at the battle in front of the castle, so he ended up staying there."

"Don't bother lying to me." She lowered her voice. "I have more eyes in the sky than you do on the ground. I'll find him and hold you to your word."

"I'm not lying, and I will keep my word but can't with him over in the castle. I didn't see it myself but someone said he caught fire from an attack and was burning. But the priestesses put it out and carried him into the castle while we pursued east." When Leyta mentioned "fire," Lil'iek's mouth dropped open slightly and her eyes saw past Leyta.

"Attacked?" Lil'iek was almost breathless. "Who saw it?"

Leyta's nerves set on edge as if she'd stumbled onto something without meaning to. "I don't know. I heard it third-hand. The fight was such a frenzied jumble. If you'd like, I could send a message through my ranks for any with knowledge of it to bring word to you or Tek'ouk'iek."

"No. No, thank you." Lil'iek, suddenly cold, turned and walked away.

Leyta eyed the early morning sky, seeking peace in the light of the growing dawn. To the north, another pollen cloud rose, not as big as the previous ones but still potentially lethal. *And what of the maelstrom of sentiments we put out today? Did we transform enough monstrosities to finish us off?* The allies regrouped and mourned once they were out of the field of rotting carrion and the feast it provided. She wished the fog would return, considering the carnage and desolation before her, clarity was worse than the uncertainty.

Qosku followed Syago around the edge of the broken spire in search of the trapped Alexandre. The tower, though new, felt old in its ruin. Qosku watched around for movements, looking for wounded allies and envious enemies but seeing neither. All lay in destroyed waste beneath faint morning sunlight. Both of them had slight burns on their skin, several cuts and bruises, and a sore weariness so thorough Qosku thought he might never feel relief again.

Suddenly, they could hear voices inside the tower ruin. Syago stopped, holding a hand out for Qosku to be silent. Given that he moved stealthier than Syago, Qosku somewhat resented the gesture. They inched closer to an open doorway and peeked in.

Two Razhod disciples—wounded and covered in dirt, but inexplicably alive—rummaged through the rocky debris inside. One stood with his sword out in anticipation of enemies. He whispered loudly, "We need to go. Now."

"I'm coming," the other responded, using his sword to leverage a rock over. "I'd just hoped to find their book. Thought maybe it would be here and I could actually look at it."

"It isn't here," the other pressed. "And you wouldn't find it beneath all these rocks if it were. But there is one up at the coven, sneak a peek there. With the holy sword maybe they'll let us look, or even elevate us to full Razhod. You have it still?"

"Yes, let's go." The one raised a cloth tightly wrapped in the shape of a sword with his other arm before slipping it into the holster of a small side pack. They moved out toward the opening Qosku and Syago watched through, and Qosku and Syago skirted around the wall to hide. Syago readied his sword to attack but Qosku gripped his hand.

Syago looked at him and Qosku whispered, "They go to home, yes? We can follow."

Syago's eyes flickered in deep thought. "Yeah, but I doubt we could stalk them the whole way through the wilderness without them knowing. Might as well finish the last of them off here."

"But there could be more, and you sense Alexandre, yes?" Qosku reminded him. "We follow Alexandre to the rest."

A light twinkled in Syago's eyes. "Oh, that's clever, Qos. Very good."

The disciples walked away from the ruins, now running north while warily looking about. Qosku and Syago waited almost an hour before considering it safe enough to pursue. It didn't occur to them until they'd already gone that they ought to inform someone of their plan, but once the thought crossed their minds, they brushed it off, thinking the hunt wouldn't last more than a day.

"Do you ever think about how the Razhod get so many Unaka in their cult?" Syago asked as they made their way across the plain between mounds. He added hurriedly, "I don't mean like it's your fault. I'm just wondering how and why. And why they're so powerful."

"I confuse by it also," Qosku responded. "I never meet any Unaka who want join them. And I never see Razhod who I know. I thought maybe it from the old cults, maybe they become Razhod. Many people are hurt by Asturion soldiers and want for be free. They want escape, so they become violent. But I never saw a Razhod before so I don't know, except for the one we just killed. He tried to persuade me."

But I still don't know what happened to Chaska, or if that was even the Razhod. But then how did Chaska appear at the Razhod tent at Tiakanawu? Maybe that was also a hallucination, and before too.

"You think the coven recruits desperate or vulnerable people? I suppose that makes sense. Hard to imagine why people would do this otherwise."

"Maybe we learn it at end of this hunt," Qosku concluded.

"I hope so. We can't do this anymore, fighting them. I can't."

Qosku wanted to counter this but felt instead that he agreed, a realization that deeply unsettled him.

CHAPTER SIXTEEN

CASTLES IN THE SKY

Based on *Leyta's Journals*, cc bastica 430;
The Hunter's Parchments, cc bastica 404;
The Nordvargor Testaments, cc bastica 913;

1st of Maiod–26th of Hulior, 247

With the departure of the Fomorions, the allies rested easier, taking an extra day to recover and search out the battlefield wreckage. This spilled over into Beltan, which would normally have been a grand festival but here was shorter and more somber. The armies split, returning to their places. Andala led the chamands back to Bokhor. Lil'iek and the last three Roah'riik went south back into Thornwood. The armies, sleep deprived, rested long in the care of those who'd stayed on.

Leyta did not sleep so well. Syago and Qosku were missing, as was the last relic piece. They'd found one in the rubble of the tower, which they guessed to be the Razhod piece and a good sign the group was truly finished, though they were too tired to celebrate any of this. She took comfort on finding their own still where Syago reported leaving it in Voium. She'd even laughed a little as it was extricated out of the cathedral privy. The search for the third had scraped the field and tower exhaustively and had come up with nothing. She wondered if the Fomorions had taken it, but they hadn't taken anything other than tents and food. This meant that either one of the two enemies had hid it. By the end, she was so sick of the relic, she locked the other two pieces up.

They attempted a counting of all the enemies and still lacked the bodies of Knave and suspected some missing Razhod disciples. All known Razhod and the main leaders of the Chaos were confirmed dead, or destroyed in the case of the dolls. All the bodies, save the demon's, remained in the bags they'd been placed in. And beyond her last sighting of Syago and Qosku moving across the field, she knew nothing of them now. Trusting in them, that they would return, possibly with the news she lacked, she tried not to worry about it. Even the chamands, now with their powers returning in the wake of the Razhod's extermination, couldn't gain any information other than to say some spirits saw the pair heading north past Bokhor.

After they'd resettled in Cantlgrym, the Razhod invaded Leyta's dreams. Not only them, but also Jester and the revived Queen. And now that the madness of war was past them, the Seeping became a central concern. Leyta's headaches and nausea had diminished, but her fatigue hadn't and now her hair was beginning to fall out. She hid it by wearing a wimple more often in place of a net or braids. Even though not married, none noticed as her style fit in with being Castellan. She wasn't really surprised as she'd been up front on the wall when it started, but the direction of this blight concerned her as most with this problem died soon after. She hadn't seen many others as bad in the Seeping as she, but maybe they too hid theirs well. It had once been a stigma, people with it were avoided, but none of the fears of curses had ever come true. Just the horrors of watching someone's body ulcerate until nothing was left. She didn't feel that now, and hoped for a miracle that she never would, but sensed that she was not free of it.[34]

Missing a cure for the Seeping was not her only struggle. Monstrous feldinals tore apart the world and assaulted the castle walls. The heresy was still true, dyne was still transforming the world around them, mal-adapting it into an aberration they had to fight. She wondered if maybe a solution lie in the dydatris pieces. But without a solution, the hope still wasn't enough to lift her despair. The pieces were difficult to understand given they weren't complete, but they also contained an ancient language. What she could glean from studying them was that the dydatris could bring more power in dyne. And escalation could only make the spiral worse. It also offered no salvation from the Seeping.

With everything weighing on her, she thought she'd give it another couple of months, then resign if she still had not recovered more of her sentiments. It almost kept her going, wondering if her void was the message from Deova Bondua that they needed to live without dyne, to save the world. But they

---

34 The Seeping was literally the seeping of blood from the stomach, from the throat, from the skin.

couldn't. They'd pillory her with the other heretics before listening to her. Especially with the monsters already damaging the walls as is.

She picked up the class for younger children who'd returned to the castle after a month. This helped more than anything else, easing her despair. It even rekindled other sentiments, but with how frequently she was interrupted with her other duties, she soon had to leave it to Balgor.

She took inventory of the situation: no enemy sightings, work had begun to cleanse Voium of the Seeping, and Balgor had learned much from the relics, expressing excitement. Balgor had also organized a small force to go north and free Roza from her battle grave as he'd promised. Leyta was dismayed to learn on his return that Roza had decided against coming back to Cantlgrym. Though it was probably for the best, Leyta had hoped for a chance to make it work. More unsettling was that after two months, Syago, Qosku, and the last relic were still missing with not even a rumor to hold onto. She set about getting the classes back into sequence and called for a vigil and celebratory feast. The training regimen resumed along with its use of hunting and gathering parties, as did trade with other cities, though much thinner and more sporadic. They scheduled the vigil and feast to take place the following week.

After a day of this activity, feeling exhausted again, she made her way up to Balgor's study for the promised meeting. The two relics lay before him on a table, surrounded by a mess of parchments left by Seumas where the Fomorion scholar wrote furiously. She drew a chair up and sat next to him, leaning on the table while resisting the urge to put her head down and sleep immediately.

"It's incredible, Leyta," Balgor said. "Layers of meaning, I've only scratched the surface. This part is a diagram of dyne, how it functions. The laws of it all."

"Any laws we can use now?" she asked.

"Well, not yet," he said, faltering slightly but then resuming his animated pace. "But I haven't translated it all. You'd have better luck with it, be much quicker as you've already got the language. Though the missing piece is key to what we lack. Perhaps calling an angel to us through Osmos might help us find the last piece and gain answers."[35]

---

35 Their notes on the item remain vital to the continuing development of dyne as a science and practice.

"When we last summoned Osmos and spoke to an angel about the relic and Tiakanawu, it maimed and killed some of our priests for insufficient devotion. Then it promised to return with an army to fight the Razhod and the devils next time we call. I'm not desperate enough to do that again." She sighed. "The relic might have to stay another of those unsolved puzzles. But I'm glad you got as far as you did."

She wanted to be more excited, but instead felt hollow. If they found the third piece, it could only result in more dyne; to preserve civilization they somehow needed less. She mumbled some approval, and he set down his quill. "I see Cantlgrym is taking its toll on you. I apologize for being less helpful these past days. If it makes you feel better, this has come at the cost of my own sleep as well."

She smiled and shook her head. "You'd have to run around the castle for it to make up in any way."

"Perhaps I'll get on that tomorrow." He tried a small light laugh. "Though I'm also pulling extra weight since Virgow still struggles with his burns. The Seeping is also getting him pretty bad too, and I suppose you as well by the look of it."

She smiled weakly. "What I do need you to do tomorrow is begin work on the Chaos remains. They're still in the bags we transported them in, stuffed in a cell. I think everyone here believes they're cursed. You can do it with your students if you need. I'd rather have you take a team to back you up, but we need to start it soon. It could be important."

"Of course, I'd completely forgotten about them." His smile softened. "I did notice a difference in the Jester doll compared to the others, but it's all foreign dyne to me. I suspect the one piece we're missing, Knave, is the key. So unless Syago and Qosku turn up with his head, I doubt we'll learn any-thing." He grew quiet at mentioning them. "I'm certain they died honorably."

Denial, straight and true, shot through her. But she couldn't fault him his words. Instead, she said, "I hate not having closure."

"And we may never have it. Or it may happen that we don't like what we find."

"No," she said it quietly.

"Perhaps it's time we take our turns at resting. Our conversation about these relics can wait."

The pace settled in the following days, which turned into yet another as Lügosa festival approached. Still she'd heard nothing of Syago and Qosku. Even when Syago had hunted devils on his own, rumors had reached her. Now, there was nothing but silence. The relic, she now assumed, was lost or merely stolen, which was just as well in her mind.

The day of the feast arrived and tournaments filled the day, followed by the traditional dances, play, and theatrical ceremony. After this, people gathered in the hall for supper.

She'd decided to resign that day, and focus on teaching young children until her health improved. Festival preparations had kept her mind off of everything, the heresy and the people she missed, but their absence returned to full attention as she took a seat for the feast. So many empty seats that should've been full. She looked at some of the other keepers and saw that they felt it too. They were clearly wounded as well, lasting trauma in their minds if not their bodies. She even felt sympathy for the hard-edged Virgow at the other end of the table. She disliked him and hid the secret of her commitment to Lil'iek, whom she'd not spoken to since the Gravespire battle.

They had a beautiful toast to the days now past, those they'd lost, and the days to come.

She nearly announced her resignation there, but decided to hold off until after the meal. Though it was only a time, for halfway through her plate, a shift in the mood of the hall swept through, subtle and curious at first then clear as day. Horror welled up in Leyta as she recognized the feeling. Numbness spread as her body refused to respond to her commands. Her head fell limply to the side, and she slouched in her seat. Chatter faded out into a deafening silence, broken only by the tinkling of silverware on plates. Some fell to the floor. Mass paralysis in the greathall again, this time from some type of venom, and they waited involuntarily for their captor to make the appearance.

Jester walked in, tall and proud in his same costume, trailing a small entourage of dumbhead brutes, a couple Fomorions, and the demon Knave. His triumphal bearing gave away what the sorrowful mask did not. Victory.

Two men picked up Leyta's seat, careful not to topple her, and moved it to the side of the table. They turned her head so she could see Jester sitting in a new chair placed at her headseat of the table. He pulled off his hooded mask and placed it next to his plate. The faceless head still disturbed her as much as the mask had, but it was noticeably more real than the doll's head. He wore the missing piece of the dydatris around his neck and a crude eye pendant that she assumed must grant him some form of vision now that his puppets were all destroyed. Once he took the remaining two relic pieces at the castle, he'd have all three together in one.

"All right," said Jester, leaning forward over his plate in false excitement. "*Now* you may begin eating."

He grabbed a handful of vegetables and shoved it in his lipless mouth, chomping loudly as food flew everywhere against the stillness.

"What? Is something smelly in the food? Or did the drinks upset your bellies?" He threw the napkin over his shoulder and dabbed at his mouth with the table cloth. His voice sounded more harsh this time, more unhinged. "Why so glum, everyone? Is it something I farted?"

He leaned over his plate again and whispered to Leyta, "Did I interrupt a good joke again? My mistake. But I know what would cheer you all up... food fight!" He flung a piece of mash from his spoon. It hit Leyta in the face with a splatter and slid down, wet. A speck of annoyance masked the swelling panic inside her. She'd doomed them all. Let their guard down.

"You know you brought this on yourself, Miss Castellan. You can't beat me, you never could. The only thing you've accomplished is forfeiting all opportunities for a nice clown. Now it's mean clown time. And mean clown doesn't play fun games."

He turned back to his messed plate and said, "Bring me the relics and give me the rest of my power." Large hands brought him the two relic pieces and he fit them onto the other two pieces, holding the completed relic aloft for everyone to see.

"Now dawns a new age," he proclaimed while rising from his seat. "Liberty, mischief, and ugliness will now flourish under my lawless reign. You killed my royal group, and for that I will forgive you. I hold no grudges. But with them gone, it does mean everyone's going to have to really pull their own weight here. I, for one, will have to fill in for King, Queen, and Knight in addition to Jester. I adopt those roles unto myself as King-Queen-Jester-Knight and Knave will remain my chief assistant of roguery while you assist with clowning. The only rule is no rules. This has been a long time in the making, it is long deserved, so enjoy it while we have it... or face the consequences.

"Now for my first act as Multi-Ruler of No-Rules, I first crown myself, which is my privilege." Knave handed him a metal crown, different from what King or Queen wore. This was just a brass ring with jeweled tiers rising out of the base. Jester tore his mask in half, separating it from the upper hood with the bell jangles. He fit these together so that the bells hung over the crown, tossing aside the mask part. "And I think a legitimate ruler always has good hair, don't you? And some kind of face?"

A henchman gave him a handful of rushes. He took the straw and fitted it in at the center top of the hat where he'd cut a hole. It poked out above his jester bell-crown. Another handed him a makeup set. He took a pallet of lipstick and drew on his faceless head a red mouth, fitting a crooked frown over his bared yellow teeth, and purple eyes that only smudged to dots. "There, now I'm ready to be your King-Queen-Jester-Knight. Now everyone's happy!"

Silence in the room.

"But wait, there's more. For my second and final act, for now, I will make use of my new royal powers. See I'm a rather skilled archemist in addition to bard, in case you hadn't yet figured it out. It's how I managed my puppet that you destroyed. But I know people need to see some verification of my authenticity. So it's time I raise the stakes in this charade."

The Clown King stood and removed the dydatris from his neck. A servant carried the chair back to the wall as he placed the artifact on the stone floor and ran his fingers along it, lovingly. "Now, rise, and fly!"

The markings on the relic glowed, and the castle trembled. The tremors increased until Leyta thought it would bring down the walls. But the structure remained firm until the tremors began to fade. Even as she wondered how the piece worked, she quivered to think of what powers he would have with all three pieces in one. Then, as her mixture of fear, sorrow, and anger drained from her, she understood. The piece allowed him to use not only his own sentiments, but those of all the others in the castle. A castle that now moved.

A boom like thunder followed by a gust of wind swept the brambletops as Lil'iek descended from them with her youngest son on her back. Something stirred inside her, a growing emptiness that confused her at first till she realized it sounded like how Tek'ouk'iek had described using dyne. Except that she wasn't using dyne; she didn't even know how. She halted, as did her oldest child and her cousin. Evidently they'd felt it too. They looked at each other then climbed back up to the top; the whole village went up top. From the top of the forest, she saw the spires of Castle Cantlgrym, normally unseen from this distance, rising up into the air on a slag of stone. It hovered in the air and stayed there, defying explanation.[36]

It left her dumbstruck, and frightened. She wondered if it was some kind of attack or maybe a new innovation of dyne achieved by the palemen. Of a sudden she missed both Fal'iek and Tek'ouk'iek for their quick, analytical thinking and general knowledge of the Asturions. She was at a total loss what any of this meant. The whole village was abuzz.

"It must be the dydatris," she heard Tek'ouk'iek mutter in her mind. It seemed like what he would've said, and she knew this must be his spirit communicating with her on the wind. It made sense.

She nodded and mumbled under her breath, "They must've found the last piece, maybe after the battle, and didn't tell us."[37]

She went to the Quoarn'riik gathering, more accustomed now to walking in herself since both of her men were gone and she'd earned enough authority through respect to represent her family as matron. She hoped this break in tradition would open it up to further change.

"We don't know if this is bad or good," Tok'olk was saying. "It might be—"

"Nothing the palemen do is ever good," Hucayali'koh said. "Not for us. They only cause problems that spill over onto us then neglect to help us, if not attack and rob us directly."

"We need to get over there," Lil'iek said. "I need to go and find out."

"You?" said Hucayali'koh. "But what could you do?"

"I'm sorry," Tok'olk began, "but I worry we'd just provoke them. We don't want their attention on us."

"I think it is dangerous, chieftains." Lil'iek's level tone caught their attention. "It's always a mistake to trust them without care. Remember that Virgow is in that castle. I've no question that if this is not his doing, then he'll somehow turn it against us.

---

36 Possibly the most incredible claim of this entire work. I need only point to the vast multitude of written attestations that, in spite of variations in the tellings, it did indeed happen.

37 See *Sol Sistere de Selbst* by Himetuks Himi'n

"And that drain you're feeling on your emotions? That's what it feels like to use dyne. That castle is lifted up by their dyne, which they're using to somehow take from us. I don't know how but we need to get them to stop. A castle floating on our sentiments can't depend on ours for long until it falls."

"Then that's their loss, not ours," Mi'qamac said.

Lil'iek was already shaking her head. "No, it could cause untold destruction. Tek told me many stories, Fal'iek too of the things he'd seen. It could kill us or drive us mad, if not allow them too much power over us."

There was worry and fear in Chief Tok'olk's eyes. "Lil'iek, we—"

"We call the grim'iik," she said. "We must get there, and we must hurry. I'll go without your sanction if I must, for everything I've fought for could be lost here if we miss our opportunity."

The chieftains exchanged looks then nodded. Lil'iek motioned to Guaran'upik, and they retrieved the grim'iik skull. Fearsome and large, more so than the other skulls they carried.[38]

Arriving again at the forest tops, Cantlgrym still in view, the three Roah'riik placed their hands on the skull as the rest stood around watching.

Breaking custom as she always did, Lil'iek joined her hands to the skull and felt it, far away. It refused their plea at first, annoyed. Then it came, enraged at their persistence. The massive ten-pace wingspan visible from afar, it brought its own wind as the wings halted and drifted down to perch beside them. Its neck and head were featherless with a red bulge that sat atop its bare head like a crown. Its wings were full of dark feathers with colorful endings. Beady eyes watched them, and they, through the skull, pressed their need to get to the castle in the sky. Reminding the sacred beast of their goodness to him, admiring his greatness, and showing how this threat endangered Thornwood, they achieved its consent to take three and no more.

They knew better than to ask for more.

Those eyes focused in on Lil'iek, seeing her with a visible glimmer of admiration and respect.

Lil'iek, Guaran'upik, and Machi'guenk went while the others took the skull back down. She prayed as it lifted them up into the air. But her prayers only found emptiness, no hope.

---

38 *See Gybiaaw Blackbraid: On Yaotl Mictlan*

Hope was always gone, Fal'iek had said. *There was only ever us and our actions, confined by the world we're in. The most we can do is push hard for what we need then adapt when we don't get it. And when we cannot adapt, we accept our fall with grace and dignity. Only us saves us.*

Tek'ouk'iek had echoed this. He'd come to resemble Fal'iek more and more in their marriage. She reminisced sardonically, *Did I do that to him, or did the war? Either way, I am that now, fighting their battle with only their spirits behind me.* She ran her fingers over her feq'uok, feeling their hairs and nails on it, feeling their bodies and souls in her mind and heart. And all the ancestors wisdom too.

CHAPTER SEVENTEEN

Hidden Far, High, Deep

Based on *Annals of Syago,* cc bastica 391;
Writings of Qosku, cc bastica 400;
The Nordvargor Testaments, cc bastica 966;

Maiod–Huniod, 247

Qosku and Syago made their way warily through the rocky pass, weary from the long walk and uphill climb. They'd left Shruumoth Forest the day before, having camped the night there, and since been on what seemed like an unending path through bramble-filled ravines and rocky hills. Surprisingly little had attacked them out there. This allowed them to keep a steady pursuit of their enemies, who were a likely reason for their luck. In fact, the occasional light attacks put food in their hands without having to forage, both of them needing to eat extensively due to their conditions, Qosku's werebeast and Seeping, and Syago's devil arm.

Few words passed between them in the quiet journey. Syago thought the silence mingled with stilted conversations to be awkward at first, but realized that they were comfortable just being in each others' company. They didn't need to talk constantly as they understood each other regardless. But the silence felt more stark to Syago, as Alexandre was less present in his thoughts. This left the devil's arm stronger now in its appetites and passions, tasking his mental discipline even more.

At one point in a gorge with walls covered in ferns and moss, a stream running through, Syago sensed the change in Alexandre, its presence grew stronger, which meant their quarry wasn't moving. "They've stopped again. Too long for a single incident, so I guess it's for the night."

"We rest now," Qosku said, dropping the small bag that held his armor and weapons when he didn't need them.

Night fell with a newly waning moon, and Qosku allowed the transformation, keeping it under tight control. It helped heal his wounds quicker, and held off the Seeping. Syago had left before the blight but his passage through the town had upset his stomach and bruised his throat. Both had supernatural healing and fortitude, however even these could not completely heal and protect Qosku from his ulcerations. It was still causing hair loss. Even Qosku's fast-healing werebeast was beginning to lose hair, and Syago wondered if it would do something similar to his devil arm. But Qosku saw improvement in beating back the fatigue.

They ate and Syago slept in a crevice between two boulders with Qosku's beast some distance further south. Sometime before sunrise, Alexandre sent out a weak and fading alarm to Syago, waking him. He went to Qosku, now back to normal. "They're moving, let's go."

Qosku stretched and rose to his feet, and they were off. They came to an end of the fern gulch at a waterfall hoping to find the end in sight, a remote castle or tower. But the waterfall climbed out of the thin woodland of ferns and brambles then turned to stony cliffs. The journey would stretch on still, not short like they'd believed. But there was no canoe for him to use.

Qosku, following his gaze, sighed then walked back down the ravine. Curious, Syago followed him to a carved out mushroom husk. Syago had noticed it but not given it any thought. Husks were common. He dragged it to the water with Qosku, then saw the hole. They made a quick patch using mud and weeds, then found some branches from a dead tree, panned enough on one end with some trimming to serve as paddles. And they were off up the river, pushing hard against the current to keep up through the dark and winding vine covered cliffs while watching the tops for signs of ambush. The way the mists and later sunlight illuminated the whole ravine would've been beautiful if not for the expectant wariness that things were hiding in them, waiting to kill the two travelers. The increased demand on their bleeding intestines slowed them and left them vulnerable.

They paddled quietly, the lapping of the river the only sounds at dawn's fading light. A giant snake attacked them one night, swarms of bats another, swarms of bugs one more still. The river led them out of the cliffs to find the sun shining on a small bunch of large brush with gorgeous leaves, coloring red and orange. Neither had seen them before and were tempted to go pluck what looked like luscious fruit, but both knew that anything beautiful was usually deceptive in nature. A lure, a trap. There were no general laws, no reliable patterns to determine the safety of a food item. Only trial and error. Instead they slowed the paddling to admire it briefly and ate what they already had, then camped on the opposite shore. Syago remembered Fal'iek talking about watching what other animals ate to test their safety. *At least there's fewer pollen or spore clouds up north.*

"What you think about, Syago?" Qosku asked as they ate one evening before sleep.

Startled slightly, the question reminded him of when Leyta asked it. Syago replied quietly, "My father... and mother. And the Razhod. What they're about, how to beat them. Sometimes I think of my old hobbies, sparring and tournaments. But this past year of fighting devils and Razhod, it's taken those loves and twisted them. Broken them." He'd thought of Leyta off and on in their journey, longing for her, to touch someone warm. He missed feeling wanted dreamt of their future, but also dreading it as well. There'd been so many opportunities for one of them to lose the other, he considered that maybe Deova was blessing him in spite of his cynical doubts.

"What about your father?" Qosku pressed.

"He left me an impressive legacy to follow," he said, shifting uncomfortably. "It was everything to me, then I discovered the legacy I aspired to wasn't as bright as it sounded. He wasn't the hero I'd thought. But then neither am I..."

"You're hero to me, Sy," Qosku said. "Impressive and kind. And brave and honest."

The words sunk in him, that innocence of ignorance of the same he'd held before. "I'm not the hero you think I am, Qos. I've done things. I talked with my father in that... cave, and feel better now. I have my own crimes to pay, so I can understand him, but now I have my own guilt and my own future to stress over. Now I wish I knew more about my mother, but it seems I can't."

"You are hero. I did bad things too. I killed my lo- my friend. And betrayed my twin sister who I think was captured by Razhod. Nobody fights back in this world and stays clean. I learned that from the marshes. This world is too dirty to stay clean."

He felt it true; he'd forgotten about Qosku's tragedy and expulsion. He still couldn't get over it, but he supposed these things took time. "I think you're right. I just wish we'd quit with the lies that make it harder to realize that. If we stopped idolizing a clean tale of ourselves, of our history, and instead looked at the dirt, maybe we'd be better prepared for it when it does come."

"What Alexandre think about?" Qosku asked after a pause.

"Justice, holiness. Philosophy and theology mostly. Right now he's watching the cultists for anything concerning, I think. He's also very placid and calm, kind of like you but more... philosophical? It amazes me how he can dwell on it so endlessly for centuries and not go insane."

A moment passed. Syago thought about how much more confident, Qosku had become. Less troubled and less awkward, in all much more comfortable in his own skin since Gravespire. No, since the marshes. With all that this younger boy had endured and defeated, he was undeniably the toughest and strongest person Syago knew.

"What about you, Qos? What's on your mind?"

After a moment's pause, Syago thought he might not answer when said, "My ancestors. And Lügos."

Syago didn't know Lügos very well despite his being from Tolgrym, and he wondered how close they'd been. He didn't want to press, so he asked, "Why your ancestors, didn't your parents abandon you?"

"Maybe, maybe not. All I remember is an attack on our yaqta and they sent me and my twin sister Chaska away. We ran with the other children and I took care of her. Many ran or died. All the mountains here can hide the ones that ran. I searched the ones we know. But maybe there is another, maybe the Razhod know it."

"Do you remember your family well?"

"No, I just... want them. I need family."

"Wait, you never told me you had a twin. What happened to her?"

"I not certain. I think she died in ritual sacrifice by the Razhod disciples. I think they turned her into gravespawn like Roza, or maybe just hypnotize her then use her for their rituals. I saw her captured at Tiakanawu, but don't know what happened since. If she's still alive I will free her."

Syago saw him fall quiet and knew the monster transformation would come soon, so he let the silence reconvene. He did notice the improvement in Qosku's command of Asturion and later complimented him on it.

The journey of the two warriors dragged on many days, days became weeks, far longer than they'd anticipated but Syago confirmed that there was no denying the accuracy of their pursuit. Qosku trusted him and didn't mind the journey hardly at all, in fact he enjoyed the tranquility of it, in between violent and disturbing struggles for survival. It reminded him of his journey to Castle Cantlgrym from the Unakan colonies, though now with a smaller party. They even passed by several Unakan ruins, whole villages and fortresses abandoned then overrun by plants. Now nearing a month, both felt weary from it all.

They soon left behind the vines and ferns for icy cliffs and full snow drifts as they traveled further north. The river was hard to paddle up, getting thinner and faster. Eventually it disappeared into another waterfall that fell from a vast glacier above. They docked their canoe where another, nicer one of wood sat and followed the footprints.[39]

"At least they don't know we're following them," Syago said as they climbed a thin faded staircase up to the top of the glacier.

"Or they know and lead us astray to traps," Qosku said.

"I doubt it, but good thinking," Syago muttered into the cold air. "Wait, maybe we should just turn back. We're not prepared for this and we've come far enough we could find their trail again with a better group... no, I can't leave Alexandre and they might still disappear."

He'd renewed this debate with himself numerous times, usually terminating it before Qosku could join in.

They used furs from small animals to patch together an outer coat that was still insufficient against the frigid wind but better than just a tunic and gambeson. The air thinned, making them breathe harder for less. And the Canker still sapped their food intake and strength. Qosku wasn't vomiting anymore but neither had his digestion fully recovered, leaving black bile in his stools and sometimes blood in a cough. All his hair was now gone, though his beast still retained some. But at least he was free of being male. He could even die happy, he felt. It was ones less weight to carry in their pursuit.

---

39 And I suppose you'll complain about the level of detail of this trail they walked. But you may need to walk it yourself. So it must be written down in as many places as possible to ensure it is not lost. In fact, I consider this account comparatively light in that regard.

The snowy trail eventually went up the side of a mountain, instead of winding around the peaks or through the valleys on the other side of the ridge. On the mountain sides, slippery rocky ridges pushed them into the glacier, which they evidently would have to cross. It was gorgeous and frightening, a field of ice tower ridges with shadowy crevices below. It looked impossible to traverse yet there was a path of bridges that marked an experienced and tested path, which made it easier.

Below they could see broken remains of older bridges. Qosku had heard from old Unakan friends that spoke Amoyara who supposedly knew from someone else that these glaciers moved. But that seemed impossible, however so did the Apugaka Mountains being alive.

They spent that night in a snow cave that trapped their heat and they were fortunate to face nothing worse than an occasional flurry of snow. The next morning they crossed the deep, dark chasms, slipping and nearly falling several times.

One particularly brutal attack from a pale ozor nearly took them off the ice ridges. Later, a standoff with a herd of odd goats. They stopped intermittently to admire the beauty of the view, rows of peaks and ridges, capped in white, spread out before them beneath gray skies. Qosku looked at Syago and realized for the first time how good Syago looked against that backdrop with his light brown skin and dark hair that blew gently in the chill breeze, like he belonged there. This made Qosku uncomfortable. He'd always thought Syago a good-looking person but never felt attracted to him and didn't want it to start now. Being alone together didn't help it, in fact was probably the cause of it, so he committed to avoid looking at him or being near him. At least with Syago, Qosku knew there was no chance of love unlike with Lüg. The need to keep hiding himself, his innerself, grew tiring but at least he succeeded, for the other option, of being open, he was not yet ready for. In fact, this entire trek was giving him too much time to think. When he wasn't reminiscing on his wounds, he'd be consulted by his memory ghosts, Lügos about how to care for his illness and Chaska about exploring more. She'd have loved this trek, turning over rocks or poking plants, even cutting them open to examine their insides. And he'd look at Syago or despair about his bleak and shrunken future. And his impending, ulcerative death.

And then Alexandre slowed to a stop during the day. Syago knew this to mean the holy sword had finally arrived at the disciples' destination.

Alexandre couldn't communicate. Something dulled the sense, visibly worrying Syago, who quickened his pace ahead of Qosku along the path, one small and old and hidden to all except those right on it.

They climbed steep, rough ridges, then walked warily over a snow-covered field of broken stones to a thin ridge that bridged one low peak to a higher one, minding the sheer cliffs of ice on either side of their narrow path. Qosku noticed porous rocks and obsidian in the path. Obsidian of the kind the Unaka collected from volcanoes. Once at the end of this thin ridge, it was a direct climb up a stony wall into the clouds. The ridge flattened and they saw through dense fog a cave, massive and dark. The edges of the cave were warped, but more carved out than the last cave of horrors they'd entered.

"If there was ever a good time to turn back for help," Syago said, "it is now."

Qosku smiled and stared at him. Would the debate run its course again? "And Alexandre?"

"He's... strong," Syago said, clearly unsure.

"Soulblades were destroyed before. And Razhod returned when they had opportunity."

"But if we go in, we'll likely not be able to come back out for help. It could be beyond us in there." Syago looked out into the fog that obscured what would've been a good view. Qosku only looked at Syago, having already made up his mind.

"Or it could be our only chance. They're weak now."

Syago stared at the fog, then nodded. "Death or victory. Let's go."

They ate the last of their food, then entered the cave, a long deep entrance that dropped like a ladder down a hole. All around, Qosku saw less of the smooth teeth common to most caverns and more of a twisted, bubbly aspect in between jagged protrusions. Qosku realized this was a dead volcano the Razhod had carved out a home in. They descended onto a staircase which opened down into a wide crack. Syago grabbed a torch from the wall and lit it. The crack, full of stony teeth and bulges, forced them to crawl, at one point on their bellies, down away from the last of the daylight. Their noisy movements only made them more nervous as they squeezed through, so vulnerable. But no monsters came, nor other people. Eventually the crack opened up before a large gate—like door. It took a good amount of strength to push them open, and complete forfeiture of stealth. But none hid behind any of the doors, only more darkness and more doors. They went down a spiraling stairway. They walked for what felt an agonizingly long time, tense, though long only because of the slow pace. Qosku noted the workmanship of the stone; he was no craftsman but he knew Unakan stonework when he saw it. Hope flickered in him, yet he would've remembered living in a cave if this had been the place he'd fled as a young child.

Eventually they saw the Unakans themselves. Small rooms off to the side of the hall, behind ragged curtains, held eyes that reflected the torchlight. Moving closer, the torch revealed their gaunt forms in iron chains, watching and waiting. Prisoners or slaves? Qosku spoke to them in Unakan, asking about their captivity, about the Razhod, about his family. They stared, nothing more.

The pair moved on and soon the civilization expanded, first into small mining and blacksmith operations that branched off of the stairway, all of the workers in iron or steel chains. They backed out before they could be seen and returned to the earlier prison cells. They soon realized that they weren't really prison cells, but living quarters. The chains only joined limbs of an individual and sometimes people to each other, but never to a wall. They increasingly ran the risk of getting reported. They didn't know that the ones earlier on wouldn't report them, but given their state and isolation, it seemed unlikely. So the two agreed to dress like the captives, rest and eat of the food, and sneak in on one of the unused chain sets they found. They could keep their belongings with them, as all carried sacks throughout.

They soon labored in another adjoining area sorting food. It was frogs and mushrooms, though Qosku had no idea where any of it had come from. Then they pretend-sorted rocks for ore until a taskmaster approached their area. This all gave them plenty of information, and no information. None understood his language, or none responded, and when they could be heard speaking, which was rare, it was unintelligible to Qosku. It was known that Unakan varied by region, but he'd hoped some of it would be similar. They saw no sign of the Razhod except occasional cultish markings on walls. Taskmasters would wear painted skulls or animal heads and they too were chained, but with smaller, nicer bronze manacles.

Syago focused on finding the disciples while Qosku focused on his parents and sister. He became increasingly certain he'd never see his parents again, but he would see Chaska. If she was turned into a gravespawn and made their captive that way, like Roza had been, he had to free her.

The two moved down the stairs to a network of porous chambers. Qosku saw none looking like his parents and knew that if they ever had been here, they'd be long dead by now.

After a few days of this, more started noticing them. Getting uncomfortable with the attention and what it might bring, they slipped into a room and saw sick Unakans sleeping on stone beds. No, more than sick. Their skin blotchy in places as if burned, and they coughed blood, like the Canker had done. A lone girl cared for them, her eyes milky white with blindness. They wore not chains, but rough cords. Seeing them, his own end, made Qosku vomit once again.

They left and went down to another room, slipping through heavy doors to find a small uncarved cavern with a massive dark pit. They looked around for another passage to sneak through but saw only a ledge on the far side of the pit, rising up and stretching out over it, like a waka altar. Then Qosku realized the pit moved, a swirling black lake of fog. He recognized the red stain on that altar and before he could turn away, in the middle of the dark whirlpool, opened up a single pale eye. He hurriedly grabbed Syago to bring him back to the door they'd come from.

They returned to the peopled cavern accepting that it was too late to hide. Qosku wanted to proclaim their freedom, ask for their support, but he knew better. Already alarm might be going out and that could only hasten it. But as they re-emerged, the people ignored them. Qosku noticed many on this level had smaller chains of brass or silver. The higher status taskmasters even had silk binding their hands. But all were bound. *A hierarchy of chains.*

Qosku asked one of them, "Your masters, where?"

Finally one pointed down a tunnel, and down they went. The maze of descending caverns and tunnels opened into yet bigger, more porous caverns and tunnels, each more full than the last with quiet activity. The silence horrified Qosku. Not even whispers. How could they be kept under such control?

As their search deepened, they finally glimpsed an Unakan disciple, notable for the robed clothing. From the shadow of a corner overhang, they looked for a room to hide. They watched the disciple go to a large stone door, where he bowed down. In the darkness before them dwelt the glowing red irises of a full Razhod. The man was a shadow except for those coal eyes. He took out a lever-key and unlocked the door before unrolling it, bidding his disciple to follow him in.

As they disappeared, Qosku pushed Syago to follow. Confused, Syago hesitated so Qosku rushed ahead with Syago in tow. They approached as the disciple vanished into the room. He slid the door shut, but Qosku grabbed Syago's boot knife and jammed the handle into the key hole, hoping to at least stop the lock. The door slid shut and the handle thankfully fit.

He looked back at Syago watching the slaves that had gathered in a multi-layered circle around a twisted effigy of blackwood they'd just placed there, and praying in dull voices, faces down. Qosku had seen them begin to gather when the disciple entered but hadn't paid it any attention, instead watching the disciple. He realized then that their faith in the Razhod controlled them, each wishing to become a disciple. Perhaps some feared them, but now devotion and ambition reigned.

Qosku tugged on Syago's arm to get help with the stone door while the slaves were distracted. They slid it only a crack then slipped through, weapons ready.

The small room was empty save for an altar in the middle and seven small red-curtained alcoves, all closed. After a quick survey of the room, they silently approached one curtain. Standing ready in front of it, they looked at each other and pulled it open to reveal a bald Unakan Razhod meditating in dark priestly robes. Glowing red-on-black eyes stared at them without really seeing anything. Qosku hit first with a quick kick to the man's head. The Razhod's reflexes almost caught the kick but not fast enough in the ambush, and he dropped back, unconscious and bleeding. Qosku looked at Syago quizzically as he stopped his sword thrust. "Why didn't you kill him?"

"I had a thought," Syago said while pulling out some old rope. "We need him to stay alive for a time so he doesn't die and tell the living Razhod about our intrusion. If we kill him, he wanders as a spirit; if he sleeps, he's trapped."

"Then we must move fast on the others in here. And with much care. He probably won't last the night with the blow I gave." Syago nodded and they checked the other curtains. Qosku wondered at the meditation and remembered hearing that Razhod don't sleep, instead they fall into a kind of trance. *But where did that rumor come from?*

The second man didn't even react when they opened the curtain on him, so deep was his trance.

They saw one more curtain left, but as they approached it, the curtain opened and the disciple they saw before came out. This disciple was a young Unakan girl. Chaska.

Qosku's heart stopped and she gasped, her hand flying to her mouth. For a moment they stared at each other, and Syago glanced between the two, confused.

"Chaska? Is that really you?"

She responded in the affirmative. He looked at Syago and asked in Asturion, "You see her also, truth?"

This appeared to confuse him more, but he nodded. Qosku hadn't been sure what had happened before, had wondered if it was a hallucination, but this confirmed that she was still alive as their captive.

"Qosku," she began. Her voice choking with emotion as she ran to embrace him. The hug was strong and tight. "I—oh, I missed you."

"I missed you too," he said, tears streaming down his face. "And I am so sorry about what I did to you."

"No, it was good. It made me strong. And it brought me here, to the Crimson Covenant."

His insides went cold. She wore the disciples robes, not chains. Nor was she a gravespawn under a spell. She was a mortal human and one of them, by choice. The embrace separated, and she regained composure, not shedding tears as he did. She looked so normal, but more confident. Devotion filled her thin brown eyes.

He gaped at her, speechless.

"Join us, Qosku. They'll have a place for you. It's difficult but so worth it in the end. And they can help you with... that problem."

"Chaska..." he began, breathless with disbelief. "I don't understand. Do you know who they are? What they've done? How can you do this?"

She jumped on the answer, as if she couldn't give it fast enough. "I know who they are better than you do. I live here. They're not fake or weak like everyone else, Being part of them is worth more than all the misery in the world. They've helped me so much. Stay with me, learn from them. They are the only truth." Her shining eyes pleaded.

"Chaska, how did you get like this? I just don't understand."

"They took me in after that terrible marriage, and they began instructing and training me to follow them." Her eyes looked up as she recited, "We say '*By pain we learn, on the stairs of agony do I ascend. Only the strongest survive, only the eternal thrive, in the great kingdom of chains.*' And it's all true." Her voice picked up speed in urgency. "Mortality doesn't matter. I even sacrificed someone for them, it's hard but good—"

He couldn't help his horrified expression. "No! Chaska, none of this is good. They're enemies of all life. And look at what slaves they made here."

Her voice dropped to a dismissive tone. "It is all fine. Our bonds make us appreciate our liberty and drive us to earn better chains, which are only manifest as physical chains in place of unseen bindings. Freedom is power and power is freedom. Embrace the power with me and be free!"

So much of her words resembled the dogmatic terminology and aphorisms memorized in the other religions and cults he'd seen. But in the end, they were all just different methods to embrace contradictions and delusions. And with such fervent conviction.

"This is all lies, Chaska!" He had to keep himself from yelling. "They've lied to you, put a spell on your mind."

"No, no. It's beautiful if you just open your eyes and heart to it and cast away the lies of society. Look, there's two meditating in here. When they wake I'll have them speak to you."

"Chaska, they're dead. I had to kill them so we can finish the coven and take the sword back."

Her face widened in horror. "No, no, NO! You shouldn't have done that. They accept impressive challenges but not murder. Qosku, maybe if you turn yourself in, you can serve out a sentence, but killing them in here, like that, is unforgivable."

His world was spinning. "What? What do you mean? You'd turn me in to die? Your twin?"

She went to the door. His own twin sister. Qosku tackled her, desperate to restrain her the way they had the others but perhaps bring her back. She resisted him, fought him. She was stronger and fiercer than he remembered. A fanatic's fury. And had evidently trained as well, but not as much as he. She tried everything possible to attack him. His eyes ablur with tears, and not wanting to hurt her, he struggled to pin her and she bashed her head against the ground trying to headbutt him. He grabbed for her again as she slipped free and she tripped, hitting her head on the altar with a sick crack. Then she was still, her blood on the altar. He looked in horror at what he'd done. This time her death *was* unmistakable, and his fault. Cradling her face, he closed her eyes and mouth and wept onto her.

Syago stood speechless, then solemn. He gave him a moment of mourning, then they wordlessly hid her body to rest in an alcove. She was still so beautiful, just as he remembered. And sincere in being happy to see him, such a wonderful person that they'd taken and ruined. He consoled himself that she'd found fulfillment here, whatever shape it took it'd been evident in her face. Just like her, to find something redeemable in a terrible thing.

Mentally, Qosku was already moving on from grieving to revenge. He'd been grieving his whole life, it seemed, and he was done with it. But it wasn't a revenge of anger so much as guilt, guilt that had faded at finding her alive then come crashing down again as he did finally kill her. He had to fix this. He needed to use the turmoil of violent, crushing emotions within, vent them, preferably on those most responsible for all this misery.

He took one last look at the sister he didn't know anymore and wiped his face, resiliently collecting himself. "Now what we do?" Qosku asked. "Where is Alexandre? Where do we go to kill these- these..."

"It's below, but not far."

"Then we take their disguises and get Alexandre. Or kill more Razhod." He spoke the idea as if it was obvious, or as if it was his decision. Either way Syago didn't disagree. They pulled the still unconscious bodies out and carefully removed their black robes. *These are the ones responsible for her death. It was they that trapped her mind.*

As they donned the robes over their travel-worn clothes, Syago said, "This is a doomed plan, we could be against an army here. We should go back."

"We can't, too many have seen us. They would chase or wait for our army to come here with a trap. We can't get army up this mountain, but we can sneak in and be quick. I am not leaving. I'm finishing them."

"I suppose you're right." Syago sighed. "I'd always dreamed of fighting the Razhod like my father did, or something like that, but now... Well, if we die at least I died as my own hero, as who I am."

Hearing Syago speak so freely stung Qosku. Dynfist teachings emphasized self-awareness and being present, being free of any bitterness. Being authentic and real. Syago had just done this by admitting his foolish dream, not weighed down by regrets. While Qosku hid inside, as a coward. Though he was no longer frustrated with his body, or identity, Qosku would die with a secret inside. Leyta's voice echoed in his head to fortify and strong forth. And Chaska, she'd have told him to be bold. He watched Syago fiddle with a belt on the dark garments inside the robe, tightly fitted over his chestplate. Why did he have to look good in black? The feeling wasn't strong, but it was there, a nagging fear. He was so tired of hiding it, fighting it.

Qosku opened his mouth several times before words finally came out. "Syago... th- there's something I need to tell you. Before we..." He'd almost said die but cut off. Worse, he'd committed himself to telling Syago by starting it.

Syago stopped and looked at him. Qosku continued before it could get harder, his eyes dropping to the ground. "I... I am different. I'm a-a t-twist. I mean, I don't like girls. It's- it's boys, but I'm not wanting to kiss anyone. I'm woman inside a man body. I don't know why, but it's who Qosku is. But really I'm just me and my training." Qosku hated that his Asturion worsened in his nervousness and that he couldn't keep his eyes on Syago. When he finally looked up, he saw Syago staring at him, first blankly, then in confusion. As understanding dawned, his expression grew dark and disgusted. It stayed in that form for what felt like an eternity to the uncomfortable Unakan, who fought to not tear up. His hands sweat and heart hammered against his chest.

Then Syago's expression softened and he seemed to look at him, really look at him, almost into him. He stretched out his hand for Qosku to clasp and said, "Okay. I mean it is different and I'm not sure how I feel about it, but we're still friends. If anything, it just means you're even tougher than I thought. I'm more than happy to protect you and fight beside you."

Qosku took his offered hand uncertainly, and they shook a single quick but firm pump of their arms then broke. They both stood and prepared their belongings. Qosku watched Syago out of the corner of his eye, his movements more stiff and guarded than usual. However, as Qosku changed openly, not afraid to look at his own naked self or be seen by Syago, both regained their usual casualness perhaps more consciously than normal. All of it Qosku appreciated with growing relief. Syago even looked Qosku in the eye with a nod as they moved the bodies. They then retreated to two separate alcoves to pray and eat before their hour of evil.

He felt a rush of relief at how the confession had gone, the acceptance he'd longed for leaving him whole. He'd accepted himself, gotten his body to accept him in turn, meeting him halfway. And now his friends had begun accepting him in his sphere as he'd always accepted them in their sphere. The circle was complete.

CHARITY THY NEIGHBOR
What passes when that power possesses?
It overflows, over the brim it goes
Never ending, it must be ever sending
Flood the cyclicity with that full felicity
Everywhere necessary a kindness antiquary
For minds ever under sorrow's grind
Need thy frothing friendship for which we fight
And as any story goes, tragedy follows
Then as love brings on, night's misery sings dawn
Be a cure to other's wrongs, a harmony to their songs
Be a light in someone's darkness, not a darkness in their light
For a tale's best plot is conflict enriched
Yet the consequence of conquest comforts not conscience
So then,
Bear forth love
That every story end
With some of beauty's mercy trend[40]

---

40 This unfortunately is our last poem from Qosku, thankfully not destroyed like many others and evidently written after his confession to Syago.

CHAPTER EIGHTEEN

JESTER'S CARNIVAL OF SAD MARVELS

Based on *Leyta's Journals,* cc bastica 450;
The Hunter's Parchments, cc bastica 406;

sometime in Hulior–29th of Septimosk, 247

Days and days passed into months and still the castle flew, floating over Lake Laomain. They waited and waited for help to come, for it all to end, but instead the terrifying charade continued on. Leyta assumed help had been sent, and uprisings had happened inside as well, but if so, she saw and heard none of it. Confined inside the gloomy halls, mostly the dungeons, Leyta only noticed the lifted state of the castle from the constant drain on her sentiments. Occasionally a window would give her an unusually strong breeze. It took from all of them, all the time, and wore her down physically and emotionally, more so than she was already from the Seeping and depression. It was a miracle she could move at all. She worried most about the youngest keepers, what was being done to them. If Leyta could get permission to see them, at least their endearing smiles, they would lift her despairing heart and she theirs.

On Leyta also fell the tasks of deep cleaning as Jester and his henchmen put everyone to work redecorating the floating Castle Cantlgrym. She'd been coerced into an extravagantly pretty dress that was too tight, restricting her movement. Their treatment was similar to what they had endured at Castle Covadongar, but now more cruel. Now there was no King or Queen to restrain Jester's "playfulness" or Knave's appetite.

This gave her some motivation. She rebelled internally against the great drain, unending in its oppressiveness. She fortified and refused to bow down, refused to be weakened. She ripped the dress for better mobility, but Jester ensured that it got stitched back up for her.

Bartolain de Barberochester lost his bed "privilege" and thus had no place he could sleep. He fell physically and mentally ill. He was offered the impossible task of putting together his own bed out of discarded materials, then none ever saw him again. Guilliom de Cantarchar lost food rights due to an "attitude" and became sick. He was told to go find his own food, and then he too disappeared. These were all clarified as "liberty that forbids none but encourages independent work."

Jester's nightly choir rehearsals were the biggest concern to her, knowing that power he had. Even those who didn't attend for the free supper could still hear his dyne-empowered song echoing throughout the castle halls. Halls with blood smeared over the floor as if something recently killed had been dragged through. She heard the eerie singing as she washed it.

She was miserable, not only for the burdens and things done to her, but also for having failed as their leader and not getting them out of it. And the Seeping still ate at her. She'd lost all her hair, which she hid with a wig and a small wimple. Her insides bled, leaving blood in a cough and runny black bile from the other end. All this thinned her out, making her gaunt as death. But she'd made it past the point where most died, and her illness had largely flattened out. Finding suitable herbs also brought relief. At least her skin wasn't ulcerating, yet. It felt more an early decay than the dripping death she saw drawn out in the old texts. It was such a great misery on top of everything that only her resolve to spite Jester and save the children carried her.

But she was not alone. Lil'iek found her on the third day, a welcome surprise. The Huntress crouched in front of her, behind a statue Leyta scrubbed blood splatter off of. "Lil'iek! I—"

She shushed her and looked back at the snoozing guard. "I can't get rid of him or they'll know I'm here. So we only have until he wakes. I flew in on a grim'iik, not important. What's important is that I think Knave finally stopped searching for me. I can't find the weapons or I would give you your scepter. And... have you seen Knave?"

"Wh- no." She looked at the guard who stirred.

"I'll come back," she said before hurrying off. Leyta rose to act as though she'd been speaking to another stray keeper further down the hall; nothing else would make sense and she was used to the blame.

Four days later, an agonizingly long time to be without speaking to her, Lil'iek returned. "I've lost them," she said, breathless from having knocked out the guard.

"What?"

"Guaran'upik and Machi'guenk, the two I brought with me, they haven't come back and I don't know what happened to them. I spend most of my time hiding from Knave. I've only seen Jester once, he nearly caught me. So they definitely know I'm here, and I'll be taking that guard with me. We can start picking them off—"

"What? No! I've gained that one's trust. He lets me get away with things."

"Leyta this isn't the time for sneaking extra privileges—"

"I'm not talking about privileges! I'm talking about a plan. I've started a new scepter and am looking for the others. I've narrowed down the possible locations."

"Leyta, we don't have time for that, he's powerful now. We have to move and my plan will protect you—"

"I don't want protection. I want to save my people. We have to overthrow him, not just take out his men. If he can raise the castle, he doesn't need them. They're a luxury. Just get me a scepter and information on him."

"Fine, but one more thing. Virgow is still here?"

Leyta rolled her eyes. "Now who's asking for privileges in a moment of crisis? Yes, he is here."

The Huntress stared at her. "All right, I'll come back when I have something more."

Lil'iek ran off again as the man awakened. Leyta didn't see her again but continued her work planning and preparing. She regretted arguing with Lil'iek, of course if she could dispatch the guards that might make an easier time of finding other things she needed, but she also feared that it would end the patience of her powerful enemy and any chance they had of real success. The Clown King would just as soon execute her.

Sixteen days went by without a word.

Then she found a single note. It read: *No fight, only flight.* This unhopeful note didn't help. Then she realized that she wasn't sure if Lil'iek had written it or if by *flight* it didn't mean simply jumping off the wall to one's death. As the agony of wait drew on, such a path sounded more and more sweet.

But the Clown King beat her to it. Six days later in the midst of scrubbing another blood smear in one of the lower hallways. The brute posted to monitor her suddenly informed her it was time for the festival. Having not been outside, or near anyone else, she had no idea what festival this was.

She dropped her red and brown rag and stood, wiping her bloody hands on the blue and white dress in a protest that now felt useless.

He brought her to the great hall. The walls and ceiling were lavishly decorated in the sorrowful royal colors of the Jester costume, drapes and streamers hung everywhere mismatching and asymmetrical. Candles burned on the walls and above the iron chandeliers. Bright sunlight also streamed in from the small windows above. A series of rugs patched together to resemble a red royalty carpet led up to the master's platform where sat an odd construct... A mountain of furniture and weapons, on top of which sat the Clown King in a single chair. She even noticed bones among them. It was the oddest throne Leyta had ever seen. She noticed ropes and chains passed behind it, evidently stabilizing it enough to hold the lean figure of Jester, who leaned thoughtfully against one hand.

There were no floor rushes, not even old stale ones. But the floor was clean regardless as people hadn't been entering from the outside. As she was brought up the hall, she noticed the animal heads held up on standing pikes, lining the patched carpet. Each of the heads, rat, gurow, bomog, malwolf, yama, baingoat, and so on, had the mouth peeled down into a frown. *So this is what the other keepers have been doing.*

"I have the best throne of all time," announced Jester loudly, for he had to yell in order to be heard from so high up. "What think ye, puny girl?"

"It certainly fits your ego," she said, speaking loud but not yelling.

"Friendemies, join us!" he shouted, and from the side entryways, Balgor, Virgow, Seumas, Bishopess Yanet, and Roberton, the new head friar. Each was followed by an idiot henchman or one of the two Fomorions. Leyta guessed the two giants to be either outcasts from their clans or still under the Clown King's spell. Each of the masters of the castle wore strange combinations of costumes clearly intended to appear humiliating. Virgow wore a dress akin to Leyta's, Balgor wore barbarian clothing, ill-suited to the scholar, Roberton wore the pomp of a royal court attendant. Bishopess Yanet wore dancer's clothes, tight and revealing on her aging, holy figure. Seumas had the guise of a prison taskmaster and executioner, dark work pants and belt over his heavy body and iron studs on the belt. A hood obscured his face and, though not being a warrior, an axe hung at his side next to the whip and chain.

Then she realized with a pang of horror that three of the guards had been keepers. She'd both taught and disciplined each of them and guessed this turn to the enemy's side was an effect of the constant exposure to Jester's choir. He'd molded their young, emotional minds to be complicit if not fully bought in. Or was it an act? Yet they seemed to enjoy prodding the masters along. *No sign of Lil'iek or her companions, which could be good or bad.*

They came to stand by her, looking each other over and evaluating the room. Some began to whisper but Jester's overly loud throat-clearing interrupted them. "We musn't forget our Lady that is Dead." He raised his hand lazily and one of the curtains fluttered. Roza emerged from it, moving stiffly to stand beside them. Leyta was surprised to see her but then realized of course Roza would come to their aid, or try to. Freed from the Razhod, she must've fallen under Jester's power. "Goodie, you're all finally here and ready to go! First, we shall begin with a little demonstration, a joke or game, if you will follow me."

He jumped from the chair to grab a drapery and slide down it, tearing it slightly. He landed softly in front of Leyta, then strode to an adjoining door. In front of the door hung two bodies. The limbs were bent and twisted at odd angles, broken into eerie designs, bone splinters protruding, with excrement and urine already leaking out at the bottom among the blood and drying.

The naked and broken bodies of Guaran'upik and Machi'guenk brought tears to her eyes. She'd never really known them, but she felt for Lil'iek and all of the awful things the Clown King had done. He stopped in between them and mused, "I almost forgot about these two. They didn't like the games I wanted to play, so they killed themselves. Some people can't handle being sad."

"Foda you—" She cut off at a glare from his expressionless, faceless face.

He abruptly turned, and guards pushed her to follow. He led them up a stairwell to a door that hadn't been there before. She noticed the wall had been opened by dyne, and the proceeding staircase, on the outside of the castle, also placed by dyne. Winds tore at them as they ascended to the roof. She'd only been up here once when she'd first arrived and wanted to do some forbidden exploring. The pointless emptiness of it had dulled her excitement. But now, all of the masters and their watchers gathered to look out across the great expanse that had been the Kingdom Republic of Nevermore.

Once everyone stood on the roof, Leyta realized there was a near equal number of them, foe to foe. The Clown King turned to face them, the dydatris still hanging from his neck. She suspected the odds were not as good as they looked. She understood the use of the relic as his scepter, a foci for an under-experienced dynast. The floating castle functioned more as an archemical work, being embued with dyne, his specialty.

He stretched out his arms. "What sad fun?! Such a pretty day, and I'm going to ruin it as I do everything. See Voium out there, our closest neighbor, competing with the castle for intellectual ego? Remember the recent trials of Voium. First, a massacre. Second, overrun by your military. And third, tainted by a Razhod curse. And fourth, my doll's captivity. It's a running joke, one that I must continue."

He held up the dydatris, and the top of the main castle tower burst into flame. The tower fire went from yellow to white and, in a massive surge of energy, drained from Leyta and the others with such force they fell to their knees. She watched in shock as the fire shot from the tower in a dense stream to the distant Voium. The stream pressed for a moment, tearing at her eyes, ears, and heart. She closed her eyes and plugged her ears until it faded. Jester lowered his arms slowly, breathing heavily. In far distance, the city fire raged. Leyta thought of who might be there: elementists and priestesses were supposed to go in and work on cleansing it of the Seeping, but other than them, it was likely still empty.

She also felt the sting of its loss as an important symbol and resource for the kingdom, and her personally, now dead forever. Bishopess Yanet had fainted, and Seumas clutched his chest in pain. Above them, the main tower, having served as fuel, stood as a charred skeleton of its former magnificence, the roof completely gone.

"What?" asked the Clown King. "You don't like my contribution to the running joke of Voium? WHY AREN'T YOU LAUGHING?!" His voice took on power, enhanced beyond his normal bounds with the relic, to something that thundered through them, causing Leyta to bend over and clutch the ground in delirium. "Nobody ever likes my anti-jokes. What do you think you're doing?!" he snapped at Roberton and Balgor, who were tending to Seumas and Yanet. Yanet sat up, awake and apparently fine, but Seumas still clutched his chest.

"Leave them be, he's hurt and needs help," Leyta shouted at him. "If you had the decency and nobility you pretend to, you would allow it or help him yourself."

He walked up to her before she'd finished, grabbed her by the front of her dress, and dragged her to the edge. She resisted, but his strength and dexterity greatly outmatched her. As he held her over the edge, she looked straight at his "face," the paint renewed and still disturbingly ridiculous beneath his fake crown.

"Will you be telling me what to do now?"

"No," she said carefully, wanting to protest but also not wanting to fall. The castle grounds below filled with keepers emerging to see the noise. She also saw observers peeking out of windows, and felt herself slip in his ironhard grip. With great care and deliberation she spoke, "But you were going to tell them what to do as well. You must play by the rule also or we won't either."

At this, that repulsive head tilted slightly. "Now you're getting the idea." He roughly placed her back on the roof and walked back to the stairwell. As he passed Seumas, he pulled out a small vial and shoved it into Balgor's hand. "Give this to him, it will cure the ailment. Now let us return and resume the court."

The guards shoved and prodded them to follow. Leyta went first and looked at Balgor, who looked at the vial with a frown. His guard jabbed at him with a halberd and he ignored it, bleeding. She returned to the new throne room to find Jester using a metal shield as a platform to levitate himself back up to the throne seat. The ease with which he controlled the metal sparked envy in her. The rest of the leaders filed in, Balgor and Roberton held up Seumas, who appeared relieved of his heart pain but still weak. As the Clown King resumed his seat high above them, keepers filed into the room. The entire castle was present.

"Welcome, one and none," said Jester, spreading his arms out. "We have much to discuss before our enjoyment of the sad things of our new non-kingdom. First, the rejoining of our two friends, formerly known as King and Queen, but which we will now dub Fire and Ice!"

Loud bursts of fire and darkfire drew everyone's attention to two statues on either side of the throne. Leyta hadn't noticed the gargoyles before, taken from the castle's flying buttresses outside. The gargoyles had symbols painted all over them, the same symbols visible on the King and Queen dolls. She understood, the spirits that had inhabited those dolls now took the statues as their surface anchors. The gargoyles slid forward, stone grinding on stone, to place them just in front of the throne as protection.

"And now for the return of Knave!" Jester shouted as Knave flew above them, his great wings flapping as it perched on the chandelier, eerie girl's face peering down at them. "Now let the inaugural tea party-feast begin!"

As people moved to assume seats, eyes turned to Seumas, now convulsing on the floor with his face turning purple.

"What did you do to him?!" Leyta yelled, running to his side as Balgor knelt over him grimly.

"I didn't do anything," said Jester. "You gave him the poison."

"WHAT?!" Balgor roared. "You said it would cure his illness!"

"And you believed me. But I did tell the truth, it did cure the ailment and now it's doing something else."

"YOU LYING—" Balgor strode toward the throne but cut off when instead of confronting him the other two Fomorion giants simply stepped aside. A plume of darkfire popped in his face. He brushed it away, glaring at the two gargoyles.

"Anything else, fat man?" asked the Clown King. "No? Good, resume your seats."

The loud splatter of Seumas vomiting black brought attention back to the sick one. Leyta ran her hands over him. "Will you at least let an apothecary retrieve herbs so we can ease his pain?"

"Of course nobody is stopping you," said Jester, with the same threatening air implied in all pledges of freedom. "But you won't be able to stop his pain, I recall this being a strong dose."

"What is it?" she asked, looking down at Seumas, whose skin grew more and more purple. Her own stomach churned, reminded of her Seeping sickness and what it might have in store for her. "What's happening to him?"

"I actually don't know," said the Clown King as he leaned forward in his seat. "It's a new mix, untried. I put in everything I had left, added a little bit of dyne and poof, mystery mix curative. It did the base function, curing his heart, but what comes next is a surprise even to me. Isn't this fun?!"[41]

The old master writhed on the floor, eyes white and mouth foaming. She glared at Jester, then at the guards, daring them to do something to stop her from running for the herbs. She knew little about herbology, but

---

41 I can't find any solid theory on what this might be and can only conclude that something from Knave, like a drop of blood, was mixed in. Body archemy works so rarely with or without demon parts, it is effectively a dead study.

it didn't matter. The guards, Knave, and Jester were all in that room and this left her the opportunity to pry at what she believed a location of her scepter while gathering the herbs. She made for the storeroom, then turned instead for Roza's old quarters, still untouched since the battle as far as she knew. Entering, she stifled her nose against the confined smell of dead animals, long cleaned up but still a trace.

She found a number of strange things but no scepter. She knew the one hidden in her own room was already gone and this room held no herbal medicine either. Roza hadn't needed any as a gravespawn. She turned to leave when Lil'iek suddenly appeared at the door, again panting from a hard run.

"You look like you've been having fun," Leyta said, looking at a bandaged gash on her arm.

She turned, following Leyta to the storeroom. "Not really, a lot of hiding and waiting in uncomfortable places."

"Your two—"

"I know," Lil'iek said softly with a hint of anger.

"Lil'iek, your plan," she said. "We have to start it now. We have to start something."

"Agreed, but yours isn't lost either." Lil'iek held up Leyta's scepter. The dynast gasped and ran to it. "Good to see I picked the right one, I wasn't sure. Your guard led me to a stockpile of weapons and other things too, but since I couldn't carry them all with me, they'll have moved them by now. I'm surprised he didn't burn them."

"Something's happening to Seumas, I don't know what to do."

"I doubt we can do anything, it's late in the poison and he's old. Maybe if you can get the relic; it's powerful."

"Do you think if we start a fight in the throne room that we'll get enough support from the rest?"

"Yes, but without weapons... they might just be in the way. And I suspect he's not laid out all his cards yet. The main thing is he has control of the field right now. We have to change that, introduce our own element he can't control or predict. Otherwise it will be a massacre."

"Like what?"

Lil'iek shook her head, then pulled some herb pouches out of her sack. "Take these for Seumas, or anyone else. I'll follow you and watch. As soon as you start something, I'll move. Or if I see an opportunity, I'll start and you take it, we'll go from there. It's all we have right now."

She nodded and they left, she stepped over the brute who'd followed her, dead from Lil'iek's stealthy knife to the throat. His absence wouldn't be noted for some time, though Leyta felt a pit in her stomach for the man. He'd been one of the few to stay on with Jester, easily manipulated, and seemed like a genuinely decent person. But Lil'iek either didn't care or didn't see another way. At least the man was now free. Leyta stuffed the scepter under her dress by tying it to her leg and returned to the throne room in a hurry. She grabbed several herbs together in a handful to put in a tea.

But on arrival she found she was indeed too late. Seumas, or what had been Seumas, now lurched as a creature with arms as tentacles and long fangs jutting awkwardly from his mouth. His eyes were bulged and veiny, changing to darker colors. His entire form grew, purple and covered in veins. He foamed at the mouth as people backed away. After staring in horror and deep sorrow, Leyta had the mind to stuff the herbs back into the pouch as she backed out of reach from his writhing tentacles. He didn't appear to be grabbing at anything in particular, just clawing at the general area. Whatever her Seeping sickness would do to her, it was not this.

"Tea-Dinner is served," announced the Clown King. "The rest of you should really take your seats before something happens to your plate." Those standing reluctantly moved to the tables. All except Leyta, anger and sadness swelling in her as she watched the creature in its evident misery.

"YOU'RE A MONSTER! YOU'RE EVIL!" she screamed up at him, tempted to draw her hidden scepter there but the awareness of the statues pointed at her reminded better.

"That's 'you're evil, King-Queen-Jester-Knight' to you," said the Clown King. "And of course I am. Isn't that what King and Queen told you when they were here? They talked of their noble work but warned you of me. Well now you've removed the nobility and left the clown to take over. What did you expect? More candy and laughs? It's all downstairs from here, young missy. Now sit."

"You've betrayed your- your creeds. All that you pledged, freeing us. You haven't freed anything but instead wrapped it up in your own twisted sense of control."

"I control nothing, only the laws of survival do. Strength, sweetheart, that's what wins in the end. Rulers only make you pretend they aren't just another gang like me. At least in my case, I'm not a gang-ruler with silly laws. Instead I'm a force of nature that reacts as any force does to opposition." His voice adopted a polite, intellectual tone as if in a deep debate, irritating her further.

She breathed deep before speaking. "If that is true, then it is our choice, our will to depose them and live leaderless. A truly free society would be willful and voluntary, not forced. Your violence has made you just as bad."

"I only embody what society has done to me. You have brought me on yourselves. You will do so personally, again, if you do not sit and partake your tea."

Fuming, breathing, she walked to a seat near the front of the tables.

Lil'iek followed Leyta back to the greathall, then watched the interaction from the shadows. There was one other door to enter the hall, but it too was visible. As she pondered her options, she felt a familiar cold touch her neck. It wasn't a knife, however, but the tail-blade of Knave. He, it, hung from a tapestry behind her, leering with child eyes.

Chills shot through her. It hissed then pressed her toward the greathall. Once she entered, Jester's joyful clapping was drowned out by the pounding in her ears. Two things struck her: the loss of her advantage in the face of certain death, and being pushed toward the back end of the table near Virgow, who sat in some kind of dress.

He was burned all over. This shocked her, but it shouldn't have. He had been the other burn spot, pulled out by his nearby soldiers. She saw also that the Seeping had taken a heavy toll on him. She'd hoped to find him in her time lurking through the castle but hadn't been able to, had suspected he'd been below in the catacombs where she'd not reached. Maybe once the chaos started, she could slip a blade into him. But before she could meet his eye, she was turned by Knave to face the throne.

"—to join us for our tea-party-dinner-feast? We're serving justice. Perhaps you'd like an opportunity to taste it now, as I hear you've a hankering for burnt meat." Several gasped as a guard pulled Virgow to his feet, put the cane in his hand, and shoved him toward her. Jester continued, "This one should taste like what you had before as they were cooked together."

Seeing him wince and struggle to walk gave her pleasure inside. But as he halted before her, his bad leg wobbled and dropped him to his knees. With a grimace and great, slow effort, he rose back to his feet with the help of his cane.

"I hear crutches work better than canes," she said. "My dead husband told me as much. Did you know him? Ever meet him?"

The marred Unakan veteran gave no answer, stared at her with his usual stoic mask. She saw through it, though. Between those wrinkles, burn patches, gleaming sweat, and remaining eye, and absurd costume, he was tired. So very worn out he'd not be disappointed at all if death came, for it had already come many times only to pass him over for someone else. That he was still alive at all was the most incredible thing. Yet his ego and sense of performative toughness couldn't let onto any of this. His commitment to dying an unwavering war hero and martyr, void of any guilt or shame, were the only things carrying him now. The act itself was costing him tremendously.

"Did you kill him?" she asked.

"No, he burned us both. He attacked me."

"Attacked you because you murdered the rest of us at Tiakanawu, then blocked us from restitution. There are many at fault for our struggles, but we didn't expect to find enemies among friends."

He gave no response to this and she stopped short of further condemning him, for she realized she couldn't kill him. Not only would killing him be the reward he wanted, the Asturions watching wouldn't understand it, even after what she'd just revealed to them. If she killed him, they'd see only another vengeful, cruel Kimoc striking down an ailing old war hero. But letting him live? A Kimoc demonstrating considerable restraint would leave an unforgettable impression. Or not, probably not. They might not even survive to tell the tale.

Better to let him suffer a little more. Plus this anger was killing her, it was time to let it go. "But I want nothing more from you. You are now as ugly outside as on the inside, that is justice enough for me."

A brief pause, then Jester began a slow clap that echoed through the hall. She expected him to kill one of them anyways, but he simply had her resume a seat beside Leyta. Virgow made his way back, where he seemed to shrink into his chair like a withered leaf.

The dishes and trenchers arrived soon after Lil'iek and Virgow sat back down, and Leyta initially felt relief in that the darkelan season meant no animated meat until she saw that the meat was still alive. A white rabbit pinned alive to its plate set right in front of her. Also in front of her was a large bowl of beetles, a jar of ants, and a glass jar of spiders among others along the lengthy table. She doubted whether all of it was truly edible, though she knew which parts of the insects were. Her parents enjoyed fried insects, being wealthy, but less of the spiders. They were edible only in the abdomen, a fact she knew from her friends and a rough darkelan at Cantlgrym years ago. She didn't dare try the tea either. She looked at the other keepers wondering how far under his spell they might be, but most looked as unhappy with the setup as she felt.

Knave flew from his high perch and walked along the table, glaring at each of the keepers while picking at the "food." She took comfort in that his child's head didn't resemble anyone she'd known.

Her mind returned to Seumas, who interrupted the conversations of disgust with a loud crack. He'd risen from his spot on the floor to bite at the table with his new maw of long fangs. The executioner costume had completely broken off and he looked like a demon. A tentacle slapped the pinned rabbit to himself, and he gnawed on the head, killing it with a wet crunch.

"Oh, Seumas wants to join you," said Jester. "But those manners will need improvement. Diegon!" The henchman presumably named Diegon moved up and prodded it with a spear. Surprisingly quick, it snapped the spear away and took hold of Diegon. The man yelled as it pulled him to the floor. Out of sight below the table, he screamed and thrashed as the creature snarled and gargled. Flecks of blood flew up. Again Jester announced, "You know what he needs? A playmate. In any case, an army has gathered around the lake and that won't do. Osmos, come. Bring me another friend from the Abyss to be our new Knight!"

The name Osmos brought a hushed chill throughout the room. Dirt etched a circle on the floor in front of the throne. Several people crossed themselves, but Leyta only clenched her eyes shut against what she knew would be another terrifying experience. She peeled them open as noise filled the room. Candles on the walls flickered and plateware rattled and shivered. Quickly the marks finished on the floor, glowed, and the loud thud of Osmos's appearance echoed in the hall and jolted the table. The gate's immensity reached high and wide between table and throne, a tall trapezoidal frame with statues. Great stone doors opened first to utter blackness. Then a multitude of human arms reached out, stretching inhuman lengths, to grab the nearest living thing, a Fomorion giant. The bearded cyclops roared in defiance, beating at the comparatively thin arms, but they held and bent like wet cloth.

The ohancanu's roars turned shrill as the arms dragged it into the darkness. Leyta looked at the children along the table who gaped in terror, wishing they could look away. Jester gave a cry about it taking the ohancanu instead of one of the people but the Door of Infinite Spaces gave no heed and didn't need to. The giant clutched at one of the statues on the dais, but soon his hands peeled away and he vanished into the void. The stone doors slammed shut.

On the Clown King's request, the central door eye opened and turned its door hinges again, sliding them open to reveal an arctic ocean, dark and cold. The Bottomless Abyss. It was a long time of cold nothing, then suddenly a massive, spidery crustacean of spiny shell emerged dripping water, scratching over the floor on eight long legs, ridged and bladelike. From the jagged carapace bulk waved six antennae, bulbous and vacuous black eyes swiveled. Massive sharp pincer claws all protruded from a spiky shell of dull blue and oil black. The mouth was several ridges of jagged teeth. It had a second mouth above that, one that looked humanoid. Leyta realized one claw, the larger one, also had a mouth at its juncture.

The demon, a destitution, foamed from its razor-ridged mouth as it eased into the room. From the doorway also reached a thick flaplike tentacle lined with frills and little feeler nobs sticking out, the rest of its bizarre form swirled just inside the doorway. The insanity grabbed at the destitution's leg, either trying to eat it or trade places but the destitution avoided it and the insanity retreated back through the door. The demon's humanish mouth slobbered a single word, *"Give."*

"Take one of the boys," said Jester casually. The destitution rushed at Trebor de Moray, who sat at the end of the table. Before the warrior could flee, the larger claw swung down with a smash against the table. The table's items bounced and flew. The pincer clamped down on Trebor and lifted him up with his chair. Trebor's face was screaming but there was no sound in his suffocation. Leyta heard a snapping sound, unsure if it was the chair or the young man's spine, or both. Both chair and Trebor went in to the creature's open maw with a squishy crunch. The creature gurgled in delight.

"Now my new, good friend," began Jester. "We have need—"

But the destitution wasn't done. It snapped a claw at another young girl, who ran screaming. Unable to watch any more, Leyta drew her scepter. Her rage then ignited lightning around its head, but it barely noticed. The claw snatched Mariaciela and drew her into its maw as well. Jester was screaming for the demon to stop but it only seemed to quicken its ravenous pace, reaching for another girl before even finishing the second. The girl escaped the claw, her dress tearing on its ridge, but one of the eight legs snapped down, pinning her to the floor right next to Leyta in a splat of blood. Lil'iek ran past it, cutting with her hellknife. With the lightning not doing enough, Leyta switched to fire, using the candles. Claws reached for another, and another against the fleeing children while the destitution feasted and even began chewing on the table itself. The Clown King shouted for control behind the looming gate.

Its shell protected it too much from dyne. Backing away, Leyta had an impulse that was both dangerous and brilliant. She shouted, "Osmos bring me a portal to the Halls of Celos, a soldier of Heaven." Osmos turned its gate eye.

"No. Osmos you're dismissed," snapped Jester.

"*The order stands,*" Osmos said, opening its eye again.

"What?! But 'tis I that called you!"

"*There is already a standing request from that other side,*" Osmos said as the gate swung open to a world too bright to see into.

A shining golden spear shot out and smashed into the demon. No, not a spear but an eight-winged creature like the one she'd seen before, but this one had shining gold feathers instead of white. It spun back from the demon as its warm radiance filled the hall. Its voice thundered. "DEMONS AND DEVILS SHALL NOT RUIN THIS WORLD SO LONG AS BUT ONE ANGEL OF HEAVEN STANDS AGAINST." The beautiful sheen hurt Leyta's eyes, and she couldn't look at it, couldn't even see it, but also couldn't look away. Eyes opened along its wings, and this time she saw through the mass of gleaming feathers into its center. It had no body, just an area the wings joined and, somehow in the center of its conjoined wings, was a wide mouth. The angel struck at the demon with metallic feathers.

The great hall exploded into commotion, starting with the crashing of the table. Food and wood splinters flew everywhere, people ran, and Leyta sprung from her spot with scepter in hand. The Clown King shrieked for containment of the angel, and the guards ran about in the confusion. Jester yelled, "STOP!" and a concussive blast of wind threw everyone and everything back. But instead of stopping or even slowing, the frantic riot continued. The horrifying maw of fangs in the center of such a glorious angel hissed, then it pounced on the demon, biting its leg with a juicy crunch.

Leyta tore her gaze away and made for the throne, relying on the chaos to provide cover. The spiny bulk of the destitution rolled into her path with the bizarre angel on top, his warcalls of holy justice echoing over its growling. The angel rose, evading the destitution's acid foam while shooting rays from the wing-eyes at the shell. The shell deflected them, and Leyta watched in horror as one incinerated a boy right in front of her. She shouted at the diligence, its known soldier rank of Heaven, to stop. But it continued shooting, its blade-like wings sliced through another boy, and the maw continued snapping. "THE GLORY OF GOD IS NECESSARY AND YOUR MORTALITY IS NOT."

Leyta almost screamed at him. *What have I done? I've made it worse by calling the angel down.* Diligence and destitution circled each other, slick tongues from both lashed out, then the two suddenly shifted as Roza flew in with a booming punch to the angel, following the Clown King's orders.

It spiraled away into a pillar, crashing through it, and the demon righted itself. The destitution pinned Roza to the ground with one of its legs, skewering her on it. Leyta readied her scepter when Knave suddenly pounced on her, raking claws and snapping barbed tail. Claws hit her forearm as she avoided the more lethal tail, but it was too quick. The girl-face cackled then growled, eyes bleeding. It paused, face twitching. Leyta shoved it off and scrambled away. The agony pursued her through the mayhem. It pounced again, taking her down to the floor. She pushed her hand against the child's face, smearing the blood.

Then her struggle was abruptly halted as Osmos, all but forgotten in the madness, opened its doors once again. This time to the dark swirling

clouds of the Hellpits. Knave screeched frantically, flapping its wings, but something unseen pulled it toward the cosmic doorway where shadows moved. Jester screamed for the gate to close and leave. The demon's tail whipped forward, sickle blade narrowly missing her chest, but the bony cord of it wrapped around her arm, dragging her with it.

"But why that demon?" shouted Jester.

"*The Abyss owes the Pits,*" Osmos said. "*And this one does not belong here.*"

Both Leyta and Knave screamed as they slid along the floor toward the gate. She attacked Knave as he flapped and scratched at the ground, but she couldn't break his hold. Giant furry claws reached out of the haze for them both. Then Lil'iek was there, severing the tail with a single cut of her hellknife. Knave flew into the waiting furry arms within the gate. The Clown King screamed, "Knave, NO!" Then lightning rolled over the entire room, brought on by his fury and use of the relic. The possessed gargoyles also released jets of fire and darkfire, burning and freezing the broken furniture in front.

The lightning charge ended, leaving Leyta and Lil'iek panting on the floor, numb and nauseous. Blood gushed from her nose, and Lil'iek vomited. The gate, thankfully and finally, vanished but left the two otherworlders to continue their monstrous battle atop everyone else. Leyta could barely take it all in, much less map out a way to resolve it or rescue her people. The people slowly resumed their panicked fight as Seumas terrorized them, the other masters worked to contain him while also fending off the remaining henchmen with improvised weapons. The demon and angel smashed through a stone pillar and into the throne tower. The loud crash brought the stack of furniture tumbling down on the eternal foes. Jester did not fall, but instead seemed to vanish. Leyta and Lil'iek searched for him among the curtained ceiling as demonic acid and angelic light burned away the curtains and nearly walked into the path of the gargoyles, torch jets almost catching them. Then the two women had to back away as the destitution barreled toward them with the diligence in its vice grip. Both had severe wounds by now, strange blood oozing and flying; Roza's corpse body was still stuck through by one of the pointed legs. They hit the shattered table again as Leyta and Lil'iek dove aside.

Unable to find Jester, Leyta raised her scepter and put all her anger over Seumas into lightning on the demon. The sparks crackled around it but the destitution acted as if it were nothing. The demon shifted his bulk, ignoring the burning of its eyes and feelers, and grabbed the angel wings with its pincers, ripping them off. The angel's ray attacks abruptly stopped as the giant pincer tore two more wings, then shredded them further.

Strengthening her hate with the memory of Jester's atrocities, Leyta hit the demon with that lightning and then fire from the area. *At least all my power has finally returned, even if it's still not enough.* The destitution turned to her, then to Lil'iek, who darted between its legs, slicing at one with the hellknife.

Before Leyta could focus a new attack in Lil'iek's support, Jester swung down on a drape and kicked her in the side, "Hiyah!" knocking her to the floor. He casually dropped a flask that burst into flame, her clothes catching. But she was ready, a hard swipe of the scepter moved all the fire off of her and at the Clown King, her quick timing saving her from the burns. He didn't scream as he caught fire, didn't make a sound, but instead held up the relic, and the fire strengthened. Unharmed, he walked to her. She got to her feet, meeting him face to faceless.

"Isn't this madness fun?" rasped Jester, opening his arms as if for a hug. "Burn with me."

"No," she said, and kicked him in the chest. He stumbled back into the fast approaching tentacles of Seumas. They latched onto his arms as she moved for a better angle. The tentacles burned with the fire, and Seumas shrieked but held, pulling him in. The Clown King fought the pull, burning his foe and winning. Leyta couldn't take control of his flames, so she moved around to the side and pushed all the anger she felt for Jester into the air. The wind blew the fire away from Seumas. Jester fought it with the relic, canceling her wind. The weakening of the fire around the Clown King's body allowed Seumas to pull him in and sink its fangs into his shoulder. He ceased the fire and sighed deeply. "At last it ends. This miserable tale, my joke life. Remember me with pain, will you?"

"I'll do my best not to remember you at all," she said through gritted teeth as she moved fire to aid Lil'iek in confronting the destitution. Seumas's jaws stayed slurping.

"Ah, that's the spite I always enjoyed in you. Perhaps you will make the change I needed as a boy after all." Then Jester died, And Seumas halted his horrendous bloodsucking long enough for a second, bigger bite that broke bones, swallowing his human flesh.

Her body suddenly felt a surge of sentiments and everything in the room began floating, a strange sensation but with terrifying implications. *The dydatris!* She reached into Seumas's yawning mouth and grabbed the relic on Jester's chest, ripping it off just before he clamped down. She immediately willed the falling castle to stop and everything slammed back onto the ground, sentiments drained again. As stars flashed from the blow, things lifted again, and this time she halted it slower. She struggled to balance her own sentiments into those around her. But with her own sentiments fading back to the emptiness she'd had before, she found it harder to guide the relic. Even by using others' sentiments, she needed to put in her own. She did what she could with increasing nausea.

The hall calmed slightly, many people had left, several still fought the guards or each other, and the demon still came at Lil'iek in between the lurches. Leyta wanted to hit the destitution with something but couldn't lose focus on the castle. Seumas, however, finished the clown corpse and lunged at the rival aquatic demon. His burnt tentacles wrapped against its wounded legs but the small claw thrust in, stabbing and clutching the smaller creature. Seumas gurgled in pain, then stopped as the destitution tore it apart, and Roza, free of Jester's spell, worked to stop the remaining legs while Lil'iek was able to move in and finish it, carving out its main carapace, while Leyta lowered the castle. Waves of nausea rolled, her sentiments burning out.

The conflict finally over, she focused on easing the castle back to the ground. Tipping and weaving, she channeled her sentiments and those of the world through it to ease the great rock back down into the lake. So great was the effort that she collapsed as the island castle settled back down, uneven and ungentle, but finally safe. She passed out and slept feverishly for days after.

CHAPTER NINETEEN

THE DOOM BELL CALLS

Based on *Annals of Syago,* cc bastica 399;

sometime in late Huniod, 247

Syago and Qosku had finished their brief respite when a deep thrumming sound began, faintly audible. It sounded like a large bell tolling assembly. Qosku looked like he'd had a good cry. Syago didn't blame him, but had his own worries about his devil arm. The tingling spread throughout his whole body, the hunger and anger were more ever-present. In the absence of the Judgment Sword, it had sped up whatever change it was enacting. He felt the scaly skin all across his chest and down his side. It could have his whole torso by now, he was scared to look. Distant Alexandre didn't like this prospect either, but was more affronted by the bell and its dark surroundings.

Wordlessly they completed their disguises with weapons ready beneath, and walked out the rolling stone door. A throng of Unakan were walking toward the bell's toll. The civilian-slaves in their dark rags and various types of chains, and the disciples in dark robes.

They saw the hooded figure of a Razhod emerging from another doorway down the hall. Syago saw inside a dense library of old books and a stand in the center with a single black tome, as if enshrined.[42]

The two heroes fell in line until they arrived at a giant cavern and saw a large bronze bell, a crack through it, being rung. A steady, heavy

---

42 Though a few references to this book exists, its title, author, and contents remain entirely unknown.

thrumming. Oddly, it appeared to have no effect on the porous cavern it-self. Perhaps it was built well enough or dyne had been used to prevent it from causing damage. It did have an effect on Syago: his devil side tingled, thrilled by it and eager too. He realized then that it'd subtly affected his cognition, making him want to go toward it just as it'd made him more eager to fight, quick to anger, and always hungry. It was at home here.

Stalactites and stalagmites jutted throughout the entirety of the mas-sive cavern like teeth on the inside of carnivorous maw gloomily lit by candles. Everywhere candles. But the walls were more of the same bubbly stretches of holes. The people of the mining empire flowed to platforms that surrounded a central colossal stalactite that jutted down over a dark chasm across from the bell. A stone walkway connected to it and hung suspended by numerous large chains. A few cloaked figures, the Razhod, walked that path as both disciples and slave worshipers knelt in rows throughout the cavern. Although it was an incredible sight, Syago's attitude was more calculating in this grim setting. They watched the flow of people, silent and motionless, then began heading towards it, weaving through the worshipers while avoiding eye contact. The people of the crowded walk-ways parted for their esteemed disguises as they passed beneath the bell for the bridge to the door.

They walked the same floating path, reaching the door the Razhod went through at the same moment the bell stopped, mercifully. They stepped through and the doors closed behind them, without anyone pushing them shut. The doors locked. They didn't pause long, ascending an unlit spiral stairway until they reached the final room where the Crimson Coven of the Razhod gathered.

Only four witchlords and a disciple stood in the room, Syago noted in surprise, recognizing the disciple as one who'd taken Alexandre. He and Qosku, still in disguise, split to stand opposite each other, each next to a Razhod. They made brief eye contact with each other through their raised hoods but avoided it with the others.

Embedded into the wall, Syago noted an eerie figure of obsidian that resembled a furry, horned man devil stood tall and imperious in priestly robes, holding a large tome in one hand and a scepter in the other, vaguely resembling Bophormothul the Necromancer but with a different, more human face. On the wall around it was an ornate outlay of silver Syago could barely make out in the room's dimness. At the base of the statue, in its robed belly, sat what appeared to be a massive door etched with crude symbols. And in front of the statue an altar on a raised dais held swathed Alexandre, frightened as Syago had never felt it before.

He estimated the situation. Four full Razhod between him and Alexandre, with Qosku close and ready, following his lead and he Qosku's lead as well. The odds were terribly against them. He'd never been able to kill one alone, always only with help, and he wasn't certain he and Qosku were enough. He considered calling Alexandre to him and then running. This seemed the best plan, but fear held him in place. Then he realized it wasn't just fear that paralyzed him, but his devil side. The arm had taken enough of his body to make him stay. He warred within himself between fear, desire, rage, hate, courage, terror. And then, he was out of time and the decision was made for him.

The Coven of the Rippers knelt in unison and said, "We are ready, Teacher, and bring what is needed."

A Razhod walked up and laid a small sack of items on the altar next to Alexandre. Somehow, Syago understood his old stolen amulet was in that sack. To his surprise, the sack sunk into the altar, into what must've been a hole.

Another Razhod addressed the statue. "Teacher, I bring you a disciple who is ready for the final sacrament toward his ascension, bearing the necessary sacrifice as required by the Crimson Covenant. We now invite him." The disciple, a tall Unakan, walked forward and knelt in obeisance at the altar before the statue, prostrating himself onto the dais while mumbling a prayer, then removing his cloak and shirt. The bare-chested man looked tough, muscular, and confident with scars from being whipped. Syago sensed his anticipation, though it was hard to tell in the dim light. Razhod were known to see in the dark, so Syago guessed what little light there was, was only for the disciple.

Together, all in the room knelt and chanted, with Syago and Qosku following: "Defy the void. End the pain. Embody the power. Destroy the illusions. Break the fetters. Reject the lies. Avenge the wrongs. Upend the Law. Come into the darkness."

A chill went through Syago, and he made a stunning realization. They were speaking a different language, one he'd never heard before. It did not

even resemble any other language he knew. And yet, he understood it. The devil arm understood it and now he did too.

The disciple prostrated himself over the altar. "I am ready, and pledge myself to the Crimson Covenant with this offering, my lords and masters." The presenting Razhod returned to his place in the circle, kneeling, while the disciple initiate stayed at the altar. Syago heard the muffled cries of an infant suddenly become loud as the man unwrapped a bundle in front of himself. Panic quickened in Syago, a desire to act now and rescue that infant. But he again hesitated too long and the screaming halted, replaced by gurgled crying fading to nothing. The disciple said, "The sacrifice is finished, my lords and masters, and my Lord Teacher the High Priest."

A deep voice grated out of the statue as if crushing Syago in his place, *"Good."*

Ice-cold fear shot through him, but his devil side shivered with pleasure. The chandelier candles went out completely, removing all light and giving his heart another chilling pause. His devil side trembled with excitement. The darkness was profound, all encompassing, deafening. Yet instead of an initiation ceremony, as Syago expected, he heard a sickening splatter and the man screamed. His shrieking continued, and he begged for help, for mercy. No one else moved except Syago, who fought his quaking and his devil arm's urge to act. The screams whimpered, then abruptly stopped with a loud snap, crunch, and more splattering. Then only darkness and silence. He wanted to look but knew he would only see the burning red irises of the other Razhod and they would see his, not burning, not a Razhod.

Syago felt the first heartbeat, a thrum on the cavern walls followed by a deep breath that filled the room from the statue's unseen, trumpet-like mouthpiece. Another followed and another in sync with deep, ragged breaths. A low hum picked up among the witchlords; Syago tried to imitate it and realized it was a chant.

Stone ground on stone and itched at his bones and skin and Syago knew the statue door, actually a tomb, opened. He nearly called Alexandre then, but he felt petrified in place. He couldn't move. Then he despaired further, for he couldn't see how they could ever permanently defeat the enemy.

Alexandre, noble and courageous in its desire for justice, was also terrified for its and his existence. His devil arm throbbed in a repulsive kind of ecstasy. *Why did I ever think we could be a team?*

He chanced a look ahead and saw, in the darkness, burning irises open, and he looked away. Syago somehow knew what he'd seen. The eyes of the risen Great Lord of the Deep, Barthandeon, moved forward as if floating. Syago would've thought it a regular human body but for the voice that emerged. That awful voice filled the room, heavy, deep, and rough, and inhuman. "Ahh, it is good to live again."

Syago hid his eyes to not be spotted. The Dark Sage's gaze moved around gently as he spoke, watching. "Nearly seventeen years have I been entombed, awaiting the last remnants of my old body to be destroyed so that I could regenerate. A long torment as you, my fellow Oblis of the Raix, very well know. A cruel punishment we've all born since the dawn of time.

A brief pause. "I understand there are some among you that question the efficacy of my method. Certainly the problem of locating and destroying all remnants of my body was taxing, a cost I hope to reduce. Over the eons, we who have never received our own bodies have had to acquire them. We as ghosts take new bodies every time we die, usually by lying to our disciples with false promises then stealing the body in a ritual. But by resurrecting the same body I come back stronger and immune to whatever previously killed me."

Syago saw the familiar glow of Alexandre's blade emerge. The silhouette of the Dark Sage lifted it, unwrapped it, and allowed it to shine spitefully against the evil room. This light only revealed the shadowy forms of the Coven. The figure of an arm moved across the blade, which flared yet brighter. Syago felt anxious for Alexandre, but the sword instead turned to an old, raw hatred Syago had never before beheld in it. The Dark Sage put it down and continued his lecture by holding up his hand. "No blood or burn, though indubitably it wants to. A sarcophagus that learns. My physical transformation has furthered visibly, and while I obviously wonder at how far this will go, it lacks negative effects thus far. While you pass through death briefly, the hell you experience as an empty spirit makes it feel eternal, completely exposed to our affliction. I was able to reduce the agony by dwelling in my crypt as a recovering corpse. When *you* obtain a new body, whether by temporary theft or our disciples' gullible offering, you must force it to your will, train it to your mind, and grow accustomed to it. But I need only awake and arise, for I conquered this body long ago."

Syago's head swam with all that this meant. Kask and Davagis were merely pawns, always had been. They were never elevated out of being disciples into being Razhod, but instead were tricked, murdered, and then had their bodies taken by their masters. The real Kask, who had not been a great swordfighter, had died before the Battle of Tiakanawu, his spirit switched out by another with helleyes and centuries of swordfighting experience. Same with Davagis and the rest. Except for the Dark Sage. Perhaps even that original, Count Barthandeon, was never truly one of them either. They'd thought he was the first Razhod, the founder, but this sounded far older than two centuries. It explained why the witchlords were so powerful; they'd been making war across uncounted lifetimes. *But why?*

"Let us continue on our quest to avenge the wrongs wrought against us by the enemy and, most importantly, of alleviating our endless suffering in both life and death. Our salvation from the eternal torment will come only through improvement toward the eventual triumph over the Tree of Life by the Tree of Doom. Ending the suffocation is the only thing that matters, not mortal lives or days wasted, but obtaining our own relief by any means necessary. In our eternity, all else is as snow blowing briefly by in the wind before melting to nothing."[43]

They're in pain? From what? He considered the scriptures' words on hell and torment of the damned, that demons and devils were cast out to the lower hells as punishment. But these were body-hopping ghosts, not devils or demons like he'd slain. *Perhaps another group cast out of Heaven into another hell, and the endless agony had driven them to madness and revenge, or just a will to escape at any cost.*

Barthandeon continued, "We'll persevere in telling our disciples that they can become one of us for now, I know you sometimes sympathize with them and other victims, but never forget mortal life is already short and painful. Death even more so in the shadow of eternity, they pay a finite price compared to us. I urge each of you to ponder changing to my method which will betray fewer servants. No doubt the next Teachership rotation will determine the future as the mantle is passed to the next High Priest of the Eternally Dying, carrying the greater share of our pain and bulk of the power. Now that the coven branch down in Nevermore has finished their work-—"

---

43 Tree of Life legends are common, but the only other references to an opposing dark tree are Nordvargr's Doomwood, mentioned once, and Lustmord of a gloomtree, twice. It may just be metaphorical as it was for them.

He stopped, the red irises flickered, disembodied in the dark. "It has just come to my attention that we have two new guests who've not been introduced to us. Show forth our craven intruders, rudely unintroduced. Let the lights aid them."

The candles above lit, bringing back the dull visibility to the room. *Run, you fool!* Syago thought, but couldn't. Something shoved him and Qosku forward. Knees trembling and heart racing, he dismissed the pang of horror he felt and straightened up to face his foe, the foe of his family for generations, of humanity for eons. He and Qosku stepped into the middle and dropped their hoods and cloaks to stand openly.

Ancient, wizened eyes of that hellish red on black observed them calmly. The Great Lord of the Deep, the Dark Sage of the Inferno, opened robed arms in display of his existence, fully embodied and enthralled with tenebrous powers. He stepped over the disciple's gored corpse and down the dais steps gracefully in soundless black robes so dark that no light reflected off of them.

The Dark Sage stood seven feet tall, and horns stretched from his forehead, twisting forwards then back. Dark rust-red hair like a thick beard surrounded his hard, gaunt face, bristling backwards and bringing to Syago's mind the other name: Devilface. His lightless robes shifted on their own, and Syago realized it was made of that strange shadow substance. A grimshade.

"I am Qosku," Qosku said, stepping forward as he punched his metal fists together, clashing the claws. "I have come to free my people. You slave them no more. You die now, and all your other bad peoples."

Alexandre flew into Syago's hand, at his call. "And I am Syago de Odiru Parlain, eighth Holy Knight of Alexandre, and fifth Holy Knight against the Hellfaces. I too—"

"We would find a more worthy foe in that Nevermore clown of course," the Dark Sage interrupted. "I'd enjoy fighting him as most of you did, a once-in-era opportunity by your accounts. Yet I must make due with these who withstood him."

"Everyone that faced us is dead," Qosku stated.

"Come and let us surprise you too," Syago added, keeping his voice equally flat. He'd never been more certain of his death, and never more afraid of it. But he stood against fear, against the coming pain and spiritual enslavement the situation promised. He stood prouder than ever before, representing his legacy at the end of a generations-long war. And to his surprise, his devil side wanted to fight as well. Though it be against a favored being, it wanted violence more than anything yet he would remain cautious with it. Though futile, he counted his advantages. A small platform limited the Dark Sage's movements and dynal activity. Still, he doubted they could defeat the legendary Dark Sage of the Inferno but if they did, four angry followers would confront them next. The heroes would not survive, but they would try.

"Ahh, this is adorable," said the Dark Sage, coal-eyes studying them. "Two heroic wishfuls come to take us on. But they've really no idea the allegations they make. I shall have to sacrifice them of course, we need an offering in any case. If only they knew the whole world they seek so pitiably to defend, perhaps they might acquire some sympathy for us. But first, there are some among our number whom they cannot see. Reveal yourselves, my brothers and sisters of the Crimson Covenant."

Up above the hooded Razhod, about sixteen silvery spirits suddenly appeared floating in the air. They stood together in the air and looked down on the two heroes with the same smoldering helleyes. Like the embodied witchlords, they didn't move, didn't smile or frown. Just watched with a kind of cosmic hate unseen anywhere else in the realm as they waited for a body to steal. He even recognized the woman that had spoken to him in the cave, whom he now guessed had been the man he and Qosku had fought. Their spirit forms looked different to Syago than the other spirits he'd seen, as if less bright and vibrant but somehow stronger and more real. *Pain*, Syago thought. He couldn't tell how he knew it, but they suffered even now.

The Dark Sage spoke again, but still not to his prey. "I'll give them their opportunity of combat in the sacrifice. Forget not their perspective, these feebleminded mortals console themselves with their place as important pieces of the universe; in reality unwary minor pawns of cosmic games between us and the enemy. Never our target, only in the way. Mortals do occasionally serve as entertainment and alleviation. But humanity is its own enemy. Neglecting and abusing each other, they do the labor for us. A truly disgusting species. As we've divided kingdoms, raised them up and razed them down, they've called us wicked and evil. But humans too do wicked things when in pain, it's their excuse to blame whichever king or pest that festers. How then can we be bad when our ceaseless agony leaves us no better choice? If we are evil, it is only because our foe, whom they worship, made us this way. Who could stay sane, much less good, under such unrelenting pain for so many millennia? We are merely doing what we have to, having tried all else. They have the peril they deserve. We only seek to escape our hell imposed on us, a foe our enemy deserves."

His coal-eyes turned back on them, hardening with his voice, and yet he still did not address them.

"I would pity them, but they're hardly worth our attention. Merely victuals for our spirits to consume in the judicious study of revenge against our true adversary, the focus of our immortal hate. They will burn as the books they've burned on the sacrificial pyre of deicide."

He turned again to the other witchlords. "Even with their minor, temporary victories over us, we are endless and untiring. Pain is the most universal foe, the infinite and eternal enemy of all, and we have the greatest portion. We will change this." He snapped clawed fingers and Vilekor appeared in his hand, the sickly yellow-green metallic shard gleamed dimly in the dark. The long and twisted darkwood staff seemed a perfect fit in his hand. "It will serve us now as we sacrifice the two redundants to our spirit pacts and break hated Alexandre. In time, our savior will come. Greater than us all, none will stop him. Not even the enemy. We will be free." Alexandre glowed furiously in Syago's hand, ready to fight. "Retreat now, fellow Oblis of the Raix. The sacrifice to our sworn greater spirits is ready, and to please them these common mortals must be free to fight back. We begin."

The four Razhod jumped to the back ledge of the crevice beneath the watching ghosts, freeing up more of the platform. As Syago moved forward with Alexandre, Qosku also springing forward, Devilface clicked Vilekor on the ground and lightning jolted through them both. Their knees buckled, and it ended with them gasping, heads swimming and aching, almost forgetting the situation. But they recovered quickly. The Dark Sage spun the staff, then a small burst of wind popped at the airborne dynfist as Qosku attacked. It threw him back, and he rolled, catching the ledge before falling off it. Syago ran ahead with Alexandre but slowed when Vilekor snapped forward. It came on suddenly, a surge in his body that choked him, and he began to sweat profusely. He held up Alexandre in front of him, devil arm also resisting, and the heat weakened. Barely able to move, Syago waved Alexandre and the glowing blade seemed to throw off the invisible sentiments that pushed the water out of him.

Qosku returned but his second charge got halted by the shade cloak. It shifted violently, then exploded in a flurry of small shade bats that swarmed about the two, beating and cutting them, knocking them back despite their efforts to fight it off. After a moment of this rapid beating and cutting, the shades regathered into the single form of a robe, snapping out from the Dark Sage's body like a giant whip. Qosku tried to dodge but was flipped in mid-air and slammed into Syago. The two tumbled over the edge, caught it, and hurled themselves back up. Devilface already stood in front of them, every bit as fast as the legends claimed.

They attempted a dive-roll to either side but Devilface snapped Vilekor back and forth, clipping both on the shoulders and tossing their roll farther than they'd intended. They rebounded and darted in as he switched Vilekor for Mordios. He whirled it around, deflecting both of their hits before almost halving Qosku with the scythe then hitting him down with the butt while the shroud grabbed Syago and slammed him on the ground. Syago got a thrust of Alexandre in, but the cloak pushed it away and the scythe forced him back, tripping him. Devilface permitted them a moment to rise.

They approached more warily, carefully before a sudden sprint. Devilface vanished, and they snapped to a halt when a ball of fire combusted where he'd stood. Their reflexes saved them, only getting singed by the flameburst. He reappeared with Vilekor in hand, and they shifted to flank him. The shroud shivered again, bursting into a bat swarm, knocking them back.

The swarm regathered on him in a different spot, further along the platform. Before they could even blink, he sparked more lightning on them, wave after wave as they buckled down guarding against its jolting force. Syago was paralyzed until his devil side absorbed the brunt of the burns and moved Alexandre up, deflecting sparks back. Gasping, Syago understood then. Devilface dealt with the confined combat area by using concentrated blasts that targeted them instead of broad or heavy assaults. Of course he'd mastered this in his long existence. And everything else.

Syago and Qosku stood panting; bruised and bleeding all over. Devilface was unfazed and untouched, his expression ever the calm cruelty of a priest performing a ritual or study on inhuman subjects. The two warriors looked at each other briefly, many things passing between them.

Not giving them more than a moment to breathe, the shroud whipped out as fire swirled down from the candles. Syago focused on fending off the whip, finally cutting it. The end piece dropped to the floor and slid off the platform. The rest of the whip withdrew, and the fire continued to swirl around Devilface, preventing them from attacking. Behind the fire, he raised Vilekor and a head-pounding sound vibrated through their ears as the fire wall advanced toward them. Clutching their heads against the sonic attack and backing away from the blaze, Syago dimly wondered at why the other Razhod didn't wear similar shrouds. His ears rang, and through the fire, he saw the statue tomb behind the advancing Dark Sage.

Syago and Qosku seemed to develop the same plan at the same time, looking at each other as they charged the inferno. It sped up as it crashed on them, Syago using Alexandre to cut a partial path into it. He rolled, roughly, to his feet. The sound blast stopped as he tossed Alexandre, shouting Qosku's name. Then grabbing the swinging staff, devil arm pulsing, he pulled himself into the shroud, legs kicking and arms punching. It felt like jumping into a mound of soft, dry snow.

Cold, soft darkness resisted and mulled around him, but he felt that solid body in there. The shade material surged around him, swallowing him, and he realized it had left Devilface to entrap him. It wrapped around him, all was darkness and suffocation crawling down his throat. It felt an eternity until the shade suddenly stopped and tore free. Then Syago heard it, Qosku was using Alexandre to hammer away at the statue tomb. Though clumsy with the mighty soulblade, he still cut through the ornate stone with heavy attacks. Seeing what he was about, Devilface went at Qosku. Qosku, now faster and better protected than ever, danced about the small platform, avoiding the hits while still bringing down the tomb. Pieces of obsidian fell off and the sarcophagus gaped open. The shade cloak shifted about before moving toward Qosku. Syago stomped his foot on it, then threw himself on it.

Devilface finally cornered Qosku and knocked him back onto the main platform.

Alexandre flew to Syago at his call, and he twirled it hard, lifting himself up above the statue to attack the wall above for a cave-in. The statue crumbled beneath the rubble.

Syago dropped down next to Qosku as the shade sought to rejoin its master. No, he realized in surprise, it attacked him. As the tomb broke, the grimshade wrapped around the Dark Sage in a stranglehold, binding arms and legs and prying Vilekor from his hand as he brought fire down on it.

Both the fire and the staff dissipated on the separation. The whole room shook, cracking and groaning from the structural damage. The other living Razhod jumped down to the main platform. Two came for the heroes and the others to the Dark Sage, attacking the shroud to pull it off.

Syago braced himself to fight the Razhod that approached him, then suddenly turned and ran for the exit with Qosku at his side. The Hellfaces followed, blades in hand. Fast, the heroes kept pace ahead of their pursuers down the spiral stairs while Syago slashed at the ceiling with Alexandre, bringing rubble down on the stairwell as they fled. Once they emerged from the stalactite, Syago turned and began sawing at the platform bridge while Qosku held off the Razhod who were bottlenecked at the doorway. The bridge lurched as Syago cut through, nearly throwing the two heroes in the disconnection. Syago used Alexandre to carry himself upward as Qosku leaped far to a nearby ridge, barely grabbing it. Syago's rise brought him into the central stalactite's side, and he cut at it with heavy hits, cracking it. His arms were weary from battle, but Alexandre's mighty blade, glowing, still cut through stone.

The doom bell rang pounding cacophony as the bell tower crashed with the bridge. Syago, gliding up and around, only cut into the stalactite twice when a crack began that tore at all the sides, the entire ceiling now raining down rubble. As the stalactite broke from the ceiling under its own weight, one Razhod leaped for the swinging bridge with the aid of Zurrogiath and barely caught it, the other got knocked out of the doorway before he could make the attempt and fell, calling up Grievore just in time to ease his landing. But, in a mass of crumbling ceiling, the stalactite dropped atop both remaining Razhod with a deafening crash.

Syago dropped down next to Qosku, both gasping for air in the clouds of dust. For a moment they saw nothing except gloomy haze. Looking around warily, Syago healed from Alexandre while they listened and watched. They walked uphill as the crowds of stoic worshipers gathered about them. Qosku began speaking to them, proclaiming freedom, Syago surmised, but they appeared more angry than happy. He'd just destroyed their rulers and bishops. Dust rose around them as the collapsing finished in the cavern center, rocks still fell on the outer areas and groans followed the expanding cracks above. Syago put a hand on Qosku's shoulder. "Qos, we have to go. They won't listen, they're trapped by centuries of enslavement."

Qosku nodded, and they turned for the exit cave, even darker now with dust filling the room, stifling all the meager lights. Before they could leave, a spirit appeared faintly in the crowd, silvery silhouette, tall and bearded, the ghost of the Dark Sage.

"Have you learned your lesson?" Syago challenged, feeling a surge of awe and pride in what he'd just accomplished. The ghost of the Dark Sage watched them, immobile. "Come back again," Syago shouted. "We'll beat you—every time!"

But the ghost didn't respond, wasn't even listening. It walked through the crowd, which parted in fear. Syago clutched Alexandre, unsure what to do against a spirit. The phantom came on fast, becoming a blur as it moved into Qosku. Qosku fell on hands and knees, gasping. He clutched his head and growled. Syago knelt by him, "Qosku, fight him. Don't let him in." He took Alexandre and placed it in Qosku's hand.

"Grrr, can't. I can't, too strong. Hurts too much, moving my b-body." And it was true. Qosku's skin rippled and twitched, even his voice changed as he spoke. "W-won't let him use me. Won't h-hurt you- anyone."

Then the hair came, the arms and chest expanded, then the rest of the body. Devilface's ghost inside him forced the werebeast transformation. Syago tried everything, putting arms around his friend, meeting his eyes, but none of this, nor Alexandre, stopped the possession. Qosku bulged in size, an arm knocking Syago back. The slave worshipers watched in horror at what was likely their first exposure to a werebeast curse. Even to Syago the transformation appeared quicker and harsher than usual, continuing past its normal stopping point. Syago backed away from the frightening sight, wrestling with his options and possibilities. He refused to believe this would be permanent, the Dark Sage had said they need a ritual to permanently steal a body, and Qosku was still in there; this was only a temporary, forced possession.

He had to find a way to slow or stop it without killing it or letting it kill anything else. He wouldn't kill his friend but thought that maybe Qosku would prefer that to being lost to the beast or the Razhod, or to killing others.

It finally finished its growth with a roar that thundered the cavern. Much bigger, with longer teeth, claws, and even horns. The snarling black beast had advanced far beyond any ozor Syago had seen, larger and more fearsome. And Syago supposed, more in the control of the Dark Sage than if he'd stayed human.

It charged.

Syago tried to move and guard but a claw shot in too fast and knocked him over the crowd of fleeing Unakans, gashes on his devil arm bleeding. The crowd of slaves also got tossed aside as the behemoth plowed toward him. He used Alexandre to carry him above the approaching beast, toward the opening they'd come in through. He landed softly and ran, thinking he had time. But a small turn of his head showed the abomination flying through the air in a great leap, almost on him. He dove into the tunnel as it smashed into the wall, sending cracks up after him. The monster of Qosku charged him, plowing through the collapsed enclosure. Syago's devil arm snapped out to grab a slave and throw him at the monster. *NO! Foda, I've just got to run.* But as Syago frantically fled ahead of the collapsing tunnel and pursuing mammoth, he saw it hit itself against the cave walls in the pursuit and realized his guess was correct. Devilface did not have complete control and Qosku forced his own way back in by trying to halt or even trap it. He shouted for Qosku to fight strong.

But Devilface was still much stronger, evident by the wanton violence as it emerged from the tunnel into the small chamber. It gored slaves and disciples that fled in terror, claws raking them apart. It hurled them at Syago, knocking him down. He rolled back, barely avoiding a claw swipe at the spot he'd been at, then rose with an upslash that cut the behemoth's arm deep. It snarled and Syago dashed back and to the side, narrowly avoiding a rush from the monster. Syago felt cramped trying to maneuver in the tight tunnel against such a colossus. He cut again at the leg, then cursed and shouted an apology to Qosku for what he must do.

Then suddenly, a citizen slave leaped at him, and another. Their efforts to hold him down were strong, then weak, then strong. Their bodies convulsed but grasped him tight, and Syago realized they also were being possessed by the other Razhod spirits, just as the assassins must have been. His devil arm went berserk. More came at him, swarming, and he had the strange sensation of a spirit trying to possess him directly, struggling against both his own will and Alexandre's, though the devil mind was keen to the newcomer. He wrestled in every sense of the word, the alien mind distant, yet Alexandre confronted the intruding will so that Syago could focus on the more physical danger.

Adding to the riotous chaos, Syago saw the grimshade pool reaching out of its room to grab at everything, pulling Unakans in, pulling in the two Razhod they'd tied up in the adjoining room, even grasping at the roaring behemoth. Seeing his change, he fled into an upper tunnel. The mammoth entered behind when Syago's devil arm, ignoring Syago again, grabbed a boy and flung him into the jaws. The needles of that maw clamped down and mashed the worker to red ribbons. On impulse, Syago ran forward and used his devil arm to punch it in the nose while cutting high on the walls. The tunnel came down, and in the haze of dust, Syago felt stones pummel him but only partially trapping his legs while the majority of it catching the behemoth.

Syago came back to his full senses, realizing that he'd been hit harder than previously thought. The haze cleared, revealing the beast's unconscious form. Unconscious or dead? Fear leaped in him, and he hurried to pry away the stones, then changed to slapping at the monster's face before freeing it. Finally it did wake, slow and groggy but still inhuman.

Syago looked on warily with Alexandre in hand, but no attacks came. In contrast to the frenzied violence moments before, the abrupt cessation and stillness felt haunting. "Qosku?"

It groaned and shifted. "If you be Qosku, come forward and return to your true form," he said, not sure that this would prove anything, let alone work. He sought to think of an identity test question but realized that the Dark Sage might be able to learn them through his network of loyal spirit spies, or for all Syago knew, occupying the same body. The abomination crawled out of the stones, slow, allowing them to roll off. As it came out, Syago saw the full beating it'd taken, all bloody from his cuts and the stones.

The beast first reverted to the normal beast form, healing some, then slowly back to Qosku. Qosku curled up on the floor, naked and shivering and still wounded. The memory of Qosku's other secret suddenly returned to Syago but somehow it didn't bother him now even though the sight of the twist, naked, ought to repulse him. He felt some shock at seeing the scarred mess around his crotch, then intense sympathy for the journey behind it, what it'd cost and why he'd felt it so necessary. Such a lonely, hurt life behind him. A sense of profound remorse and brotherly love filled him, tempered by weariness. He picked up his friend and carried him up the hazy tunnel, looking around for something to clothe him in but seeing only the eerie citizen slave eyes watching him. He realized he didn't even know if the Razhod were all gone, if their ghosts wouldn't attack again. The full sense of the dangerous situation reemerged, and he hesitated. But no attacks came.

The people came out of their holes, expressionless and watching, and Syago stopped, surrounded. One finally emerged with a bundle of old brown cloth. Weathered and dirty, but sufficient. Another brought Qosku's old possessions, torn clothes, gauntlets, and small travel sack. Syago took them all, and the dynfist friar suddenly jerked awake, fear in his eyes. Syago set him down, and Qosku stared in frightened confusion at him for a moment, then, disarmed by Syago's smile, dressed himself. They sat a moment, the Unakans gathered around.

"I'm not going back with you," Qosku said suddenly, quietly. "I can't. Well, maybe I go back for goodbye or visit but not to stay."

Syago looked at him but said nothing for a moment. He knew of many reasons why Qosku couldn't return to Nevermore. He didn't think any of it was insurmountable, but still, maybe Qosku would be better off in a different path. "You should stay with them," he said, tilting his head at their quiet audience. "We just eliminated their rulers and freed them. They've no experience governing themselves, they need guidance. I can't do it, I am not one of them. But you could be, you are."

"I don't think they want me," Qosku said with a frown as he looked around. "And I don't think I could, we barely understand each other. I was thinking more like... well, I think there should be a community for people like me. For werebeasts, or twists, or both. We can't be anywhere else, but we could be together. But I might come back here, or stay here awhile to help and then leave..."

"It's a lot of responsibility. A lot of possibilities to sort through, I don't envy you on any of it. What will you do about your- your womanself?"

"I don't know." He looked at the ground. "I don't see any way to actually become more physical woman except in disguise, so maybe I just one inside. For now, call me she."

He nodded. "I am in need of my own change. If you'll aid me." Syago pulled off his gambeson then his tunic beneath it to reveal that nearly his entire torso was scaly red with purple veins from the devil arm, all the way up his neck. There'd be no hiding or controlling it anymore. It was consuming him, mentally as well as physically. Holding back the rage and hunger had been tolling him already, but now? "You need to kill me, Qosku. My thoughts and actions are less my own anymore, I'll soon lose control over my feelings and become more completely mad. I've lived out my life best I could, enjoyed as much as I was able, served a purpose, and now I don't think I'd even be able to make it back to Nevermore before becoming wholly and permanently lost. I'll write down some last words of what I saw in there and give it to you. You'll slay me, bury me, then get Alexandre and my parchment back home for me."

Qosku's eyes glistened, but he nodded. This gentle boy, no, girl, had done what she knew to be necessary before and would do so again. They took their time. Syago to write down the Razhod speech they heard, then go through it again, then give it to Qosku with Alexandre. The sword didn't really like her, considering her also an abomination, but she was nice and humble. And it understood the situation and so awkwardly accepted it all for the time being.

They decided to do it at the mouth of the cave and made their way back up that long winding path with other Unaka accompanying them like a funeral procession, quietly holding candles.

The disgusting red monstrosity that was now most of his body felt angry that this had to be, and wanted to kill and eat his Unakan friends. But it could not stop the gentle sunrise over snow-capped peaks and wisps of clouds, or the somber ray of endless light in his heart.

They watched the dawn for a moment, enjoying the icy breeze, then the small friar rubbed her arms looking down in that awkward way of trying to start a farewell but being unable to. Syago held open his arms and walked up to Qosku. Qosku carefully returned the tight embrace.

"Thank you," Syago said, feeling as though never before had any two words been so insufficient for the meaning behind them. "I've learned much from you and will miss you. Visit my tomb sometime, when you can."

Qosku nodded and mumbled something through his tears. They broke the hug, wiped their eyes, and cleared their throats. Qosku then took

Syago's belongings and added her own, saying she too was starting anew.[44]
She raised shining Alexandre at the devil of Syago, who stood against the
winds and sun, arms out, and freed him from his pain and mortal prison
to go in search of his mother with his father.[45][46]

44 This journal became the primary source for his accounts in this narrative. Several have questioned its legitimacy, as any manuscript. The number of self-incriminating experiences detailed here fits the criteria of embarrassment—he likely wouldn't have made them up and then given it over for others to read so they're likely true.

45 The last lines were likely added by Qosku afterward. Though some have speculated that Syago wrote them in advance.

46 The Razhod ghosts were probably waiting for him to die so they could take his spirit away.

CHAPTER TWENTY

BEGIN

Based on *The Hunter's Parchments*, cc bastica 423;
Leyta's Journals, cc bastica 476;

31st of Octubre, 247
5th of Novumbre, 247

Lil'iek stood in the courtyard of Castle Cantlgrym in wait of the dydatris ceremony. In the days following the destruction that was, a quick and mostly unanimous decision was reached across the dynasts of Nevermore that the dydatris relic should be destroyed. Not just broken into pieces but rendered unusable and unfixable. Some had argued for its usefulness in the right hands, but the terrible sight of what happened to Voium, still in frantic reconstruction to appease the frustrated and despondent refugee population, reminded everyone why this was not a good idea. The distrust of leaders remained from the brief civil war and the possibility that the Razhod might resurface again and steal it also played a role in the decision.[47]

She didn't want to be there, at the castle again. But as the only remaining Kimoc with any ties to the palemen, she needed to be sure it happened and make her people's presence known. Her public forgiveness of Virgow had worked; they respected her people now. For now. And she had moved on, enjoying her children and a new lover in secret. She'd even brought her children, that they may see the paleman society and those palemen too might see that her people had sweet and innocent children, being raised up by strong parents.

She thought of Syago, now missing five moons since the Battle of the

---

47 See *Sol Sistere de Selbst* by Himetuks Himi'n, and once the truth is worse, it can begin to get better.

Gravespire. Qosku, as well, having grown fond of both of them. She took comfort in that the two warriors had gone together and that Syago had done similar things before. Lil'iek wasn't worried at all for them. The eternals watched over him more than any and the winds confirmed that he would be fine. Patches of leaves and mud still covered her recovering wounds from the last fight. Healing and building bridges had been more on her mind since the castle's fall than finding justice for the wrongs done to them. It wasn't that she'd let go of it all, only that she accepted the grim reality of what was possible and probable, as her husbands had done.

Lil'iek wondered at the future of Quoak, of all of the motherwood. With Quoak and Koah decimated from the war and betrayal, they'd reluctantly had to combine or face destruction from the wild, and even then it seemed insufficient. They still lacked warriors, not people. There was talk of establishing an Asturion-style settlement in Quoak, perhaps bringing in some refugees in a sort of unity treaty. Trust had grown, but Lil'iek knew from the oral histories that Tolgrym had been founded in a similar way with Kimoc traditions being completely wiped out. They'd decided to bide their time on it, however trappers and elementists had already begun setting up an outpost between the river and abandoned castle. It would happen anyway, regardless of their decision. She only hoped it wouldn't be as bad as the elders feared.

The Cantlgrym courtyard teamed with counts, barons, archpriestesses, chamands, and elementists. Most notably stood Roza, the gravespawn and former mastra at Cantlgrym. She wore a hooded robe to shield her from the sun, and hide the giant hole in her midsection. She stood back and apart from the rest, though everyone's unease remained. Roza, to her credit, didn't care, and Lil'iek wondered what she would do now but admired her resilience.

She couldn't see the relic, laying in the grass in front of Balgor. Castle Cantlgrym towered in the background, still beautiful despite its scars from the last fight, and despite its slight tilt from an uneven landing. Balgor made his speech, though she couldn't hear it over the wind, ironically, and couldn't really concentrate anyway. Thoughts of the war ran through her mind, the terrors, the unpredictable chain of events, and the future implications of it all. It was said among the Asturion elementists that the relic would change dyne forever. Even after the relic's destruction, they would still have its language mapped out. She lamented that Tek'ouk'iek, who would've been excited by all this, was not around to see it.

The rebellion had simmered down to a sentiment that leaders were acknowledging, for the moment. The Razhod would likely appear again, she had no specific reason to believe this other than a skepticism borne out by experience. They always came back, even when you didn't think they would, they still did. She trembled to think of this and wondered at how it could be possible to survive against the plague that was the Hellfaces. Lil'iek worried more for Leyta, who'd been unseen by anyone other than Balgor and other close Cantlgrym associates. She was reportedly ill, or as Lil'iek had come to suspect, mad. It wasn't an uncommon end for dynasts and many Roah'riik suffered similar fates due to the constant strain of engaging with the wild so intimately, mind to mind. Lil'iek felt a different illness stalking her, drinking. She needed something to alleviate the trauma and grief she'd accrued, and with the increased trade from the palemen, cider was suddenly very available. Pushed on them, even. But it hadn't yet consumed her as she'd seen it do others. She would be fine holding it at bay.

Balgor's voice raised and everyone clapped. He hefted a large hammer, taking aim. Apparently the relic wasn't empowered by dyne in a way that protected. They took this as a sign to mean that the builders intended for it to be destroyable. Though they'd heated it to make the destruction easier. The scholarly giant hammered down on the gold relic with a loud, metallic chink. A few more hits, and he stopped. He dropped the hammer and everyone clapped again, everyone except Lil'iek, who watched these momentous occasions with both relief and wary unease. Her children watched quietly with her, holding onto her. She stayed for a moment, loving the feel of their little hands clutching her.

A soft knock at the door didn't give pause to Leyta, who poured through her books, studying frantically. "Who is it?" she called out.

"Balgor," the big voice responded. "May I come in?"

"Enter." She released her grip on the knife beside her. Without easy access to dyne, and no consistent power even when in possession of her scepter, she had to rely on other means to defend herself.[48]

Balgor stood before her, and she looked up at him, seeing sadness in his eye. "What's wrong? What happened?"

"Leyta, what are you doing? It's midnight. This isn't necessary or good for you."

"But Jester's still out there. I know it. Probably he's behind Syago's and Qosku's disappearances. Your refusal to accept it doesn't change anything."

"We destroyed his body, Leyta. The real one. You did it more than anyone else. He's verifiably dead this time."

She looked at him long and hard. They'd all said that she'd been there too, but she felt certain she would've remembered it. She recalled the fight, hazily, and nothing of the end. A trick of Jester. "So then, you're under his spell too. He sang to you and tricked you into seeing it and thinking I'm mad. What else do you think? That Knave is gone too?"

"Yes." His calmness unsettled her, it was hard to read. Removed in its studiousness. "You overspent your dyne Leyta and it affected you. There's no shame in it."

Then behind him, in the window, she saw Knave fly by. She ran to the window, knife in hand. Knave was gone, but on the shores of Lake Laomain stood Jester, watching her through dark mask. "There! Do you see him?" She pointed.

Balgor came to the tight window and peered out and around, then shook his head. "Can I see the knife?"

Confused, she handed it to him, then looked out herself. Jester was gone. He haunted her in this way, appearing only to her, then disappearing before anyone else could witness it. The Seeping too taxed her. It was killing her, so slow but so unstoppable. However, she at least wasn't dying from it the way Virgow had. His skin had ulcerated, and he drowned in his own blood the day before. Perhaps Jester didn't need to kill her after all, only wait for her own time. She turned to Balgor, who was at the door. "I need to keep the knife, Leyta."

"Why?" she asked. "Well, fine, it is yours after all. But can I have my scepter back? Have you fixed it?"

"No, I'm still working on them." He then let out a great sigh. "I'm sorry,

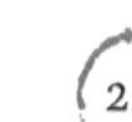

but... the academy is closing, Castle Cantlgrym, I mean. They want you to take up a new place at a new fort in Maolgon. You'll teach there, and they'll help with your Seeping, more than we're able to here."

"All right, I'll think about it if you can get me more information. But I need something to defend myself with in the mean time, do you understand?"

He nodded. "I'll stay in here with you, would that satisfy?"

She shrugged, returning to her studies, studying how Jester and Knave might've pulled such a deceit. She suspected they had the dydatris, that alone explained the potency of this illusion Balgor and the others were under.[49] The work was tiring, but it did give motivation to replace her despair and emptiness. If she thought too much about the heresy or her nightmares, she'd become practically incapacitated.

Days later, she sat in a wagon with Balgor as it entered Maolgon. Thinking about how she'd not heard of this new fortress, she asked about it.

He sighed again, a common act for him in recent times. "Leyta, I must tell you the truth. It's not a fort. It's an abbey. Saint Foucal's Abbey Asylum."

She stared at him, stunned. "How could you?" Her voice trembled, breathless. "You betrayed me. You."

Great tears streamed out of his eye, faintly visible from the bars of light shining into the dark stable area from outside. "I'm sorry, Leyta, I didn't want it to come to this, but there's nothing I can do. You're sick, you almost set fire to a group of people. And this heretical theory you keep bringing up, the bishopess isn't happy about it. They could do worse than send you here. This'll be good for you, safe, I'll make sure of it."

Jester had done even worse than slay her, he'd confined her to chains in a cell with the sick and insane. On a rebellious impulse, she made a run for it after they arrived, determined to hunt Jester and Knave on her own. But when she exited the gatehouse stables, once her eyes adjusted to the bright sunshine, she stopped in even greater astonishment. Instead of a city bustling with indifferent activity, she saw people gathered around the stables in anticipation of... her arrival?

Still squinting against the sunlight, she looked at the people surrounding her with celebration. All of them, young and old, were smiling, beaming

---

49 *Moonspell Hell Light de Lostregos* or *La Epica de Black Lava Gojira* explain the illness better than my clumsy words.

at her. "What is this?" she asked though they couldn't hear her over their own cheering. Trumpets howled and flutes whistled. Balgor and several guards walked past and helped part the crowds for her to walk through. Balgor grumbled, "How did they know we'd arrive today? All that secrecy for naught."

As she numbly followed them through the crowds, people reached out their hands, touching her dress. She stopped and asked again, this time louder, "But why? What is this for?"

"You saved us all!" replied a man holding his boy on his shoulders.

"You're my biggest hero!" an elderly woman also said.

A little girl jumped out in the path in front of Leyta to proclaim, "When I grow up, I want to be just like you, wise and powerful and beautiful."

A small boy at her side asked, "Can you teach me how to slay demons and evil men like you did?"

As realization dawned, her surprise turned to horror. They didn't know! "BUT HE'S NOT DEAD!" she screamed, on the verge of tears. She could hear Jester's song now, faint and eerie, but there. Haunting. "I didn't save you from anything. You're falling into his spell and need to wake out of it. BREAK THE SONG, WAKE UP!"

The crowd's calls of adoration quieted, confusion masking their faces. And through the crowds, she saw Jester's bell-tails bouncing in step with her, vanishing before she could point them out, then reappearing. She ran at him, pushing through people and swinging a fist to catch him off guard. In surprise he ducked away and fell backwards on the ground where she realized it wasn't him, just a regular man in a jester's motley. The crowds exploded in cheers as the clown pretended to be slain by her as they be-lieved she'd slain the real Jester, though now with all silliness. Someone threw down small doll figurines of the rest of the Royal Chaos for added effect. Everyone laughed as if she was joking.

They laughed!

She shouted some more but was hurried on by Balgor. She tried to reissue more warnings, but Balgor motioned for music to begin again. The clamor picked up and not a few men shouted marriage proposals to her while others passed her small notes or gifts they'd made for her, saying how much they loved and appreciated what she did. But it wasn't true. They couldn't see. The danger, it was still there, everywhere. She'd failed them, not saved them.

She was a crying, trembling mess when she finally got to the abbey, secluded in a northern corner of the city against the wall. Inside its walled enclosure was a small garden that she admitted looked nice, definitely not the dungeon she'd expected. But what brought her joy was seeing the children run to her. They surrounded her, chatting. And they talked less of her supposed victory and more of interest in her as their new sister in asylum. The handful of children, each varying in age, weren't sick or mad as she'd expected—well, she noticed a few odd ticks among them, but she immediately adored each.

She turned to Balgor, who spoke with Abbess Alana de Eyre, who Leyta actually knew quite well from Voium. "I can't stay quiet about this," she insisted. "If you're going to make me stay, will you at least let me study and practice?"

"I'll tell you what, Leyta," Abbess Alana began, her tone level, not as condescending as Leyta had expected. Kind but blunt as equals. "We'll give you our most important task, one I know you'll enjoy. We need a good teacher and mentor for these children. If you commit to that, we'll help with your studies."

"And we promise to pursue the Royal Chaos," Balgor said, trying and failing to inflect confidence in his voice. Leyta at least appreciated the attempt. "We'll get them, don't you worry about that, and we'll let you know of all our developments. I'll even look into your theory about dyne on the outside."

Leyta was about to object, condemn their treachery and concealed condescension to hell. But she realized it wasn't their fault they were being deceived, perhaps they were as much victims as she. Maybe if she played their game for some time, everything would be fine. Maybe they'd stop him after all, they were competent enough. And she was so tired of leading the fight. She was still a powerful woman and hated being confined as she was, but teaching the children did appeal. It was her once favored pastime. If nothing else, it was at least one way in which to fight back. The children tugged on her dress now, asking to show her their rooms and hers. And she saw Navidsom, whom she'd sent there, standing in the doorway and smiling instead of grieving.

She nodded at her peers and went with the children. As she walked with them, answering their thousand questions and asking some herself, she found another startling realization. All her emptiness, sorrow, and anxiety seemed less. Or at least she noticed it less. She thought she even felt a touch of peace and joy again.

Maybe I can do this after all.[50]

It is done.

---

[50] There's no record of Qosku returning to Nevermore. But Syago's possessions somehow did. I've speculated that that most loyal of friends secretly dropped them off and made a clandestine visit to Leyta. I see no reason to doubt it.

GLOSSARY
DEFINING OUR TERMS

ANDREW WROTE THIS PART

Angels: Beings of the overworld Kingdom in Heaven, Halls of Celos, embodied in various forms. They come from the classes of Seven Virtues: Chastity, Temperance, Charity, Diligence (Devotion), Patience, Kindness, Humility. These parallel similar classes of Seven Blessings by the lesser known Celestians, neither which are as safe and innocent as they sound.

Alerhas: Plants with pollen that infects lifeforms' wounds to germinate, then grow roots in the body, usually killing it. The alerha then drives the body to infect more and spread its pollen.

Apus: A type of eternal or "god" for the Unaka, based on specific mountains in the Apugakas, their name for the Barbathors.

Archemist: Using dyne and alchemy to manipulate the elements, the needed symbol is etched into an appropriate object which then activates when touched. The person touching use their sentiments to power it.

Archdynast: A dynast at the top of the dynal hierarchy, including elementists who are not dynasts such as archemists. Like all dynasts, they require a foci, usually a scepter or staff, that lets them aim and direct their sentiments into the elements. *See Dyne*

Asturions: Called the palemen by the Kimoc for their whiter skin, came from overseas several hundred years ago. They brought castles, swords, and more monsters according to the Kimoc. According to the Asturions they brought peace and prosperity.

Bards: Minstrels, musicians, poets, story performers, dancers, jesters, fools, and the like. They specialized in using music and/or art to convey sentiments into people and animals. Dyne puts the sentiments into the art that then seeps into human bodies through perception.

233

Barons: Minor lords within towns or cities, generally under a count with the absence of kings. They're responsible to fund expeditions and defend the domains.

Baw'kook: Fomorion in Asturion, these half-human half-animal were giants and usually only seen raiding. Included the ukuku, ohancanu, wookalar, goatmen, wolfmen, and so forth.

Bolas: Stones on the end of a cord that when thrown wrap around the target, binding them.

Bomogs: Bomok in Kimoc. Burly bulls with thick fur and curling horns used for meat, wool, fertilizer in the outside, and pulling warwagons.

Canker: Unakan word for the Seeping. A blight corruption caused by the Razhod soulstaff Vilekor, seems to emanate from the metallic rock on its top getting heated.

Chamands: Summoners and necromancers accepted of the covens in Bokhor, they summon spirits with a bell but can also be warriors. Shunned summoners were witches, or witchlords in the case of the Razhod.

Claymore: A type of two-handed sword.

Counts: The lord of a town or city by male birthright. Wife would be countess until husband dies. They're usually over barons, like lower level lords. The count typically must be an archdynast to lead the defense of his domain and fund the expeditions.

Crenellations: The blocky, peggy lining that runs along the ramparts/ battlements of a city or castle wally wall.

Culicida: Legendary carnivorous fungi that exhales poison gas.

Daemogs: Thinner bulls that run in bigger herds and snort fire. Their farts also are flammable.

Deepwraiths: Grimshades or shadowmen in other languages. An odd shapeshifting shadowy creature of stealth and death.

Demons: Otherworlder monsters like devils but from The Vast Abyss, an arctic oceanic underworld. They're classified by the Seven Afflictions: Agony, Terror, Despair, Violation, Sorrow, Bondage (Slavery), Destitution (Starvation), and Insanity.

Deova Bondua: The Sanator, The Holy One, Our Blessed Lady in Heaven, Sofia the Savior, The One True Path, and the Eternal of the Palemen (Kimoc wording).

Devils: Underworld monsters like demons but from The Infernal Hellpits, apparently a mostly subterranean otherworld. Classified by the Seven Deadly Temptations: Greed, Gluttony, Lust, Wrath, Pride (Arrogance), Envy, Sloth, and Hate and Apathy.

Duende: Urisg brownies or the Kourii are other names for them, not to be confused with the Xanas. This tiny people are said to be dangerous and live in the marshes.

Dyne: Originally the power to move the elements, like a ruler over them as dynast or but also through archemist and bards. The real power is through sentiments identified in the Vision: Red is anger, hate is brown, fear bright green, anxiety less bright green, sorrow is blue, joy is yellow, pride is orange. But note that only some are used while others have less useful effects or are just not as explosive, common, or sustainable.

Dynfist Monk/Friar: Like a dynast or bard, they use dyne to shoot their sentiments into something. In this case the careful practice of putting it through their own body for greater bursts of speed and strength. Deleterious health effects may follow. It's more distinctly religious, called Takanaku among the Unaka.

Elementist: Anyone that can use dyne.

Emaions: Greater spirits with specific but broad powers, such as a Belfegor the Behemoth or Nimrød the Reptilium, that can be summoned. Spirits of fire, lightning, shadow.

Eternals: The Great Ones "gods" of the Kimoc, Unaka, and Amoyara pagans. But each group views theirs differently. Often associated with natural features.

Feldinal: Furacán in Kimoc, Amoyaran, and Unakan. They're oversized animals often with strange humanoid mutations, similar to demons and devils but less lethal.

Flambard: Two-handed sword with a wavy blade, like flames.

Foci: Usually a scepter or staff serving as the tool of a dynast to guide their sentiments in the practice called dyne. For archemists the foci would be the object they write on, for bards and dynfists it's their bodies.

Fomorions: Baw'kook in Asturion, these barbarian giants were half-human half-animal and usually only seen raiding by humans. Tribal collective that included the ukuku, ohancanu, wookalar, goatmen, wolfmen, and so forth.

Gierra: What the Asturions call their earth.

Grievore the Violator: A flambard soulweapon greatsword, maybe just short of a greatsword. But two-handed life-draining soulweapon wielded by the Razhod.

Grim'iik: Gigantic blackbird that stalks Thornwood and mountain valleys and is worshiped as an eternal.

Grimshades: Deepwraith or shadowmen in other languages. An odd shape-shifting shadowy creature of stealth and death.

Gurows: Large, vicious crow-like animals.

Hellfaces: Tauntname for the Razhod who'd had black eyes with red irises that glowed in the dark, these helleyes along with scars earned them it. Barthandeon, their leader, had one more unique: Old Devilface.

Hellweapons: Handcrafted by shamanic, necromancer figures specifically to slay otherworlders. Different materials grant narrow but spectacular abilities, usually at a dark tradeoff. Not to be confused with Soulweapons.

Kimoc: The tribal peoples of the land of Nevermore. Even though the desert canyon peoples and the forest peoples are quite different, the Asturions call them all Kimoc to simplify things.

Lifeless: Undead, animated by forces of one religious narrative or another. Or by forbidden magics. Oft called zombi by the Bokhor summoners.

Mabin'guarik: Fearsome forest beast with a vertical maw on its chest, bulky clawed arms, and a cycloptic eye on its head.

Machicolations: The extensions of the wall battlements that enable soldiers to shoot down through a small hole at siege assaults or battering rams while staying covered. If in a shooting mood.

Malwolves: Large wolves with tusk-like teeth, yellow eyes, and either thick black fur or no fur at all but hairless black skin. There's probably some reason for this.

Mastozon: Mastozan for women specifically, who'd be second class of an already second-class word meaning mixed blood/skin. Of both Asturion and Unakan/Kimoc ancestry.

Mewil'ishyuuks: Basically a huge sacred deer with wicked antlers. For some reason they let the Roah'riik ride them and worship them.

Mordios The Reaver: A soulweapon warscythe used by the Razhod. Said to kill instantly on touching blood. Had been a favorite weapon of Barthandeon.

Morion Helmet: Openfaced helm made to go with armor that has a collar. Morions have a rim around the edge and a small crest or fin along the top.

Morwolf Hounds: Smaller wolves that somehow cooperate as pets and hunting companions.

Mother/Mamak Yoaom: The motherwood, or eternal "goddess" of the forest, but like she is the forest.

Muru'unkuy: Massive boar-like animal with tusks and extra bad smells.

Nevermore: The Kingdom Republic of Nevermore is the undisputed(?) name for the largely unmapped realm herein which we find ourselves.

Ohancanu: Barbarian giants who are the most human of the Fomorion/Baw'kook collective, would be human except for their size and cycloptic eye. Balgor is sole proof they can be intelligent and peaceful, not that you've given them a chance.

Osmos: A mystic cosmic gate that connects gierra to the otherworlds (overworlds and underworlds), for a price. The osmosis of the cosmos. Do NOT summon unless prepared to pay a toll.

Otherworlder: Any being from the otherworlds, typically broken down to overworlds and underworlds, though gierra is sort of considered an underworld as well by the Church. Either way, better just not summon Osmos at all.

Ozor: Even if you think you can pay, or have nothing to lose, don't summon Osmos. Oh and ozors are just extra large angry bears.

Pauldron: Basic medieval terminology you really could've looked up on your internets. But guess I shouldn't complain you're here instead. Pauldrons are shoulder plates of armor.

Penaga the Slaver: Penaga the Punishment, as well. A barbed warwhip soulweapon wielded by the Razhod.

Pillory: Same, but medieval arm and neck brace to punish criminals, expose them for public mockery.

Piory/Abbey/Monastery/Convent: Sorry I'm not doing four of these, even if there are minute differences between them. They had monks, friars, abbots/abbesses, and sometimes priests and bishops. Religious communities wouldn't be so isolated in Nevermore anyways, but cloistered in some corner of a town or maybe on a mountaintop fortress.

Quelk: Like an elk, but with a q and more sinister.

Quervosks: Like big ravens with extra temper and razor beaks.

Quoarn'riik: Like a chieftain among the Kimoc, but also shamanic and usually elected by the women. This varied by people and tribe.

Razhod: Witchlords, the Crimson Coven who held the Crimson Covenant. When alive, they were called Hellfaces as well due to their hellish eyes. Not to be confused with their followers in the cult.

Roah'riik: Hellhunters and helltamers among the Kimoc, more so the forest tribes, who use bones as a telepathic medium.

Saqra: An eternal of the Unaka, but one that can be summoned and so also emaion or greater spirit. Known for dark tricks, he also had a mysterious cult.

Seeping: The Asturion word for Canker, or blighting corruption. It causes the body to ulcerate and seep blood as if from burns, caused by the metallic rock on the soulstaff Vilekor.

Soulweapons: Weapons with greater spirit emaions in them. The powers of the spirit are then embedded into the weapon pending good relations between wielder and weapon spirit. Not to be confused with hellweapons, these are sentient, durable, and select who can wield them. They also have extra sharp blades, control over weight and balance, and can fly. The Razhod destroyed all but Alexandre who in turn destroyed them.

Tamboc: Unakan fortresses usually on the tops of mountains.

Takanaku: The practice of dynfist as found among the Unaka.

Ukuku: Ozormen Fomorion/Baw'kook, so ozors are like large bears and these are even bigger and more half-human bearmen. Said to be the most peaceful giants.

Unaka: Mountain dwelling peoples that worshiped the sun, moon, and mountains as eternals and supplied the entire realm of Nevermore with metals while barely getting credit for it.

Warscythe: Since scythes were used to shear harvests during a gathering expedition, these are only different in that the blade was retrofitted to point more up. Not a common weapon.

Witches: Outcast summoners and necromancers, different from witchlord Razhod who were a class of their own.

Wookalars: Boarmen of the Fomorion/Baw'kook barbarian giants. Large hairy walking swine with tusks.

Woshik: Various home arrangements of skin canvas, often with furs or art on it.

Xarampions: Lizard-like creatures with frills and long hook claws. Also smell terrible.

Yactas: Unakan town or village, usually mountaintop or plateau.

Zupayk: Another Unakan eternal that can but should not be summoned. See Emaion greater spirit.

Zurrogiath the Desolator: A great-axe soulweapon light for its size. It rapid rusts and rots anything it touches. Wielded by the Razhod.